FIRESTARTER

Haemas wandered lost in a vast, despairing darkness thick with the stench of burning and smoke. Somewhere ahead, a voice called her name over and over. Painfully, she forced open her gritty eyes and blinked up at Kevisson's haggard face.

The corners of his mouth tightened. "Now *control* it."

She lifted her head from the smelly blanket, her neck and shoulders stiff. "What—?" Without warning, the hungry flames leapt up in her mind again, roaring and eager, followed by an explosion of real fire from the campfire's dead ashes. Back in the trees, the tethered pack animal bawled and strained at its rope.

"No, you can't let it come back!" Kevisson's fingers dug into her shoulders. "It's feeding on your fear—and your guilt. I don't know what really happened at Tal'ayn, but you don't deserve to die for it."

Tal'ayn . . . her father . . . Sorrow stabbed through Haemas, and the flames roared higher. She smelled acrid smoke as the leaves overhead caught fire . . .

By K. D. Wentworth
Published by Ballantine Books:

THE IMPERIUM GAME
MOONSPEAKER

MOONSPEAKER

K. D. Wentworth

A Del Rey® Book
BALLANTINE • NEW YORK

A Del Rey® Book
Published by Ballantine Books

Copyright © 1994 by K. D. Wentworth

All rights reserved under International and Pan-American Copyright Conventions. Published in the United States of America by Ballantine Books, a division of Random House, Inc., New York, and simultaneously in Canada by Random House of Canada Limited, Toronto.

Library of Congress Catalog Card Number: 94-94418

ISBN: 345-38973-5

Manufactured in the United States of America

First Edition: November 1994

10 9 8 7 6 5 4 3 2 1

For Mom,
who loved this book first,
And for Dad,
with whom I would have loved to share it

Chapter
One

Haemas blinked.

Between one breath and the next, the warm dining hall had gone cold as the winter-wrapped mountains outside—and silent, so mind-numbingly silent. The crackling fire in the great stone hearth had burned down into red coals and the platters heaped with roast ebari and baked whiteroot were mysteriously half emptied. Two of the delicate green crystal goblets had tipped over, and red wine stained the tablecloth like blood.

She saw her father's ornately carved chair tumbled on its side, and an icy knot of fear formed in her stomach. Only a second ago she had been sitting across the table from her stepmother and cousin, half listening as they discussed the boring details of last night's gathering at Rald'ayn. She slid out of her seat, confused, then stopped as her toe bumped something soft and yielding.

She looked down. Her father sprawled at the foot of the table on the plush maroon rug, one gnarled finger grazing her boot. Her throat ached. She wanted to run, to scream, to do anything but just stand there, gazing down at his white and empty face.

"What's the matter, skivit?" her cousin Jarid asked from behind her. "Having second thoughts?"

She tried to turn around, but her body wouldn't answer.

Jarid walked into her field of vision and nudged her father's shoulder with his boot. The gray-haired head rolled loosely. "Going after your own father like that." He crossed his arms and smiled his familiar crooked smile, as always, in perfect control. "And at such a tender age, too, only fifteen. Not even properly Named. Whatever will the Council say?"

1

Every muscle in Haemas's body ached with her effort to move. "I don't understand." Her voice was only a hoarse whisper. "What's wrong with him? What—what happened?"

Jarid arched a golden eyebrow. "You killed him, of course. I always knew it would come to this."

A drop of ice-cold sweat trickled down her temple as she fought to move and failed. Jarid must have a mindlock on her motor centers. "Let me go!"

"Before the Council arrives?" His voice was mocking. "I think not, my girl."

She closed her eyes and reached for every bit of psionic strength she possessed, trying to break Jarid's hold. Time blurred as she hurled herself against her cousin's will, but he was so much older and better trained that she found herself lost in a red haze of pain.

"Damnation!" She heard his voice from a great distance away. "Who would have thought it?"

"What are you going to do now?"

Alyssa, Haemas thought, sliding down a long blackness. That was her stepmother's voice.

Jarid answered, but she could not make out the words.

"Then do it!" Alyssa's voice was also fading. "Let the Barrier k . . . her, the sooner, the bet . . ."

The Desalayan mountainside, littered with jagged gray rock, sloped sharply down from Haemas's feet. Her boot slipped and the sound of falling scree echoed hollowly across the mountains. Her startled breath puffed white in the chill air. Shivering, she hunched against an exposed rock face and stared about with bewildered eyes.

The orange sun hung low in the west, the sky a riot of rose and gold. She thought she recognized the rolling, soft green valley far below. She must be about halfway down the outward face of Kith Shiene, the sheltering mountain that stood between the Highlands and the outside world, but only a second ago, she had been in the dining hall with Jarid. She tried to remember how she had come here, but a fevered pounding began behind her eyes and the details retreated behind an impenetrable curtain. She felt sick, dizzy, unreal. Then, out of the confusion, one compelling certainty leaped at her: She must get away. When the Council learned she had killed her father, the punishment would be death.

Below, pale-blue psi-active ilsera crystals had been embedded in the mountainside, each one as big as the head of a full-grown man. Since the first handful of Kashi had realized what their developing Talents meant and seeded themselves into these mountains in order to remain apart and stabilize their gene pool, the unTalented chierra had remained below, breeding randomly and overrunning the land. The Barrier had been erected to prevent the chierras' superior numbers from invading the Highlands.

The crystals shimmered as Haemas approached, triggered by her brain waves, and her heart began to pound. She had entered the Barrier once before, several years ago, as part of her training, but it had been a wrenching experience.

She clenched her hands and edged into the pulsing blueness, trying to shield her mind from the Barrier-generated pain as she had been taught. At the first touch of the light, though, she doubled over and struggled for breath. A raw, scalding agony burned through her body, relentless as an avalanche. She clenched her hands and fought against the pain, but it was as if she'd never learned to shield, as if she weren't Kashi at all.

Her breath came in aching gasps as she inched downward, focusing on the need to keep moving above everything else. The frigid mountain wind blasted through her thin indoor clothing, but she was quickly drenched in sweat. With each step, the pain thickened until a red haze swirled behind her eyes. Every comfort she had ever known in her life, every affection, every certainty, seemed distant and unreal.

Her foot slipped. She lost her balance, slid, then tumbled several yards over dirt and loose rock, her right shoulder coming up hard against a jagged outcropping. Throbbing and bloody, she clung to it until her sight cleared slightly; then, taking a ragged breath, she lurched back onto her feet and stumbled on. When she finally reached the far edge of the blue shimmer, the false agony gradually faded, but the pain in her wrenched shoulder remained.

Shivering, she edged ever downward.

* * *

Ten hours now, Jarid thought, and still the Lord of Tal'ayn lingered on that indistinct sill between life and death. Jarid's aunt by marriage, the Lady Alyssa, had sent for the best healers from every High House, but they all said nothing more could be done.

Jarid watched as the remaining eleven High Lords stood around his uncle's bedside in tense silence, their bent heads ranging from sun-bright gold to the palest silver.

"And you say the seneschal is dead, my lady?" Lord Rald turned to the young white-faced mistress of Tal'ayn.

Alyssa nodded, her golden eyes narrowed with anger. "Jarid found the body in the same room, not even cold, and my husband was as you see him." She reached down a trembling hand and brushed the cheek of the unconscious gray-haired man in the great canopied bed.

Lord Senn patted the woman's slender shoulder. "What of his daughter, the Lady Haemas?"

"Gone." Alyssa's bitter voice choked. "I have Searched for her myself, but she seems to have fled Outside."

"You're sure it was her?" Rald leaned one arm against the mantel and shook his head. "If I remember correctly, the child is only fourteen or fifteen."

"She's fifteen." Aaren Killian's pale-gold eyes met Jarid's for a heart-stopping second, then turned away, dismissing him. "Tal and I have already agreed on a marriage contract. She will marry my oldest son, Kimbrel, as soon as she's Named in a few weeks."

His oldest son. Jarid's jaw tightened. Someday he would make Killian regret refusing to acknowledge his birth. He shoved through the onlookers to Alyssa's side and took her arm. "What difference does it make how old my wretched cousin is? I *saw* her do it!"

"Jarid Tal Ketral, isn't it?" Rald nodded at him. "I remember you from the Council's last Temporal Conclave. You were quite promising, if I recall correctly."

So the old fool had noticed him, Jarid thought behind his tightly woven screens. He was careful not to let the inner smile reach his lips. The rest of these old fossils had better learn to pay attention to him, as well, or he'd displace the whole lot.

Rald drew his ebari-leather gloves out of his belt and thrust his right hand into one. "Well, of course she must be found. I'm sure we're all agreed on that. We can't afford to have even a half-trained traitor of that age running wild among the Lowland chierra. Who knows what ideas might get into their heads? It could even breed rebellion. They're barely kept in check as it is."

The others nodded. Senn turned back to the younger man. "Then we will trust you, Jarid, to look after things here at Tal'ayn." He hesitated, gazing down at the ashen face of the injured man. "Both of your uncle's brothers are dead, and the line has thinned out so much in recent generations that, with the girl missing, the question of succession is unclear. In spite of everything, you might even have a claim on the estate yourself."

Jarid's face burned. He felt the simmering rage that rose to the surface every time the question of his parentage came up. His mother, Danih, had been a weak, sentimental fool, and it seemed the whole Highlands knew how she had cuckolded her husband, then foisted an unwanted Killian bastard on her brother, Lord Tal, before having the sense to die.

He glanced at the bold profile of the Lord of Killian'ayn. Killian was tall and angular, with piercing pale-gold eyes much the same shade as Jarid's. The other man peered intently down at the still figure on the bed, seeming not to even notice Jarid.

Alyssa held out her hands to Lord Senn and bent her head to be kissed.

"You have my blessing in this time of sorrow, Granddaughter," Senn said softly. "I grieve that such tragedy comes so soon after your marriage into this fine old House." He pressed his old lips to her smooth forehead. "Twenty-three is terribly young to be widowed."

Alyssa tightened her fingers over his hands. "Perhaps, the Light willing, that will not come, Grandfather."

Senn looked around the circle of powerful men, all fellow Househeads. "A Searcher must be sent to the Lowlands to bring back the girl."

Again the heads nodded. Jarid watched them closely

without detecting the least shade of suspicion in their surface thoughts.

The Council filed out, Senn waiting until last. He touched
Alyssa's cheek. "I'll contact Shael'donn and arrange for the
Search," he said quietly. "You just tend to your husband."

She nodded, seeming to swallow back her tears, and
gave him a wan smile.

Senn patted her arm. "It will be all right." He opened the
door and followed the rest. Jarid walked beside him up the
main stairs to the family courtyard.

The mountain wind drove chill raindrops into their faces
as, one by one, each Council member stepped onto the covered platform, inset above and below and on the four mid-
points with pale-blue ilsera crystals, then wrenched the
energies into alignment with his destination and disappeared.

Jarid turned around and saw Alyssa's green-gold eyes
staring at him from the open doorway.

"They *knew*!" She drew her thick black silsha-fur cloak
closer around her body as he approached.

He took her shoulders in his hands and drew her back
into the covered stairwell. "They did *not* know." He pushed
a lock of burnished-gold hair out of his face. "And watch
what you say out here. You know the walls have ears."

Alyssa jerked away from his hands and glided down the
worn stone stairs. *Chierra ears*, her voice said in his mind.
Those can be quite easily taken care of.

Don't take them so lightly, Aunt. Jarid followed, his
heavy outdoor boots echoing hollowly down the long stairwell. *It was chierra ears, after all, that spoiled our plan.*
He held the door open at the base of the stairs and she
brushed past into the main house.

A chierra serving woman, stooped over her scrubbing,
moved hastily out of their way, bowing her head. Jarid
caught sight of her reddened eyes. It was old Jayna,
Pascar's wife. Still mourning her husband, the seneschal, he
supposed. Alyssa jerked off the heavy cloak, threw it across
the wall rack, and swept by the old woman without even
noticing.

Jarid followed Alyssa's black-clad back along the corridors to the family wing. Inside the spacious apartment, he cast his mind about for other presences, but there were only Alyssa and himself, if one didn't count old Tal and the chierra nurse in the main bedchamber.

Alyssa gripped her fingers together and glared at him. *I told you this would never work!* She paced to the window and looked out into the growing dusk. *They could read us— they know!*

Don't be such a coward! Jarid walked into her private bedchamber, then threw himself backward on to the rich, gold-worked spread. *Are you sure you're really a Senn?*

Lineage is your problem, my dear, not mine! She followed him inside, locking the heavy door, then pressed her back against it, watching him like a bavval on the hunt.

Blood pounded in Jarid's temples, but he held on to his anger, hiding it deep inside. Alyssa was an idiot, but he couldn't afford to let go, not yet, not with so much at stake. He took a steadying breath. *They didn't know. On my part, I radiated shock and outrage, and you, of course, were properly subdued and grief-stricken.* He folded his hands behind his bright hair and smiled. *In a little while, we can send Uncle on to the Light, and then I will simply make myself indispensable running this great House and all its lands.*

And our marriage? She fingered the embroidered red flowers on the collar of her black gown. Her narrowed golden eyes, shot through with green streaks, followed his every move.

In time, he replied, *after my uncle has been properly mourned*. He reached up and seized her wrist, pressing his lips to her warm white skin. *Now—my boots, wench!*

She resisted his strength for a moment, then collapsed against his broad chest, laughing and knocking him back across the wide bed.

He laid a finger across her soft red lips. *Although we must be careful for now, we can still enjoy ourselves.*

She stood and braced herself, tugging on one of his gleaming black boots. *And the brat?*

Lying back, Jarid sighed as the boot slipped off. He wriggled his liberated toes. *My sweet cousin? Don't worry about her.*

Alyssa dropped the boot to the floor, then took hold of his other foot and strained backward, stumbling as the second boot gave. She threw it to the floor beside its mate.

Jarid pulled his long legs back up on the bed. *We'll make certain to find her before the Searcher, and then she'll meet with an unfortunate accident, too. Such a sad story.* He stretched and settled comfortably on the pillows.

Alyssa sat on the bedside looking down into his face. Then she leaned over and snuggled against his chest.

Jarid took her shoulders and flipped her roughly over on her back. His eyes, pale as newly drifted sand, bored down into her more golden ones. *Everything is going as planned.*

Hunched on the downward side of a scraggly, wind-stunted tree, Haemas tried to think. Her shoulder still throbbed and her right arm was all but useless. She pressed her cheek against the tree's rough bark and told herself she had to go on.

Far below, a tiny glittering ribbon of silver threaded the broad valley floor. A river, she thought, trying to imagine it something like the rushing mountain streams she knew, only much wider. The darker blue-green of trees dominated the sloping sides of the valley, with the valley's center a patchwork of bare brown fields and green pastures.

Her eyes drifted shut as she tried to imagine the people down there. They would look like the chierra who had served her all her life, but these would be free, paying tribute to the Kashi Mountain Lords, but not service. They would be uniformly dark, none of them possessing golden eyes and hair, the genetic tag heralding the presence of Talent in her kind. Their eyes would be brown, unreadable chierra eyes. They would have only five fingers and five toes, not six like the People of the Light, and they would be both head-deaf and head-blind, as she seemed to be now.

Left-handedly, Haemas pulled herself onto her feet and started downward again. Before her, the early-evening sky was a creamy gray-green, the suspended sun orange and huge. Through the pain in her shoulder, she thought she could feel that the air already seemed warmer, but she might just be imagining that.

Far above she suddenly heard the sharp crack of falling

rock. Glancing upward, she saw nothing, but she quickened her pace. The darkness thickened as she picked her way down. Scattered stars pierced the night sky, cool and disinterested.

Then she felt just the slightest feathery brush against her thoughts. Heedless of the rocks, Haemas hurled her aching body to the ground, stretching out in the chill dirt and grass, trying to blank her mind, thinking only of dirt and rock and the cold evening air, trying not to remember her father's still, white face.

Somewhere up above in the Highlands, someone was casting a mental net for her, but she dared not look. She could only press against the cold ground in the darkness until, at some point, she fell asleep.

Fear . . . pain . . . wrenching sorrow. Summerstone drifted on the cool night breeze through the forest, reaching for the faraway traces of strongly broadcast thought. There! She located the source far away on the side of the mountain: a small one of power, such as never came down into the lower altitudes alone. And it felt young, still malleable, perhaps enough so that they could make it understand the coming danger before it was too late.

Listen, she said to her sister. *Do you hear?*

Windsign coalesced her scattered body and steadied herself against a gray-blue trunk. Her smooth green head cocked. *Yes, but it is so far away. We will never get there before the males take it back to the high places.*

Excitement diffused Summerstone's body and she had to concentrate to hover near her sister. *A few of the quiet-minded females can hear a little. We could send one to help it, perhaps bring it to us.*

Windsign hesitated. *But what of the mountain males?*

We cannot let them stop us this time. If we fail, it means the end of this When.

Then we must try, Windsign said. *Send a quiet-minded one to fetch it down from the mountain.*

The touch on her cheek startled Haemas awake. Her eyes flew open and she stared up into the calm brown gaze of an older chierra woman.

"What a place to rest, my girl." The round, plump face crinkled into a broad smile. "Oh, to be that young again."

Haemas sat up, then hunched over against the pain in her sore, stiff right shoulder. The woman gathered the full skirt of her long, unbleached dress in one hand and leaned over her, clucking in sympathy.

"Have you taken a fall?" She fussed at the bloody edges of Haemas's torn tunic, now also soaked with the heavy morning dew. "Well, that's what comes of climbing these hills at night."

Alarmed, Haemas lurched painfully upright. The sky and the rocks spun in sickening circles around her.

The chierra woman watched her shrewdly. "You don't look at all well."

Haemas wove haltingly down the hillside in the early-morning light. The woman followed, then slipped her arm around Haemas's waist from behind, bracing her. "Let's get you down the mountain and out of them torn, wet clothes lest the Mother take you before your time."

The Mother ... the term jarred Haemas. She'd heard these Lowlands chierra were pagans, worshiping some sort of fertility goddess instead of the Light and its power. Chilled and aching, she looked sideways into the pleasant, homely face, then gave in. As it was, each step cost more effort than she thought she had left. After a while, the woman hummed an old folk tune as they walked. Eventually, a rough path asserted itself and the way grew easier.

"Yes, just lean on my shoulder, young chick." The woman's voice was soft. "Idora knows the way."

It wasn't seemly for the daughter of a High House to give over so to a Lordless chierra stranger, and yet, Haemas thought wearily, what did "seemly" have to do with her anymore? She rested the weight of her throbbing shoulder against Idora's maternal softness and concentrated on moving first one foot and then the other.

Hours later, it seemed, they arrived at someplace warm and bustling. Haemas straightened her aching back and blinked in a daze. Work-roughened fingers reached up and brushed her face, fingered a stray tendril of her hair. She drew back in alarm.

"Sisters!" Idora chided. "Let the child be. She's had a

rough time, as you can well imagine." Her strong arm pulled Haemas away. "Come with me. Talk will keep."

A score of steps later, Haemas found a cot at her knees. At Idora's urging, she painfully stretched out on it, pillowing her hot, aching head on her undamaged left arm.

Idora smoothed the long, pale-gold hair back from her face, then disappeared. When she returned, she brought a steaming mug redolent with strange spices. Putting an arm around Haemas, she braced the girl up long enough to sip at a hot and unfamiliar tea that burned a fiery track down her parched throat.

"Enough for now." Idora's voice was businesslike as she lowered her back to the cot. "Sleep for a while. You be safe here. Dream of the Mother's arms."

Haemas sagged back down on the clean, rough blanket as her eyes fluttered closed. She dreamed of nothing at all.

Chapter
Two

The stone shrine faced the rugged foot of towering Kith Shiene. Idora paused in the doorway and stared up at the late-afternoon shadows outlining the infamous pass into the Highlands. It was said that attempting the strange blue light would kill a person faster than an arrow through the heart, though she couldn't imagine why anyone would even be interested in trying. Fortunately, she'd had very little to do with Kashi Lords. But if even a tenth of the stories told about them were true, much strangeness went on up there—minds taken over, chierra forced into involuntary servitude generation after generation, bodies used and thrown away. She shuddered. The Kashi seemed to think that just because a thing was possible, that made it right. Even living this close to their lands was risky, but on that Idora had no choice. It was here the Mother had bid her shrine be built.

She glanced down from the jagged granite peaks to her light-haired charge and shook her head. How had the Mother known exactly where the lass was to be found? Here at the edge of the Great Forest, it was well known the Mother's power waned, yet, last night, Idora had heard Her Voice more clearly than ever before, telling her exactly where to look. Somehow this troubled girl must fit into Her plans.

She laid a hand on the girl's shoulder and felt the slender body trembling through the homespun shift. Although the youngster had the height of a grown woman, Idora doubted she could have more than fourteen or fifteen years at the most. Her eyes, a strange shade of pale gold, were never still, and, despite Idora's patient urging, she had yet to speak a single word. What had happened up there in the Houses of the high and mighty Kashi Lords to send Idora

12

this terrified child? And what would happen when they came after her, as they surely would?

Guiding the girl to an old blanket, she settled her beneath the setting sun to breathe the Mother's fresh air. Idora had cared for enough young ones in her time to appreciate the healing power of the Mother's world. The breeze picked up, carrying damp smells from the stream.

Knyl, one of the younger sisters, shyly handed the girl a wooden bowl of dried beans and showed her how to sort them. The girl picked up a handful and idly let them slip through her six fingers onto the blanket.

Six fingers! Idora sighed. No matter how much some might insist Kashi and chierra had once sprung from the same roots, there were enough physical differences to remind her that they were also worlds apart. She wondered what life was like up there. Were the Kashi really as rich as everyone said, and were their lives truly so easy? Could they really speak with their minds and travel in the blink of an eye?

She watched the girl scoop the spilled beans back into the wooden bowl, using her right hand haltingly. She could already see the shoulder was not going to heal right. Perhaps if she immobilized the arm—

Suddenly the lass's light, almost blank eyes darted around the clearing. Her young face froze; then she struggled to her feet and bolted toward the huge, blue-capped trees a hundred feet away.

"Mother above!" Idora clutched a double handful of her skirts and followed.

The girl was gasping raggedly by the time she reached the shade of the outlying trees. Staring wildly as if something were close on her heels, she threw her arms around the huge, rough-barked trunk and held on. The tree shivered and slowly pulled a thick, ropelike root out of the dark earth.

The spreading branches with their lacy blue leaves collapsed downward, lying nearly flat against the trunk. The girl leaped back and watched as the exposed root slowly snaked out along the ground away from her and punched a new hole. Shuddering, the whole tree moved a few inches forward as the root disappeared back into the earth.

"What is it?" Idora panted up behind her. "Did you hear your folk? Be they near?" She brushed the exotic light hair out of the young one's eyes. "Are you well enough for someone to take you back up the mountain? We can send for someone from one of the Kashi Houses down here to take you home."

Pale eyes wide, the child shook her head. Knyl and Cerissa ran up, questions in their eyes, but Idora waved them away. "Go back to your chores."

"Yes, Sister." The two younger women lowered their eyes and turned back to the keep. The tree closest to Idora quivered, pulling up two roots at once, then plunging them into the ground farther out to drag itself away. The Kashi child stared at the trees with puzzled eyes.

"Have you never seen a Wanderer before?" Idora took the girl by the arm and pulled her gently toward the sprawling, gray stone keep. "They be a sign of the Mother's special blessing. There's some what says the Wanderers sing, but I never heard them. All the same, we try to stay out of the grove so they will remain with us for a long time, blessing us with their shade and fruit."

The girl watched for a moment as the edge of the grove crept toward the stream, then allowed Idora to take her back.

"Don't you want to go home?" Idora asked as they stopped to retrieve the blanket with the pile of spilled beans. "Talk to me. We'll give you refuge if that's what you want."

The girl dropped to her knees. Idora saw her hand close convulsively around the hard, dark beans.

"I've never had a Kashi come down from the mountains in all my years of serving the Mother, but I know you speak our language, or we speak yours. It's all the same thing."

The girl dropped the beans into the wooden bowl with a clatter and stared silently at the blanket.

"Mother above and below!" Idora reached out a hand to the girl's chin and tilted her head back to peer into those strange eyes. "I must be just a stupid old woman after all. You can't speak, can you?"

The girl clung to her work-roughened hand, then picked up the last of the beans and poured them into the bowl.

* * *

Haemas heard the murmur of the sisters' soft voices in the next room. Idora had sent her to bed, but she didn't dare sleep. Even she, unTalented as she was, had been taught enough about Searching to know better than that. Yernan, her old tutor, had always told her the "unguarded mind" was easiest to follow.

Idora's low voice spoke steadily, interspersed with the quieter tones of the other sisters. Haemas pressed her cheek to the doorjamb and listened. There was a warmth to this place that went beyond blankets and fires; she had never felt anything like it in the vast halls of Tal'ayn. But if she stayed here at the very foot of Kith Shiene, *they* would come. It was only a matter of time, and very little time, at that.

The image of the dead-white face at her feet leaped into her mind again. Tears welled up and the awful, aching sorrow swept back until she couldn't bear it. Her head began to throb. She pressed the heels of her hands over her eyes.

Speech seemed to have left her now; every time she tried to speak, the words just weren't there anymore. But it didn't matter. How could mere words ever explain away the horror of what she had done? How could they explain what she herself did not understand?

Reaching under the cot, Haemas pulled out the simple gown the sisters had given her to replace her torn tunic and breeches. She pulled on the soft clothing in the dark, then stuffed her light hair under a worn wool scarf she had found among the sisters' things, hoping that if she met anyone, it would hide what she was. In the other room, the voices droned on. When she was finished, she slipped through the darkened rooms to the back door.

The heavy beam was already in place for the night. Her right arm was all but useless, and she had to tug at the bar one-handed. It wouldn't budge. Frightened, she kept at it; she had no choice.

If she stayed this close to the mountains and lower-lying Kashi lands, her people would find her, and then, in payment for all their kindness, the gentle chierra sisters of this peaceful place would be forced to share her death.

Birtal Senn balanced the ornate silver-hafted dagger on the tips of his blunt fingers. A good weight, although only moderately skilled workmanship. Perhaps he should refuse to purchase it. After all, a man in his position had a responsibility to encourage excellence.

He let his eyes rove the new tapestry, acquired just last winter, that hung on the opposite wall of his study. The red and yellow threads portraying the Coming of the Light to Kaenen, the first true Kashi, were simply the best and brightest he'd ever seen. Now, there was a prize worth a man's gold.

He stretched, then sensed the serving girl's nervous presence outside his study. He seized control of her mind and made her knock more loudly than she'd intended. "Enter," he said, then smiled. They hated it when he did that.

Trembling, the young chierra pushed open the heavy door and stood there, her brown eyes cast down to the floor. His appraising eye noticed her front teeth were crooked and her skin tended to dark cream, not to his taste at all.

He lifted a silver eyebrow and laid the dagger aside. "Yes?"

She closed the door and advanced a few hesitant paces. "A young Lord to see you, sir." She twisted her hands in her white apron. "Shall I show him up?"

"Just one?"

She nodded.

"Bring him up, then, and have Tchirna send up refreshments." He turned his back on her and sorted through his papers for a map of the western Lowlands.

Her reply was almost too low to make out. "Very good, my Lord."

He heard the door whisper shut. What a little idiot, he thought. It seemed the new chierra girls taken from the Lowlands were more timid every year, not that this one had anything to worry about. With those teeth and that skin, she was as plain a young thing as he'd seen.

A few minutes later, the door opened again. A tall, lean-bodied Kashi walked through and pulled off his long gray cloak. He carried himself aloofly, as if he had iron in his backbone and stone in his jaw.

Irritation flickered through Senn. The Andiines were such a stiff-necked, self-righteous lot, as though foregoing the pleasurable duties of House and family to dedicate themselves to the dreary job of teaching Talented Kashi youngsters made them somehow better than everyone else. Of course, most of them were second or third sons, or non-lineal nephews, unable to inherit anyway, and the Order did allow them to hone their Talents to a razored edge. In a crisis like this, there was no one better trained to whom he could turn. He gestured with the rolled map at a seat by the fire. "I am Lord Birtal Dynd Senn."

The young man dropped his cloak over the drying rack by the fire and turned oddly dark eyes on Senn. His hair, too, was a darker variety of gold than Senn had seen in many years, more a shade of golden *brown*.

"What's your family, boy?" Senn watched him closely as he sat down in the opposite chair.

"I am not a boy." The dark eyes, the muted gold of late-afternoon sunlight, bored into his own. "If I were, you wouldn't have sent for me."

Senn leaned back in his chair, stroking his beard. "I sent for the best Searcher the Andiine Brothers could provide." He laced his fingers across his belt. "Your family?"

The young man seated himself. *I presume you're asking if I am full-blooded. Does this answer your question?*

Senn frowned as the volume of that reply made his head ring. "Ellirt knew I needed the best. He wouldn't send me anything less."

"I'm a Monmart, if it makes any difference—Kevisson Ekran Monmart."

Both surnames denoted minor families, neither one of them High Houses, but still respectable; Senn had known a few from each line down through the years. He wove his shields tighter, smiling vaguely. "Don't let a curious old man put you off." His own bright-gold eyes narrowed, studying the seated figure opposite him. No matter what he said, the fellow carried more than a touch of chierra, there could be no doubting that. Still, it happened occasionally, for all the laws against degrading the gene pool. Some hot-blooded son would get a chierra girl with child, and then his family would foolishly let the baby live, thinking they could hide it away among their servants. And once it survived into adulthood, it was sure to breed more mixed brats. Senn scowled at the thought. If Kashi Talents slowly filtered into the chierra population until no one could tell where they were likely to pop up, the Kashi would lose their advantage and the chierra masses would overwhelm them. Someday such idiocy would be the downfall of the Highlands.

He folded his hands over his belt. "I've never seen you at the Temporal Conclave."

"I attended once, before Yjan Alimn died." Monmart's dark-gold eyes glittered. "Master Ellirt believes you're toying with forces beyond our control. He's forbidden us to participate." He drummed his long fingers on the arm of the chair. "The Search, my Lord?"

Was there a trace of impatience in that voice? Senn couldn't be sure. Young Kevisson's shields were quite as tight as his own. "Yes," he said, unrolling the parchment and smoothing it out on the table. "Take a look."

Weighting the corner with a pen stand, the younger man bent over the aging map and followed Senn's finger.

"You are familiar, I take it, with the events at Tal'ayn a few days ago?" Senn's thick finger stopped at the inner circle of the Highland caldera, on the rocky inner border of Kith Shiene, where a dark outline indicated Tal'ayn's holdings.

Kevisson Monmart shook his head. "Master Ellirt said you would tell me anything I need to know."

"The young heir seems to have escaped over Kith Shiene, through the Barrier, and on down into the Lowlands."

The golden-brown eyes fixed him with a penetrating look, unnerving in their steadiness. " 'Escaped,' my lord?"

"She attacked her father." Senn straightened, grimacing at a twinge in his lower back. "It's just a matter of days before my granddaughter Alyssa is left husbandless."

"She must be quite strong."

"My granddaughter?"

"No, the young Tal." Kevisson's finger traced the route from Tal'ayn to the Lowlands, a dark-blue mass on the map divided by the lighter-blue ribbons of the rivers. "In order to overcome her father, a fully trained Lord."

"He was drugged," Senn said contemptuously. "Any untrained nobody could have done it, given half a chance." He glared at the Searcher. "She is to be brought back *alive* before the next Council meeting."

"I'll need something to focus on." Kevisson rolled the map into a tight tube and handed it back to Senn. "I've never met her or her family."

Senn pulled a yellow strip of silk out of his pocket and unfolded it on the table. "Her birth gift from her mother's line," he said, holding out the carved black obsidian ring in the palm of his hand.

Kevisson took it in his long fingers and clasped it tightly. Finally he nodded. "This will do."

"When will you start?"

The Searcher turned his powerful, almost-animal eyes back to Senn's face. "Now," he said.

Lyrdriat, the third moon, was just rising, adding its pale-gold crescent to silvery Sedja, the first and biggest moon in the night sky. The air was cool, but lacked the damp chill of late spring in the mountains. Haemas picked her way in the semidarkness along a mountain-fed stream that led away from the chierra shrine, climbing over the gnarled roots of the true-trees lining the stream bank. After having grown up beneath all the restrictions attendant upon the daughter of a High House, it was strange being out alone in the night by herself.

She finally stopped when the first blush of rose and pale green appeared above the mountains in the black sky. Bracing her tired back against a sapling, she eased down to the grass and closed her eyes. Surely she was far enough away from the stone keep to be out of the sisters' reach, and she had felt no more stirrings of Kashi Searchers since early that evening.

The world felt dull and muffled, claustrophobic, now that she was locked up inside her own head. It was as if she had lost something she hadn't truly known she possessed until it was gone.

Jarid's sarcastic, handsome face rose up smiling in her memory. Scowling, she tried to think of something else, but the image remained, mocking her. "What's this?" it asked insolently. "Killed your own father?"

A throbbing ache centered itself behind her eyes. No! she told herself. She would not think about that!

She wrapped her arms around her ribs and watched the

sun rise with aching, dry eyes until she was exhausted enough to sleep.

The fire in the great hearth was blazing higher than she had ever seen it before. Haemas stood in front of it, amazed at the heat radiating against her face.

"Failed again, have you?" Her father's gruff voice came from behind her back.

Suddenly cold, despite the fire, she did not dare turn around.

"Get that from your mother's line, I suppose." She heard the hollow clang of a metal cup against the heavy wooden table. "Though both the damn Killians and Sennays are supposed to be Talented. At any rate, I expect to whelp much better brats soon out of . . . of . . ."

She heard the cup scrape as he picked it up again. "Alyssa," she finished for him. "Alyssa Alimn Senn." Hugging her arms around her body, Haemas shivered.

"One of Senn's get." The cup banged down again. "By the Light, a fine, plump creature, full of curves, not another one of those damn Sennay beanpoles like you and your blasted mother."

Haemas watched the yellow-orange flames leap higher and higher.

"You pay attention to the wench after we're mated, girl. She has a few years on you." He chuckled and she heard the chair scrape as he pushed it back. "Maybe you'll pick up a few pointers on how to be a real woman."

Eight years, Haemas thought. Alyssa Alimn Senn, who was to become her new stepmother on this day next week, was just eight years older than herself.

"Darkness and everlasting damnation!"

The heavy silver cup came flying almost over her shoulder at the fireplace, clanging against the back wall and bouncing back out through the flames. Haemas jumped aside and watched it roll on the thick brown rug.

"Bring me some more mead!" he roared at her. "By the Light, I intend to have this place properly run after I get . . . Alsa in here!"

Haemas bent to pick up the metal cup, still cold to the

touch even after its trip through the flames. "Alyssa," she said faintly.

She woke up with a start, more tears running down her face, but she wiped them away, suddenly determined to be done with crying. Jayna, her chierra nurse, had always insisted "tears buy no bread."

No one could undo what she had done. Nothing would ever bring her father back, just as nothing would erase the pain of not being loved by him or her own shame over not being able to love him herself.

Kneeling at the stream's edge, Haemas dipped a handful of cold water to drink, then more to bathe her scratched arms and hot face. High overhead, the orange sun indicated she had slept longer than was wise, and her stomach clamored for food.

Food, she thought wistfully. She had neither money to buy it from anyone she might meet nor any way to find her own. The plants here varied from those of the high plateau where she had lived at Tal'ayn, and besides, she wasn't a kitchen maid or a field hand. She recognized nothing of which she could be sure. Perhaps she could at least make a fire and drive the chill out of her bones.

As clouds drifted across the sun, she gathered a pile of tiny twigs and dead leaves, then settled on her knees in the undergrowth. Taking a deep breath, she tried to compose her mind. She could almost hear old Yernan, her tutor, shouting for her to concentrate.

"When properly trained, your mind will generate the spark!" His red-cheeked old face had puffed up like a bellows and his bushy white eyebrows had met over his beak of a nose.

Closing her eyes, she concentrated, turning inward until she knew nothing of the forest and the stream, nor anything around her, going deeper and deeper into her mind, looking for some spark of mindtalent still left, some sign that it wasn't gone forever.

There was nothing.

When she opened her eyes, the sky had gone gray and brooding. Her head ached with a sullen ferocity, her stomach twisted with emptiness, and beneath all that was a growing despair.

Chapter
Three

The twisting branches of true-trees, thick with oval, blue-green leaves, towered over Haemas as she waded through whispering ferns and beds of tiny white anith flowers. The air was filled with the wild, clean fragrance of growing things and the rustling shadows were deep and cool, but the dense brush caught at the cumbersome long gray gown and made her progress even slower. She wished she still had her tunic and breeches, but at least she had gotten away from the shrine with her boots.

She stopped and squinted up at the sky, which was barely visible between the branches shifting in the breeze. It was late afternoon by the angle of the sun. She had been walking all day, with very little sleep the night before, and nowhere could she find any fruit or berry familiar to her.

Finally, almost ravenous, she snagged a purple berry from a low thorny bush and sniffed. It smelled edible enough, so she popped it into her mouth as she picked her way along the stream. It was sour, but she made herself swallow anyway, then ate several more; if she didn't get some real food soon, she knew she would just fall down and never get up.

After she finished, she stopped long enough to drink from the stream's clear water and wash her sticky fingers. Her left hand tingled where the dark-purple juice had stained it and could not be washed off.

When she looked at her rippling reflection, a twisting shadow caught her attention up ahead where the stream curved. She watched for a moment, her heart pounding. There it was again—a flicker of movement against the lighter brown of tree trunks.

She turned and ran back along the stream in the opposite

direction. Her feet seemed increasingly clumsy, though, and it was stifling even here under the thick shade. Wiping her forehead with the back of her hand, she struggled forward, roots and half-buried logs catching her feet every step of the way.

She burst into a clearing and saw a man sitting on a stump across the stream, watching her.

"Having a spot of trouble?" he asked, his voice casual, friendly.

She blinked. The air rippled and *two* men sat on stumps, dressed in faded blue tunics, holding longbows. The ground tilted sideways suddenly and she found herself down on her hands and knees, wrist deep in spiny grass.

"Are you lost?" he asked.

She tried to regain her feet, but her head was so light that it seemed in danger of floating off. She blinked again and the men resolved back into one dark-haired person. She looked down at her hand. It looked insubstantial, almost transparent. She heard splashing, then flinched as the stranger tilted her head back. She heard his sharp intake of breath as he gazed straight into her eyes. "Mother preserve us!" He yanked the scarf off and spilled pale-gold hair down her back.

She grabbed for the scarf, but her fingers clutched only empty air. All her movements seemed to be in slow motion now. Studying her hand, she wondered how she could have missed.

"Well, you be quite a prize to fall into a man's lap, all alone and unprotected." He grinned insolently at her, his teeth very white in his tan face. "Have you a name then, prize?"

She stared at him uneasily. There was something wrong with his face, but she couldn't quite put her finger on what it was.

"No?" He held her scarf out of reach. "Be reasonable. If you don't give me a name, how will I know who to send to for the ransom?"

She reached up to push him away, but suddenly there were three of him. Squeezing her eyes shut, she tried to quiet her stomach's flip-flops.

"You don't look at all well." A strong, cool hand touched

her forehead briefly. "That won't do. There's very little demand for the return of dead loved ones." She felt him grasp her hand and force apart her fingers. He sniffed. "Mother around us! Vriddis berries? How many did you eat?" He shook her until she opened her eyes. "How many?"

It didn't matter, she thought wearily, nothing mattered. Her eyes fluttered closed again.

"Kashi idiot!"

She heard him walk away, the leaves and underbrush whispering as he passed. Haemas's arms and legs seemed heavy and her mouth very dry as the cool breeze played across her face.

"Drink this!" A strong arm pulled her up as a slab of bark pushed against her mouth. She tried to push it away. "Drink, damn you, or I'll hold your high-and-mighty Kashi nose and pour it down your throat!"

Thick, pulpy liquid trickled into her mouth and she choked. It tasted like laundry water at the end of wash day.

"More!" the voice ordered.

Opening her eyes, Haemas turned her head away. The man tilted the bark up and relentlessly poured more down her throat. It burned like soap all the way into her stomach. The man walked away, and she coughed until he returned.

"Drink a bit of this," he ordered. "It's just water, but it will cut the taste."

She sipped the cool water for a moment before he took it away.

"If you drink too much right away, it'll dilute the antidote." He sat back on his heels and watched her.

She blinked slowly, but he remained just one man, dressed in a patched tunic the same shade of blue as the true-trees.

"What possessed you to come down here all alone?" He took a sip of water himself. "You don't even know enough to keep from killing yourself."

She braced herself against the tree trunk so she could study his face. He had black hair and darkly tanned skin with strong cheekbones and a crooked nose. Then she realized what had seemed out of place before. He had blue eyes.

"Where be your people?" he persisted. "And why are you dressed like that? Anyone who didn't get a good look would take you for one of us."

In all her life, she had never seen blue eyes before. They glittered like points of ice in his tan face. She glanced around, finding the scarf by her side, and looped it over her pale hair. Then she stood and wavered away from him.

"Oh, no, you don't." He scrambled after her, bringing her up short by the back of her gown. "Sorry, you'll not be leaving just yet." He forced her into the stream and up the far bank with him.

His grip was too strong for Haemas to break away, and her feet still didn't seem to be working that well, but at least he was taking her away from the mountains, so she decided that she could afford to bide her time.

Kevisson rolled the black obsidian ring in the palm of his hand, reading the faint traces of personality that remained. He had a fleeting impression of loneliness . . . despair. The girl had been solemn, reclusive—

Kevisson?

His head jerked up. *Yes, Master Ellirt?*

Come by my rooms before you leave. I need a word with you.

On my way. He threaded the ring onto a heavy golden chain and settled it around his neck, then wedged the last of the trail food into his pack and lashed the leather ties. Looking around the small room with its thick walls and bare flagstone floor, he couldn't think of anything he'd forgotten. He probably wouldn't be gone long anyhow. After all, his quarry was only a girl.

He stepped out into the empty corridor and heard raucous young voices down in the dining hall. The air was filled with the inviting smell of tonight's roast savok, but he had no time to eat. He could munch a handful of trail food after he got started.

He paused outside Ellirt's heavy wooden door.

Come in, boy. Come in.

Kevisson pushed the door open and walked into the spacious room. The older man stood by the fire, his white-haired head bowed.

"Put the pack down and have a seat." Ellirt didn't turn around.

"With all due respect, Master, I need to be off." Kevisson sank uneasily into a chair close to the hearth.

"You want to make a good impression on old Senn." Ellirt reached for the chair behind him, running his fingers over the carved arm before he lowered his round body into it. "I don't blame you. We don't get many requests for help from that quarter. The Houses are usually too busy trying to cut each other's throats to turn to us."

Kevisson hesitated. "It's more than that."

"Yes?" Ellirt settled back and locked his fingers together.

Kevisson watched the shifting yellow flames. "I got a sense of something . . . out of joint when I talked to Lord Senn. I felt—I don't know—urgency."

"A youngster drugs her own father and then burns his helpless mind?" Ellirt snorted. "That could give a person a sense of urgency, all right!"

Kevisson shook his head. "No, that's not it. Lord Senn seemed to be holding something back."

Ellirt leaned forward, his sightless eyes staring. "Birtal Senn is a powerful man, Kevisson, second only to old Tal himself. Don't let his age fool you, and don't cross him. The High Houses are squaring off over this matter, and we don't want to be caught in the middle. It runs deeper than rank; if Tal doesn't recover, important alliances are going to be broken and remade in the next few weeks. You just find that young delinquent and dump her off in his lap as soon as possible."

Kevisson didn't repeat his doubts. "I understand," he said, rising. "Now I really had better be off."

Ellirt rose, too, and walked beside him to the door, one hand on the younger man's shoulder. "If you have any trouble at all, link back here to me immediately. Do you understand? Just me, nobody else."

"Of course, Master." Kevisson tried to keep the surprise out of his voice. "If that's what you want."

"Very well, then." Ellirt patted his shoulder. "Off with you now, and don't tell anyone else where you're going."

Kevisson shouldered his pack as the door swung closed behind him with a soft thunk. Don't tell anyone where he was going? He looked back down the torchlit hallway. He'd never heard of such a thing in all his years of training here in Shael'donn.

The wind was still blowing as he entered the courtyard and headed for the portal. Stepping onto the covered platform, he reached out with his mind and activated the dormant energy in each inset ilsera crystal in turn, recalling the subtly different frequency of the portal above the Barrier.

North . . . south, he recited in his mind, feeling each crystal warm in turn, east . . . west . . . above . . . below! As he completed the sequence, he reached for the Barrier crystals' harmonic signature. The world around him dissolved and he flashed through a silent gray otherness into the portal on the rocky slopes of Kith Shiene.

He could feel the strength of the Barrier blazing just below. Strengthening his shields to the maximum, he steeled himself and started through the thick wall of pain that had kept chierra Lowlanders out of the Highlands for the last five hundred years. Even though he had done this before, sweat trickled down his face as he strained to keep his shields tight. By the time he reached the other side, he ached all over.

He paused beside an outcropping of jagged gray rock and cast his mind ahead, seeking some sign of the girl, but there was nothing. Although it didn't seem possible for someone of her age and limited training, she must have made it through the Barrier and then walked on down the mountain. Kevisson shook his head, disappointed. He'd hoped to find her before she got that far. Well, the orange sun hung just above the horizon. In another hour or so, he could reach Lenhe'ayn, the minor House that oversaw this region, and claim lodging for the night.

He could start again from there in the morning.

"What in the seven hells have you got there, Cale?"

Haemas's head ached and her feet were worn to rawness as she stumbled into a firelit clearing.

"Don't look big enough to eat," one man said. Several male voices laughed.

"Maybe we can use it for silsha-bait," another put in.

The man released the back of Haemas's gown and she sank to the ground next to a crackling fire.

"Keep a close eye on this," the man instructed the others. "And give it a bit to eat."

Another man walked up and fed several sticks into the yellow flames. Haemas looked up at him. Dressed as poorly as her captor, he was thick-necked and shaggy with a dark, scraggly beard and a jagged scar running across his heavy cheek.

"Mother above." His dark chierra eyes stared down at her. He snatched one of her six-fingered hands before she could resist. "If I hadn't seen, I wouldn't have believed."

Haemas yanked her hand back. Chierra, she thought uneasily, a whole camp of renegade chierras, running free with no Lord to make them obey. They wouldn't dare harm her, would they? She closed her hands into fists and buried them under her arms.

"Leave her be, Mashal. I had enough trouble catching the whelp without you scaring her off." The first man walked back into the flickering firelight.

"I were just looking." Mashal threw a last piece of wood into the fire.

"I think we can all remember what happened the last time you just 'looked' at a female, Mashal." The whole camp snickered, and the big man scowled.

An older man with a fringe of white hair outlining his head walked around the fire and handed Haemas a rough wooden bowl filled with thick stew. With a shock, she realized he had only one hand; the other arm ended in a scarred stump. Tearing her gaze away, she balanced the bowl on her knees and wrinkled her nose at it.

"Don't got no fine dinnerware, Lady." His weathered face smiled at her. "Just dig in with your fingers."

"Don't call her that!" Mashal's heavy face twisted. "She ain't no better than you or me or anyone else here!" He held his knife up and let the firelight play along the finely honed edge. "Her kind bleeds, same as ours."

The old man bobbed his head. "Sorry," he mumbled. "Just habit, you know. I served them so many years. . . ."

The first man stepped between the two. "Leave him be, Mashal. He don't mean nothing."

"I know." Mashal rubbed a big hand across his face and looked down at Haemas. "But demons take it, Cale, what do you mean to do with her?"

So, Haemas thought, the man who had brought her here was named Cale.

"Sell her, of course." Cale ran a hand back through his black hair and smiled. "She'll be worth a rare amount of gold to someone." He leaned down and glared into Haemas's face. "Now eat that or I'll dump it in the fire!"

With a start, she remembered the bowl of food and picked up a warm chunk of meat with a thumb and forefinger.

"That's better." He settled on the ground beside her and nodded approvingly. "It's powerful hard to sell dead folks these days."

Mashal shoved a thick log nearer with his foot and sat next to Cale. "How much do you think you'll get for her? There's a big difference between what one of those Lowland farms will pay and a real Highlands House."

Cale reached out and tucked a bit of strayed pale-gold hair behind Haemas's ear, grinning as she flinched away. "I don't know where she be from yet. Haven't been able to get a single syllable out of her."

She fished another piece of meat out of the broth and ate it doggedly, refusing to meet his chill eyes.

"How about it, prize?" Cale asked. "What's your name?"

She found a piece of firm whiteroot and took a bite.

"Not a word for the man who saved your sodding life, then?" He made a clucking noise. "So much for the high-and-mighty manners of the highborn."

Suddenly her stomach knotted. She pushed the bowl away and hunched her arms around her knees. Later, when they were all asleep, she would slip away.

"Finished?" Cale peered sorrowfully into thc half-full bowl. "I guess we should all be getting some sleep, then." He reached into his pocket for leather thongs and took hold of one of her wrists.

Frightened, Haemas scrambled in the other direction, wrenching her injured shoulder, but he held on, first tying one wrist and then binding the other securely to it. Then he took a turn of thong around his own wrist and tied it off.

"Just in case you had any ideas this party were over." He winked one of his odd blue eyes at her and tossed her a ragged blanket. "Pleasant dreams."

Haemas pulled the blanket around her tired, aching body as well as she could with her wrists bound and closed her eyes. Exhausted as she was, though, sleep refused to come. She stared into the wavering yellow circle of firelight as the flames died down and the other men settled around the edges to sleep.

It had been two full days now, and she still hadn't felt anyone else Searching. Maybe they believed she was dead and had given up. She thought again of her father's white face as he'd lain at her feet that night. She remembered nothing of what had come before. Whatever had possessed her to do such a thing? If only she could remember!

These stupid chierras thought they were going to ransom her. She shook her head. They had no way of knowing the only thing anyone from the Highlands would pay for now would be her death.

"No, she isn't dead." Sparks flew as Jarid thrust the log into the orange heart of the fire with the poker. "At least not yet."

Thunder rumbled outside the thick walls of Tal'ayn, heralding a storm that would break before the night was out. Perched on the window seat, Alyssa huddled deeper into her fur-lined shawl. "You know what a clumsy, gangly thing she is. She probably fell off the mountain and cracked her head open." Her green-gold eyes watched him pace the length of the bedchamber. "I don't see why you have to go."

"What you 'don't see' could get us both killed, my dear aunt." Jarid's restless gaze wandered the room. Cluttered with lacy cushions and powders and ointments, it was unbearably fussy. He shoved an armful of cosmetics to one side of her dresser and scowled. "I have to find the little wretch before the Council does."

Tucking her slippered feet beneath her, Alyssa sipped at a cup of hot tea. "Well, I've Searched two whole days now and found nothing."

"Then it's fortunate I am not you." Jarid stared at the

trusting face of his aunt by marriage, carefully shielding his distaste. She might be an idiot, but Alyssa's Testing had given a Plus-Four rating, strong enough at least to pick up anything he was careless enough to broadcast.

He leaned against the window seat and brushed her golden hair aside to stroke the warm curve of her neck. Sighing, she pressed her cheek against his hand. Outside, the faraway thunder rolled again.

At any rate, he thought as he looked down at the top of her bright gold head, she was a pleasant enough diversion, and actually rather pretty until you knew how little lay behind those even features and incredible green-gold eyes. Well, Alyssa had her uses—for now. Jarid moved away. "I'll Search for her myself," he said abruptly. "Tonight."

"What about the other Searcher?" She rose from the chair and followed him to the canopied bed. "The one Grandfather sent for. He might sense you."

Jarid stretched out his six-foot frame across her bed and closed his pale-gold eyes. "Don't be stupid." He began the relaxation ritual, counting his breaths, centering down. From somewhere far away, he heard his own voice tell her, "Lock the door and don't disturb me. This will probably take some time."

Concentrating on his breathing, he loosed his mind into the gray otherness, looking for the pale spark of life he could identify as his cousin. As his Search ranged farther and farther, he began to think that perhaps she was dead or in some way beyond his reach, but then finally he hovered above her presence, congratulating himself.

As he watched her, though, it seemed that someone else was there, watching with him. Jarid cursed and slipped away without making contact. He would have to follow her in person and then finish off the little skivit.

After a long time, he opened his eyes again, cold and cramped. Curled up in a chair, Alyssa watched him with troubled eyes. "Did you find her?"

He arched his back and smiled as the first spatter of raindrops struck the window. "Oh, yes," he said. "I found her."

Chapter
Four

When the toe punched her ribs, Haemas couldn't remember where she was. Her right shoulder throbbed as she bolted upright. Trees surrounded her on every side like a wall of rough brown pillars, and thin early-morning light filtered down through the whispering blue-green leaves.

Cale squatted beside her to untie the rawhide thong binding her swollen wrists, his face impassive. "We're leaving in a few minutes, so you'd best get on with your breakfast." He nodded at the wooden bowl near his foot.

Haemas massaged her wrists, then tried to work out the stiffness in her shoulder. Movement, however, only made the pain worse. She gave up and pulled the bowl over with her left hand. It was her leftover stew from the night before, cold and congealed and thoroughly unappetizing. She pushed it away.

"Well, that takes care of that. Now, I suppose, like all females, you require a bit of privacy?" Her captor regarded her with his strange blue eyes.

She pulled the ragged blanket around her shoulders, not sure what he meant.

"You know, bodily functions?"

A sudden heat flushed her cheeks. She turned away.

"I thought so." He sounded unconcerned. "Go right ahead, but—" He reached out, gripping her arm tightly above the elbow. "Make me and boys come looking for you and there'll be no more privacy on this joyride."

Haemas stared at his hand on her arm for a second, then nodded.

"A 'yes' would do just fine."

She jerked her arm, and he let go as a chorus of muffled chuckles were heard around the camp.

"I'll have you know," he said to her rigid back, "that in some circles, I'm considered excellent company!"

When she returned, she was surprised to see that they had produced a string of large horned saddle animals from somewhere in the forest. The creatures had shaggy, dappled blue-gray coats and four large, bulging black eyes. The one closest to her bent its long thin neck and sniffed suspiciously at her, while its lower jaw circled with endless chewing.

Around the clearing, the others were already waiting on their mounts. Cale swung up on the creature's back with practiced ease, settling into the simple, hornless saddle. Then he motioned to her.

She had ridden horses in the Highlands, but never anything that remotely resembled one of these—*things*.

"You aren't going to make me catch you again, are you, prize?" Cale crossed his arms and grinned insolently down at her. "Although that might be fun."

Mashal, sitting on a huge, potbellied beast, rubbed a hand over his black-whiskered face and snickered. Haemas walked hesitantly over to Cale's left foot.

"No, no, the other side," he said. "Don't you Kashi know anything? Always mount an ebari from the right side."

She gave the beast's swishing tail a wide berth and walked to the other side. Without waiting, Cale reached down and grasped her right wrist, yanking her upward.

Landing behind his saddle, she sagged forward, dizzy with the pain in her shoulder. He kicked the ebari and it followed Mashal's scruffy beast into the forest. Still trying to catch her breath, she held on with her left arm and tucked her right across her chest. Every jolt from the big beast's loose-boned gait wrung another deep twinge from her torn muscles.

She closed her eyes. It would take a healer to knit the muscles properly again, but Healing was a rare mindtalent. Chierras didn't know how to Heal.

Giving herself up to the creature's plodding rhythm, Haemas tried to clear her mind and think about nothing.

Kevisson tied the last lace on his pack, then turned around. Myriel Lenhe's tall, well-rounded form, wearing a green satin tunic over flowing breeches that clung to every curve, leaned against the door frame. She had a soft oval face and classic Kashi skin, white as frost. Her lips quirked into a knowing smile.

He bowed slightly. "I'm sorry, Lady Myriel. I didn't realize you were there."

That, of course, was a lie; he had sensed her waiting outside the door. What he hadn't realized was that Lord Lenhe's daughter would be brash enough to come in without knocking. Fortunately, Myriel's mindtalents didn't seem sensitive enough to pick up the difference between his polite lie and the bare truth.

She beckoned the servant waiting in the hallway to follow her in. "Mother sent up some breakfast. She didn't think you'd be ready to leave yet, since you arrived so late last night."

The crockery clinked as the young servant girl set the heavy tray on a table close to the hearth.

"That's all, Cenda. You may go." Myriel's golden eyes didn't even glance at the chierra girl as she spoke. "*Brother* Monmart," she said, accenting his Andiine title, "why don't you eat your breakfast before it gets cold?"

So he wasn't a Master yet, Kevisson thought behind his shields, that didn't alter the fact he was still the best Searcher in Shael'donn. He had trained three times longer than most Kashi men. He settled in a cushioned chair and caught the sweet musk of her perfume.

She seated herself gracefully in the opposite chair and uncovered his plate. "I'm told the psi-ratings of the Andiines are uniformly quite high." She fingered the ash-gold braid looped over her shoulder.

"We vary, of course, but many of us do test relatively high." Kevisson bit into a piece of mellow white cheese, studying her. What did she want? She was of marriageable age, of course, and quite striking, but he had long ago resigned himself to the fact that, between his appearance and his lineage, *he* would never be considered marriage material by any but the poorest of Houses. That was part of the reason he had originally considered taking vows at Shael'-donn. He had more of a future there than anywhere else.

She sighed. "My rating, I'm afraid, is not very high. I received only slightly over a Plus-One at my Testing four years ago."

Kevisson's eyebrows arched before he could keep the shock from his face. He swallowed a half-chewed mouthful of fresh bread and cheese. "My Lady!" he said, trying not to choke. "Why are—"

Myriel managed a cold smile. "Mindtalent seems to be diminishing in our family, Brother Monmart. My father intends to have it otherwise."

Kevisson skimmed discreetly at her surface thoughts for a moment, picking up anger, frustration, but only the barest glimmer of personal attraction. "I don't understand."

"Surely you must realize, Brother Monmart, that if an heir is born to this family with *no* trace of mindtalent, we'll have no more right to this land than the chierra field hands. The Council will rescind our grant and give Lenhe'ayn to a new line that demonstrates high potential." Myriel rose and walked to the window, gazing down at the courtyard. "The shame . . . the reduction in rank . . ." Her voice choked off and she took a deep breath. "Nothing like that has happened among the Houses in at least two hundred years."

"My Lady, you must know marriage is out of the question for anyone in training at Shael'donn. We dedicate ourselves both to the training of young Talent and the development of our own. We have no time for family."

To his consternation, Myriel turned away from the window and, putting a hand over her mouth, laughed. It was a cold, bitter sound that raised the hairs on the back of his neck.

"I'm sorry." She dabbed at her eyes. "But did you really think we were speaking of marriage?" Her eyes glittered like newly minted gold coins.

He stared at her for a long moment. Then, snatching up his pack, he started for the door.

She rushed after him, laying a restraining hand on his arm. "Please forgive me." She looked contrite. "I'm not very good at this."

Kevisson looked at her coldly. "Just what is it that you *do* want from me, Lady?"

"A child." Her face colored. "We . . . need at least one

infusion of new, strongly Talented blood to improve our line, and several would be even better. And we heard that . . . sometimes a man from the Order is willing to give a child to the daughter of a great House, even though they never marry."

Kevisson frowned. "It has been done, Lady, for various reasons, but . . ."

"You do not wish to."

"I have never considered the possibility." He leaned against the mantel over the hearth. "My Talent is strong, but my appearance has always been—held against me in the higher circles." He studied her with his golden-brown eyes. "Most likely any child of mine would resemble me."

Myriel turned away. "That would hopefully breed out after several generations. But your strength—we need that desperately."

If she had said it didn't matter, that Lenhe'ayn would cherish his child no matter what color its eyes and hair, he might have been tempted. But he knew he would never give his flesh and blood to be despised as he had been all these years.

"I'm flattered, Lady, but I must refuse." Kevisson held the door open for her. "Perhaps if you would contact Master Ellirt at Shael'donn, he could find someone more—deserving of this honor."

Myriel did not meet his gaze as she swept through the door ahead of him. "Perhaps," she murmured, toying with the end of her braid.

As he followed her back down the narrow hallway, the surface of her thoughts teased him with the faintest twinge of regret.

Hunger . . . stomach-cramping hunger beat insistently at Haemas. Rousing herself, she looked out into the leafy dimness through which they rode. The ebari's flat, round feet thumped over the leaf-covered forest floor as Cale's back swayed before her.

This was no time to think about food, she chided herself. Then another wrenching wave of hunger swept over her, and she suddenly realized it was coming from outside. *She* wasn't hungry, but something nearby did hunger—something sleek and powerful.

Taking a ragged breath, she groped within her mind for her shields, but they were still gone, as they had been ever since that last terrible night at Tal'ayn.

She twisted back to look over the ebari's rump. Nothing, just blue-green vegetation and silence. The certainty grew in her, though, that *something* prowled after them through the shade-shrouded forest.

She turned back around and huddled against Cale's quiver and blue-green shirt, trying to shut out the all-pervasive hunger. The ebari snuffled uneasily beneath them and swished its tail. Up ahead, another ebari whined as if in answer.

Cale gathered his reins, stopping the horned animal under a large spreading tree. Slipping off, he called out to the others to come back.

Mashal rode up, a frown creasing the scar across his heavy face. "What in the blazes are you stopping here for?"

"Something's wrong." Reaching up, Cale pulled Haemas to the ground. The ebari squealed and rolled its four black eyes.

Haemas wavered on rubbery legs for a moment, then backed up to the comforting solidity of a tree. The forest seemed alive with hunger and crafty, confident stalking.

The rest of the men forced their now plainly nervous beasts back to Cale and Mashal. The white-haired old man dismounted and gripped his reins tightly in his one hand as his ebari tried to bolt into the forest. "I don't like the feel of this," he said in a low voice to Cale.

Haemas had a sudden strong impression of sleek muscles and powerful, curving claws. She looked to the rear again.

"Holnar! Tie those ebari down or we'll lose them!" Cale threw his reins to the old man and reached for the longbow across his back. "Mashal, you watch after our guest here!" Eyes trained on the overhead foliage, he notched a red-fletched arrow into his longbow.

The big man grabbed Haemas's left wrist and pulled her away from the panicked animals. A split second before she heard the low snarl, she knew where the stalker was. She looked up into the arching branches that shut out the sky.

A sly, gleaming blackness curled up there, radiating hunger while it studied them with calculating yellow eyes. She felt the hunger in its crafty mind ... and a surprising sense of familiarity. Somehow, it seemed to know her.

Mashal gasped. "That's the biggest silsha I ever saw!" He released Haemas's wrist to notch a white-fletched arrow into his own longbow.

The silsha snarled again. The ebari strained against their reins.

The old man had tied off several of the shaggy animals to a tree, but the largest ebari refused to go any closer, shaking its horned head back and forth in its frenzy to be free. Holnar stumbled and the ebari dragged him out from under the tree before he could drop the reins.

A streak of gleaming black hide flashed from above, knocking the dappled ebari to the forest floor. Cale stood ready with his bow as the two creatures thrashed together. Holnar lay stunned against a large knobby root a few feet away.

Watching the struggle, Haemas found no room in her mind for her own fear. The predator's sense of excitement and impending victory overwhelmed her, and she inched closer as the ebari kicked one last time. The black silsha raised its bloodstained muzzle and snarled defiance at the men surrounding it.

Holnar stirred and groaned. Cale took careful aim, then froze as Haemas darted between him and his target.

Locked into the silsha's yellow gaze, she felt they were intimately connected, as if this beast had come just for her. From behind, Cale called, "Mashal, get her highness out of there!" Off to the side Holnar groaned again and the animal flattened its small tufted ears at the fallen man, rumbling low in its throat.

Find ... hunger ... protect ... anger ... hunger ... find ... Its thoughts beat relentlessly at her mind.

She stroked the shining midnight coat. *Eat.*

It lowered its long, sharp-muzzled head and tore at the ebari's soft underbelly. Resting one hand on its strong-muscled back, Haemas felt its warm breath as it tore into its meal. Dimly she heard the others dragging Holnar back out of the way, then realized they were moving the remaining ebari out of sight into the forest.

She ran her hand across the length of the satiny coat. Let the chierras go; she didn't need them.

After it had finished feeding, the silsha snuffled warm breath gently into her face, asking her for something, or to do something. Haemas couldn't quite make it out. Puzzled, she held the massive head between her hands and gazed deep into the molten yellow eyes. *What?*

A sudden *whoosh* just over her head made her jump as a red-fletched arrow narrowly missed the black beast. Screaming its defiance, it leaped into the tangle of intertwined trees that roofed the forest.

As she jumped for a limb to follow it, an arm snagged her from behind. Struggling blindly, she fought until she was dizzy and breathless.

Cale lowered her to the leafy ground under the tree. His normally tan face had gone white, his blue eyes staring at her. "Mother above, below, and beyond!"

Mashal seized his arm and pulled him back. "This demon's spawn is crazy!"

Haemas paid no attention. As the black creature moved out of her awareness, she began to have room once again for her own thoughts, and in those thoughts came the realization that, for the first time since she had fled the mountains, she had linked with something outside of her own mind.

The little idiot might at least have had the grace to fall off a cliff, Jarid thought testily, stepping out of the portal just above the Barrier on Kith Shiene. He'd tried killing her at least a dozen times in the last ten years, though. The whelp always had such damnable good luck.

Tightening his shields, he thought that he would like to know exactly how she had gotten past the Barrier, anyway. It should have been the end of her in that condition.

And she wouldn't have gotten away at all if it hadn't been for his uncle's chierra seneschal, Pascar, who'd spoiled everything at the last moment. Well, the idiot had paid in full measure for that mistake.

Now it was left to Jarid to tie up the final loose end. If

the Council ever got its collective hands on Haemas Sennay Tal, he wasn't sure his tampering would hold up to trained inspection.

Feeling the Barrier seethe about his mind, he ducked his head and scrambled down the slope. Tendrils of pain kept seeping in through weak spots in his shields, forcing him to patch as he moved and not letting him pay enough attention to his feet.

Every time he slipped, he determined the pale-eyed little skivit would pay for this when he caught up with her. On the Barrier's far side, he stopped to catch his breath and drew the map out of his pack. He was still a long way from the spot he'd marked last night after his Search.

He stuffed the map into his pack and decided to hike on down to Lenhe'ayn. It would be the middle of the night before he got there—the perfect time to "liberate" one of their horses.

Chapter
Five

"That one's bred out of the Highlands for sure." Holnar gestured with his stump at the girl. "All the really powerful families live up there."

Leading his restless ebari through the shadow-filled forest, Cale glanced up at the pale-haired girl riding silently in his saddle. Her strange, light-gold eyes stared straight ahead, seeing nothing, as nearly as he could tell.

"There's no knowing what you've got hold of when you're dealing with the likes of them." Holnar spat into the brush. "Watch out the lass don't mess with *your* head, same as that beast."

Cale looped the reins tighter around his wrist. "If she could do that, she would've been at it already."

"Has it occurred to you there's something not quite right about her?" Holnar felt the back of his head gingerly, then kneed his ebari up to the front of the line.

"It's occurred to me there's a lot not right about her," Cale muttered at the old man's back. Two whole days now, he thought, and not a word, not even a sound out of the brat. It wasn't natural. *They* talked, at least everyone said they did. Of course, he'd never gone up to a Lord personally and tried to have a conversation. In fact, he'd never even seen one up close before, but everyone knew they didn't spend all their time talking in their heads.

He wondered uneasily just *what* he had gotten hold of.

Mashal dropped back to walk beside him. "I'll lay you odds *she* called that thing down on us!"

A skeptical look spread across Cale's face. "Don't be ridiculous."

"No?" Mashal glared up at the oblivious girl and lowered

41

his voice. "Think! Have you ever seen a silsha around here this time of year, or one so big?"

"Well—"

"The Mother-take-it thing knew her, I tell you, and she knew it." Mashal stumbled over a root and scowled. "You saw how it was. She meant to go with it!"

Cale sighed. When he'd first got a look at those Kashi eyes, the girl had seemed like a bit of gold on the hoof, so to speak. A quick ransom note, a few bags of coins, he'd thought, and no one would ever be the wiser.

"You should have let her go with the damned thing. She's naught but bad luck and here you are, taking her straight back to our homes and families!"

That raised a sore point that didn't bear thinking about. Cale winced as Eevlina's jowly face floated into his mind.

"Leave her deep in the forest for the Old Ones," Mashal insisted morosely. "Admit it, you haven't got the faintest idea where to sell her. For pity's sake, Cale Evvri, she don't even *talk*."

"A female that don't talk," Cale mused. "An interesting concept, at any rate." He twitched the girl's leg. "Don't you agree, prize? A female that don't yammer on all day at a fellow should be worth her weight in gold."

The impossibly light-gold eyes flicked down at him for an instant, but then she was lost in her own world again. Her indifference nagged at him, infuriating and yet worrying at the same time. He brushed a leaf out of his hair and scowled. What exactly did go on in their heads anyway, these high-and-mighty folk from the mountains? Could she be talking to them right now, calling them down to take her home? "Go on with you, Mashal," he said uneasily. "You're just jealous. I caught her, and I'm going to sell her."

The heavyset man snorted and jogged through the brush up to Holnar's ebari, catching onto the stirrup to help himself keep pace.

"Just see if I don't then!" Cale shouted at Mashal's back. "I bet you a horse that I sell this whelp back to their high-and-mightinesses before the season is out!"

The look of triumph Mashal threw back over his shoul-

der gave Cale the squirmy feeling that perhaps this was
going to be harder than he had thought.

Kevisson fingered the hard roundness of the obsidian
ring hanging on its golden chain around his neck and repeated his question.

"A light-haired lass, you say, my Lord?" The homespun-
dressed woman squinted up at him from the ground. Her
weathered face was strong, her brown eyes wary. "We do
shelter many who pass this way. Just how long ago would
that have been?" *You yellow-eyed oaf*, her mind added for
good measure.

Kevisson plucked a vague impression of a slender young
girl from the surface of the woman's thoughts. He smiled
reassuringly at her broad chierra face. "Two or three days
at the most. My youngest sister has run away and my
mother is quite worried. Are you sure you haven't seen
her?"

"Your sister, my Lord?" *Your sister, my foot and ankle,
too!* Her face skeptical, she picked up her skirts and swept
her arm at him. "Come inside and I'll tell you what little
I do know."

Kevisson swung down from the black Lenhe mare he'd
borrowed. A second woman in homespun, this one younger,
appeared to lead it around the back. He followed the first
woman into the gray stone keep, bending his head as he
came through the doorway.

"I am Idora, first among the Sisters here at the Mother's
shrine." She indicated he should sit on the simple wooden
stool before a wide cooking hearth. "We've nothing fancy
here."

Kevisson sank onto the offered seat. "My sister?"

"Yes, the poor young one." Idora sat on a second stool
and retrieved a bundle of knitting. "I found her on the
mountain early one morning when I were returning from a
difficult lying-in clear on the other side of these woods. She
were fair-haired, all right."

Kevisson picked up a figure from Idora's memory:
Haemas Tal, bruised and feverish, exhausted.

"So quiet, she were. The poor thing never made a single
sound the whole two days she were here." *She never told*

what were done to her, if that's what's on your high-and-mighty mind.

He leaned forward. "But she's not here now?"

"No, my Lord." *And I wouldn't be telling the likes of you if she were!* "We meant to return the lass once she were better, but something scared her off."

Kevisson sifted carefully through the old woman's surface thoughts, but the image eluded him. "What was that?"

"I never knowed, my Lord." *Probably the thought of you chasing after her!* "Something troubled her sorely late one afternoon and she slipped off the same night. We never seen her again."

"Do you know where she went?"

Thank the Mother, I do not! Idora shook her gray-haired head resolutely.

Kevisson listened at her thoughts for a moment, but could find nothing helpful, just a confusing combination of resentment and concern. "Did she leave anything behind?"

Idora considered. "Her clothes," she said finally. "They was all torn and bloodied from the mountain." Her chin lifted. "They was ruined. I'm sure the young Lady didn't want them no more."

"Of course," he said quickly. "It's just the sentimental value they would have to my family."

There's not one ounce of decent sentiment in your whole clan! "And which family is that, my Lord?" Idora stopped knitting and looked at him craftily out of the corner of her eye.

"Monmart," Kevisson said, thinking how scandalized his mother would be at having her name dragged into this affair.

Idora put aside her ball of gray wool and the knitting needles. "Not a Highlands House, is it?"

Snobbery even in this humble place. Kevisson smiled thinly.

"Wait here, my Lord." Idora disappeared through the back door. A few minutes later, she reappeared with an armful of soft gold and blue cloth.

He picked up the gold overtunic, noting the ripped, bloodstained shoulder, then examined the loose blue breeches with both knees torn out. Touching the clothes she'd worn so recently heightened his impression. Her face swam into clearer focus in his mind: pale eyes, high cheekbones, a delicate high-bridged nose.

He folded the clothes and felt in his pocket for a coin. "You have been a great deal of help, Sister," he said, pressing the silver hexagon into her palm.

Little enough for the likes of you! Idora's mouth set stubbornly. "This be far too generous, my Lord."

"It's a gift for the poor, Sister."

"Well, then." The coin disappeared. "It would be a sin to refuse." She resumed her knitting.

Kevisson unfolded his legs and stood up, wincing a little at the saddle-stiff muscles. Getting soft, he chided himself. "Good-bye, Sister."

"Good day, my Lord." *And may the Mother take you before you darken Her door again!*

Idora watched the stranger ride away. Mounted on a real horse, too, she thought angrily. The cost of that beast's grain would have fed a chierra family for a year.

"What was all that about?" Knyl asked in her soft voice, staring after the Kashi's back.

Idora's mouth straightened. "The Mother has not seen fit to tell me yet, but I feel She has special plans for the light-haired lass."

"But she ran away." The younger woman opened her apron and tumbled out the whiteroots she had just dug for supper.

"She went into the forest," Idora said. "Straight into the Mother's arms." She thought for a moment. "But with the likes of that one after her, it's a good thing I asked the Mother to send a shadowfoot to protect her."

Knyl's dark eyes grew big. "A silsha?"

"Just wait until his high-and-mightiness tangles with that." A gleam of satisfaction crept across her face. "In fact, I wish I was going to be there to watch."

Ignoring her bound wrists, Haemas turned over on the hard ground, away from her captors, and closed her eyes. A sense of the silsha's dark sleek strength lingered. She concentrated on the link to the world outside her own head, savoring what she'd thought was gone forever. She could feel the ebari's thoughts around her now: tired, hungry, and still a bit nervous. Then she shut them out, trying to picture, instead, the silsha's compelling yellow gaze. It had seemed to want something from her. She wished she knew what.

The low murmurs of the men standing the first guard, the hiss and crackle of the low fire, the whisper of the evening breeze through the branches all faded away, and the darkness carried her into sleep and a dream. . . .

She stood at the dining room door, her palm pressed to the satiny wood.

Jarid turned his light eyes to her—eyes so much like, yet totally unlike her own. "Come in, cousin."

She glanced at the long table. "Where's Father?" Only Alyssa, her stepmother, and Jarid, her orphaned cousin, were waiting to eat.

Something was wrong. Pascar, the old seneschal, moved quietly around the huge table, lighting the tall, twisted candles for the evening meal. Jarid's eyes followed him impatiently. "Out!" he demanded as the last flame took hold. Pascar dropped his brown chierra eyes and bowed, then closed the door behind him.

Haemas slid into her accustomed place. Jarid lounged back against the intricately carved wood of his chair and stretched his arms over his head like a carnivore limbering for the hunt. "You want to know where your father is, skivit?" He winked. "Why should you care? He's never had any use for you."

Alyssa's amused eyes gleamed over the hand she used to mask her smile.

Haemas realized her own hands were clenched around the table's edge. With an effort, she dropped them back into her lap. "I don't believe I'm hungry," she said faintly, holding her shields very tight so no sense of her unease would escape. "Please excuse me." Nodding to her stepmother, she began to rise.

"Not so fast, cousin." Steel rang in Jarid's arrogant voice.

Without meaning to, Haemas found she had dropped back into her seat.

"I have a little something for you." Jarid's sense of inter-

est in her became stronger, sharpening into something closer to ownership. "Something that I trust you will not find unappealing."

Haemas tore her gaze away from Jarid's compelling, ice-pale eyes. "I want to go."

"Very well, then, skivit, by all means, go." His tone mocked her. "But first you must drink a toast with us."

Frozen, she watched as his steady hand poured deep-red tchallit wine into the green crystal goblets set before each place. His sense of triumph was so strong that she knew he was not even bothering to shield. Jarid handed one goblet to Alyssa and the next to Haemas, reserving the last for himself.

All three portions came from the same bottle, yet the moment her hand closed around the slender green stem, Haemas knew something was wrong with it. Her hand jerked away as if the glass had burned her.

Candlelight reflected on the green crystal as Jarid raised his goblet high. "A toast to the Heir of Tal'ayn."

Alyssa rose beside him, her hand draped casually over his shoulder. "To the Heir!" she agreed merrily. Watching each other, they sipped the bloodred liquid.

"What's this, cousin?" Jarid turned the full force of his magnetic gaze on Haemas. "You won't drink with us? We can't have that."

The compulsion to drink flowed over her, more powerful with every passing second. She closed her eyes, fighting his will, gripping the hard arms of her chair until her fingers were numb. Abruptly her cousin showed her a gruesome image in his mind: her father lying dead on the floor.

"Father!" Haemas gasped. "I won't let you!"

Casually Jarid doubled the force of his compulsion. Her hand crept toward the cup. "But," he said softly, "you've misunderstood. You know a touch of Foreseeing runs through the Tal line. No, I'm afraid my unstable cousin is the one who will do that."

The struggle generated a white-hot haze inside her head, through which she could just barely see her hand as it closed around the goblet's green stem again.

Jarid nodded his approval. "Just one sip."

She picked up the cup and put it to her lips. . . .

... "No, no, I wouldn't hurt him!" Her heart thumping wildly, Haemas bolted upright in the darkness. Her head throbbed and hot tears streamed down her face. "I wouldn't!" Her panic increased as something snared her wrists and would not let go.

"Demonfire and damnation!" a male voice exclaimed in her ear.

Haemas cried out and struggled, frantic to get away. A red glow arose in the darkness a few feet away as someone prodded the fire back to life.

A hand clamped over her mouth and an arm caught her shoulders. Gradually her struggles subsided, as she remembered where she was. After a moment, Cale released her, but she just sat there, staring at her bound wrists, trying to control her ragged breathing.

Cale brushed a twig out of his hair. "I suppose we'll never know what *that* was all about."

Haemas tried to massage her aching shoulder with her bound hands. "I'm ... sorry," she said. "I was ... dreaming."

Cale's mouth dropped. "Holy Mother above!"

She blotted her damp cheeks with the back of her hands, realizing every eye in the camp was on her.

"Did it just talk?" Mashal demanded, throwing a large branch on the fire.

The flames hissed and popped as they all stared at Haemas. "Well, prize?" Cale tugged on the thong that led from his hand to her wrists.

She raised her chin. "My name is Haemas."

Mashal scowled and turned away, poking the fire viciously.

Cale shot him a triumphant look. "And what House would you be from, young Haemas?"

She looked away into the blackness outside the fire's yellow light. "That's none of your concern." Then she found her blanket and rolled back into it as well as she could.

Mashal snickered. "Within the month!"

Somewhere out of the darkness came the snarl of a silsha.

* * *

Windsign shared the shadowfoot's frustration as it prowled the outer reaches of the quiet ones' camp, wary of approaching the girl again. She saw the scene through its eyes—the tangled vines, the moldering leaves, the bright circle of frightening, unnatural light. *The shadowfoot is nervous*, Windsign said. *They have fire and weapons.*

He must try again, Summerstone said, *even if it costs his life. We will all die unless we gain her help.*

At midmorning the following day, Jarid jerked irritably at the knobby head of the nag he had liberated from one of Lenhe'ayn's outer fields. Flattening its ears, the black gelding eyed the stream suspiciously and refused to cross.

Cursing his luck, Jarid seized control of the animal's distastefully dull mind and forced its unwilling legs into the shallow water. It was no big secret to him why the Lenhe field hands had not worried if this beast strayed. The only thing more important in its stupid mind than sloth was food.

Where in the seven hells was his fool of a cousin going? he wondered as he released the horse's mind. He'd tracked her to a chierra shrine the night before, but none of the women there had known anything, so he'd stolen an ebari saddle and bridle and moved on.

The idea of women having a religious vocation made him laugh, anyway. Trust the chierras to get everything backward.

Glancing upward at the canopy of leaves and branches, he tried to calculate the time, but too little sunlight filtered through. His stomach insisted it was lunchtime, though. Frowning at the thought of making another meal on trail rations, he cast his mind through the forest until he found the clear, unshielded thoughts of a Lowlander not too far away.

It was an old peddler driving his wagon down a narrow track on the forest's near edge. Jarid cursed. It would take him some time to catch up.

A half hour passed before he could reach the boundary of the forest. The old peddler lay sprawled against a tree trunk while his equally elderly draft ummit watched him snore, chewing its cud.

Jarid dismounted and quickly touched the man's wrinkled forehead to establish a link. *You are sound asleep*, he told the peddler sternly. *Sound asleep.* Then he searched the old man's stores, finding an appreciable quantity of real ham and fresh bread, along with a barrel of last fall's callyt fruits.

Making a sandwich of the ham and bread, he squatted down beside the old man's unconscious body and sorted through his recent memories. His name was Cittar and he had traveled these back areas for the last thirty years, selling mostly to the chierra settlements located far away from the Highlands.

Jarid found no memory of the girl, however. Standing up, he bit into one of the sweet yellow callyts and munched thoughtfully.

It was apparent from the old man's memory that he traveled quite a range in this area. Even though he hadn't come across Haemas Tal yet, there was still a possibility he would, especially if a bit of direction were added to his mind—a marked compulsion to ask after strangers and to seek out young, unaccompanied, light-eyed, fair-haired girls. Jarid smiled to himself.

Crunching the callyt core, he laid three of his six fingers along the old man's lined brow.

Chapter
Six

Haemas flinched as a blue-and-red-fletched arrow *thwa-ng*ed into the bark of a tree just ahead of Cale's nose. Their ebari mount squealed and danced nervously, and the chierra hauled back on the beast's reins. He stood up in his stirrups and addressed the swaying treetops. "That's not funny!"

Her heart thumping, Haemas clutched at his waist to keep from sliding off the back of the anxious, horn-tossing ebari.

Mashal yanked the smoothly worked shaft out of the tree. "Jassfra," he pronounced, his heavy-jowled face breaking into a scowl.

"Oh." Cale grimaced, then twisted around to follow the arrow's trajectory back into the trees. "Are you sure?"

A lithe figure jumped down feet first through the branches and hit the ground with a muffled thump. "Better listen to him." No more than sixteen or seventeen, the girl gave them a merry grin as she straightened, fingering the bone-handled dagger sheathed on her belt.

Haemas stared in amazement at her short-cropped hair; it was as deeply red as the heart of a midwinter fire, a color she'd never seen before.

"Dammit, Jassfra, do you always have to show off?" Cale reined the ebari in until its chin touched its chest. It stopped prancing and only rolled its four black eyes back at him.

The self-assured redhead slung her longbow over her shoulder. "I missed you, too, lover. Lor, *what* have you got there?" She reached for Haemas's leg. "Is that what it looks like?"

51

"None of your damn business!" He swatted her arm away. "Keep your paws off. It's mine."

Bracing her hands on her hips, Jassfra stood back and looked him full in the eye. "You weren't so selfish last winter. You remember, Tenth Night, when you said—"

"Never mind that!" He kicked his ebari and reined it in a wide path around her. "I want to get home now. We've been out a long time."

"And don't I just know it!" Wrinkling her turned-up nose, Jassfra hooked her long legs over the lowest branch above her. "Eevlina has been looking for you these last two weeks. You'd best go on in." She pulled herself up and disappeared into the blue-green canopy of leaves again. "Give her my regards!"

"I'll be sure to do that," Cale muttered under his breath as they rode on.

Haemas stared back over her shoulder. No girl of the Highlands would ever have spoken so to a man, not to mention carried a knife.

As they continued through the forest, the trees grew much larger and farther apart than before. Overhead, the interlocked branches shut out most of the sun, and the trunks stood like massive columns, big enough that five men couldn't have ringed arms around them. They rode a well-marked trail through a cool, dim silence scented with the menthol resin of leaves crushed beneath the ebari's hooves.

Occasionally, as they passed another unseen sentry, they would hear a whistle or a figure would lean out of its leafy hiding place to wave down at them. Cale's moody silence grew darker as they progressed.

Finally they broke into an open space, and their ebari swerved around a deep fire pit where a haunch roasted on a spit. A black-haired woman looked up from a bowl where she was sorting red berries. Her broad face split into a smile. "Cale!"

He nodded, sitting very straight in the saddle. "Amina."

Haemas's mouth watered as she caught a whiff of the roasting meat. Then a squat, gray-haired old woman emerged from a triangular split in one of the huge tree trunks. Cale reined the ebari to a stiff-legged stop in front of her.

"Cale Evvri." The woman rested her fists on her ample hips and regarded him with an icy expression. "I expected you and your misbegotten bunch of males back at least two weeks ago!"

The rest of the ebari-mounted men caught up with them, crowding into the large clearing.

"Fine lot of *horses* you brought, too." Her bushy gray brows knotted together. "I suppose this means you've got nothing at all to show for more than a season's work."

"Now, Gran, you don't really want horses. They're so flighty, like, and—"

"Don't you 'now, Gran' me, you halfhearted excuse for a man!" Her massive breast heaved as she stared up at the girl behind him. "And, I might ask, just what in the seven hells is that?"

Cale swung hastily down from the saddle, then pulled Haemas off like a sack of grain and held her before him. "This is much better than some old horse, Gran. With this, we can *buy* horses, lots of them!" He tilted Haemas's face up so the woman could see her eyes.

Eevlina scowled. Snatching a stick from the ground, she thumped him about the head and shoulders. "*Buy* horses?" She snorted. "Why in the Mother's good name would we ever buy something when we can always steal it?" She swung at his ear. "Have you lost your mind?"

Cale dodged out of her range. "Now listen here, Gran, after I ransom this whelp for lots of money, you can buy anything you want. You ought to give currency a chance. You might like it."

"You're a great big lunking lily-livered disappointment to me, boy!" She gave him one last withering glare, then turned away. "Your mother should've listened to me the day you was born. 'Leave it for the beasts,' I tells her. 'Who needs another worthless male to feed, and a funny-looking one at that?'" She shook her head as she stooped to reenter the tree.

Mashal stared after her broad back as it disappeared into the dark interior. "I didn't think she'd go for it."

"Shut up." Cale's blue eyes narrowed thoughtfully. "On the whole, she took it better than I'd hoped."

* * *

Small but surefooted, the black mare picked her way around the gnarled roots and rotting logs that littered the forest floor. Kevisson relaxed in the saddle, his golden-brown eyes half closed as his mind ranged farther and farther away in a standard spiral Search pattern, trying to locate the young Tal. How could she have gotten so far? Idora's memory plainly showed that just three days ago the girl had been weak with injuries.

Abruptly the mare shied to the right and threw up her sleek black head, her delicate nostrils flaring in alarm. Kevisson grabbed the coarse mane, then reached for her mind to see what had frightened her. Replaying her memory, he saw the small, bluish-gray body with a tiny pointed face dash across the mare's path: a common skivit. He grimaced and swung down from the saddle, anchoring the mare's tossing head with one hand as he sought to calm the high-strung creature with his mind until at last she stood quietly.

Then, tethering the mare to a tree branch, he slipped her bit and fitted on a feed bag of oats. She was a beautiful creature, he thought, but a perfect example of the inbreeding that was going to make her species useless on this planet unless something were done. Instead of breeding for color and conformation, the Lenhes ought to have developed a strain that could digest Desalayan grasses and grains without dying from a lack of trace elements, not to mention one that wasn't terrified of its own shadow.

At any rate, it wasn't the mare's fault that she was an inbred ninny. Kevisson patted the arching, glossy neck and settled back against a neighboring tree, focusing again on his job.

Where was Haemas Sennay Tal?

He strongly suspected from Idora's account that the girl had sensed someone Searching for her and fled into the woods. Unforgivably clumsy. He shook his head. That's what came of teaching amateurs the basics of Search techniques. These days any idiot with a Plus-Three rating thought he could Search as well as a Shael'donn master!

Pulling the soft blue-and-gold clothes out of his saddlebags, he tried to pick up a sense of the girl's mental signature, the qualities that would make her stand out even in a crowd of hundreds. His fingers traced the embroidery around the high collar, a fanciful pattern of moons and stars worked in silver with a large sunburst dominating the middle. Her image crept into his mind much as he had begun to see it before at the chierra shrine: tall, slender, sad . . .

And young, he thought, so young to have attacked her own father and killed a servant. He pushed farther, looking for more. Quiet . . . grief-stricken . . . He waited, but that was all; he sensed no trace of anger or hate, nothing to indicate she was capable of murder.

He closed his eyes and began to count each breath, letting more of the tension in his muscles flow out of his body with each exhalation. Gradually he achieved readiness for the more extensive trance that was obviously going to be necessary. He let himself sink deeper and deeper into the center of his mind.

When he was ready, he pictured again the solemn face, the unusually light-gold hair and eyes, the sense of grief and determination that clung to her clothes like a dim perfume. Then he loosed his mind into the gray otherness for what seemed like hours until he finally found her.

His mind emerged from the grayness with hers as an anchor. Go softly, he chided himself as he circled the bright silvery center of her thoughts. Too close, and he would just frighten her into running even farther.

She was in a place of trees, he realized—giant trees— and other minds hovered nearby. Someone had to be helping her, although these seemed to be only chierra—he sensed no one with any Talent.

Gingerly he picked at the edges of the girl's thoughts, trying to determine the strength of her mind. As she wasn't old enough to have been Tested yet, there had been no record in the Highlands he could depend upon. Nevertheless, Kevisson had no intention of being mindburned like the old Lord, her father.

A sense of power did radiate from her mind, but it had a strange, muted quality about it, quite unlike anything he'd ever come across. Although he would have liked to probe deeper, he withdrew, maintaining the barest thread of contact between his quarry and himself.

Opening his eyes, he glanced around the forest and

stretched his stiff shoulders. As long as she didn't become aware of his touch, he should now be able to ride straight as an arrow to her.

The black mare swished her silken tail and regarded him over the feed bag with heavy-lidded, half-dozing eyes.

Well, Kevisson thought, even a horse could be right occasionally. His Search *had* kept him up very late last night.

He settled on his side and closed his eyes.

Eevlina tore off a greasy mouthful of roasted tree barret, then wiped her stubby fingers on her bodice as she chewed. "It's plain to me now, boy, that I'll never get one bit of use out of you. I should have packed you off to your father's people long ago."

Cale toyed with a bit of berrysauce on his wooden plate, glumly watching the shadows from the fire flicker across Eevlina's face.

"You've never shown the slightest smidgen of sense." The old woman scraped up the last red smear of berrysauce on her plate and sucked it off her little finger. "I must be going soft in my old age to let you stay on so long."

Cale set his dish down by the crackling fire and picked up a stick. "Well, now that I've gone to all the trouble of catching one of those high-and-mighty Lords, the least you could do is let me try, Gran!" He poked angrily at the glowing embers.

"That?" Eevlina glanced at the pale-haired girl hunched up in the shadows, then dissolved into gut-rolling laughter. "High-and-mighty?"

Cale got up stiffly and checked Haemas's bound wrists. She stared off into the darkness as if he weren't even there. Then he settled next to Eevlina again without looking the old woman in the face. "She'll grow," he said shortly, his eyes on the dancing fire.

"You bet your worthless life that bit of stuff will grow!" The old woman glared at him. "And then where will we all be? It'll be jerking us all around like we was puppets on some string, the way all them Lords do."

"No, no!" Cale fought the exasperation in his voice. "I'll take her back long before that. She's worth a rare amount of money, Gran. I just know it."

"Money again!" she exploded. "And can we eat money in the dead of winter, or wear it when we're cold, or ride it when we're on the run?"

"You can get all those things and more, Gran, when you've got money. Really, it's the coming thing. Everyone says."

" 'Everyone says!' " she mimicked. "And I suppose we'll all jump off the top of the nearest tree, if everyone says?"

Cale threw the stick into the fire and stalked moodily into the darkness.

"Money!" Eevlina snorted at his retreating back. "You have a distressing streak of silliness, boy."

Cale snagged Haemas by her wrists and hauled her roughly up to her feet. Damnation, he thought, dragging her after him, the brat was almost as tall as he was.

He yanked her around the huge tree to a small clearing, where a few silver shafts of the first moon's light filtered down through the trees. "All right." He shoved her back into the shadows against the hard trunk. "I want to know what House you be from and I want to know now, or I'll beat it out of you!" He glared at her, breathing hard.

Moving away, she tugged fretfully at the thong cutting into her wrists. "It won't do you any good."

Cale reached out and took a handful of her gown, pulling her close to his face. "You had better pray you're wrong about that."

The girl glanced up into the treetops swaying in the evening breeze. "I can't go . . . back."

"Don't feed me that load of—" He tightened his grip and pushed his face into hers until he could smell the faint scent of woodsmoke in her hair. "What House?"

She flinched and turned her head aside. "Tal."

"Tal," he repeated. "That's one of them Highlands Houses, isn't it?"

"If you take me back to Tal'ayn, they'll kill me—and probably you, too, for that matter."

"I don't believe you."

"You can prove it—at the cost of both our lives."

Cale squirmed as seeds of doubt took root in his mind.

He loosened his hold. "Why would your own kind want to kill you?"

The girl stared silently up at Sedja's silvery crescent, her aquiline profile very different from the snub-nosed ones to which he was accustomed. "It has to do with my father," she said in a low voice. "He was very important, you know."

Cale straightened. "All the better, then."

"Not exactly." Her pale brows knit together as if she had trouble finding the words. "I seem to have . . ."

"Blast you, have—what?"

"Killed him."

Cale stared at her drawn face in dumbfounded silence, having expected any excuse but that. She brushed angrily at the shiny trail of a tear on her cheek with her bound hands.

He shut his eyes and leaned his forehead on his two fists. Wouldn't Eevlina just love to hear this? Maybe they should use the brat for silsha-bait, as Mashal had suggested.

Then he had to laugh—fat lot of good that would do. This particular brat seemed to be on very good terms with silshas. Something clicked in his mind; maybe he could make that work for him. "Back there on the trail, how did you know the silsha wouldn't attack you?"

She considered, her young face standing out white in the moonlight. "I saw in its mind that it didn't want to hurt me."

A grin split his face. "And what about a horse, then? Could you see into its head?"

"A horse?" She nodded slowly. "I suppose so. Why?"

"Because we just may be able to do a little something for Eevlina after all, prize." He stretched his arms behind his head until his joints popped. "There be a nice little fair coming up in a few days." He winked at her in Sedja's silvery light. "A *horse* fair."

"A horse fair," Jarid repeated to himself as he worked the stiffness of a deep Search trance out of his muscles. It was as good a place as any to run the skivit to ground. What was the name of that town he'd picked out of the chierra bandit's mind? He thought for a minute, then had it—Dorbin.

A few feet away, the old peddler grunted in his sleep and resumed snoring with his gap-toothed mouth open. Jarid smiled. It seemed they all had an appointment to meet in Dorbin in a few days.

Cittar glanced uneasily at the tall, bright-haired Lord riding beside his old wagon. It bothered him that he couldn't remember exactly how they had met. Clucking to his elderly ummit, he prodded it with his stick over to the less rutted side of the road.

The Lord looked at him with inhuman golden eyes and reined his dark-brown horse over to give the wagon room. Cittar ducked his head and let the ummit plod on, listening to the tinkle of the tiny bells hung on his wagon. What in the name of the Mother could this silent Kashi Lord want from him?

But suddenly his doubts faded like water draining down a hill after a hard rain. Cittar swatted at one of the pesky insects buzzing around the old ummit's shaggy gray hindquarters and thought instead of the Dorbin Fair. Although he usually went to Dorbin later in the year, he had the urge to swing by now instead. If he took the next fork, he could reach the town in a day or less.

He nodded to himself. "She might be there," he said, then wondered if he was talking about the middle-aged innkeeper, Cynnalee Kochigian, who welcomed his old bones most times.

An image floated up in his mind, the milk-white, pale-eyed face of a young girl—a *Kashi* girl. He mulled that over, feeling angrier at the face with each passing minute. His gnarled hands twisted around the stick, clenching it tighter and tighter.

What was there in that young face that made him so hot, so ready to—kill? The clatter of hooves made him glance up as the Kashi Lord spurred his horse into a ground-covering lope and disappeared up the road ahead of him.

Chapter
Seven

A light breeze ruffled the pale-gold tendrils around Haemas's face as she struggled to pull herself up one-handed into the tree fork. From there, she eased out onto a broad, overhanging limb. An iridescent lightwing perched on the branch just above her head, and she held it there with her mind for a few seconds, listening to its vague thoughts of flight and food.

Then, releasing her hold, she filtered her awareness outward through the leaf-shrouded trees and the encampment. Other minds, like tiny sparks of light, came to her notice—skivits and tree barrets and other such wild creatures; she could touch nothing else. They had always been there, but she had paid no attention to them. Nowadays, though, she found them a comfort when, to her impaired psi-senses, people still felt no more alive than the wind or the trees or the clear green sky.

Frowning, she slid farther out and settled on her stomach. Below, the matriarch Eevlina presided by the fire pit, glaring fiercely and wielding her knobby walking stick like a scepter. Several men sweated under a large iron tub, trying to place it on the fire to please her.

Haemas sighed. As far as she could see, nothing ever suited that one.

"Move one ladylike muscle and I'll slit your refined gullet." The thin cold blade of a knife pricked the tender skin at the base of her jaw. Noiselessly someone slipped down beside her and grasped a handful of her hair. "What are you doing up here?"

"St—staying out of the way," Haemas faltered.

The blade eased off. "Well, I have to admit the sense of that." Jassfra let go and lounged back against the main trunk. "Knowing Eevlina, that is." She cocked her head. "I thought Cale was supposed to keep you tied up all the time."

"He doesn't need to; I can't go back." Haemas sat up and steadied herself with one arm around a smaller branch.

Jassfra ran her thumb along the knife's sharp blade. "If 'twas me, now, I'd be off in a flash, back to all them big fancy houses and jewels and such, and folk to wait on me day and night."

"It's not what you think." Haemas studied the hearty redhaired girl with her athletic build and confident air, trying to picture her as the pampered daughter of some High House, groomed first for duty and obedience, then marriage and childbearing. Jassfra took for granted the freedom women and girls had here in the camp to live as they pleased. None of the men ever dictated what a woman could do or where she could go, as Haemas's father had always done with her.

Without warning, the chilling image of her father's dead hand flung against her boot washed over Haemas again, bringing back the aching despair. Her stomach tightened and she felt sick. Why had she done it? If only she could remember, then perhaps she could find some peace. Her head began to throb, a fierce brightness simmering behind her eyes as it did every time she tried to remember that night. She pressed her fingers to her temples, suddenly cold and clammy despite the warmth of the air.

Jassfra slid the bone-handled knife into an ebari-hide sheath at her waist. "What happened to your blade?" she asked. "Did Cale take it from you? I'd like to see me one of them fine Highlands knives."

The thought of handling a real weapon as these chierra women did brought a blush to Haemas's cheeks. She drew a steadying breath and shoved the memory of that terrible night to the back of her mind. "Kashi daughters are never given knives."

Jassfra snorted. "That's stupid! How are they supposed to take care of themselves, then?"

"They—aren't." Haemas eyed Jassfra's lithe, well-muscled frame with secret envy. "Perhaps you could show me. . . ." Her voice trailed off as a sly hunger nudged at the edge of her consciousness.

Food . . . hungry . . .

She braced herself and slowly stood, curling her twelve bare toes over the rough bark. "Maybe you should get down now."

"Actually . . ." Jassfra pulled herself up. "I was thinking it's *you* should get down."

. . . protect . . . find . . .

Something in the branches far above rustled. "No." Haemas craned her head back. Strength and cunning enveloped her like a blanket. "I'll be all right."

"I don't like you up here hanging over our heads!" Jassfra grabbed Haemas's arm. "You get down right—"

A low rumbling growl interrupted her.

Jassfra's eyes followed Haemas's glance above. The branch immediately overhead shook; then the silsha's narrow black nose broke through the leaves. Blinking its fierce yellow eyes, it thought, *Come! Come now!*

Haemas eased her arm out of Jassfra's stiff fingers and stretched her hand up to the whiskered face. The silsha rumbled deep in its broad chest. She ran a finger along its cheekbones back to its tiny tufted ears and its eyes narrowed in appreciation.

Jassfra's boots scraped as she slid backward down the trunk and thumped hard when she hit the ground. Angry, excited voices below tried to shout over each other. Haemas listened, but she couldn't make out most of what was being said. Finally one voice won out.

"Mother above, girl! What in the seven hells do you think you're doing up there?"

That was Eevlina, Haemas decided. She dangled one foot over the side of the branch.

"Do you or do you not have another one of those damn silshas up there with you?"

Haemas scratched the beast behind its tufted ears. "Yes."

"Then get rid of it!"

The silsha leaned its sinuous body companionably against her. "It's not hurting anything."

"Get rid of it, you little wretch, or you'll get what's coming to you if I have to climb up there and give it to you myself!"

An argument ensued, too low for Haemas to make it out. Then she heard Cale's voice.

"Well supplied with water and food up there, are you?"

Haemas pressed closer to the silsha's warmth.

"Blanket and all, too, I suppose?"

Haemas sighed. *Wait*, she told the silsha. It rolled over on its side and playfully stretched out a foreleg ending in wicked four-inch claws.

Slowly she climbed back down the massive trunk, favoring her shoulder. When she reached the ground, the whole camp was crowded around. Jassfra stood, feet braced wide apart, an arrow notched and aimed up into the leaves.

"If you kill it," Haemas said, "I'll call another one—when you're all sleeping!"

Jassfra's hands didn't move, but her brown eyes rolled down to look at the girl.

"You'll do no such thing." Eevlina grabbed Haemas roughly by the shoulders and shook her. "Don't they teach you to obey your elders up there in the Highlands?"

Haemas stiffened against the pain in her torn shoulder muscles. Above, the silsha picked up on her discomfort and rattled their ears with an angry snarl. Closing her eyes, she reassured it that she was all right. "He won't hurt anyone. I promise."

"You'll bring another one in the night, you say?" Eevlina threw up her hands, then glared at Cale. "We'd be safer, then, just to kill *this* little monster!"

After a strained silence, Cale smiled thinly at Eevlina. "I'm thinking a tame silsha could be a rare wonderful thing to have along on a raid."

"Oh?" Eevlina's heavy face creased doubtfully. "Well, call it down, girl. What are you waiting for?"

Come down, Haemas told the silsha. *Quietly.*

The foliage trembled as, with one great leap, the silsha bounded to a much lower branch, then landed on the leaf-covered ground at her feet. White-faced, Jassfra stumbled back, realigning her arrow on the beast's chest. The silsha flattened its ears, but Haemas placed a hand on the black-velvet head. Blinking its hot, yellow eyes, it curled lazily around her legs, the flick of its restless tail the only sign of movement.

Eevlina paced warily around Haemas, her face creased in a heavy scowl. "What's to keep that black-hearted beast from eating the ebari or even, Mother preserve us, one of us?"

The silsha licked its lips.

"We could feed it," Haemas suggested.

"Feed that demon-spawned creature!" Eevlina snorted. "The very idea of wasting our food on that—that thing!"

"I'm sure it would be much happier hunting," Cale broke in hastily, "just as it has *always* done."

"See that it continues to do so!" Eevlina threw back her shoulders with all the dignity she could muster, wielded her stick to clear a path through the crowd, and stalked into the trees.

"He be asking for you, Lady," the chierra nurse insisted.

"I can't possibly come now." Alyssa unlaced her fingers and tried to stare the woman down. "Tal'ayn does not run by itself, and his Lordship very well knows that. I'll look in later tonight, when I'm not so busy."

"Begging your pardon, Lady." The woman dropped a hasty curtsey. "But that's what you said *last* night. He's rare fit to be tied, he is."

Where was Jarid, Alyssa thought angrily, when there was real work to be done? How dare he go off and leave her up here alone with this horrid mess? With a visible effort, she controlled her anger. "Very well. I'll come in for a few minutes, but I want it understood that this inconvenience is not to be repeated."

Keeping her eyes on the floor, the old woman nodded. "Thank you, Lady. I know the sight of his dear wife will speed his Lordship's recovery."

A faint line appeared between Alyssa's golden eyes. Did she detect an underlying current of sarcasm in the old chierra's words? Straightening her shoulders, she glided ahead of the servant through the doors and into the main bedchamber.

The old woman's homespun skirt rustled as she fussed

with the pillows. Then she bent over and whispered to the still figure in the great bed. "A visitor, your Lordship."

The gray head stirred restlessly on the pillow. "Alyssa?"

Alyssa closed her eyes as she sought to weave her mental shields so tightly that he would read nothing from her. "I'm here, Dervlin," she answered in a cool voice.

"How . . . long?"

"Two weeks." She moved closer to the bed, disgusted, as always, by the stale medicinal smells of the sickroom and the sight of his haggard white face upon the pillow. "You had an accident."

"Accident?" The gnarled hand on the bed strained to reach for her.

How she hated the touch of his old man's hands! Alyssa affected not to notice his hand, looking down instead to brush an imaginary speck off her brown velvet skirt.

"I . . . I don't . . . remember." The hand dropped back to the mattress, exhausted even by that simple effort.

"That's exactly why you must rest, Dervlin." She twitched at the corner of his blanket. "Stop wasting your strength harassing the nurse to bring you visitors and get on with your recovery. The healer was quite firm about that on his last call—*no* visitors."

The startled brown eyes of the chierra nurse glanced up at her, then fled back to the patient again. Alyssa grimaced. Unfortunately the healer had said no such thing, and the creature was very well aware of it. Her memory would have to be adjusted to agree with Alyssa's official version. She sighed. She would leave that chore for Jarid's return; he was much more proficient at it.

"Try to rest now, Dervlin, and I'll come back to see you later." Much later, she amended mentally, trying to hold down her pace to a brisk walk as she headed for the door.

After closing the heavy, carved doors behind her, Alyssa leaned against them and locked her hands together to keep them from shaking. Why didn't the old bastard have the good taste to simply *die* and let them all get on with their lives?

Jarid had promised his uncle would be gone in a matter of days. Now he actually seemed to be recovering. She ran a hand over her burning cheek, then straightened her back.

She had a house to run, as well as an estate—both of them almost totally hers at last.

The image of her grandfather's face began to coalesce in her mind.

Grandfather! A feeling of uneasiness washed over her, but she quickly hid it behind her shields.

Alyssa, child, how is your husband? Lord Senn projected an aura of warm sympathy.

Worse, Grandfather. She leaked a nuance of deep despair through her shields. *Much worse.*

Setting her water bucket down in a rare patch of golden sunlight, Haemas shook her head as she held up her blistered palms. Alyssa had always insisted her stepdaughter was too "boyish and unladylike" to do anything but disgrace the name of Tal among the High Houses. If Alyssa could see her now, fetching and carrying for a bunch of chierra thieves . . .

She rubbed her stinging hands over the breeches they had given her and sighed. Alyssa had always been so condescending, even that first day when Dervlin Tal had brought her to Tal'ayn as his Lady.

Haemas remembered Alyssa's tiny, perfect figure and sighed. Even though she was so much younger, Haemas was a full head taller than Alyssa and her stepmother never let her forget it.

"Do try to stand up straight, child," Alyssa had said in that refined voice of hers. "No one will offer a matrimonial contract for a big lump like you if you don't at least try to move gracefully. And eat something—you're no bigger around than a rail."

Move gracefully, Haemas thought. She wondered what was happening at Tal'ayn, now that—

An icy shiver gripped her and a warning throb behind her eyes made her gasp. It would not do to think about any of *that*.

Just overhead, she heard the leaves whisper as the silsha slipped along a slender branch. She looked up and laughed as the great beast reached down with a wickedly clawed paw. Matching his foot with her hand, she marveled at its size. Even with her six fingers spread wide, the silsha's paw was much bigger.

"There you be." Cale rounded a tree and stood there, glaring at her with his strange blue eyes. "It's time to leave."

Haemas looked down at her boots. "I'm not going."

"Don't recall nobody asking your leave on the subject, your high-and-mightiness." He folded his arms across his threadbare shirt.

A rumbling snarl broke from the silsha, and Cale's dark face paled. "And look at this! We can't even get the ebari into camp as long as that—*thing* be anywhere near!" He glanced uneasily at the black beast draped over a low-hanging limb just above his head. The silsha wrinkled its lips back from fierce white incisors, then washed its foreleg with its rough tongue.

"Eevlina told you to send it away." Cale moved prudently out from under the dangling claws. "Get rid of it. It's high time we was off to Dorbin."

Haemas sighed, then looked up into the narrow-muzzled black face. *Go away and hunt*, she told it reluctantly. *Far away.*

The silsha slitted its yellow eyes and panted. *You come away! Come to trees!*

Haemas conjured up images of indolent wild ebari and fat tree barrets. *No, go and hunt now. Come back and find me later.*

Small one must come. The silsha stretched out a foreleg and touched her face with a velvet paw.

No! She motioned at the beast. *Go hunt!*

A wave of frustration emanated from its mind as it rose to all fours and stretched its long body sinuously. Then it leaped effortlessly into the higher branches. Loneliness washed over Haemas as an angry growl reverberated back through the trees.

"Finally!" Cale blotted his perspiring forehead with his sleeve. "Now maybe we can get down to business."

Haemas turned and followed him back through camp to the waiting ebari on the other side. "You mean now you can go *steal* something."

"Of course." He seized her from behind and hoisted her into the saddle.

"Quit blathering with that demon's whelp and help your old Gran onto this Mother-forsaken beast." Eevlina gathered her tattered homespun skirt and glared over her shoulder.

Moving to her side, Cale hastily bent over and locked his hands together, grunting as he took the heavyset old woman's full weight. Then he looped Haemas's reins over his wrist and swung up onto his own shaggy ebari. He kicked his mount, towing hers along beside him.

Haemas settled back, adjusting to the ebari's thumping, loose-jointed gait. If Cale thought that she, a Lord's daughter, however disgraced she might be, was going to steal horses for a bunch of chierra bandits—well, the joke would be on him. She would never find the nerve to pull it off.

She reached out for the silsha's mind, but either it was far out of her range or it had shut her out in some way. What was it old Yernan, her tutor, had always said to her? *Shut the world out or it will shut you out.* She closed her eyes and began to block out the distracting information that her senses provided. First, sight, of course. Then she closed off her awareness of the forest noises and the voices of the raiders discussing their strategy for Dorbin. Then she blocked out the ebari plodding beneath her, the ever-present twinge in her stiff shoulder, the hard curve of the saddle.

Still unable to center, she paused, wondering what she had forgotten. Then it came to her—the smells. She shut out the sweaty musk of the ebari, the damp scent of green things underfoot, and the faint acridness of perspiration.

Finally she floated without distractions in the center of her own thoughts, trying to see if the silsha followed. Gradually she became aware of a line, some sort of tie that led from her mind to—somewhere else.

It was not of her making. She had never seen anything like it. Following the line through the gray otherness, she tried to see where it led. Just when she was beginning to get a glimmering of the source, she felt herself falling.

"Mother above!" Cale's voice exclaimed.

She hit the ground with a head-bouncing thud.

Cale leaped down and pulled her up into a sitting position. "If you aren't the most accident-prone youngster I ever seen!" he grumbled. "Didn't anyone ever tell you sleeping were meant for beds?"

Haemas blinked, trying to see through the spots dancing in front of her eyes. The back of her head throbbed with an insistent ferocity. She closed her eyes and checked for the invisible tie; now that she knew where to look, it was easy.

It was still there.

Pulling the rough gray cloak closer around his face, Jarid congratulated himself on the effectiveness of his disguise. The old chierra still making his way up the road to the rocky cliffs of Dorbin would remember only that a youthful thief had pushed him down and torn his cloak from his hands.

The fact he had willingly handed it to a Kashi Lord had been blocked from his mind forever.

Jarid smiled. He could almost relish staying among these simple, unresisting minds, where a Talented man could take anything he wanted. It was quite unlike the Highlands, where he'd had to fight for everything he wanted, then fight even harder to keep it. For the first time he understood why many of the lesser Houses had moved down to the lower elevations. Even a relatively unTalented Kashi could live like the highest Lord among these five-fingered animals.

He stepped up to the stone-block gatehouse before the town wall of Dorbin, projecting an image of brown chierra eyes. The heavy-browed guard gave him a surly look. "What be your business in Dorbintown?"

Jarid held out the copper. "I've come for the fair."

"You carrying any iron or other metal goods?"

Jarid stiffened as the man pulled his cloak aside to check his belt. *Brown hair and brown eyes and an empty belt,* he projected strongly at the guard. *You see only brown hair and brown eyes and no sword or dagger!*

The guard blinked, then rubbed his whiskery chin. "No iron," he said. "One copper."

Jarid flipped the coin at him and pulled the hood tight around his head again before he entered the town. Puzzled, he put his hand on the shoulder of a solitary man standing in front of a disreputable-looking tavern. "Why is no iron brought into Dorbin?" he asked, laying a compulsion on the half-drunk man to answer.

The man's bloodshot eyes blinked mistily at him. "Dorbintown be famous for its iron, friend!" He patted Jarid's shoulder. We don't allow no shoddy outside metals to be sold at our fair!"

Jarid released him and watched the man maneuver unsteadily down the unpaved street. No outside metal. He fingered the cold blade of his dagger underneath the cloak. Then it should be all the more exciting and puzzling for this dull, provincial town when a certain pale-skinned young girl was found here with a contraband dagger buried up to the hilt in her Kashi back.

Chapter
Eight

Haemas's head still ached from her fall when they rode out of the forest's leafy silence into the soft gray light of dusk. Jagged limestone cliffs rose in an unbroken wall on the other side of a reed-choked river, and she smelled the dankness of mud and wet stone.

Cale reined his ebari in and indicated the cliffs with his chin. "Dorbin lies above on the other side."

She rubbed fretfully at her throbbing forehead and squinted; she could just make out a single squat tower in the distance, but the effort made her head hurt even more. Closing her eyes, she sagged back in the saddle. They had been riding all day. All she wanted was a few hours of uninterrupted sleep.

"Oh, no, you don't!" A rough hand shook her arm. "Don't you go sleeping on that ebari again!"

Haemas cracked her eyes open.

Eevlina's grizzled face stared back. "I've got big plans for you, whelp, and you'd better come through," the old woman said, then whacked the girl's ebari across the hindquarters with her stick. Haemas grabbed for the creature's long neck as it leaped forward, nearly jerking its reins from Cale's hand. He cursed, then rode back under the trees, towing her mount after him.

"We'll camp here tonight." He swung a leg over and dismounted, then tied his ebari to a tree. "We'll hit Dorbintown tomorrow."

Haemas pulled one foot from the stirrup, then slid down the beast's warm, hairy side and stood there, clinging to the saddle, trying to make her knees lock.

"How about calling us up a nice juicy tree barret for dinner?" Eevlina's voice bellowed in her ear.

Talk to something and then eat it? Nauseated, Haemas blinked at the old woman's beaklike nose for a long moment, then let go of the saddle. Her knees buckled and Cale caught her arm.

"I told you we should have rested," he said to Eevlina as he steered the girl away from the ebari's milling feet and eased her to the ground. "She's not made of iron, you know."

Haemas pressed her fingertips against her aching temples. She wasn't cut out for this. What point was there to a life that existed only to roam the Lowlands and steal? She had to get away from these people.

Cale's footsteps walked away. "Gran," he said after a moment. "Brew up some of that assafra root what's good for headaches and the like."

"For her ladyship over there, I suppose?" Eevlina's voice was caustic.

"Only if you want her fit to get you a few horses tomorrow." Cale paused. "Shame to come all this way and get nothing, though. I hear there's always some fine stock at Dorbin Fair."

"One piddling fall on the head and the whelp's half dead," Eevlina fussed. "Them lords and ladies must be an all-fired puny lot!"

Haemas heard the sound of wood being broken for a fire and then, a short time later, the crackle of flames. She hunched against the scratchy tree bark, shivering in the cooling air and longing for the silsha's companionable warmth.

She would have liked to see if it was anywhere near, but her head ached too much to even think about trying to find it. Every time she tried to concentrate, the throbbing intensified until she could hardly see.

She must have dozed off, for the next thing she knew, Eevlina was pressing a wooden cup of hot liquid into her hands.

"Drink this," the old woman ordered harshly, then surprised Haemas by laying a work-roughened hand across her forehead. "No fever, at any rate."

Haemas sniffed at the cup and wrinkled her nose at the acrid-smelling dark liquid.

"You drink that, you little wretch, or I'll skin your scrawny, pasty-skinned body myself!" Eevlina's gray eyebrows knit together, marking a fierce line across her ravaged face.

Haemas gulped hastily, trying to swallow the foul-smelling stuff quickly so she wouldn't have to taste it. Just about the time the first swallow hit bottom, though, her throat began to burn and she started to cough.

"Don't suppose I made it a mite too strong, do you?" Eevlina wiped her callused hands on her skirt and stood up, smiling craftily. "I must be getting old."

Cale gave the old woman a dark look as he thumped Haemas's back. "That'll be the day."

When she could breathe again, Haemas wiped at the tears on her cheeks. "My head does feel a little better."

"Course it do," he said stiffly, taking the cup back. "Nobody in these parts knows herbs better than Eevlina." He tossed a tattered blanket at her. "Shut up and get some sleep."

Hugging the worn material to her chest, Haemas pillowed her head on her good arm and curled up next to the tree. Lying very still, she could hear the trickling of water as the river swirled against the gray cliffs.

She awoke with a start, a cold shiver running through her that had nothing to do with the mild spring night. She had been dreaming, but for a moment she could not remember of what. Then she knew: Jarid.

But it had been so strange, not really like a dream at all. He had seemed to squat next to her as she slept, whispering threats in her ear while she lay powerless to wake.

Hugging the ragged blanket around her shoulders, she stood up and nervously surveyed the meager camp. In the scant moonlight filtering down through the trees, she could just see Cale sleeping a few feet away from her, his dark-haired head turned away. Eevlina and the rest were only featureless lumps rolled up in their blankets closer to the waning fire. Overhead, the treetops rustled in the night breeze.

"Here, what do you think you're up to?"

The fierce whisper startled her, and she whirled around. Holnar's bearded old face emerged from the shadows.

"I . . . thought someone was here," Haemas said, "in the camp."

"Likely story." He spat into the dirt, narrowly missing her foot. "You just thought you'd get out before the rest of us and keep all them horses for yourself!"

Haemas stared at him.

"Go back to sleep." He shoved her elbow irritably. "Go on, or I'll wake Eevlina and then you'll really be sorry!"

They would all be sorry if that happened, she thought, but she lay back down, this time beside Cale, and closed her eyes. As she drifted back to sleep, though, a nagging thread of fear insisted that somehow her cousin with the bright-gilt hair had really been there.

Famished from expending energy on his Search, Jarid left the privacy of his room at the inn and went downstairs into the noisy common area where he slid onto a long bench close to the hearth and ordered a cup of tea. When the haggard serving wench brought it, he cupped his hands around the clumsily made white mug and let the warmth of the dark tea seep through into his hands. So close! A crooked smile played across his lean face, but no one at the crowded table paid him any heed. He permitted this bunch of cattle to see only a shabby stranger with dark hair and dark eyes—a man just like every other in this Light-forsaken town.

The bedraggled little beggar should be arriving tomorrow, however, according to the plans he had lifted from her sleeping mind. Then he would finish this miserable business so he could return to the Highlands and take up his rightful place as Lord of Tal'ayn.

Jarid chuckled to himself and shook his head. Imagine his skivit of a cousin taking up with a bunch of chierra *thieves*, of all people! Uncle Dervlin should be turning over in his grave right about now.

That is, if the evil-tempered old man had finally had the sense to die and leave them all in peace.

Out of the corner of his eye, he saw the peddler walk

through the inn's front door and sit down at a long table littered with crockery and tankards.

"Cittar!" The innkeeper, a tall bony widow, broke into a broad smile as she wiped her hands on her apron. "What brings you here this time of year?"

"Cynnalee, darling." The old man rose and pressed his whiskery lips to her work-reddened palm. " 'Twas your beauty what brung me, and nothing else."

Snatching her hand away, the woman buried it under her apron, managing to look both scandalized and pleased at the same time. "Go on with you," she scoffed. "It never brung you this early before."

Cittar pulled off his battered hat and smiled up at her. "It's true I resisted for a long time, Cynnalee, but this year it seemed I could hear you calling just as clear as morning." He gave her dry, lined cheek a gentle pinch. "Would you be having a bit of your best ale for an old man?"

She nodded and picked up a tankard.

In his dark corner, Jarid laid a coin on the table and slipped his hood down lower over his face. Although he'd rendered the old man unable to recognize him during their meeting on the road, it did no good to play with the Fates. He paused at the door just long enough to see the peddler draw the woman into his lap and nuzzle her neck.

Outside, late arrivals drifted into town for the fair, carrying the awkward lumps of their trade goods on their backs or towing plodding, heavily laden ummits behind them. Jarid surveyed the thatched roofs in the moonlight across the small town and the straggling rows of people headed for the common.

Tomorrow, he thought with a sense of satisfaction, she would come straight to him.

Kevisson lifted the saddle to the back of his flighty black mare, still puzzling over the brief mental contact that had touched him earlier. After a brief skittering against the edge of his mind, he'd sensed nothing more, but he hadn't imagined it; someone had traced *him*. For a moment, the young Tal girl crossed his mind, but he dismissed that idea. She hadn't even felt his touch when he had created the subliminal line of contact between them.

Tightening his shields, he swung up on the compact black mare and turned its nose on a path that would lead them deeper into the forest. If the girl and her companions remained stationary again today, he would finally catch up. Then it would only be a matter of biding his time until he could spirit her away.

He pulled the jet-black obsidian band off its golden chain—a birth gift from the girl's maternal family line, Birtal Senn had said—and slipped it over his sixth and smallest finger. Then he pictured her face as the chierra sister at the shrine had seen her. But a sense of unease crept over Kevisson as her somber face floated in his mind. *Stomach-wrenching fear . . . shame, bitter as gall . . . suffocating black terror.*

In the name of the Blessed Light! He snatched the glass ring off his finger and stared at it, the blood roaring in his ears. The searing emotions remained, although they were not as intense. He took a deep, steadying breath, then ripped a bit of cloth from the hem of his tunic, hurriedly wrapped the ring to keep it away from his bare skin, and stuffed it into his pocket.

Kevisson's hands still shook as he gave the mare his heels and let her pick her way around the deadfall and snags. The arching forest of redthorn and spine-wood soon gave way to gnarled old giants that shut out the sky, and he kept a careful watch for chierra minds up ahead. Finally he caught a faint glimmer of light reflecting on water up ahead in the cool, impenetrable shade beneath the oversize trees. The thirsty mare nickered softly.

Kevisson dismounted and led her under the low-hanging branches, ducking his head. Pulling eagerly away from him, the mare buried her muzzle in the secluded pool. He waited a few blinks for his eyes to adjust to the dimness. Leafy vines trailed from the branches of the trees, mottled with yellow green; to his surprise, the sides of the pool were formed of quarried white stone blocks. A set of broad steps led down into the water on his side.

Kevisson shivered suddenly and pulled his cloak more closely around his body. It was much colder here where the sun didn't reach, and oddly quiet. A fine mist steamed off the water's mirrored surface.

He walked closer and knelt, peering into the still water. Five oddly cut ilsera crystals had been set into the white stone border below the waterline. Their faint pale-blue glow brightened as he watched.

The whole effect made him think of some sort of portal, but that was ridiculous. No one would ever build a portal in water. Then his skin prickled; perhaps it was ilseri.

The mare raised her dripping muzzle and twitched her ears. Kevisson reached for the trailing reins. He had never seen an ilseri, of course. The Old Ones, as some called them, had retreated into the deep forests long ago, when humans had first come to Desalaya. No one had encountered one within living memory. It was quite possible they were all dead now, but occasionally an artifact was found.

As he tugged the reluctant mare away from the pool, a faint hum began in his head, like a cloud of nits, growing louder by the second, and painful. The reins slipped through his nerveless fingers as the mare snorted and trotted away through the trees. Kevisson fell to his knees, weaving his shields tighter, but the sound knifed through his brain as if he had no shields at all. A numbing cold swept over him. He doubled up in the grass, clamping his hands over his ears in a useless effort to keep his head from bursting. Try as he might, he could not shield against it.

A boneless hand slipped under his arm and pulled him to his feet. Kevisson sagged against a smooth, cool body, struggling to walk, unable to open his eyes.

The overwhelming, echoing vibrations finally began to recede. He felt the warm dance of sunlight on his face, but his very bones ached with cold. The supporting arm propped him against the rough bark of a tree, but his legs would not hold him, and he let his back slide down the trunk until he rested on the ground.

He hunched there, hands tucked under his armpits for warmth, and tried to stop shivering. The alien vibration in his head continued to fade until it was ... gone. Forcing open one heavy eye, he looked blearily around and saw that this blessed patch of sunlight was at the edge of the forest. Broad fields swept toward the horizon. He tried to get to his feet, but fell back as dizziness overwhelmed him.

Closing his eyes, he leaned back again against the comforting solidness of the tree trunk and let the sun bake the bone-deep cold out of his body. When he finally stopped shivering, he took stock of his situation. Although he seemed to be at the edge of the forest, that couldn't be. From any direction, the forest's edge had to be at least forty miles from the secluded pool.

He cast his mind about for the mare, but she was nowhere to be found. He reflected ruefully that she was probably on her way back to Lenhe'ayn, along with his saddlebags and every scrap of clothing and provisions he had brought with him.

Dusting his hands off on his brown breeches, Kevisson stood up. He would just have to finish his assignment, then return to Lenhe'ayn and reclaim his belongings. Squinting up into the cloudless green sky, he tried to calculate the hour, then stopped. The orange sun hung midway between the horizon and its zenith: Third Hour or so.

But when he had found the pond, the day had already progressed well beyond the Sixth Hour.

He backed against the tree. What had happened at the pond must have been a shock to his mind. He could have understood if he had lost an hour or so, but it seemed to be *earlier*, not later.

Finally he shook himself and checked for his link to Haemas Tal. It was still there; in fact, she seemed quite close now. If he had traveled forty miles between one breath and the next, at least it seemed to be in the right direction. He started hiking down to a road just visible below the forest's edge. Whatever the truth of what had just happened, he still had a job to do.

Eevlina smeared a last dab of dark stain across Haemas's cheek and stood back to survey her work.

Haemas rubbed her nose with the back of her hand. "Stinks."

"Humph!" Eevlina wiped her hands on her tattered homespun skirt. "No one will suspect anything amiss with a natural smell like that. You be still until that stain dries or I'll take my stick to your other end."

Arms held out from her sides, Haemas backed away and wandered over to watch Cale pack instead. At least her head didn't hurt anymore. The old woman must know something about herbs. All this fuss just to steal some horses, she thought, leaning against a tree trunk, and for what? She'd bet her own weight in ilsera crystals that these chierras didn't have a supply of old-style grains, and without that, the horses would eventually sicken and die. Nonnative stock simply couldn't survive more than six months on native plant life.

"Enough laying about!" Eevlina limped over to the nearest ebari and glared back over her meaty shoulder. "The morning's half over. Are you worthless excuses for human beings going to piddle the whole day away here on your backsides, or are we going to go get us some horses?"

Mashal whooped and launched himself up into the saddle, his scarred face split in a fierce grin. His ebari squealed and tossed its horned head. Holnar smiled, too, as he accepted his reins from Jassfra and pulled himself one-handed up into the saddle. Cale leaned over to give the old woman a hand up. His brows furrowed as he took Eevlina's weight and then strained to boost her up into the saddle.

Haemas waited by the beast she'd ridden up to this point, but Cale swung her up on his own ebari to sit in the saddle in front of him.

"I can ride by myself!" She twisted around to look at him as he settled behind her.

Reaching forward to tuck a bit of stain-darkened hair back under her hood, he shook his head. "Not this trip, prize. Today I'm keeping a close eye on you. And don't forget to keep those inhuman hands of yours out of sight."

He kicked the ebari and reined it into the file of riders in front of them as they started for Dorbin.

Chapter
Nine

Blue and red and yellow banners waved gaily above the entire width of the town common as customers wandered from stand to stand, searching for a bargain to entice the coppers out of their purses and pockets. The air was filled with the smell of baking bread as well as roasting pullets and fresh spice cake.

Jarid Tal Ketral sauntered unrecognized through the laughing people, listening to the music and waiting for events to take their scheduled course. He had the peddler ready to leave the inn and primed for action at his first sight of a certain young Kashi face.

And as for his cousin, he had already picked up the first vague thought patterns of the thieves as they entered the town's dusty streets.

A glimpse of glossy dark braids framing a round, pink-cheeked face caught his eye. Jarid stopped at a booth made of a rough-hewn plank over two barrels. The buxom girl, dressed in a red smock covered by a crisp white apron, turned back to the counter. Her cheeks blushed a bright crimson when she caught him watching her.

She dropped her dark liquid eyes. "Ale, sir?"

"All right." Jarid fished in his pocket and flipped her a silver that mirrored the sunlight as it spun.

She caught the glittering hexagonal coin between her palms, then gazed at him with wide, troubled black eyes. "I haven't enough coin to change this, sir."

He reached out a hand and cupped her chin. "Did I say I wanted change?"

Backing away, she began to protest, but he slipped past the outer surface of her mind and stilled all thought of fear or resistance. The tiny crease down the center of her forehead relaxed; her even white teeth smiled at him. "That's most kind of you, sir," she said with a trace of Lowlands lilt in her voice.

Jarid traced the smooth curve of her neck with his finger. Not bad. A little soap, the proper clothes, and this one would clean up very nicely. Maybe he would have her brought up to Tal'ayn when—

"Get your bloody hands off me daughter, you backwoods scum!" A massive hand gripped Jarid's shoulder and whirled him around to face a tight-lipped father's rage. The dark-haired girl just laughed and passed Jarid a foaming tankard of rich golden ale. Jarid laughed, too, as he maintained his hold on the girl's mind and snaked a tendril of thought into the hot red core of the man's anger.

The hold on his shoulder eased into friendly pressure and in a minute the father was thumping him on the back and laughing with them. "I didn't know you was coming, lad," he said. "Why didn't you send word?"

Jarid sipped at the tart ale. "And spoil the surprise?" Abominable stuff, he thought, far too bitter for his taste. "Now, perhaps—" He hesitated while he sifted through the girl's mind for her name. "Perhaps *Mairianda* could go with me to look through the horses. I have my eye out for a likely beast."

The thought that he couldn't spare the girl flashed through the man's mind, but he found himself saying "Sure, lad. Go on ahead. I'll watch the booth."

Jarid slipped his arm around Mairianda's plump shoulders and drew her down the row of stalls. Her black eyes sparkled as she looked shyly sideways at him.

Too bad he still had business to take care of, Jarid thought regretfully.

Kevisson's link to Haemas Tal grew stronger with each passing moment; she had to be in the gray-walled town just ahead of him. He eased down onto a large boulder on the side of the dusty road and took the weight off his aching feet. He hadn't walked so much in years.

You're getting soft, he told himself. Usually the Andiine Brothers of Shael'donn worked with the mind, not the feet.

Well, after this assignment, he should certainly be back in shape.

An old woman limped past, trundling a pushcart heaped high with round whiteroots and leafy greens. She glanced at him, her lively brown eyes almost buried in the deep network of sun-wrinkles. Then, making the four-cornered sign of the Mother over her heart, she spat into the dirt at his feet and moved on.

Evidently Kashi faces weren't too popular around these parts. Kevisson sighed as her stooped figure halted at the gate and waited for the guard to search her vegetables. Then she dropped a coin into his outstretched palm and passed through.

Well, he didn't like to do things this way, but neither did he want to have his head smashed in some alley before he could find the girl. Kevisson closed his eyes and concentrated. It shouldn't take much, just a heightening of his natural coloring, and these people should perceive him as chierra.

As he approached the gatehouse, the guard watched him with a bored expression. "What be your business in Dorbintown?"

"I want to buy a horse." Kevisson watched the guard closely, suddenly conscious of the warm sun beating down on his shoulders.

"Any iron to declare?" The guard's eyelids drooped with boredom.

"No."

"One copper." The guard yawned and held out his sun-browned hand.

Kevisson felt through his pocket but felt only silvers, much too rich for a chierra farmer attending a rustic fair. He dropped one of the shiny hexagons into the man's hand, projecting the impression that it was only a copper.

Glancing at the coin with an indifferent expression, the guard waved him on into the town. Kevisson smiled to himself as he crossed the boundary. He wished he could be a skivit in the woodwork later, when someone found a silver hiding among the day's proceeds.

A considerable number of riders, as well as many people on foot, surged down the street, mostly headed in the same direction. Kevisson fell into the flow, catching excitement from nearby minds. A fair—they were thinking and talking about a fair in the center of the town.

He tested his link to the girl; sharp and clear. She was very close.

The pair of young men in front of him turned aside at a two-story inn, waiting at the door as a middle-aged woman with a worried expression and an older man, tugging on his tunic, emerged. The man jammed on a worn hat, then jerked his arm out of the woman's grasp, arguing with her all the while.

Kevisson dodged around them and continued down the street, following his link. Their angry voices carried behind him.

"What do you mean, you have to go now?" she cried. "Go where? You've barely just arrived."

"Leave me be, wench. No one owns Cittar!" the man replied loudly. "I has to go. That be all there is to it. I just has to!"

The trip into town proved uneventful, although the six coppers Cale paid to the guard at the town hall aroused Eevlina's protests. After proving to the guard that they carried no metal, they followed the swelling crowd of would-be customers to the common where the horses, along with the rest of the animals for sale, were tethered in a long curving line. Flags snapped in the breeze and everywhere there was laughter and singing. As they rode past, Haemas twisted in the saddle and glanced back wistfully at the savory morsels for sale at several booths.

"Turn around and quit gawking." Cale dug his heels into the ebari's sides and it lengthened its bone-shaking stride. "Folks'll think you never been to a fair before!"

Haemas turned back around, amazed by the sheer number of strolling, exuberant dark-haired people. "I haven't." She caught a scrap of music on the breeze and pushed herself up on the saddle so she could peek over the ebari's branching horns. The horses' glossy backs gleamed in the sun up ahead, blood bay and golden chestnut and ebony and iron gray, and she'd never seen so many people together in one place in her whole life. "It's too crowded," she said uneasily. "We'll never get away with it."

"You just do your part." Cale reined the ebari in. "Let us worry about the rest."

Clinging to her saddle with both hands, Eevlina eased her bulky body down to the ground. Jassfra dismounted, too, and they both passed their reins up to Holnar. Eevlina tugged her stained gray bodice down over her sagging bosom, then pointed her stick at Cale. "Meet us back at the same place we camped last night. I'm not about to go traipsing over the whole countryside just to find the likes of you."

"We'll be there, Gran."

Haemas watched the old woman shove a huge wicker basket at Jassfra, then limp toward a large, open-sided pavilion set up in the center of the wide grassy common. Cale dismounted, then reached up to pull Haemas down. The instant her feet touched the grass, a prickly feeling crawled down her spine. "Someone's watching us."

"Where?" His black-haired head craned around.

"I don't know." The awful feeling, like fire mites crawling over her skin, was growing more intense. She glanced nervously at the laughing, chattering people crowding past.

"Come on." He jerked her arm impatiently. "I don't see no one looking at us, but I do see the horses."

"No, it's true! I—feel it."

He stopped and studied her face with his strange blue eyes. "*Feel* it?"

"Like the silsha."

"Oh, quit making excuses and get on with it." He dragged her over to a nervous chestnut mare decked out with bright red ribbons in her cream-colored mane. Haemas offered the flat of her hand to the mare's twitching muzzle. The pink nostrils flared, then lowered to sniff, tickling her palm.

A short, energetic brown-eyed man wiped his hands on his worn black leather breeches and walked around the mare's flank. He grinned broadly. "That's amazing. I trained this here gorgeous creature myself since she were a wee filly, and I ain't never seen her take to anyone so fast."

Haemas stroked the mare's warm neck, then scratched

behind the velvety ears, listening to the creature's mind. "But didn't you just trade for her yesterday?"

"You wasn't there when old Groengin and I struck the deal!" The man peered suspiciously into Haemas's face. "No one were."

Thrusting himself between her and the trader, Cale smiled thinly. "Looks to be a mite too fine for our purse, anyway." He snagged the girl by the neck of her ragged tunic and dragged her toward the next horse. "Thanks all the same."

"Did Groengin send you to queer my deals?" The trader's brow furrowed. "I'll fix that old bastard! He traded me fair and square!"

Cale marched Haemas past the next three horses before he stopped. "Are you trying to get us killed?" He peered over the back of a tall black gelding.

"Sorry," Haemas said, rubbing her neck. "I wasn't raised to be a thief."

"You wasn't raised to do *anything* useful, but you're going to learn." Cale straightened up cautiously. "Now, get to work. Eevlina and Jassfra should be ready soon."

"Ready for what?" Suddenly Haemas shivered even though the air was balmy. The crawly feeling of someone watching her was overwhelming.

"Never you mind. Just get on with it."

She stretched out a hand to the long-legged black gelding. It flicked an ear at her, then turned away.

The watched feeling increased again, and a spot right between her shoulder blades began to itch. She turned around just as a man and woman pushed past Cale. The woman had long dark braids and a shy smile, but a curious *doubleness* overlaid the man's face. He had brown chierra eyes and hair, tan chierra skin . . . and bright-gold hair with pale-gold eyes.

Haemas blinked hard, trying to see what was truly there.

Brown eyes.

Gold eyes.

Her breath caught in her throat; she couldn't separate the two. He had to be Kashi, sent to punish her. Slipping around the gelding, she pressed her forehead against its smooth neck and tried to breathe slowly.

The gelding nickered, then lipped at her sleeve. Closing her eyes, she reached out with her mind for her pursuer, but nothing was there, as nothing had been ever since *that* night.

"Enough already!" Cale grabbed her collar and pulled her away. "We'll have every horse trader in the whole of Dorbin breathing down our backs. All you have to do is talk to the beasts a bit, not make love to them!"

She looked over her shoulder and caught another glance of the double face. "Someone is after me. We've got to get out of here!"

"That line were old before Eevlina was born." He marched past several ebari and a skeletal ummit, then stopped in front of a swaybacked gray mare and her colt.

"Can't you see him?" She ducked down behind the placid mare. A chill washed through her. She seemed to feel someone only a few feet away, laughing at her, the same way he always did when— Her mind raced. Was it Jarid?

She darted around the mare, keeping her eyes on the ground, swerving past clumps of people, knowing only that she had to get away.

Suddenly a black boot snaked out and tripped her. She crashed hard into the ground, stomach first. Stunned by the impact, she sprawled in the short grass, an iron band constricting her chest, unable to get her breath.

The black boots walked up to her nose. "Well, Light bless me if it isn't the skivit underneath all that dirt."

Kevisson swallowed the last bite of savok stew and stood back, feeling much better. The woman behind the roughly made counter looked pointedly at the wooden bowl in his hand.

"More stew, sir?"

"No, thank you." He sopped up a smear of savory brown gravy with the remaining crust of black bread, then stuffed it into his mouth and handed her the bowl. Fortunately, his silver had been in his pocket when he'd encountered the pool, or he'd have gone hungry—not to mention lacked the money to pay his way into Dorbin.

Testing his link for direction, Kevisson began to trace it

again through the crowd, although he wasn't sure just what he could accomplish in front of so many people. More than likely, he'd have to track the girl when she left with her friends and capture her somewhere in the countryside, perhaps when they all slept tonight.

He passed a dancing circle of girls with tiny blue and white spring flowers braided into their hair, their slim hands tracing graceful figures above their heads. Behind him, the feda pipe slowly increased its tempo until the crowd's clapping hands could not keep up. A shout finally went up as the dance ended, dancers and piper alike exhausted and laughing.

Then several fiddles took up the slack, weaving lively harmonies around each other as Kevisson worked his way across the common. He slipped his hand into his pocket and closed his fingers around the hard obsidian ring. Even through the cloth wrapping, the sense of his quarry was so strong that he felt sure he would see her any second.

Passing the final food booth, he saw a string of animals staked out up ahead. Suddenly a slender, dark-haired figure darted past him and continued on a short distance before tripping and sprawling face first in the grass.

He started to pass by as several people stopped to help, but the ring in his hand vibrated with Haemas Tal's closeness. Kevisson glanced around in a quick circle but saw no one who fit her description.

Closing his eyes, he tested his link to be sure. Then he looked again as a Kashi man with bright-gold hair seized the gasping, smudge-faced waif and hauled her roughly to her feet.

Somewhere on the common behind him, the fiddles reached the climax of their tune as Kevisson and the Heir of Tal'ayn locked eyes for the space of a heartbeat before the Kashi jerked her away and the crowd closed between them.

Chapter
Ten

"Take a strong hold on this ragamuffin, Mairianda," Jarid instructed as he jerked Haemas's prone form up, "and haul her straight back to your father. He can use her to take out the slops."

Mairianda seized the struggling girl's arm with both hands. Her soft, round-cheeked face smiled at Jarid as if he were inviting her to a festival.

He reached across and shook Haemas until her head snapped. "Now stop that and, for once, behave yourself like a Lady! I'm not going to take you back." He let a sly smile seep across his lips. "After all, you did both of us a favor."

His cousin stared at him, her eyes enormous, and touched the livid bruise spreading over her cheek with the back of her hand.

He read the doubt and suspicion playing through her mind. "I'm sure you realize you can never return to Tal'ayn." He felt her shame rekindle as the white-hot memory of her father lying dead at her feet resurfaced. He schooled his voice to reasonableness. "Go with Mairianda."

Yes, skivit, he thought to himself with satisfaction, go with Mairianda. I had planned to have the satisfaction of burying my own dagger in your heart, but if the old peddler finishes you off, no one will ever trace your death to me.

"Mairianda will take care of you." Jarid reached for Haemas's mind, reassuring himself that she was not shielded. Ever since that fiasco at Tal'ayn when his young cousin had fought him with such unexpected strength, he had been plagued by a lingering uneasiness whenever he'd planned for this meeting.

Haemas jerked away, then surprised him by closing her eyes and sending a mental call for—something. Before he could tap into her thoughts directly, he was distracted by shouting and a cacophony of squealing, snorting, and neighing behind them. Hooves pounded as several horses and an ebari broke loose and raced past. Throwing himself to one side, Jarid watched in shocked silence as two more horses along the stakeout line reared and fought their bonds until they also were free.

Haemas's eyes were open now. She whirled against Mairianda and pushed the heavier young woman to the ground. The peculiar *calling* continued, and Jarid realized she was summoning the animals.

Mairianda sat up in the grass, her face smudged and her apron disarrayed, and watched stupidly as Haemas stumbled into the stream of horses and ebari. Then the chierra girl turned her black eyes to Jarid, looking at him first with puzzlement, then in awakening anger.

Belatedly he realized he'd forgotten to hold on to her mind or to shield his Kashi appearance—indeed, had forgotten everything in his effort to control his cousin. He shoved the chierra girl aside and followed Haemas, reaching again for her mind, thinking angrily that he would not come so close to eliminating her claim to Tal'ayn only to fail. He had just grasped the edges of Haemas's shieldless mind when a stampeding savok slammed his shoulder from behind and pitched him head over heels.

He struggled to his knees, stopping her flight with the full force of his mind. Defiant, but unable to move, she glared at him from ten feet away. Sweat trickled down his temple as he fought to hold her there. He could swear the brat had no shields, yet every time he had her pinned, her mind twisted in his mental grasp, leaving him without full control.

Then a tall, dark-haired man appeared behind Haemas and, bundling a long cloak around her face and shoulders, dragged her into the crowd.

What the—? Was that one of her chierra bandit friends? Stumbling back onto his feet, Jarid started to follow, but a circle of chierra townspeople closed on him, white-faced and angry, their hands clenched around sticks and hoes and whips. Jarid smiled uneasily and concentrated on regaining his chierra appearance.

* * *

The handsome male dancer tripped over the two long poles flashing back and forth over the ground in an intricate rhythm. The crowd laughed and jeered until he took up the pattern again, his feet flashing over each pole as the beaters moved it in time with the music. The onlookers roared their approval.

Jassfra, standing just inside the canvas wall of the pavilion, found herself clapping and calling out with the rest of them until Eevlina elbowed her in the ribs.

"Forget that nonsense and pay attention!" Eevlina's heavy face scowled at her. "It be almost time."

Jassfra moved the basket up on her arm and nodded, although her gaze drifted back to the blue-and-red-shirted male dancers concluding the dance. Their good-natured, sweating faces were tense with concentration, and she had her eye on one broad-shouldered fellow with a ready smile. Just once, she thought testily, she would like to go to a festival or a fair and have some plain, ordinary fun.

The notion of horses to ride on their raids all summer cheered her up, though. No one could catch them if they were mounted on horses, and the beasts would likely last clear into the fall before they went all spindly and listless from lack of Old grain.

"Are you sure it's still all right?" Eevlina reached for the basket.

Jassfra rolled her eyes. "Yes."

"Don't get fresh with me, you red-haired baggage!" Eevlina planted one fist on an oversize hip and jabbed Jassfra with her walking stick. "I'll still be stealing long after the rest of you lies dead and buried!"

Jassfra was saved from answering by a disturbance from the far end of the common. A handful of people drifted outside to see, even as the male dancers were joined by young women in beautifully embroidered green vests to begin a complicated flirting dance.

Eevlina arched her bushy gray brows. *"Now."*

Jassfra stood on tiptoe to peer over the heads of the crowd outside the pavilion. "I thought Cale was going to wait for us to start."

Eevlina took her elbow and hustled her into a dark corner behind a sausage booth. "Them's *horses* I hear out there, so if it isn't Cale and that yellow-eyed brat, it might as well be. Get on with it."

Jassfra set the basket down behind Eevlina's full skirts and extracted the ebari horn filled with carefully banked embers.

"Hurry up!" Eevlina hissed, nodding pleasantly at several gaily dressed women who glanced at her curiously.

Removing the moss stopper, Jassfra blew on the embers. The faint red glow inside flared.

"What in the seven hells are you doing down there, girl?" Eevlina fretted without looking at her. "They've almost finished the blasted dance!"

Jassfra spotted a side flap of the pavilion trailing limply in the breeze. Protecting the horn with one hand, she pressed the heavy cloth to the embers inside and watched as the flames caught and blackened the edges. Then she thrust the horn back into the basket and strolled away, nodding to Eevlina as she passed. The old woman glanced back over her shoulder at the yellow flames creeping up the side of the pavilion and followed her hastily. An acrid smell drifted behind them.

They had barely reached the opposite side when a woman's screams added to the din of animal noises outside.

"What is it?" someone yelled over the music as the spectators turned and gaped.

"I hope them worthless boys is paying attention." Eevlina pushed through the crowd without a backward glance. "I don't intend to have to do this twice. They better come up with them horses this time, or I'll learn 'em not to disappoint me again!"

Jassfra pitched the basket underneath the wooden plank of an ale booth and then hurried after the gray-haired old woman.

Jarid's pale eyes pinned Haemas with a magnetic compulsion impossible to break. Her fists clenched until her fingers were white. Whatever happened, she told herself, she would not go with him!

While still calling the horses with all her strength, she tried moving just one foot, but her feet were made of lead.

Suddenly rough wool enveloped her from behind, pinning her arms as she was lifted almost off her feet. For a second Jarid's compulsion to stay dragged painfully at her mind and she fought her rescuer. Then his hold snapped, and she sagged limply against the arms carrying her.

It must be Cale, she thought. Who else would come for her? The cries of frightened horses and ebari and people yelling swirled around her, and a new note of panic sounded in the voices.

Working one arm up, Haemas fought the smothering cloak. The hold around her shoulders slipped and she managed to claw the cloth out of her face. The man dragging her through the milling crowd of people and animals glanced down, his brown eyes widening in surprise as she managed to free her arm entirely.

Or were his eyes golden? A sick, panicky feeling raced through Haemas as she stared at the curious *doubleness* of his face and hair. He tightened his grip and dragged her onward. "Don't make this harder on yourself than it has to be." Breathing hard, he jerked her out of the way of a terrified ummit veering from one side to the other.

Heart pounding, she squirmed and twisted, but with a grown man's strength he looped the cloak back over her face and forced her onward. She couldn't let this Kashi stranger take her back, her mind insisted in a red haze of panic. Then she managed to get her feet under her as they stopped and she caught of whiff of something burning.

Smothered by the cloak's coarse material, she reached out with her mind, searching for the black gelding. Holding on to that purpose, she didn't resist when the man resumed his zigzag course across the common until, suddenly, she felt the terrified gelding near.

Here, she called to it. *Here I am! Come to me!*

She heard hooves pounding through the grass and then the horse's labored breathing, coming in short, heavy blows. She reached for control. *Knock him down.*

The confused gelding snorted, its mind radiating fear. She could feel it back away, snorting uneasily.

Knock him down!

A solid impact sent Haemas and the man sprawling. She lay dazed for a moment, then scrabbled out of the cloak.

Men and women, towing screaming children, dodged around her, fleeing back toward the main part of town. The stench of scorched fabric choked the air.

She glanced down at the man on the ground. He had grazed his temple on an ale barrel as he'd fallen; a red line disappeared back into his thick golden-brown hair. A few feet away, the black gelding pawed fearfully at the turf as the smoke thickened.

Haemas reassured the horse's mind as she stroked its shoulder. The gelding trembled but stood when she grabbed a double handful of coarse mane. Just as she almost had her leg over its back, it shied away from an ummit colliding with a barrel in front of a nearby booth. Haemas's weak shoulder refused to hold her weight, and she slipped down.

The man on the ground moved his arm a few inches, then groaned. Haemas took the frightened gelding's headstall and guided it around to the fallen barrel. Using that as a step, she hitched herself over the horse's knobby backbone, balancing there on her stomach until she could swing her leg over.

The orange flames were leaping high above the central pavilion now—she could hear the crackling even on this side of the common. The hot, swirling breeze carried bits of charred material past her face. The sweating gelding flattened its ears, dancing in place underneath her, its dark eyes white-rimmed with fear. Haemas glanced back at the man who had stolen her from Jarid; one of his golden-brown eyes had cracked open just enough to see her.

Leaning over the gelding's bunched shoulder muscles, she released its mind. Terrified, the horse plunged away from the fire and smoke through the crowds, carrying her back toward the narrow streets of Dorbin.

Cale was swearing under his breath. The entire common was filled with running, squealing animals until there wasn't one safe square inch to stand on. "I'll bet the little she-demon had this planned all along!" he told himself angrily, shoving through the mass of frightened people, dodging horses and clumsy savoks.

He caught a glimpse of her patched tunic about twenty feet away, then threw himself aside as a white-eyed bay mare swerved toward him. When he looked back up, the Kashi girl had disappeared into the crowd. He swore again. What did she think she was doing, starting this ruckus before he was ready? They'd be lucky now to get away with their own ebari!

Well, he for one didn't intend to face Eevlina without his share of the booty again. Watching for his chance, he seized the trailing lead of a panicked sorrel colt as he galloped past. The big-boned colt, at least two years old, rolled his terrified eyes and struck at him with his forelegs. Cale hung on the rope, using his weight to pull the colt's head down, and watched for an opening. Just as the colt hit the ground with both white-stockinged legs, he darted in and gripped the rope halter.

A sudden commotion made him glance over his shoulder. A fallen man was being surrounded by angry townspeople. A plump girl with long black braids advanced menacingly on him, backed up by men and women brandishing sticks and tools. Cale glanced at the fallen man, then looked again.

There could be no mistaking that bright golden hair and those light demon-eyes. It was a Kashi Lord, probably the one Haemas had been afraid of. Cale's face darkened with anger and he tugged the horse over to join the crowd. Just who did this Lord-fellow think he was, ruining Eevlina's raid?

The pale-gold eyes glanced up and a cruel smile flickered across the aristocratic features. The golden hair and eyes shimmered for a moment, then disappeared beneath the face of an ordinary chierra man.

Cale reached down with his free arm to throttle the man. "Try your demon's ways on us, will you, you misbegotten Highland—"

The intense brown eyes stared back at him.

Cale found his hand steadying Mashal's shoulder as he stood up. All around them, the circle of townspeople rumbled angrily and then edged in closer with their homemade weapons. The smoke thickened as Cale watched them out of the corner of his eye.

"Mashal, what do they want?" He lowered his voice. "Did someone catch Jassfra setting the fire?"

"I don't know." Mashal pushed Cale toward the edge of

the crowd. "But we'd best get our tails out of this place while we still have them!"

They shoved through the angry townspeople back to back, with Cale keeping a strong hold on the nervous colt. The furious faces of everyone within an arm's length of them became confused, and they made their way out of the crowd. The reek of charred wood and fabric grew stronger. The trembling, wild-eyed chestnut colt fought Cale at every step.

"Over there." Mashal pointed at a skittish gray mare boxed in between two collapsed booths. "We've got to have another beast or we'll never make it out of here."

Cale was about to protest that they had to find Eevlina, Jassfra, and even Haemas, if possible, before they left, but quite suddenly he realized the women could take care of themselves. "Hold the colt." He handed Mashal the lead line. "I'll be right back." Ducking his head, he chased the terrified mare through the thickening smoke as she dashed behind booths and shied from fleeing groups of people.

When he finally trapped the mare, he vaulted onto her back and looked around for Mashal. The big man waved to him from atop the chestnut colt.

"Come on!" Mashal yelled. "Let's get out of this skivit-ridden town before the whole stinking place burns down around our ears!"

Cale nodded and put his heels to the gray mare, following Mashal through the choking smoke. Well, he thought to himself, using his sleeve to wipe at the smoke-tears streaming from his irritated eyes, he had to hand it to her. Eevlina had outdone herself this time.

The black gelding trembled beneath Haemas and its neck was soaked with sweat. Slowing it to a walk, Haemas looked around the dusty street. Panicked people were running into their houses and slamming the doors shut while others struggled on foot to reach the town gate. Behind her, a column of dense black smoke spiraled slantwise into the clear green sky.

If she could just find a place to hide, Cale and the rest of the raiders would leave and she would finally be free of them. Then she could figure out how to escape the Kashi who was trying to return her to the Highlands. Halting the gelding, she slid off its sweaty back behind a rickety wagon.

"All I know is that the lass be here somewhere, and I gots to find her!" an angry voice said. "Leave off following me!"

Haemas glanced across the farm wagon and pressed back against the building as a white-haired old man shook off the woman clinging to his arm.

The woman stumbled against the wagon, then caught the side to keep her balance. "But who is she?"

The old man turned his back and stalked down the crowded street. Uneasy, Haemas used the wagon to remount, then headed the gelding's nose back toward the town wall.

Just as she passed the old man, though, he looked up at her with hard brown eyes and yelled, "Stop, you! Stop!" He lunged, catching her left boot.

Trying to kick his hand loose, Haemas leaned over the horse's neck and urged it to speed with her mind. The skittish gelding plunged forward, but the man wrenched on her leg until she lost her balance and slid off the horse's galloping back to fall facedown in the street.

The beat of the gelding's hooves receded toward the gate as she sprawled in the dust at the angry old man's feet.

Chapter
Eleven

Boots continued to pound by, but the shouting chierra voices seemed less anxious. Kevisson's face was pressed into the stiff grass, and his head rang with an obstinate insistency. He clenched his fingers into the black dirt and tried again to get back on his feet.

An arm reached down and levered him up. He squinted through the smoke-hazed air at a young man in a smudged blue costume trimmed in red, probably one of the dancers. The stranger ran a finger along the bloody gash in the Searcher's right temple. "It don't look too bad."

Kevisson flinched. "I'll be fine."

"Come on, then. The fire be out now, but you should get on home to your folk." The stranger shook his head. "Such a funny color of hair you have there." He laughed a little as he steered Kevisson around a collapsed booth. "Almost like—"

Bloody darkness! Kevisson jammed his six-fingered hands into his pockets. The fall had stunned him, and then he'd forgotten to shield his appearance.

"Got your breath now?" The man studied him and, when the Searcher nodded, clapped him on the back. "Well, then I'll be off." The blue-and-red vest slipped off into the milling spectators before Kevisson recovered enough wits to thank him.

He turned around slowly, reaching out with his mind for his link to the Tal girl. She still seemed to be near, but he couldn't shake the impression that she was in danger. And he couldn't get the face of that Kashi man out of his mind. He was sure the Council had sent only one Searcher, but why else would a Kashi be here in the dusty backwood town?

97

He closed his eyes. The girl had fled toward the town gate. Summoning enough strength to shield his Kashi coloring, he ignored his throbbing head and trudged back across the common in that direction. His sense of the girl grew stronger with each step, and the feeling of urgency increased.

As he neared the town gate, he heard angry voices just up ahead. He supported himself against the rough stone of a ramshackle building and caught at the shifting edges of someone's hot, unreasoning hatred and a second person's bewilderment and fear. His link to the girl ran straight into that violent tangle of emotions.

"Cittar, no!" a woman shouted; then there was the sound of scuffling.

Kevisson followed the woman's anguished voice around a group of onlookers. An old man crouched in the middle of the dusty street, one hand knotted in the ragged tunic of a street urchin. A chierra woman hung desperately on his raised arm. "For the Mother's sake, Cittar, it weren't even your horse!"

Kevisson blinked, trying to make his smoke-filled brain understand. Then he realized—his link led to the dirty bundle of rags at the angry man's feet.

He reached out to the man's mind and met a seething swirl of fear and hatred. He hesitated, but then the old man shook the woman off and drew back his fist to strike the child again.

Kevisson lurched forward and clutched his thin arm. "What's the problem, friend?" he said, sending his own mind deep into the pit of black emotion before him.

The old man's fist hesitated. A puzzled look seeped across his wrinkled face as Kevisson struggled to damp out the angry energy loosed inside his mind. Then Cittar turned puzzled brown eyes to the Searcher and the fight melted out of his wiry old body. "I don't . . ." His hand opened slowly and the girl's limp body slumped back into the dust at his feet. "I don't know."

Kevisson kept his own hand steady on the old man's arm as he tried to trace the source of all that hatred. His lips tightened as he realized that someone—someone none too neat or particular—had done violence to this defenseless chierra's mind.

"It's all right, Cittar." Kevisson released the peddler's arm. "Just a mistake, nothing more."

"What were I doing?" Cittar watched in bewilderment as the woman dropped to her knees and cradled the unconscious girl's head in her lap. "I don't even know the lass."

Kevisson brushed his fingers across the girl's clammy forehead and glimpsed the familiar silver glow of her mind, muted but steady. He straightened, feeling relieved. "I don't think she's badly hurt." He looked at the woman, who was wiping at the tears trailing down her own grimy face. "Is there somewhere near here where she can rest?"

The woman smoothed the dirty brown hair out of the girl's face and nodded. "My place, the Golden Egg, down the street a ways." She shook her head. "I can't imagine what made Cittar act so mean. I've knowed him fourteen years now and he were always such a gentle old sod."

Kevisson glanced at the old man, who was standing in the middle of the road with a dazed expression. "Perhaps the smoke confused him." He gathered the girl in his arms. Her long legs dangled, but she weighed no more than a lightwing.

The woman stood up and beat at her dusty skirts. "Maybe so, but he were acting peculiar even this morning when he got up. Do you know the lass?"

Kevisson's feet were as heavy as stone as he trudged after her in the direction of the inn. "She's my sister," he said with an effort.

"Really?" Her brown eyes widened. "That's so fortunate, with all this trouble." Then her plain, honest face fell. She dropped her voice to a confidential whisper. "You know, I think the young rascal might have been *stealing* that horse. She bolted the instant Cittar told her to stop. You really ought to watch her a mite closer." She opened the door to the inn and stood aside. "Up the stairs, third door on the left."

Kevisson stopped on the landing to get his breath and leaned back against the rough-hewn coolness of the stone wall. Only a few more steps and he would rest, he promised himself. He looked down at the still ragamuffin in his tired arms.

At least his Search was finished.

Birtal Senn accepted the silver cup of spiced mead from the apprentice's outstretched hand, then scowled as he watched the youngster retreat. It just didn't seem natural for a Kashi lad to perform such a menial task.

The boy looked over his shoulder, his golden eyes wide as he made a stumbling, awkward exit from the study.

Over in his chair before the fire, Lord High Master Ellirt chuckled. "Really, Birtal, if you're going to think such things, you ought to shield around the youngsters." He winked one of his sightless eyes. "It's hard enough to get the little rascals to do their part when they first come here."

Birtal sniffed the spiced mead, then took a dubious sip. "Don't see why they should do such menial work at all." He settled into the opposite seat before the hearth and propped his heavy boots up on a stool. "It's not as if you couldn't have as many servants here as you need. The Houses have offered enough times."

"Our students don't come to Shael'donn to be waited upon. They get enough of that at home." Ellirt reached for another log, then thrust it unerringly into the fire's crackling red heart. "They come here to learn to do for themselves." The flames sizzled as the log settled into place.

Birtal rolled the hot mead on his tongue. It was excellent, as everything tended to be in this infuriating place. He wondered, not for the first time, how every product of Shael'donn could prove to be so much better than anything the rest of the Highlands could produce.

He set the cup down with a clink. "I want to know what your boy has found down in the Lowlands."

"At last report, very little." Ellirt rose and guided himself behind his high-backed chair with one hand. "As you should well know. If I'd heard more, I would have told you."

Birtal grunted.

"What do you really want, old friend?"

"I want this whole blasted nightmare to be over!" Birtal knew he was letting his irritation leak through his shields, but he didn't care. Let Ellirt know, let the entire benighted place know that Birtal Senn had run out of patience! "I want Alyssa's man back at her side! I want to see a whole roomful of her children ready to inherit Tal'ayn!"

"Ah . . ." Ellirt ran a hand back over his sparse head of white hair. "Now we begin to get at the truth."

Birtal picked up the silver cup, then realized it was already empty and thumped it back down. "It's all very well for you here at Shael'donn to turn up your nose at inheritance and family, but the rest of us still have to carry on."

"And Alyssa isn't with child?"

"No." Birtal grimaced. "Nor is she likely to be." He studied the old man's blind eyes. How did Ellirt always manage to cut to the heart of matters so?

A tiny part of his mind whispered back that perhaps his own shields weren't what they once had been.

Ellirt picked up a silver pitcher sitting close to the open hearth and handed it to his visitor. "Has old Tal died, then? I hadn't heard."

"No, but he isn't improving, either. Alyssa tells me he's rarely more than half-conscious and that the healers say he must have complete rest if there's to be any chance of recovery. Who knows when, if ever, he'll be capable of fulfilling his duties?" Birtal took the heavy pitcher and poured himself another measure of hot mead. "The Council is growing restless. Someone has to take up Tal'ayn's seat."

"Or your faction will lose its majority?" Ellirt's face remained blandly polite.

Birtal scowled. "I've a perfect right to expect Tal's support."

"But Alyssa can't inherit if she hasn't borne an heir." Ellirt guided himself back to his seat and sank down on it again. "And Tal already has an heir."

"That ingrate forfeited every right she ever had to Tal'ayn the night she tried to kill her own father!"

Ellirt nodded slowly. "You're right, of course, but I've been thinking . . ." His voice trailed away thoughtfully. "What a strange thing that was for a youngster to do." He leaned back in his chair, locking his hands across the tooled sunburst on his belt. "Oh, I know old Tal was a rough sort, but still . . . she's so young, and said to be gentle-natured."

He paused, his sightless eyes staring unerringly at Birtal's face. "Her mother was from sound Sennay and Killian stock, wasn't she?"

"*Killian* stock." Birtal snorted and moved restlessly in his chair. "Not one head of really golden hair in the whole pale-eyed bunch!"

"And so abominably independent-minded," Ellirt murmured. "Isn't there a matrimonial contract pending between Tal'ayn and Killian'ayn?"

"I don't care about the damn Killians! I just want her brought back and punished so the matter of Tal'ayn can be resolved. I want Alyssa to get on with her life."

The silence hung stiffly between them as the burning logs shifted downward, choking the fire in its own ashes. Finally Birtal said, "What's this I hear about you forbidding Shael'donn masters to participate in the Temporal Conclave? We're meeting tomorrow and, without Tal, we need at least one more strong mind in the power relay."

Ellirt rose and put a hand on Senn's shoulder. "Every time you broach those energies, you risk the lives of everyone there. And even if it was safe, what if you *could* travel across time? Would that make our lives better in any measurable way? Leave this insanity alone and put your considerable talents to some other, better use."

Birtal lurched to his feet and reached for his cloak. *I could use your support in this, Kniel.*

A somber wave of regret washed through the warm glow of friendship Ellirt projected. *Don't ask what is not mine to give, old friend.*

Birtal's back stiffened. He swirled the cloak around his shoulders and banged the door open. Ellirt's regard followed him down the corridor, but Birtal just meshed his shields more tightly and shut the old man out.

Kevisson dipped the clean cloth into the basin of warm soapy water and dabbed at the grime covering the girl's face. The greasy, dark film washed off easily, leaving her skin gleaming palely in the room's dim light.

She had a dreamer's face, he thought, with those high cheekbones and a broad forehead that gave a distinctly Sennay cast to her features—nothing that hinted at a potential for the kind of violence that had erupted up at Tal'ayn. Each winter solstice, he saw similar faces on a few of the new boys who arrived at Shael'donn for training, boys who sometimes couldn't cope with the harsher realities of life.

Her arm stirred and he stopped. The head injury did not seem serious, although he couldn't say for sure since the Light knew that he was no healer. Her almost-white eyelashes fluttered, but then she was still again.

He resumed washing the last of the brown from her face and hands. It had been, he supposed, an effort to disguise her origin, although he couldn't imagine it would have fooled anyone for two seconds once they'd gotten a good look at her fingers or eyes. Why hadn't she just cloaked her appearance by shielding?

Rinsing the cloth, he dabbed carefully at the livid purple bruise across the right cheekbone. Had old Cittar been responsible for that, or had it been the nameless Kashi man Kevisson had seen just before he stole her away?

Her arm slid across the bed's homespun coverlet, then she opened white-gold eyes and looked at him without recognition.

"Sorry." He continued working on her bruised face in a businesslike manner.

The light eyes drifted shut, then struggled open again. "Who . . . are you?" Her voice was ragged and hoarse.

"Kevisson Ekran Monmart."

Her hand came up and closed over his wrist. "You're . . . Kashi," she said faintly.

"Yes."

"You've come after me." Her stare grew defiant. She tried to push his hand away.

"I'm from Shael'donn." He shook off her grip and put the cloth back into the basin on the rough bedside table. "You had to know that someone would come." He settled a faded wool blanket over her. "After what happened, you could hardly expect your father just to let you run away and do nothing about it."

"My father is dead!" She pushed the blanket away, attempting to sit up until a hot wave of pain swept through her head and shoulder. Kevisson caught the mental backwash as she swayed, then pushed her firmly back against the pillow.

"Be still." He probed the injured shoulder as gently as he could. Light help them both, he thought, if something was broken or out of socket. "Well," he said after a moment, "that's what you get for stealing horses, I suppose, but you should live." He pulled the blanket up again. "We have to leave tomorrow, so get some sleep." He walked to the door and turned around. *Your father is not dead.*

Her drawn expression didn't change.

You didn't kill him.

She lay unmoving, her pale eyes staring up at the low ceiling.

"Your father's not dead," he said aloud.

She turned her head to look at him by the door. "What?"

He realized with a shock that she really hadn't heard his mental comment. He lifted the door latch. "He survived."

Fear and shame welled up in her so strongly that he didn't even have to read her to feel it. He caught at disturbing images that flashed through her head: her father's angry, swearing voice . . . bitter arguments . . . a lifeless body sprawled at her feet.

"You're just saying that so I'll go back." She closed her eyes. "I don't believe you."

Cale squirmed, trying to find a spot along the mare's backbone that didn't dig painfully into his posterior. Riding without a saddle was hell. He turned to Mashal. "No one's following us. We'd better head on home."

"Not tonight." The big man squinted up at the swollen orange sun hanging low in the afternoon sky. "We'll ride part of the way back and camp out. Then tomorrow we can sneak into Dorbin and find the girl. Things should quiet down by then."

"Dorbin!" Cale sat back on the weary gray mare. "Are you daft? We've just ridden for over an hour to get away from there, and we've still got to meet up with Eevlina. She's sure to have our hides for this mess as it is."

Mashal scowled at him. "We have to find the girl."

Cale reined the mare toward the forest. "Maybe you do, old sod, but I'm going home."

Mashal watched him with a grim expression.

"Don't be an idiot," Cale said amiably over his shoulder. "Eevlina'll have your ears for breakfast if you cross her."

Then visions of Dorbin crept into his head: hot food, soft beds, dark-eyed, round-breasted women who would claw each other's eyes out for the company of a real man, rich purses ripe for . . .

He shook himself. He must be sun-touched, sitting here dreaming with his eyes open. He kicked the mare into a tired trot, then found himself reining her back onto the road.

Mashal's colt turned in the direction of Dorbin. Without prompting, Cale's mare fell in beside him, and the two men rode silently down the dusty road.

His heart thumping painfully against his ribs, Cale glanced back at the shady spot under the tree, half expecting to see himself disappearing into the forest. Then he turned back to the man who looked like Mashal.

There was a curious blankness about the man's eyes, as if he were there and yet not there. The air seemed to shimmer around his head, and in Mashal's place sat a tall, lean-bodied man with pale, almost colorless eyes and hair the shade of a newly minted gold coin.

A crooked smile played across the stranger's thin lips as he glanced across at Cale. "It no longer matters at this point," he said, "and I've already wasted too much energy on you."

Cale tried to turn his mare in the opposite direction and ride like a demon for the deep, dark forest.

His body continued riding on the slow trip back to Dorbin.

Chapter
Twelve

Haemas made herself pick up a plump yellow callyt from the breakfast tray. Her shoulder still ached, her face was sore, and her throat closed at the very thought of food, but she resolutely crunched the sweet fruit and tried to make plans to get away from this stranger who meant to take her back.

The latch lifted and the Searcher slipped in with a shapeless bundle stuffed under one arm. He lifted an eyebrow as he relocked the door from the inside. "Feeling better?"

The details of the day before were not very clear. For the first time Haemas noticed he was darker than most Kashi. His eyes and hair were an odd shade of golden brown, and the lines of his lean face were straight-edged and set, as if he rarely smiled.

"Well, you look better." He pocketed the key, then tossed the bundle at her. "Cleaner, too."

She flushed to the roots of her once-again pale-gold hair. It hadn't been *her* idea to disguise herself with Eevlina's evil-smelling preparations. She untied the bundle and pulled out a long, dark-blue tunic and soft dappled-gray savok-hide breeches.

He moved to the tiny window with long-strided ease and peered down into the street. "Your prank yesterday, stampeding the animals, has put this town in a very black mood. All I could purchase in the way of riding stock was an ancient ummit, and someone will probably steal it, too, if we don't hurry."

"An ummit?" She looked up from the clothing. "But they stink!"

"You should have thought of that before you ran off everything on four legs within a two-mile radius." He turned his back to her. "You're lucky you don't have to walk. Now get dressed."

Shrugging out of her stained rags, she pulled on the soft jerkin and breeches, enjoying the feel of clean clothes next to her skin. When she finished, Kevisson turned, reached under the bed, and handed out her black boots. His strange dark-gold eyes studied her as she sat down on the floor to put them on. "You can't read me at all, can you?"

Her hand froze on her boot.

"And you weren't shielding yesterday, either, or even today, for that matter."

"That's none of your business!" She forced the boot on.

"Surely a girl of your age knows how."

Haemas felt the whisper of his mind against hers. "Stop that!" Her hands trembled as the memories of that terrible night yammered through her head again . . . the still white face at her feet . . . Why had she done it? She'd never even considered such a thing! Feeling as if she were on the edge of a mountain glacier looking down into icy darkness, she pressed her hands over her eyes. His fingers closed around her arm and she tried to jerk away.

"It's all right." His voice was low, calming. "Don't try to think about it now."

Her heart racing, she took a ragged breath and tried to make her body stop shaking.

"Close your eyes and center down."

Suddenly a black panic swept over her. She had to get away from this tiny, stifling room in this Light-forsaken town and away from this meddling stranger as well as everyone else! She jumped at him, knocking him back against the bed, then clawed at the key in his pocket.

Kevisson seized her shoulders and shook her. "I said center down, dammit!"

The torn muscles in Haemas's right shoulder burned like fire, making her vision gray around the edges. She went rigid with the pain.

Bending over, he locked eyes with her. "Clear your mind."

The warm golden brown of his almost-chierra eyes held her gaze until her eyes closed and, in spite of the fierce throbbing, she began to shut everything out, blanking each sense in turn, as her old tutor, Yernan, had once taught her.

When she had finally reached that quiet place in her mind where there was no sound, no vision, and no pain—that peaceful inner stillness—she looked again for the inexplicable link she had found before.

Still visible and strong, it led to the man beside her.

Rich morning sunlight slanted through the hall windows and a few dust motes spun lazily in the air. The long carpeted hallway smelled of wood polish and glass cleaners. Birtal Senn nodded with satisfaction; he had Senn'ayn servants working around the clock to keep the great House impressively spotless, but it was worth it. He waved aside the chierra guard at the door as he arrived at the Temporal Conclave. He was purposely late, as usual, to make the subtle point as to who was in charge here—both now and on the long-awaited day when they would finally achieve success.

Aaren Killian was waiting for him, his sharp-planed face remote. His pale-amber eyes sought Senn's. "I want to be the focus today."

Senn hesitated. Killian, the youngest of the twelve High Lords, hadn't been present on that chilling afternoon when they'd lost Yjan Alimn last year. He doubted the younger Lord really understood what was at stake. Memories of the boiling dark blueness that had swallowed the screaming youngster still haunted his own dreams, but the prevailing theory among the Conclave was that Yjan had panicked, causing his own death.

Senn considered Aaren's chances. The Killians were strongly Talented, and Aaren in particular was said to be quite gifted. "You know it's dangerous," he said noncommittally.

"That's my business." Killian glanced at the closed double doors.

"Fine." Senn opened the door and motioned him inside the dimly lit room. The drapes had already been drawn against the outside sunlight to help their concentration, and a massive table dominated the room. The members of the Conclave quieted as he closed the door. Senn counted silently, then bit off a curse. Despite his plea to Shael'donn yesterday, they were going to be one short in the relay, not a good portent for success. Still, those present represented some of the finest Talents in all of the Highlands. "Sit here," he told Killian, indicating the head of the table.

The younger Lord's eyes reflected the mellow lamplight and transformed it into amber ice. He took his seat and tented his long fingers. Senn frowned and reached for the carved, velvet-lined box holding the set of seven specially attuned ilsera crystals. If Killian managed to be the one to finally open the timeways, Killian'ayn would gain prestige and Aaren Killian could make a serious bid to be the next Council Head, a position that Senn meant for himself.

It was so damnably unfair. He'd tried operating the focus five meetings ago and simply stopped breathing during his attempt to channel the massive amounts of raw energy. If the Senn'ayn Healer hadn't been in attendance, he would have died. Now neither of his sons would agree to take the risk. His hands curled into fists, wishing he dared try again, but he was too old, too far past the peak of his Talent. Somewhere in the Highlands, though, there had to be a perfect focus—one who possessed both the strength and resilience of youth and sufficient training to employ it. Sooner or later, by trial and error, he would discover who it was, and then all of time would lie before them like a ripe field of grain just waiting to be harvested.

He opened the box and arranged the crystals in an oblong shape. He had aligned this set himself after much experimentation, and, even in their present quiescent state, he could hear their faint hum in his mind. A murmur of appreciation rippled down the table and he understood how his fellow Kashi felt. The ilsera crystals had been given to his kind long ago by the Old People, the natives of this world, for traveling from place to place, but in each generation there had been a few who claimed to have glimpsed other times in the journey through the gray betweenness, always on the other side of a realm of scintillating blue light. There had to be a way to break through and put this phenomenon to some practical use.

He nodded at the circle of expectant eyes and leaned back in his chair, centering down, preparing to help power the focus. One by one, each man in turn opened his shields and attuned his mind to the vibrational signature emitted by the crystals. It was not only difficult but painful, like the screech of fingernails across glass. Senn ground his teeth and strained to match it. So much prestige was at stake, so much glory. He would not accept failure, not again!

Killian stiffened as the power was directed to him. A hint of blue light glimmered around the crystals. Sweat beaded on Killian's brow. He spread his fingers on the table and set his jaw as the level increased, then increased again. Senn felt the jumps as each man braided his energy into the power relay. He watched Killian with slitted eyes and fought to hold his concentration, fought to make his dream happen this time.

The blueness brightened into a wheel of dancing, twisting sapphire lines that trailed off in every direction into infinity. Killian lurched to his feet, his face fierce with pain and effort. Then the lines darkened and hung low over the table, becoming a roiling midnight-blue mass. The walls trembled. Over on the sideboard, a dozen glass tumblers burst into shards. A grinding force seized Senn, shook him as a hound shakes a skivit, and threw him to the floor.

The windows shattered behind the drapes, and he felt the braided skeins of power abruptly spin apart. The dark-blue mass above the table faded. His ribs hurt with the effort of breathing as he pulled himself up from the floor. Aaren Killian sprawled at his feet, his hands clutching his head, his skin pallid and clammy, his chest barely moving.

A dozen shocked faces stared at Senn from around the room, some bleeding from shards of glass. He sank into his chair as someone wrenched open the door and sent the servant for the resident Healer.

Disappointment burned through him, bitter as gall. Not this time, then, but soon, he promised himself. He would keep trying until he found the proper focus, and then he would control time itself.

The grove still rippled with the near brush of disrupted time. Summerstone huddled beside the nexus pool, her body ringing with the pain and shock.

Windsign drifted above the ground, doubled over, her slim arms clasped around her smooth head, her large eyes staring. *That was very . . . close.*

Each time they grow stronger. Summerstone dissipated her mass slightly and let the air cradle her, warm and gentle, soothing. *We must make them understand before it is too late.*

The males will never hear us. Gray streaked Windsign's green face, outlining her dark eyes. *If the shadowfoot had brought the small one, she might have spoken for us, but is too late for that now, too.*

Perhaps not. Summerstone reached for the mind of the small one who had come down the mountain. She saw buildings of stone and lifeless wood, felt the presence of many quiet-minded creatures. *She has left the forest but is not too far away. I will send the shadowfoot again.*

He failed before.

Because he cannot make her understand why she must come. This time we will follow, and when he has brought her close enough, we will sing her the rest of the way. She will be our sister and make them listen.

Kevisson took a firmer grip on the girl's thin arm as they descended the narrow, winding stair into the inn's bustling common room. He'd enlarged his own shields to include her, since, for whatever reason, she simply wasn't able to do it on her own.

The room was filled with grumbling tradesmen, tinkers, and herders. Cynnalee Kochigian glanced up from her serving tray, and her plain, work-worn face broke into a relieved smile. "The lass do look a mite improved."

"Yes, Mistress Kochigian." Kevisson held out a hexagonal silver coin. "The night's sleep and your cooking did wonders."

"Oh, no, sir!" The innkeeper wrung her hands in her patched apron and backed away, lowering her eyes. "I couldn't possibly take so much, not—" She hesitated, glancing at the girl. "Not when it were mostly Cittar's fault, like."

Kevisson pressed the coin into her chapped palm. "Nonsense, Mistress Kochigian. Cittar is not even a member of your family. I insist."

Her bony fingers closed around the coin. "Well, thank you kindly, sir." She stepped nearer and studied Haemas. "If you don't mind me saying so, you'd best take this one home to your mum straightaway. She's still at the age to

need a fair amount of looking after, if you know what I
mean."

He smiled. "You've hit on just my plan, Mistress
Kochigian. Good-bye." Keeping a tight grip on the girl, he
opened the door and marched her out into the sun-filled
street. The early-spring air was still crisp, the grass sparkled
with dew, and the light had a crystalline edge to it that he
rarely noticed up in the mountains. The ummit he'd paid far
too much for that morning flicked a disinterested shaggy
ear at them.

"You realize what they'll do to me, don't you, if you
make me go back?" Haemas said as he stopped to check
the ummit's rigging.

"You mean the Council?" The ummit grunted as
Kevisson kneed it in the belly so he could tighten the cinch.
"I suppose they'll want to know exactly what happened."

She kneaded her shoulder with her left hand. "They'll
kill me!"

"I told you, your father's not dead—or at least he wasn't
when I left."

"He was dead!"

Catching a hint of the same dark panic she'd felt earlier,
he grimaced. "You'll see for yourself when you get home."
He made a cup with his hands. "Now get on."

For a moment he thought she would break and run; then
she grasped the saddle with her good left hand and let him
boost her up. He winced with her as she settled into the
saddle, picking up the painful jolt in her shoulder.

That injury worried him almost as much as the delusion
about her father. He wasn't at all sure she could ride long
enough to reach Lenhe'ayn. Bracing his foot in the dangling stirrup, he swung into place behind her.

She ignored him as they rode through the awakening
streets and then passed the gatekeeper at the town wall. He
found it necessary to shield her out; her torn muscles protested with every jolt in the ummit's rough gait. What they
really needed to find was a good healer.

Sitting back in the saddle, he let himself be lulled, eventually, by the easy road, the ummit's plodding stride, and
the warm sun on his face. He thought of Shael'donn and
the work he had left behind. Two boys in the Upper Form

were showing signs of becoming passable Searchers, and
Master Ellirt was depending on him to help with Testing
when he returned.

The first warning sign came when the ummit began
prancing from side to side on the road and throwing its
small head up and down. "Stop that!" he snapped at the girl
as he gathered the reins.

She turned to look back at him with frightened eyes.
"I'm not doing anything!"

He softened his shields and listened. She wasn't interfering with the ummit's slow-witted mind, although he could
sense the jolt of pain she felt with each rough bounce. He
extended his screens over the animal's mind and it resumed
its slow, plodding gait.

Haemas pointed down the dusty road at a pair of specks
in the distance. Kevisson watched as two riders grew rapidly larger, rising and falling as they galloped over the
rolling hills.

Suddenly Haemas writhed in front of him. "No! I . . . not
. . . not again!"

"What in bloody Darkness is wrong?" Kevisson snagged
her waist to keep her from falling off and tried to read what
was wrong.

Jerking around in the saddle, she struggled with him,
heedless of her injured shoulder. "Not you, too! No one—."

The sound of hoofbeats grew louder. Kevisson could
make out their mounts now, a chestnut and a gray. *What is
it? Do you know these people?* he asked her, but she didn't
hear him.

The girl struggled for breath. "No one . . . is ever—"

Haemas, listen to me! Kevisson insisted. *Who are they?*

She fought him like a wild beast until he managed to pin
her arms while somehow hanging on to the reins. Then he
picked up a mental assault coming from one of the riders,
just yards away now. "It's all right," he said to the struggling girl. "I can shield you."

He tried to enclose her mind inside his shields, but she
grew even wilder, twisting with a strength that belied her
slender frame and almost breaking his grip. "Let me—go!"

He gripped the ummit's barrel with his legs, dangerously
close to losing his balance. "Stop fighting me!"

The two riders slowed to a walk, then halted their blown horses a few feet away. The chierra man on the gray mare hung back, his face blank and indifferent. The other rider, obviously Kashi by his bright-gold hair and light eyes, studied Kevisson and his struggling passenger with a sardonic smile. "Problems?" His hawk-nosed face was proud, obviously used to being obeyed. He leaned forward and smoothed his mount's cream-colored mane with one hand.

Haemas went rigid at the sound of his voice, and Kevisson felt dark panic flooding over her. He pressed his hand across her forehead. *Sleep,* he told her sternly. *Sleep until I tell you to wake!* He sensed her fear fading and relentlessly kept up his mental pressure until her body was deadweight and her mind was quiet enough that he could enclose it in the protection of his own shields.

"Very nice." The stranger nodded his head and fingered a heavy gold chain around his neck. "Now hand her over and there'll be no trouble."

"I have a commission from the Council of Twelve to bring her back to her father's House." Kevisson shifted the girl's weight across his saddle. "You tried to take her in the marketplace yesterday. Just who are you and what do you want?"

"I don't think you need concern yourself with that, Searcher." Painful pressure built up on the surface of Kevisson's shields. "This is a matter involving only the Great Houses. You may consider your task finished now. Hand the skivit over and I'll take care of this matter from here."

The pressure increased. Kevisson drew upon his energy reserves to strengthen his shields, painfully aware that he was not yet fully recovered from hitting his head the day before. The girl groaned and stirred in his arms.

"My obligation is to the Council and Lord Senn." Kevisson considered a counterattack, then decided against it, unsure whether he even had enough energy to maintain his shield over the ummit and the girl as well as himself.

"That's very noble." The stranger drew a sword from the richly tooled scabbard at his side and held the blade aloft. It gleamed in the bright sun, obviously forged of the finest steel, besting any weapon Kevisson had ever seen in his father's house. "Of course, it won't make much difference when you're dead."

Kevisson grimaced as the mental attack redoubled. Was he just tired, or was this stranger really stronger than anyone he'd come across before? The cut along his scalp began to throb again. Behind the Kashi, he noticed the dark-haired man blink slowly and look around.

It was possible, Kevisson thought, that in intensifying his attack, the stranger had let his control over the man slip. He studied the chierra and realized he was one of the men Haemas had been traveling with before Dorbin. "She's only a runaway," he said, playing for time. "I don't see why this particular youngster could warrant all this trouble."

The Kashi man spurred the spent chestnut a few steps forward and stared into Kevisson's face. "If I were you, outlander, I would leave this matter to my betters. When I take my seat on the Council, I will remember those who helped me, as well as those who stood in my way."

Out of the corner of his eye, Kevisson saw the chierra slide off the mare and stalk silently toward the Kashi stranger. He mentally prodded the ummit to move a few steps to the left, directing the stranger's attention that way. "At least give me some idea of what this is all about," he said, "and then perhaps I can turn her over to you with a clear conscience."

The Kashi's pale eyes glittered. "Don't ask that unless you're tired of living." He raised the gleaming sword. "Now quit stalling and hand the little beast over!"

The chierra reached up from behind and grabbed the stranger's upraised arm, pulling him backward off the chestnut colt. The mental attack ceased suddenly as the Kashi's head struck the road.

Kevisson gulped a deep breath, wiped the perspiration streaming down his face with his sleeve. The throbbing in his head receded. He looked at the chierra man standing over the stranger. "Thank you."

The man smiled wearily. "Oh, you be more than welcome." He plucked the bright sword out of the dust. "And now, if you would be so kind . . ." He advanced on the ummit, brandishing the sword in a businesslike manner. "Hand the lass over."

Kevisson prodded the ummit's dimwitted mind. It obediently backed away as the man approached. "You're making a mistake."

"No, my *Lord*." The man leaped forward and grabbed the ummit's reins, then pressed the sword's wickedly sharp tip to the hollow of Kevisson's throat. "It's you who will be making the mistake if you don't hand that package down right now!"

"Well, if you insist." Kevisson's lips compressed; his Andiine vows proscribed the use of mental force except to save his own life or another from harm, and he personally found such force distasteful. Still . . .

He exerted a tiny bit of pressure on several of the chierra's motor nerves. The sword dropped suddenly from the man's numb fingers and the ornate hilt struck his foot.

Kevisson reined the ummit about, trying not to listen to the other's howls of pain. As the ummit plodded toward the forest, he sent a mental message to the gray mare and chestnut colt behind him. Seconds later, he heard hoofbeats pounding down the road and relaxed as the ummit plunged him and his passenger into the forest's cool shade.

"Now open your mind, boy, and concentrate." Ellirt rested his hand on the eight-year-old's head and activated the six crystals in sequence, then threw his mind open to their vibrational signature. Within a few seconds he matched it in his own mind and then altered it slightly to take them to Tal'ayn.

He didn't need the boy's sharp intake of breath to know they'd transferred successfully. "I hope for both our sakes you were paying attention, Benl," he said gruffly as he let the child guide him out of the portal, "because I intend it to be your turn on the way back."

"Yes, Master." The boy looped his arm through the old man's. "Over here, I think."

Ellirt could have found his way alone, but it never did any harm to let other people underestimate him. Few Kashi ever studied the mind disciplines sufficiently these days to understand the inner-sight that kept him functioning despite his blindness.

He heard the heavy door creak open, and then Benl

directed him down a steep series of stone steps. Ellirt
sensed Alyssa Senn, her thoughts angry and disordered,
hastening to meet them at the landing just below.

He chuckled. All the better, if Dervlin Tal's spoiled
young wife thought him a "doddering, meddling old fool,"
not even worth shielding against. He must be careful not to
spoil that image.

A door opened at the bottom of the stairs. Warmer air
flowed against his face. He caught a whiff of Alyssa's
heavy floral scent.

"Master Ellirt!" Alyssa's young voice was light and airy.
"You should have told us to expect you."

Ellirt hastily composed his face into benign interest.
"I've come to see your Lord husband, my dear. Perhaps
there's something Shael'donn can do for him."

"Oh, he's much too weak for visitors." She slipped her
hand under his elbow and escorted him into the main
house. "But it was kind of you to come all this way."

"Is there somewhere Benl here can get a bite to eat,
Lady Alyssa?" He patted the boy's shoulder. "You know
how young men are, always hungry."

He caught a flash of thinly veiled irritation before she answered. "Of course, Master Ellirt, although, as Dervlin is
still so ill, I didn't really think you would be staying that
long."

"Oh, nobody is ever too ill to see me," Ellirt replied
cheerfully. "Let's get Benl taken care of and then we'll
have a little talk."

Alyssa tried and failed to mask the irritation in her voice.
"Jayna, take this youngster down to the kitchen and have
the cook give him some of her special callyt pastries."

Ellirt heard the scrape of a foot as the servant dropped a
curtsey, and then the two walked out of hearing.

"Good." He turned unerringly in the direction of the
family wing. Let her figure out how a doddering, blind
wreck like himself managed that, he thought wryly. "Now,
let's check on Dervlin. There's always the chance I might
do him some good."

Not if I can help it, Alyssa thought angrily. "Through
here, Master."

Ellirt felt the openness of a large room around him. "Is

this his room, child?" he asked innocently, knowing full
well it was not.

Her hand guided him to a chair. "Please sit down. I don't
want to disagree with you, but all the healers say Dervlin
must have rest and quiet if he is to have any chance of im-
provement." Her skirts swished as she settled in a chair
next to him.

Ellirt feigned astonishment. "Really? That is most ex-
traordinary! When I was speaking with Healer Sithnal just
yesterday, he said—"

"Healer Lerik Sithnal from Rald'ayn?" Her voice was
strained.

"Yes, my dear. I suppose I must have gotten it all wrong,
but I could swear *he* said Dervlin was restless and quarrel-
some from lack of company." His chair creaked as he
leaned back. "I suppose I have come all the way from
Shael'donn for nothing, then."

Even though he couldn't see her, Ellirt's mind perceived
how the young woman knotted her fingers together and
struggled for self-control. "Perhaps—*I* am the one who
made the mistake," she said finally. "Perhaps I didn't understand Healer Sithnal."

"Do you think so?" Ellirt smiled engagingly with his
best harmless-old-fool expression. "I would be so pleased if
I could have a few minutes with your Lord husband."

"If you'll wait here . . ." Her skirt whispered over the
chair's upholstery. "I will check on Dervlin and see how he
is today. Please excuse me."

"Of course, my dear," he murmured, listening to her
footsteps recede. A sense of triumph washed through him,
but he shook his head. Not yet, you old fool, he told himself; you've just gotten your hand on the lock. We've yet to
see if there is a key.

Still, he thought, it was not a bad morning's work for a
helpless old man. He ran a quick mental check on young
Benl down in the kitchen stuffing his mouth with sweets,
then sighed. Oh, to be young and carefree like that again.

Chapter
Thirteen

Haemas opened her eyes to a blazing wood fire and the pungence of brewing tea. A lightwing chittered somewhere above in the vine-draped trees. Blinking in the leaf-filtered late-afternoon light, she had the vague feeling something was wrong, but she couldn't remember what.

Kevisson Monmart slumped beside the fire, watching her with weary, dark-shadowed eyes. He ran a hand back through his bedraggled dark-gold hair. "Do you want some tea?"

Her head was pillowed on a hairy blanket thrown over the ummit's saddle. She sat up and winced; in spite of having slept, she felt as if every muscle in her body was tense and knotted. "What—happened?" she asked; then it all rushed back to her: Dorbin, the fire, the old man—and Jarid. She remembered her cousin's mind hammering at her, the sense of helplessness and terror. Why in the name of Darkness had he come all the way down to the Lowlands after her? Jarid had never had any love for her father.

Kevisson glanced sharply at her. "Jarid?"

Her hands clenched with the angry shame of not being able to shield this stranger out of her mind.

"Look, as far as I'm concerned, you're just another Lord's spoiled brat." He dashed the dregs of his mug into the fire. "It's my job to see you get home and that's it. I don't care what you did to your father, and it's none of my business how the High Lords run their Houses—but this Jarid tried to interfere with my duties. That makes it my business, whether you like it or not."

He talked so lightly of taking her back, Haemas thought, as if it were nothing, just a slap on the wrist or an evening with no dinner, and everything would be forgotten. She

119

huddled against the saddle and turned her head to the shifting flames, watching the oranges and yellows flow over each other. If only *she* could forget.

Kevisson jabbed a stick into the glowing red coals, spraying sparks into the air. "He said he'll sit on the Council."

Haemas swallowed around a knot in her throat. No doubt Jarid would. He'd never made any secret of his desire to possess Tal'ayn.

An edge of stealthy hunger caught at the back of her consciousness . . . a faint, angry need. She looked over her shoulder into the blue-green dimness under the interlaced trees.

"Something else is going on here." Kevisson shook his head. "There's no reason for him to come after you."

A sudden sense of satisfaction filled her mind. Sitting up, she glanced around again. It felt close, very close. The ummit, tethered somewhere out of sight, snuffled and stamped its feet.

Kevisson peered out into the undergrowth. "Did you hear something?"

Over there, she thought, orienting on the far side of the little clearing. She watched a huge form, black as Darkness itself, pad into camp, dragging a bloodied, limp ebari fawn between its powerful forelegs. Darting around the fire, she threw her arms around the silsha's great neck and laid her cheek on its rumbling chest. She could feel the pleasure it was radiating all the way down to her toes. It butted its great head against her shoulder. *Come into the trees*, it said. *Come now.*

No, I'll be all right, she told it. *Stay here with me.*

"Haemas!" White-faced, Kevisson snatched a burning brand from the fire and edged toward the silsha. "Get away from that thing!"

The black beast flattened its tufted ears and snarled around the carcass in its mouth. Haemas stroked the satiny black coat with both hands. "It won't hurt me."

Kevisson closed his eyes, then opened them again with an expression of shock. "That blasted beast has got *shields*!" He tossed the branch back into the fire and sank down on his heels, watching her closely.

Dropping the mangled ebari at her feet, the silsha rolled over on its back and pawed gently at her hands with its huge feet. *Come away!* it said. *Now!*

She laughed and grabbed one paw, wrestling with it.

The Searcher's eyes never left the pair. "What is that damn thing?"

Haemas looked up at him through the tumbled curtain of fair hair over her face. "A silsha."

"But it's so big. I've heard of them before, seen a few pelts, but ..." His voice trailed away and he shook his head. "Only *people* can learn to shield, and then only Ka-shi, not even chierras. Animals can't be trained in the mind disciplines."

The silsha sat up, its yellow eyes slitted. *Leave this one*, it said insistently to Haemas, studying the crouching man. *Come to the pool!*

Not now, she told it. *Not in the dark*. She leaned against the solid black shoulder. "It won't hurt you—unless you try to force me back to Tal'ayn."

Kevisson steepled his fingers under his chin. "Isn't it time you think this through? Do you really want to spend the rest of your life down here in the Lowlands, living in some tree, while Jarid lives in your House, running your lands?"

The future ... Haemas buried her face against the silsha's smooth black fur, inhaling the clean, musky scent. It had been forever since she'd thought about more than the next ten minutes. She tried to see herself going home, walking again in the vaulted stone halls of Tal'ayn, seeing her father's hand everywhere ... knowing what she had done. Panic welled up from deep in her mind.

"I know what you *think* you did." Kevisson's quiet voice barely carried above the hiss and pop of the fire. "But your father was still very much alive when I left the Highlands, and that was several days after you ran away."

"Are you saying I should believe you instead of my own eyes?" Her face suddenly felt hot.

Kevisson stirred the dying embers and threw on a hand-ful of twigs. "Wouldn't you like to go home?"

Home ... In her mind she saw the chierra servants who had been her real family, and her secluded personal garden dug into the side of the cliff behind Tal'ayn, the striated gray rock softened by luxuriant greenery and warmed by steaming thermal pools.

Then she tried to imagine her father's stern face, healthy and alive. . . .

She shuddered.

Kevisson pondered the flames for a moment. "Well, then, look at it this way—do you want this Jarid to take your rightful place?"

Haemas's arms tightened around the silsha's powerful neck. The only problem with that question, she thought, was that the answer was no.

Supporting himself against the rough bark of a tree at the forest's edge, Jarid closed his eyes and reached out with his mind to check again. The simple, undefended thought patterns he'd detected were definitely closer this time. Someone was approaching.

He still had a few minutes, though. Taking a deep breath, he tried to center down so he could deal with this abysmal headache. Every time he blocked off one sense, though, the rustling of the leaves intruded, or the painful lump of a stone under his foot. Finally, sweating and miserable, he gave up. It had to be that wretched knot on the back of his skull. He winced as his head began to pound even harder.

He was going to make sure that little skivit and her band of brigands suffered with exquisite slowness for every indignity inflicted upon him, just as soon as he'd appropriated some supplies and another mount. He heard the faint sound of hoofbeats on the road, then grimaced when his hand dropped automatically to the empty scabbard at his side. They had made off with his sword, his horse, everything he'd had of any value, down to the gold chain around his neck.

The slow, rhythmic hoofbeats grew louder, and finally he glimpsed a youngish, plump woman riding a gaunt ebari, her gray homespun skirts hitched above her chubby knees. Stepping out where she could see him, Jarid reached for her mind.

"May the Mother cradle you in Her hand, stranger." The

woman reined in the ebari and looked down at him with deep-set dark eyes. "Are you hurt, like?"

Jarid strained to reach her mind. He could feel her before him, hear her boring chierra thought-tracings, but he could get no more hold on her mind than he could a handful of air. His face broke out in a cold sweat.

She was waiting, her hands piled on the saddle before her, watching him closely with those shrewd chierra eyes. "Have you been robbed, then?"

It must be that damned head injury, he thought. He simply couldn't believe this fat, stupid peasant could resist him unless something was wrong. "I—need assistance." He steadied himself against the ebari's shaggy shoulder with one hand, feeling ridiculously weak.

"Bandits, I suppose." She sighed. "Well, you'd best come along with me to the Mother's house." She swung her leg over the ebari's back and slid down its washboard-ribs to the ground. "The Sisters will be glad to care for you until you're fit to travel."

Jarid put his foot in the stirrup, then hesitated. "I have no money."

"Of course not!" She grinned at him, revealing a crooked front tooth. "That's why they calls them 'thieves'!"

Lord of Light! he thought, staring at her plain tan face, this peasant actually thought she was being witty. He pulled himself up into the worn, patched saddle and sat there, his mind too clouded with pain to worry much about where she was taking him. A little rest, he thought, and he would be able to pull himself together.

Then they would see what he could do. Everyone would see.

The girl lay asleep with her pale-gold head pillowed on the midnight-black of the silsha's shoulder, the animal's wickedly clawed legs stretched out on either side of her. Kevisson watched them both through the fire's shifting shadows.

He still couldn't believe it: The damned beast had *shields*. How in the world did an *animal* learn to shield? And, as if that weren't enough, apparently the blasted thing could pick up his thoughts as easily as he could its.

Taking Haemas Tal back to the Highlands would be impossible now unless he could convince her to go willingly—or he killed the silsha. Unfortunately, he wasn't sure exactly how one went about killing a six-hundred-pound beast that was sure to be faster than pure thought and would know the instant he decided to do it in.

He took a last sip of the tea in his mug and made a face; it was cold and tasteless. Tossing the dregs onto the fire, he watched the hissing droplets skitter over the glowing embers. There was so much more going on than he had bargained for.

He settled himself against the ummit saddle and relaxed his muscles. Then he counted each slow breath as he exhaled, focusing in his mind on the blue and orange Andiine pattern laid into Ellirt's floor before the hearth.

For a long time he drifted, building the intricate design line by line in his mind until he could see every whorl, every line. . . .

Kevisson!

Yes, Master. He hesitated, hating to reveal his incompetence.

He felt Ellirt's amusement. *Don't be so stiff-backed, boy. Haven't you learned anything in the time since you first came to us?*

Kevisson gave a mental sigh, then loosened his shields, integrating the link between them more fully. *I know, I'm overcompensating again.*

It's still something for you to work on, at any rate. Ellirt's calm sensibility warmed him. *But let's get to the point. You've found the Tal girl?*

Yes, Kevisson admitted, *but I've run into another Kashi Searching the girl. He's nearly taken her twice now, but all I can find out is that his name is 'Jarid,' and he means somehow to place himself on the Council.*

Damnation! Kevisson could picture Ellirt's angry face. *That must be old Tal's nephew, Jarid Tal Ketral. I don't suppose that delinquent girl has explained anything.*

Well, that's another problem. Kevisson wondered exactly how to explain this. *She seems to be injured in some way; she can't shield and she grows hysterical when I attempt to probe any deeper than just surface thoughts. You don't buy*

*this story that she attacked her father, do you? She doesn't
seem the type.*

*I was afraid this matter might turn out to be another one
of the Council's never-ending scandals.* Ellirt paused. *I
don't know what I believe about this wretched business, but
we'll never get to the truth as long as the girl stays down
there. Just bring her back here as soon as possible so we
can be done with the whole mess. Let her father deal with
all of this.*

Kevisson winced. *I'm afraid she's under the misappre-
hension that her father is dead. She's terrified to come
back.*

Dead? Ellirt's surprise was apparent. *I did find the old
coot a little weak yet, although his young snippet of a wife
would have everyone think he was departing for the next
life any minute. Wishful thinking on her part, I'm sure.*

Not dead. Kevisson let relief wash over him. The girl
had seemed so certain.

*Just throw the young baggage over your saddle and get
back to Shael'donn immediately.*

I had meant to do that, Master. . . .

But? the old Andiine insisted.

Kevisson felt ridiculous. *But she's—taken up with a huge
black silsha, and I can't get within ten feet of her.*

There was a long, embarrassing pause. *Assuming you
haven't suddenly become an imbecile, there must be a log-
ical reason why you don't simply send the beast away.*

I can't control it, Kevisson admitted, knowing it sounded
stupid. *It's impossible, but the creature seems to have—
shields.*

A black silsha, you say?

Yes, Master.

*Are you aware that the black silsha is not only extremely
rare, but also sacred to the chierra Mother cult?*

Kevisson felt weariness dragging upon him; the distance
to Shael'donn was great. *No.*

*Well, think about it anyway, and I shall mull over the
whole mess, too. You may find the Mother's Children are
mixed up in this some way.*

Kevisson could barely make out Ellirt's words. *Who,
Master?*

Walk toward the Light, Kevisson Monma . . .

He lost the link with Shael'donn as his energy reserve gave out. He'd pushed himself hard the last few days. Opening his eyes, he glanced at the other side of the dying fire, where Haemas and the silsha slept peacefully. She looked very young and helpless in the fading light, her slim arms twined around the beast's neck, her moon-gold hair strewn across the black fur.

He stirred himself enough to rummage in the saddlebag for the last of Cynnalee Kochigian's plain but nutritious food, then lay back on the saddle, munching cheese-and-berry sweetcake.

Ellirt had offered no real advice. It seemed Kevisson was on his own, for the present.

Summerstone let the night wind blow her high above the trees. Despair seeped through her, cell by cell. *She still will not come with the shadowfoot.*

Windsign answered her from the ground. *He is clever for his kind, but cannot speak plainly enough. Although she has affection for him, she simply does not understand.*

Summerstone thinned until she felt part of the dank, chill wind, until her body streamed with it through the night. *Then call him back to us. Perhaps she will follow.*

Windsign trailed her hand in the water. Concentric rings rippled outward. *Perhaps.*

Lealla stood looking down at the stranger's pale face as he slept on a cot in the guest quarters. Dark circles shadowed his closed eyes, but his breathing seemed clear and easy. More exhausted than anything else, she thought.

She turned to Esleann's plump face. "You're sure you felt his power in your mind?"

The acolyte sister nodded, her eyes fixed on the sleeping Kashi's face. "Yes, Sister. If I had not already been committed into the Mother's hands, I don't know what would have happened."

Well, that settled the matter. Lealla's mouth firmed into a worried line. "All the younger girls must go to the shrine at Litinhem." Her mind raced, working out the details.

Esleann sighed. "I'll have them pack immediately, Sister."

Lealla bent over to draw the blanket more snugly over the sleeping man. "Pick out one of the young savoks to send with them for slaughter, then turn the rest out into the forest. And send a full measure of cracked grain, as well. I've no idea how long they'll have to stay."

"Do you want me to call a shadowfoot?" Esleann asked.

"No." Lealla folded her hands. "Once the young ones are out of the way, the rest of us should be safe enough. Now hurry. I gave him a sleeping draft, but we can't risk any of the young ones still being here when he wakes."

Esleann bowed her dark-haired head in obedience and left, closing the door softly behind her. Picking up a piece of mending, the older woman settled into a chair beside the narrow bed and began where she had left off when Esleann had arrived with such troubling company.

Very strange, she thought as her silvery needle flashed in and out around the ragged tear. She'd never seen one of *them* travel alone this deep into the Lowlands before, although there were rumors that the Lords could disguise their appearance.

Well, she reminded herself briskly, it was true that trouble took advantage of the unwary, but the Mother taught her children to always be prepared.

Chapter
Fourteen

Dervlin Tal squinted irritably at the leather-bound book in his hands. Every time he was almost able to force the rebellious black print to come into focus, it blurred hopelessly again. He snapped the book shut and heaved it to the foot of the bed. Darkness and damnation, he wasn't ready to die yet! He tugged at the black silk pull beside his bed.

Jayna's gray head peered around the door. "Yes, your Lordship?"

Dervlin scowled at her. "Don't just stand there, woman. Send for the healer at once. I can't read a single word in this damned book!"

The old chierra stepped over the threshold, shut the massive door, then folded her work-roughened hands before her. "Begging your pardon, your Lordship, but Healer Sithnal did say that—"

"—I meant a real healer, of course, not that incompetent nit!"

Jayna bowed her head and continued in a determined voice. "Healer Sithnal *did* say that your Lordship's brain had received a terrible shock and it would be some time before you could expect complete recovery." Her brown eyes, deep as two wells, glanced up from the floor. "He *said* you was lucky to be alive at all."

"Lucky!" Dervlin snorted, then sagged wearily against the pillows heaped behind his back. These days, even a brief fit of temper left him weak. He swallowed; the back of his mouth tasted of burnt iron. "I want my own healer."

"Now, your Lordship . . ." Jayna ventured close enough to punch up the pillows to support his aching head. "Your old healer be dead, as you very well know. Healer Sennay died a full three weeks before you had your—your accident."

"Accident, bah!" He rubbed at the throbbing spot over his ear. "Attempted murder is not an accident!"

"I won't never believe the Lady Haemas tried to kill you," Jayna said over her shoulder.

Dervlin watched her bend stiffly before the hearth, tugging a log into place to stoke the faltering fire. Although he would never have admitted it, he found a curious comfort in her presence. An age ago, they had played together here at Tal'ayn when he was a callow, untrained lad and she the youngest child of his mother's maidservant. "Well," he said, "I'm amazed the little skivit even had the guts to try." He started to laugh, but as usual, it only made him cough.

She poured a tumbler of cool water, then fitted his trembling fingers around it. "You just lie back here and rest, your Lordship. Don't you think about nothing at all."

After sipping a mouthful, Dervlin rolled his head restlessly over the pillows. Rest? He had forgotten how. A painful brightness simmered behind his eyes whenever he tried to sleep. He felt burned, used up and useless, unable even to remember the night his pale-eyed daughter had assaulted him. "Still can't believe she ... tried," he mumbled, as sleep dragged at him. "Must be more of me in ... than I thoug—"

Warm, slanting rays of sunlight danced over her face. Haemas opened her eyes and stretched. The orange sun hung just above the trees bounding the clearing. Glancing at the sleeping Searcher, she put a hand behind her and felt through the damp grass and leaves.

The silsha was gone.

Pushing her tangled hair out of her face, she scrambled onto her knees and looked anxiously around. There was no sign of her huge protector.

Her breath puffed white in the chill spring morning air, and her shoulder ached bone-deep from sleeping on the cold hard ground. How long had the silsha been gone? Why hadn't she felt him go? She cast her mind out through the trees, but only picked up the brief thought-traces of skivits and barrets, lightwings and nits, nothing else. He was hunting, she told herself; an animal that size needed a lot of food. He would come back.

On the far side of the clearing, propped against the saddle, Kevisson mumbled something in his sleep. He turned over and his head slipped off onto the ground. "What's— wrong?" He blinked at her with dazed red-rimmed eyes.

"What did you do to the silsha?" She stood over his long, lanky form, both hands clenched.

"I didn't do anything, but not for lack of trying." He sat up and kneaded his forehead with the heel of his hand. "Sorry, I have a bit of a headache. I overextended myself last night."

Haemas's mouth tightened. He didn't care, nobody cared. The wind picked up, whistling through the glade, making her dew-dampened clothes cling to her skin in icy folds. She turned away from him and rubbed her hands over her wet sleeves, shivering.

Kevisson unfolded himself slowly, as if he'd aged twenty years overnight, then draped the smelly ummit blanket around her shoulders. "Why don't you start the fire while I fetch some water for tea?" Without waiting for an answer, he crunched off through the underbrush with a water bag slung over his shoulder.

She stared angrily after him, then kicked at the pile of deadwood they'd gathered the night before. Didn't he understand? She wasn't able to start the fire, just as she couldn't shield and couldn't read people anymore. Somehow she had lost everything that last terrible night at Tal'ayn.

When he returned some minutes later, Kevisson lifted an eyebrow at her. "What, no fire? I thought you were cold."

"If you want one, you'll have to start it yourself!" She poked at the dead ashes with a stick.

He poured water into the tiny camp kettle, then paused, his golden-brown eyes thoughtful. "So you've lost that skill, too?"

She didn't answer.

"I could show you again." He set the kettle aside and came over to stand next to her.

She looked away from his compelling dark-gold eyes, her heart hammering. This was so stupid, she was cold and hungry and dirty and—

And what? she asked herself.

Cold and hungry and dirty and—frightened.

"I was trained at Shael'donn," he said. "I do this all the time."

Shael'donn, she thought—old Yernan, her tutor, had been from there. "They never take girls at Shael'donn, do they?"

"No." He crouched in the wet grass beside her.

She stared miserably at her white-knuckled hands. Could she really learn to spark a fire again, and if so, would it make any difference? What was done was done, wasn't it? There could be no going back—ever.

"You did know how to do this at one time, I take it?"

"Of course!" She glanced up indignantly. "My father—" Terrible images from that night whispered in the back of her mind and she couldn't finish the sentence.

"Never mind." Kevisson's long fingers brushed the nape of her neck, seeking the sensitive contact points. "Close your eyes and we'll give it a try."

She stiffened, then complied.

"Fire is one aspect of the Light." His low voice spoke the ancient litany just behind her ear. "Respect and tend it as you would the Lord of Light himself."

The familiar words relaxed her slightly. She could almost hear Yernan's creaky voice reciting the same passage from *The Book of Light*.

"Build the image of Fire in your mind. Feel the heat . . . see its brightness . . . hear the crackle . . . smell the smoke."

She began to construct the image just as she had once been taught, then suddenly panicked when she felt the warm bright circle of his mind draw close to hers. She bolted onto her feet, fighting the sick swirl of fear.

He stepped back. "Take a moment to relax, then we'll try again."

Knotting her hands together to keep them from shaking, Haemas tried to get her breath. "I don't think I can stand it." Her forehead was damp with sweat, even though the morning air was crisp.

Kevisson moved around until he could see her face. "You do want to learn?"

She pressed her hands over her eyes, then took a deep breath and nodded.

"I'll help you more this time." He slipped behind her and rested his fingers lightly on her neck.

Trembling like a cornered tree barret, Haemas closed her eyes.

"Fire is one aspect of the Light itself." His other hand reached around to touch her lightly on the left temple. She felt his mind approaching hers again and tried not to stiffen as her fear threatened to engulf her.

"Respect and . . ." A sense of calm overcame her, drowning the fear with a drowsy feeling of well-being. ". . . tend it as you would the Lord of Light himself." Her head nodded now as the tight neck muscles relaxed.

"Build the image of Fire in your mind. Feel the heat. . . ."

She felt the comforting warmth radiated against her chilled face.

"See its brightness. . . ."

The flickering, weaving yellow-orange of flames danced before her inner vision, beautiful, beguiling.

"Hear the crackle. . . ."

She heard the sizzle of dry wood feeding a hungry fire, the pop and hiss of flames.

"Smell the smoke."

The woody, smoky aroma curled through the air as Fire now burned vividly in her imagination.

"Now take the spark—and Light the Fire."

Haemas reached for the flames in her mind and—froze. Her guilty fear escaped again, howling at her, yammering that she had lost the right to all of this! She could never—

Kevisson's strong, quiet voice commanded her again. "Take the spark!"

It was so close! She made herself reach out, cringing as she touched the living flame.

"Light the Fire!"

The skin-shriveling fire burned into and through her. She tried to direct it outward to the wood shavings, but it eluded her and blazed out of control. Kevisson *pushed* her somehow in the right direction. Still caught in the relentless, scorching heat, she poured the spark out into the rock-circled fireplace.

Inside her head, though, a seamless wall of flames raged,

rising up on every side until she herself was nothing but red-yellow-orange fire. Flamelets that had been her hair burned brightly around her red coal eyes.

And everywhere she turned, her father's angry face scowled at her, etched in living flame.

Just when she thought the fire would burn her into ashes, a cool wind brought the darkness.

"Haven't you got anything better than this slop?" Jarid jammed the wooden spoon back into the bowl of zeli-and-callyt porridge. Sticky gray spots spattered over the table.

The woman's plump face didn't change. Leaning over, she whisked the bowl off the table without a word. A moment later, she returned from the kitchen with a wet cloth and scrubbed the mess up.

"Our next meal comes at the Twelfth Hour, more or less." Her broad chierra face regarded him blandly. "Perhaps our poor fare will be more to your liking then."

Jarid shoved his chair back from the table and stood, not bothering to hide his irritation. His stomach was clamoring for real food. "I wouldn't even feed that sludge to a savok on its way to slaughter!"

The corners of her mouth tightened. "I regret such plain fare be not fit for a Lord's table, but we have naught else to offer."

"Never mind!" Jarid glared around the empty dining room. "I want to talk to whoever's in charge here."

"That would be Sister Lealla." The plump woman gave the table a final rub, then straightened. "Though she be making her morning reverences right now, so if you could wait a—"

"I am not accustomed to waiting." He fixed her with an icy stare and tried to insinuate a tendril of controlling thought into her simple mind.

She patted him on the shoulder. "Of course not, your Lordship. I'll be happy to fetch her myself, just as soon as she be finished."

Damnation! he swore silently. What had that fall done to him? He could no more get a grip on her than he could have seized the mind of a road marker. "Don't bother!" He shouldered past her. "I'll do it myself!" Ducking his head under the low doorway, he emerged into the morning sunshine and paused. Although he couldn't control the woman, he had seen quite clearly in her mind where he would find this Lealla.

Around one side of the simple stone keep lay a kitchen garden where several older women bent over the low neat rows, weeding. On the other side grew a young grove of callyt trees, fenced with low, bristly keiria bushes. Beyond that stood a virgin forest of true-trees, mostly spine-wood and redthorn.

Jarid ignored the stares of the women and walked through the fruit grove, searching for a break that led into the woods. He was losing precious time here. If he didn't catch up to his runaway cousin soon, that meddling Searcher would succeed in taking her before the Council. Jarid didn't know how well his handiwork would hold up to trained scrutiny and had no intention of finding out. Haemas Sennay Tal must die before anyone could question her on the events of that night. Then Tal'ayn would at last be his.

A faint path led through the underbrush into the old growth forest. Jarid followed it for a few minutes, sensing a thought-presence just up ahead. A faint smell of wet rocks and water drifted back to him. Ducking his head under a low branch, he pushed aside a curtain of low-hanging vines and stepped into a small clearing carpeted with flowering moss.

A silvery, irregularly shaped pool bubbled up from the foot of a large red slab of rock slanting up out of the ground. A hollow-cheeked woman sat with her legs folded beneath her long, gray skirt, contemplating the pool's mirrored surface. Her mind was so still that he could pick up nothing from her.

He walked closer and saw the pool had been banked with quarried white stone. At one end, broad steps led down into the clear water. The gentle bubbling of the spring, like the faint ring of crystal striking crystal, was the only sound.

He cleared his throat, but she didn't respond. "I need some supplies," he said, but the loudness of his own voice startled him, seeming to echo through the looming trees.

"It's not wise, like, to intrude upon the Mother." The woman turned her lined, sun-bronzed face up to him.

"I don't intend to stand here bandying superstitions with you, woman. I need a mount and some supplies so I can continue my journey. I have important business."

"I know." Closing her dark eyes, the chierra woman tilted her face up into the soft morning light. "Men be always in such a hurry. As long as you're here, why don't you sit for a while and open your mind to the Mother's voice?"

"Forget the religious drivel!" Jarid seized her shoulders and yanked her slight body off the mossy ground. She weighed no more than an empty sack. "Get me a mount and some supplies right now, or you're going to be very sorry!"

The water's crystalline sound grew louder, echoing through the trees until the vibration set his teeth on edge. He released her and staggered backward. His hands flew over his ears, but the sound seemed to come from everywhere, even inside his head.

Sister Lealla rose gracefully from the ground, her thin hands folded neatly before her. "There's no point fighting the Mother's voice. Open your mind and receive Her wisdom."

The crystalline resonance in the glade built up to the level of pain, stealing even the breath out of his lungs. He tried to shield it out with no success, then stumbled toward the edge of the trees.

She trailed him calmly, a faint smile on her work-worn face. "It seems She wants something from you."

Deafened and blinded by the clamor of a million crystal bells ringing inside his head, Jarid flailed for support. One hand smacked against the rough bark of a tree and he clung to it, sweat pouring down his face.

"You should be honored to serve Her purpose."

He forced his trembling legs to take another step, then another until he reached the shade of the surrounding trees. The vibrations eased and he stumbled a few more steps.

Yes, he told himself, the sound really was less. He crashed through the woods, heedless of cuts and scratches, emerging finally into the callyt grove.

Sinking to his knees under the slender young trees, he tried to slow his gasping breath. His chest ached with the effort of breathing, and even here he could still hear the faint tinkling. Bloody Darkness! What had all that been about?

After a moment, his head cleared. It had to be that blasted knot on his head, he told himself. All he needed was some time to recover, and then he'd show these dirt-grubbing peasants what a real Lord could do.

Kevisson sat by the girl's side, gauging her pale, strained face as she slept. He guessed he should be grateful that the silsha had missed out on the fire-making fiasco. The beast would have torn him to shreds if it had picked up her fear and pain.

What had made him so confident he could teach her? He wasn't even a Master yet, just a competent Searcher. Shaking his head angrily, he threw another branch on the fire that had very nearly cost both of them their lives. He glanced down at his singed tunic.

Power lay buried in Haemas's sleeping mind—too much power, over which she had no control. She was not only a danger to herself in this condition, but to anyone who tried to work with her. What he had foolishly done had only made matters worse.

Kevisson wondered what the Masters would say when he brought her back. They might think it kinder to seal off her psi-centers and let her live a quiet life. But then, what of the Council? What of her father?

Haemas groaned in her sleep and rolled over, throwing one arm across her grimy, soot-blackened face. Kevisson monitored her sleeping thoughts, then grimaced; the burning again.

Leaning over, he touched her forehead with his fingertips. *No dreams,* he spoke to her sleeping mind. She resisted him and he caught the image of an older man's angry face etched in incandescent yellow-orange fire.

No dreams! Feeling sick and shaken, he increased the force of his will until her sleep deepened into darkness. Then he sat back and watched the still, drawn face. It would almost be kinder if she could just sleep and never wake again.

Chapter
Fifteen

She wandered lost in a vast, despairing darkness thick with the stench of burning and smoke. Somewhere ahead, a voice called her name insistently, over and over, but she also felt a baleful presence, waiting to make her pay for what she had done to her father. Soon, very soon—

"Haemas, listen to me," the voice insisted hoarsely. "You have to wake up."

Painfully she forced open her gritty eyes and blinked up at Kevisson Monmart's haggard face framed in late-afternoon light.

The corners of his mouth tightened. "Now *control* it."

She lifted her head from the smelly ummit blanket, her neck and shoulders as stiff as if she'd slept for a hundred years. "What . . . ?" Without warning, the hungry flames leaped up in her mind again, roaring and eager, followed by an explosion of real fire from the campfire's dead ashes. Back in the trees, the tethered ummit bawled and strained at its rope.

"No, you can't let it come back!" Kevisson's fingers dug into her shoulders. "Concentrate on the sound of my voice. I kept you in deep sleep all last night and most of today. This time you have to control it so we can go on."

"All . . . night?" She could barely make out his face through the flickering sheet of yellow flame behind her eyes. A few feet away, the campfire licked at overhanging tree branches.

"It's feeding on your fear—and your guilt." Kevisson's golden-brown eyes bore down on her. "You have to fight! I don't know what really happened at Tal'ayn, but I don't believe you deserve to die for it."

Tal'ayn . . . her father . . . Sorrow stabbed through her, and the flames, both real and in her mind, roared higher. She smelled acrid smoke as the leaves overhead caught fire. Cursing, Kevisson beat out the glowing sparks that dropped onto his shoulders.

Haemas shuddered. No doubt she did deserve to die, but the Searcher didn't. Concentrating, she summoned every scrap of strength she had left to send the flames—away. They resisted cunningly, fading here, breaking out somewhere else, stronger than before, but she pursued them with a ferocious single-mindedness until she finally extinguished them all, one by one.

"Good. Now, hold on to that." Kevisson rubbed sooty fingers over the golden-brown stubble covering his tired face. "And no matter what, stay awake. If you go back to sleep right now, your subconscious may rekindle that blasted fire." He filled a wooden mug with water and passed it to her.

She let it roll slowly down her parched throat. "Then why did you let me sleep for so long?"

"Because," he said wearily, "every time I tried to wake you, the flames escaped. You could have died at any time. Me, too, for that matter."

She sat up, then closed her eyes as the trees swooped dizzily around her head.

"Finish that water, and then you'd better eat something."

A wave of nausea flooded over her. "I'm not hungry."

"You have to eat." He took the cup from her hand and refilled it. "And you need to get down a lot of fluid, too. You're already close to being dehydrated."

"I don't understand what went wrong." She leaned forward and pressed her forehead against her knees. "Yernan taught me to make fire when I was very small. Nothing like this ever happened."

"It's my fault." Kevisson's voice was bleak as he began packing the saddlebags with their meager supplies. "I knew something was wrong with your psi-senses, but I didn't think. Unfortunately, that nearly cost both of us our lives." He paused in the middle of emptying the tiny kettle. "You've never been Tested, have you?"

She made herself finish the water. "No, I won't be sixteen for a few more days."

Shaking the last drops out of the kettle, he stowed it in the saddlebags. "My best guess is you'll have at least a Plus-Ten Rating. That is, if you ever regain enough control to be Tested. It's control you lack, not Talent."

A Ten, Haemas thought—even Jarid had Tested only as an Eight. Then she glanced around the clearing anxiously, smelling smoke in the breeze that whispered against her hot skin.

The saddlebags slid through Kevisson's fingers as he whirled around. "Concentrate!"

She closed her eyes, thinking fiercely that she did *not* smell smoke, there were *no* flames, she would *not* let the fire come again! Sparks erupted in one corner of her mind, brightly mocking. She threw her will against them and they flared out. She took a ragged breath, trying to slow her pounding heart.

Kevisson relaxed and wiped a grimy hand across his forehead. "You can't let it get away from you again." He placed the blanket behind the ummit's hump, then cinched the patched saddle. "Once we get to Lenhe'ayn, we can rest and have a healer monitor you, but I'm not exactly sure how far it is from here. I didn't travel through the forest by the . . . usual means." He held out his hands, laced together, to give her a leg up. "Now, get on this evil-smelling beast so we can get out of here before Jarid catches up with us."

She wedged her toe into his grip and let him boost her into place. Just as he mounted behind her, she caught the faintest hint of smoke.

The afternoon sunlight streaming through Shael'donn's windows was as warm as melted butter against Ellirt's face. "What do you know about Jarid Tal Ketral?" he asked as Arldet Falt Killian made himself comfortable in the opposite chair before the hearth.

"Light above us!"

Ellirt didn't have to see the other Master to know how he stiffened at the mention of that name.

"Do we really have to talk about this, Kniel?" Arldet shifted uneasily. "That young rascal was my most painful failure."

"You are his only tutor of record." Ellirt leaned back and

propped his feet up on a low hammock. "I need to know what you remember about him."

"I was only employed by Tal'ayn for a year. Then the old Tal himself threw me out because the boy complained about my discipline."

Ellirt heard Arldet get up and pace over to the bookshelves lining one side of the room. Angry tracings dominated the surface thoughts of the other man.

"What occasioned your discipline?"

"Oh, bullying the servants, you know the sort of thing." The footsteps returned. "I caught him altering their memories and making them smart-mouth the old Tal."

Ellirt folded his hands across his chest. "Sounds like the normal sort of mischief boys will get into."

"That wasn't the worst of it, though." Arldet sighed. "He would draw servant girls to his bed at night, then block their memory, and him only fifteen!" He hesitated. "And then there was the matter of his cousin, the young Tal heir."

Ellirt pulled his feet down and leaned forward. "Haemas Sennay Tal?"

"Yes." The emotional content of the other's surface thoughts grew angrier. "You must understand, of course, that the old Tal never believed me. He always took the word of that young scamp, Jarid."

Ellirt nodded.

"I discovered Jarid was interfering with the girl's training. If I remember correctly, she was only three or four years old at the time. I came upon him one day hiding close by while the girl's tutor instructed her on the use of a portal. Kniel, I swear by the Light, the young devil was *blocking* her. Then, a few days later, I awoke one night and realized he was projecting black dreams into her sleep."

Ellirt sat silently, receiving the scene from his friend's memories: the girl-child had hair and eyes of the lightest possible gold, almost silver, and a fragile, haunted look. The boy was tall for his age and lean, with bright-gold hair and eyes a shade darker than the girl's, but still very pale. He sighed. "And you punished him?"

"Yes, although I didn't go to the old Tal at first. Damn it all, Kniel, it pains me to admit it, but the boy is kin. His father is Aaren Killian, although no one ever speaks of it."

"You know, I'd quite forgotten about all of that." Ellirt tapped his chin. "It was hushed up such a long time ago. How much do you think the boy knows of the matter?"

"The evidence stares back at him from the mirror every morning in those light Killian eyes of his. Of course, his cousin had those eyes, too, but she got them through her mother's line. I always suspected that her Killian blood was the reason Jarid seemed to detest her so." Arldet's voice was angry. "He'd have to be a total fool not to know why his supposed father at Ketral'ayn denies him, why he'll never be a Lord, no matter how hard he works and studies."

Ellirt fingered the tooled sunburst on his belt. "I don't imagine Jarid Tal Ketral is anyone's fool."

"He's a Talented, black-hearted rascal, that one." Ellirt sensed Arldet's scowl. "He stood right there in front of the old Tal, swearing with tears in his eyes that he knew nothing of the pranks of which I accused him. I truly don't know if he was just that good at shielding even then, or if the old Tal was already past his prime and unable to read the truth for himself. At any rate . . ." Arldet sighed. "I was dismissed and have not been taken on by any High House since. Jarid, I imagine, has continued to suit himself without guidance of any sort."

"Sounds like a proper recipe for trouble," Ellirt said. "What of the girl? Does she seem of a like propensity?"

"Just the opposite." Arldet shook his head. "She was a quiet, withdrawn child. I saw little of her and heard even less, except for rumors that she was not very quick at her lessons."

"A sad House." Ellirt paused to send a mental order for refreshments to one of the boys serving down in the kitchen. "Two children, both without mothers, and a father who would not face the truth."

"I was not sorry to leave that gloomy place." Arldet rose and stood in front of the hearth. "Though I've never been easy about what I left behind. When I heard what had happened between the girl and her father, I wondered if I should have tried harder to convince him before I left."

"You mean before you were *thrown out*." Ellirt shook his head. "Never mind, you are possibly being of some help now."

"Too little, too late, I should imagine."

Ellirt plucked the image of the intense, good-looking boy out of his friend's surface thoughts again and examined it. It was a strong face, with those flaring cheekbones and the typical Tal hawk nose, but a wild glint lurked behind the Killian eyes. "Well," he said, as a low knock sounded at the door, "perhaps it's not too late to try."

"Is that the only riding beast in the whole place?" The Lord stranger's pale face flushed with anger.

Esleann glanced at the elderly, broken-horned ebari and nodded. "This be all that we have, your Lordship."

Running his fingers back through his bright-gold hair, the Kashi grimaced. "Then I suppose it will have to do. Saddle it at once. I have to be on the road."

"Don't have no saddle, your Lordship." Esleann watched his eyes, colorless as ice, narrow in frustration. Suddenly she felt his mind whispering around the edges of her thoughts. She shuddered. Even though the Mother had sealed Esleann with Her protection last spring, the young woman would never get used to the nasty sensation of someone grasping at her mind.

The Kashi gave up, scowling at her and clenching his fists. "I'll get it myself!"

Esleann stepped aside as he charged past her into the simple gray stone barn. He would find nothing useful in there, she thought with satisfaction. Every animal and bit of tack of any value had been sent with the younger, unprotected girls to the shrine at Litinhem.

Ten minutes later he emerged, red-faced and empty-handed. Without looking at her again, he seized the bag of food he'd raided from their larder and hiked his leg over the ebari's bare back.

Esleann watched him ride out onto the dusty road, then jerk the poor beast's head toward Dorbin. It would be a slow trip at best, and even that depended on him not losing the ebari the first time he stopped. Lealla had kept that particular beast since it inevitably ran back to its cozy stall in the Sisters' barn at the first opportunity.

She looked back and saw Lealla walking toward her.

"You got him on his way, then?" Lealla smiled. "Good for you."

"He were a bad one," Esleann said. "Worse than usual."

"But you refused him naught?"

Esleann nodded.

"Then he won't be returning with more like hisself to rob and beat us." Lealla's dark eyes watched the stranger's back grow slowly smaller as the ebari ambled down the narrow road. "Even the high and mighty Lords themselves can't fault us for being poor, especially when it's them what made us that way to begin with."

"Did he find his way to the grove?" Esleann asked.

"Yes." The lines at the corners of the older woman's eyes crinkled. "But he weren't at all happy with what he heard there."

Esleann leaned over the cool stone fence around the keep. "I would've liked to have seen that."

"Well, that young rascal don't understand yet, but he will." Lealla nodded her gray head and turned away from the road with a satisfied expression on her weathered face. "The Mother knows his name now, and I doubt as She's done with him yet."

Kevisson tried to make out the dark shape in front of them, then grimaced. As much as he hated to admit it, only the ummit could see where they were going in this light, and ummits were stupid enough to walk in circles. He reined the animal in.

Haemas turned around and blinked at him in the cooling dimness. "Are we stopping here?"

He nodded, then slid off the ummit onto the springy, moss-covered ground. "I can't see, and it won't be moon-rise for some hours yet." He held his arms up, but she slid off by herself. Well and good, he thought bitterly. Even after everything they'd been through, she didn't trust him. "Why don't you look for some firewood?"

He turned back to the ummit and pulled off the saddle. His arms trembled as he propped it against a tree. Light above, he ached with weariness down to his very core. He tethered the strong-smelling beast downwind, well within reach of some low bushes for its fodder.

Bending his stiff, sore legs, he sat down and used a rock to clear a small bare patch of earth for the meager amount of fire they needed. They could eat what little was left of the trail food he'd purchased in Dorbin cold, but he wanted her to keep watch while he slept. She needed something to hold her attention; the greatest danger was that she would fall asleep when he couldn't monitor her.

Her slender form reappeared, her long pale hair shimmering like moonlight in the dimness. She laid down an armful of dry tinder. He arranged the fuel on the bare earth and closed his eyes to concentrate and spark the fire.

Kevisson was so tired that for a second he couldn't recall the litany, but then it came back to him. In another minute, the tiny fire crackled merrily and he looked up in time to catch the expression on Haemas's drawn face.

She wrapped her arms around her ribs and turned away. He felt her fear and despair.

"It's just a fire," he said slowly, cursing himself for not thinking, but it was too late now. "A tool, nothing more."

"I almost killed both of—"

"None of that was your fault." He rested his aching head against the ummit saddle. "It was mine. I pushed you to do something you weren't ready for, and we both paid the price." He yawned helplessly. "But now I've got to have some sleep or I'll pass out, and you'll have to tend the fire."

Sitting down on the opposite side of the fire, Haemas nodded. His eyes closed, but he forced them open again. There was more, he thought foggily—something else he had to tell her. What was it?

Then he remembered. "And you mustn't sleep." He hitched himself up on his elbows and peered at her over his chest to see if she was really listening. "Not when I can't monitor you. Do you understand?"

"Oh." The moon-colored eyes turned away from him and stared out into the darkness. He felt her despair.

Feeling as if he were falling into an endless barret hole, Kevisson let his eyes sag shut again. "Don't . . . forget."

Haemas's face heated as she realized what Kevisson meant: She mustn't sleep because she might kill them both without even knowing. She watched the Searcher across the small fire until his breathing became deep and regular.

Then the yellow flames drew her eyes, making her feel uneasy. She got up restlessly and checked the ummit. Tethered just outside of the ring of firelight, the weary beast had let its head droop to the top of the spiny bushes. It, too, slept.

She ran her chilled hands up and down her sleeves to warm them, then returned to the fire. The evening breeze picked up, making the leaves whisper and sigh. Hunching down before the fire, she tried to think ahead to what awaited her in the Highlands. Would Jarid be there when the Searcher brought her back? And was there any chance her father was truly alive, or was that just something Kevisson had told her so she would come without a fuss? Her father . . . Despair stirred inside her mind, and she knew she dared not think about that.

The breeze doubled the dancing flames over sideways, skittering a few of last year's dead leaves through the trees. Catching a faint whistling sound, Haemas stood up to listen. After another moment, the breeze gusted from that same direction and she heard it again: a high-pitched, regular whistling, almost like . . .

She glanced at Kevisson. His face was pinched and still as he lay in the grip of total exhaustion. He probably wouldn't wake for hours.

Making up her mind, she padded out of the firelight into the waiting darkness. She wouldn't be gone long, she promised him silently as she felt her way through the underbrush. She would only go far enough to see if that was just the wind whistling through a rock somewhere up ahead, or—

The wind surged again, cool against her face, bringing the sound more clearly. She hesitated, trying to make sure of the direction. Running her hand over the rough bark of a tree in front of her, she felt her way around it, smiling slightly to herself. Could that really be some sort of music the wind was carrying on its back tonight?

Chapter
Sixteen

An icy droplet tingled down Kevisson's cheek. He threw one arm over his face as he shifted onto his other side, then recoiled as every muscle along his rib cage twinged. He rolled onto his back and stiffened. Even with his eyes closed, he could see light.

He ground the heels of his hands over his eyes, then blinked up at the slivers of slate-gray sky visible through the interwoven trees. The wind whistled through the branches, and chill raindrops dripped down the leaves onto his face. Sitting up, he glanced over at the tiny fire circle. The wood had burned down into gray ash, but an armful of fresh fuel was still piled only a few feet away. Why had Haemas let the fire go out? A pang of alarm rang through his fuzzy head—had she fallen asleep?

Worried, he stumbled to his feet and searched the small campsite. The ummit was still tethered, eyeing him with placid disdain; the saddlebags lay undisturbed, but there was no sign of the tall pale-haired girl. Telling himself she was probably just poking around in the woods, looking for fruit or water, Kevisson relaxed his shields and tried to follow his tie to her.

For the first time since he had woven the psi-connection between them, he couldn't find her. His tie led a short distance into the forest and then just . . . melted away. He felt his heartbeat speed up. It would take considerable skill and training at levels she didn't possess to dissolve that tie. Had Jarid Tal Ketral found her after all?

His stomach tightened. If so, she might already be dead. If not, then he had to find her. Taking her back to the Highlands was more than just an assignment at this point; it had become a necessity. In her uncontrolled condition, she was a danger to herself and everyone around her, and the responsibility for that lay at Kevisson's feet. He had meddled with problems beyond his skill and training.

Picking up the soaked saddle blanket by a corner, he sneezed, then turned resolutely toward the ummit. He would find her if he had to search every foot of these misbegotten, silsha-infested woods to do it!

Struggling back to full consciousness from the gray otherness of Search, Jarid scowled and sat up on the side of the bed. Bypassing the remainders of his breakfast, he reached for the pitcher of water standing on the low bedside table and poured a glassful.

Darkness and damnation! he told himself. The little wretch had to be out there somewhere! He knew his psisenses were working now; he had a full purse of coins and a tolerably good horse to prove that much, anyway.

He drained the glass of water and crossed the cramped room to look out the window. The rising orange sun hung halfway above the horizon, around Ninth Hour; his Search had lasted almost three hours. No wonder he felt exhausted. If, after that much time, he hadn't found his young cousin, then the girl must be dead. Jarid could think of no other reason.

He stretched back on the rough homespun blanket and folded an arm behind his head. Well, if she lay dead somewhere in the forest with her throat slashed by chierra brigands, so much the better. That saved him the trouble of doing the deed himself, and it was only right that Tal'ayn pass to him. Haemas was soft and spineless, totally unable to make tough decisions and hold Tal'ayn against the world. Under her direction, Tal'ayn would have finished its current slide into oblivion.

Now he could return to the mountains and resume "comforting" the old Lord's widow. He'd already been absent far longer than he'd intended. Alyssa's charms lay solely in her beautiful face and body and her insatiable appetite for his attentions. It was painfully obvious that the Light had never intended her for tasks that involved heavy thinking.

He selected a callyt from the tray and sliced off a bite with his dagger. Munching the sweet, juicy flesh for quick energy, he wondered if his uncle had managed to peg out yet. Light help them all if the old nit hadn't. He closed his eyes and sent a mental call back to Tal'ayn and his voluptuous young "aunt."

Jarid?

He felt her restrained surprise. *How soon they forget.* He took another bite of the callyt, enjoying her discomfort.

I can't talk to you now. I have company—my grandfather.

Then get rid of him, he said, *and hurry. I haven't enough strength to keep this up for long.*

Well, Alyssa answered doubtfully, *I guess I could tell him I have to check on Dervlin.*

He relaxed back on the oversoft silsha-fur coverlet. He couldn't wait to return to Tal'ayn and start running the estate the way it deserved to be run after all the years of his uncle's neglect. He would refinish the ballroom floor, throw out all that ugly dark furniture with carved animal-paw legs—

All right, what was so important that it couldn't wait? Alyssa's mental tone was petulant. *Grandfather is very adept, you know.*

Jarid laughed. *That old fossil couldn't trace me if I were in the next room, much less all the way down here. And speaking of old fossils, how is Uncle Dervlin?*

Oh, Jarid! Her mental tone altered abruptly to terrified. *He's growing stronger every day. Healer Sithnal actually said Dervlin may come to table in a day or two.*

White-hot fury surged through Jarid. *Can't you do anything right? It's a damn good thing I'm coming back or you'd have ruined everything!*

How dare you speak to me that way! Alyssa's mind seethed with anger. *Not when you went off and left me to face everything alone!* She was silent for a moment. *You'll never know how beastly it's been, having to watch him get a little better each day, wondering when he'd remember—*

Never mind that. I'll take care of Uncle when I get there. Just keep the Council away from him.

That's easy enough for you to say—

Just do it. I have to go now. He broke the mental contact between them, then stared up at the cracked plaster ceiling, picturing the shining tears tracking down her creamy cheeks. She always pulled that when she didn't get her way.

Well, he told himself, the little baggage would still be good for a few more months of amusement after he returned—perhaps even as much as another full year.

Without a doubt, though, many other beautiful young girls, outfitted with suitably large dowries, currently languished in the Highland's great Houses, waiting to be wed. And he would bet his next year's beard that any number of those golden-eyed beauties would have to be smarter than Alyssa Alimn Senn.

Haemas was cold, scratched, bruised, and achingly weary from head to toe, but flames still whispered in the back of her mind, so she didn't dare sleep. She had wandered the forest all night and into the morning, first foolishly seeking the elusive music, then trying to find her way back through the maze of foliage to Kevisson, until the tree trunks wavered before her eyes and nothing seemed real anymore.

The air was chill and wet, with an icy mist penetrating down through the leafy canopy. Haemas stumbled and caught herself against a looming winterberry tree so tall that its top was lost in the canopy above. Forbidden sleep lapped at her mind like an inviting dark pool. She longed to be at peace, to go home and lay her aching head in Jayna's lap and let the old chierra nurse stroke her hair as if she were an innocent child again. She sighed and pressed her cheek to the sweet, aromatic winterberry bark that brought back memories of winter festivals and ceremonials. Everything seemed so far traveling on foot. If she had a portal, she could just step through to Tal'ayn—but that was only her exhaustion talking; no one built portals in the middle of the Lowland forest.

Then it seemed that she did hear the hum of a portal crystal somewhere nearby. Surprised, she threw open her mind. A scintillating, eye-searing blueness flared up, swallowing the trees. Crystalline chimes jangled inside her head, loud and off-key.

"But he's so old!" a faint girlish voice complained.

Haemas shaded her eyes and edged forward. The blueness sorted itself into lines writhing beneath her feet.

"Dervlin Kentnal Tal is the Lord of a Great House and first among the Council of Twelve," an older woman answered. "The Light itself must have blessed you with this union."

The bewildering blueness seemed less intense up ahead. Haemas took a step toward the voices, then another, and emerged suddenly behind a tall lacquered hearth screen in a room crammed with furniture—a study, perhaps, or a private sitting room. Her heart pounded as she touched the smooth wooden arm of a red velvet chair. This couldn't be real.

"But he doesn't even like me!" the same girlish voice said.

Haemas peered through the hinged opening in the screen. Women in rustling silks and satins and velvets milled back and forth, their cheeks scarlet with excitement. When they parted, she glimpsed the back of a petite girl whose bright-gold hair had been threaded with tiny white moonstones. The girl turned with a swish of her stiff skirts, a decided pout lingering on her red lips, and Haemas couldn't breathe. It was Alyssa Alimn Senn, wearing the same pale-blue matrimonial gown in which she'd married Haemas's father.

But that couldn't be. Haemas's hands clenched. Her father had taken Alyssa as Lady of his House two years ago. She must have fallen asleep under the trees after all; this had to be a dream.

Alyssa patted the back of her upswept hair and a tiny jeweled comb tumbled out to fall into the rug's thick, cream-colored pile. A faint strain of music penetrated the room and a crease appeared between Alyssa's striking green-gold eyes.

"They're ready for you, pet." Her matronly companion looked expectantly at the closed door. Alyssa smoothed the jeweled bodice, then composed her face into an expression of serenity. The music grew louder, vibrating with curious brittle overtones.

Haemas heard the door open, then the whisper of long skirts as the women followed Alyssa into the crowded main hall for the ceremonial. After they were gone, she circled the screen and picked up the fallen comb, fingering the inset diamonds and green kori crystals. Then she glanced at the open door. What was wrong with those musicians? They were playing such an awkward beat, their tones so high-pitched. The music jangled into her very bones, making her head hurt, her teeth ache. She closed her eyes and backed away.

The intensity of the sound lessened. Haemas opened her eyes and looked around in stunned disbelief. A grove of tall winterberry trees arched overhead, shading the forest beneath into near darkness. Through the breeze-blown branches overhead, though, she could just catch an occasional winking glimpse of sodden gray clouds.

Something sharp-edged and hard was jabbing her hand. Opening her fingers, she looked down at a jewel-encrusted comb with a single strand of gilt-bright hair still entwined in the tiny teeth.

The comb dropped from Haemas's nerveless fingers into the dark moss at her feet. The strange crystalline sound returned abruptly, and she had the sudden, skin-crawling feeling that she wasn't alone.

Her hands knotted and she made herself walk forward as her breath came hard and fast. The sound modulated to a higher, more painful pitch. Haemas fought dizziness as she concentrated on putting one foot in front of the other.

Stay, something whispered in her mind.

Stay—stay—stay echoed hollowly through the trees.

The sound vibrated so loudly now that she could barely see the ground. Groping for the rough tree trunks, she pulled herself along.

Small sister, it said, *stay.*

Stay—stay—stay echoed in her head, and Haemas realized she had stopped. She couldn't feel the forest floor beneath her feet, or see the trees; she could perceive nothing but the intense vibrating sound that hovered between bizarre musicality and pain.

Small sister?

"What?" she cried out. "What do you want? Who are you?"

Stay—stay—stay.

"No!" White-hot fear flashed through her.

Stay.

The terrible crystalline vibrations increased until she thought she would pass out, and then the blue lines sprang up before her again. She turned and fled down the nearest one.

The barret jerked sideways as the arrow pierced its cream-colored throat. It fell kicking into the damp brush. Cale limped to the creek bank, leaning heavily on his walking stick. Picking the barret carcass up by its tawny ruff, he estimated he could make it last several days—if he continued on half rations.

What in the seven hells was he doing here, anyway? He ought to be back at Eevlina's camp helping with the plans for the next raid and letting this damn foot heal properly. Why was he out here in unfamiliar territory traipsing after a crazy, half-grown Kashi girl and the Motherless Kashi bastard who had stolen her away from him?

Pulling out his knife, Cale sat down on a log and skinned the barret with quick, practiced strokes. Well, he told himself, the girl had proved fairly useless up to this point, unless you were fond of living with silshas, but that didn't change the fact that he had found her and he meant to keep her.

He pulled the heavy gold chain from under his tunic and fingered the smooth-edged medallion, thinking of how first one Kashi Lord and then the other had taken his mind and used him like a puppet on a string. Eevlina had been right: The Lords treated the chierra people as if they were nothing more than cattle.

Hiding the medallion again, he stretched the wet skin over the log. Too bad he didn't have time to work the pelt. The trail was growing fresher every day, even though his pace remained tediously slow due to his broken foot.

The image of that amused Kashi face still floated in his mind. Well, he would see who was smiling after he crept up on the sleeping bastard by night and put the same sword that had broken his foot to that pale Kashi neck.

Pulling out his firestone, Cale struck a spark, then heaped twigs on the tiny flames, cursing the wetness of the day. Finally the damp wood caught, producing an unsatisfactory, smoky fire. He spitted the halved barret carcass on a long stick and thrust it over the fire to roast.

But as he watched the crackling flames, the girl's pale, high-cheekboned face and those almost blank-looking eyes lingered in his mind. She had said they would kill her, and Cale's last sight of her had been her unconscious body slumped like a sack of whiteroots across the saddle of that smug Kashi bastard.

Fighting his impatience to be back on the trail, he waited until the meat was at least half done before bolting down a hindquarter. He wrapped the remainder in some broad leaves and stuffed it inside his shirt. Then, leaning on his stick, he hobbled back to the deep, fairly fresh ummit tracks and began to follow them through the forest again.

Several hours later, he caught a whiff of ummit stink and woodsmoke. Smiling grimly to himself, he backtracked immediately. He would wait until the deep hours of the night, then return to catch the Kashi asleep.

Kevisson stared at the tips of his boots stretched out before him. Not one sign of the girl, he thought wearily, and yet he had no sense that she was dead. The link between them didn't feel severed, just *blocked* somehow.

Jarid must have caught up with her while he had slept. He watched the flame patterns in his small fire change as the wind shifted. He could go back to Shael'donn and hope Ketral would return Haemas to her father, but that was unlikely. All the signs pointed to him simply killing the girl and leaving her fate a mystery.

Reaching into the saddlebags, Kevisson rummaged for a few crumbs of leftover food, but he'd already eaten everything. He was too tired to hunt tonight. Tomorrow he'd see what he could do to resupply himself.

Even if he couldn't find Haemas, one possibility still remained. He could Search for Ketral.

Kevisson banked the tiny fire, then closed his tired eyes and began to count his breaths, sending his mind into the deep-trance state of Search. After he had centered down, he entered the gray otherness cautiously, knowing that his energy reserve was low. He hesitated, reconstructing his impression of the other man, remembering the patterns of strength, arrogance . . . contempt.

His mind flowed out, holding Ketral's thought patterns as a map. Timeless as that other place always seemed, he still sensed that it was a long time before he found what he was looking for.

Somewhere between the forest and the foot of the towering mountain called Kith Shiene, Ketral lay sleeping in a small chierra inn. Kevisson wasted time Searching the surrounding area for some sign of the girl, but she was nowhere. Then he returned and eavesdropped on the vague surface thoughts of the sleeping Kashi, not daring to probe someone so obviously well trained.

Confused images flashed by: a huge House built into the rock of twin crags . . . an angry, gray-haired man . . . then a jangling head-splitting din that swirled through the brain, confounding the senses.

Another image formed: a young, clear-skinned Kashi woman, smiling with all the warmth of a poisonous rock bavval. Kevisson felt his strength giving out. *What of the girl?* he whispered to the sleeping mind. *What of Haemas?*

Dead, Ketral's mind answered. Then Kevisson felt the other man's awareness. He withdrew immediately, starting the long, tiring trip back to his body in the forest.

Behind him, back at the inn, he dimly sensed how Ketral bolted up, glaring around the small room, knowing someone had been there.

As he traveled back, the gray cold seeped into his mind, numbing him so that he could hardly find his body again. When he finally reached the tiny campsite in the forest, he gratefully merged with his physical self, then forced his eyes open, eager to build up the fire.

Before he could move, however, the icy sharpness of steel pricked at his throat.

"If you so much as twitch a single muscle, either yours or mine, I'll slice your Motherless head clean off!"

Kevisson tried to reach out once more with his mind, but he'd expended more energy than he could afford in the Search. His head sagged heavily backward and everything faded into blackness.

Chapter
Seventeen

Haemas made out a low, rectangular shape in the shimmering blueness before her. The agonizingly shrill vibrations died away as she ran and the line abruptly faded, leaving her alone in a large hall with an arching, high-vaulted ceiling. Polished benches of rich dark wood stretched out in long rows on either side of her. The breath caught in her throat; it was the public sanctuary of Tal'ayn.

The air was stuffy and still, thick with incense. The vast room lay in shadow except for a row of transparent bowls filled with flickering blue chispa-fire before two low tables at the far end. A trickle of fear seeped through Haemas; mind-conjured chispa-fire was appropriate upon only the most holy of occasions. Suddenly she feared to go closer.

A foot scraped as someone in the shifting blue light stood up and peered through the shadows at her. "Be someone there?" The old woman's trembling voice bore the mark of tears.

Haemas remembered that voice from hundreds of frightened, lonely childhood nights—the only voice that had ever comforted a motherless child. "Jayna?" Her brow knotted and she walked toward the lights.

The standing figure, wrapped in a long woolen shawl, put one hand to her mouth, brown eyes staring. "In the Mother's name, who are you?"

"Jayna, it's me." Haemas stopped short of the flickering circle of blue light with a cold sense of dread. The tables ahead of her were not tables at all, but biers, and on them lay two motionless bodies, dressed in colorful, richly worked garments and draped with the thinnest veils of pale-yellow silk, awaiting the funeral pyre to come.

"Mother, I don't understand!" The old woman dropped

to her knees like a broken doll, sobbing as if Darkness itself had opened before her.

Cold sweat trickled down Haemas's temples as she looked down on the two white faces under the shrouds. The nearest was of an older man, stocky and gray-haired. She raised the sheer material with her fingertips. The stern, accusing features of her father's face lay framed by the white silk undersheet. She stared at the familiar, harsh lines of his dead face—she *had* killed him. However much she had wanted to believe the Searcher, she'd known it all along. Kevisson Monmart had told only lies.

Her hand released the fragile silk and she moved as if in a nightmare to the second bier, the blood thundering in her ears. Was this more misery to be laid at her feet? Had she killed someone else, too, on that terrible night? The figure lying on the second bier was female . . . slender . . .

Frozen inside, Haemas watched her hand reach for the translucent shroud. Jayna's muffled sobs grew louder as she lifted the silk and stared at the still face of an adolescent girl. It was a high-cheekboned face, with a delicate, high-bridged nose surrounded by long, fine-textured, pale-gold hair and equally pale lashes downswept against the white skin. The folded long-fingered hands bore no ornament except for a glittering black obsidian ring . . . her birth gift from her mother's family. Haemas Sennay Tal lay cold and dead on her bier, close to her father in death as she had never been in life.

Somehow she found the strength to drop the shroud and back away, staring at her achingly bloodless fingers as if they belonged to someone else.

Cowering at the foot of the two biers, Jayna made the four-cornered sign of the Mother above her heart, her sobs echoing through the emptiness.

Haemas turned away, unable to fathom how she had come here or what she should do now. Hot tears stood ready in her eyes, but she felt too numb to spill them. Or, she wondered, was it just that ghosts couldn't cry?

Small sister-sister-sister . . .

She glanced around fearfully.

Come back-back-back.

I'm not lost, she thought. I'm dead.

Small-small-small . . .

Squeezing her hands over her ears, Haemas ran down the shadowy aisle, her heart pounding.

. . . sister-sister-sister . . .

She stumbled and fell to her knees, throwing her hands out to break her fall. The richness of growing plants filled the fresh, cool air. She made out the faint black outline of trees arching up to the cloudy night sky, and between her outspread fingers, she realized that she clutched rain-slick leaves and the damp crumble of forest soil.

Cale checked the breathing of the unconscious Kashi again, then settled back by the fire, scowling. From the looks of those dark circles under his eyes and the general pallor of his skin, the inconsiderate bastard was probably going to die on him without so much as a hint as to what he'd done with the girl. No doubt Eevlina was right, blue Outlander eyes were bad luck. Nothing went his way these days.

The Kashi groaned. Cale glanced uneasily at him, then, judging the skimpy fire to be in need of more fuel, limped into the brush to search for deadwood. A few minutes later, with as much as he could carry in his free arm, he returned to the fire. He paused to lay down the wood, then froze.

The Kashi's goldish eyes were squinting at him over the dying flames. "Don't I . . . know you?" He hitched himself up on one elbow.

Cale snatched up the sword and thrust the point against the tender hollow of the other man's throat.

"Oh." The Kashi sagged back against the ummit saddle and closed his eyes. "Yes. Sorry about the—foot."

"Sorry?" Cale leaned over, watching with satisfaction as steel nicked the pale skin. "You think that makes it all right?"

Running fingers through his golden-brown hair, the man sighed. "I would offer to heal it, but I'm afraid I've . . . never been much of a . . . healer." He opened his eyes and blinked up at Cale, his brow furrowing. "You wouldn't have some . . . tea, would you? I've . . . the most amazing . . . headache—" The golden-brown eyes rolled back and his head sagged to one side.

Damnation! Cale fingered the gold and silver runes engraved on the sword's ornate hilt. How much time could a man be reasonably expected to waste holding a heavy sword at a fellow's throat when the fellow did not have the decency to wake up and be properly terrified? He swung the sword tip away, then eased himself back to the ground, holding his broken foot out stiffly before him.

All he wanted out of this sorry rascal was information or a decent fight, and at this point, he wasn't feeling overparticular as to which. Well, what was that stuff Eevlina was always boiling up for headaches—assafra root? If he wanted any satisfaction out of this lazy scoundrel, he was going to have to pep him up a bit.

"Now don't you go thinking you can get away," he said severely to the unconscious man. "I'll be back shortly, and you'd better be ready to do some fast talking!"

He limped off into the trees, scanning the ground for tiny saw-edged assafra leaves.

Alyssa?

The ancient oak-framed mirror slipped from Alyssa's hand onto the flagstone floor, shattering into a thousand useless slivers. She stared down numbly at the scattered glass, then forced an unsteady breath into her lungs. *Yes, Dervlin?*

Darkness and damnation, woman, bring me my account books this minute!

I'll be right there. Placing one hand on the breast of her new dark-green silk gown, she fought back her sickening panic. When had the old fool recovered enough to use his mindsenses again? Why hadn't someone warned her that Dervlin had made so much progress?

Glancing down at the broken mirror, she sidestepped the silvery shards, lifting her full skirts. His accounts, she thought, then shuddered. No doubt there would be a great deal in them of which he would not approve.

Stopping by his huge wooden desk, Alyssa rolled back the top and removed the thin brown books from the third drawer. Laying her hand on the smooth leather bindings, she hesitated, wondering if she could somehow keep them from her husband for a little longer.

Jarid had promised he would return in just a few days. She thought of his strong embrace and felt the warmth return to her body. Jarid had planned everything down to the last detail. She had only to hold Dervlin off for a few more hours, and then Tal'ayn would fall into their hands like a ripe callyt.

Alyssa!

She started, then closed the drawer with a bang. *I'm coming.*

Tucking the books under her arm, she fled into her bedchamber. What could she use to gain some time? She jerked drawers open and turned over the contents in an almost mindless panic. Then she found the small gray bottle still hidden in the trunk at the foot of her bed.

Anisei . . . She lifted the bottle out, then paled. Jarid had administered a draft of the sedative to the old man on that night, but it took precise measuring. Too much and he would die of anisei poisoning and any healer who attended him would diagnose it with no problem.

Alyssa, quit sneaking around and get in here!

Her fingers closed convulsively around the small square bottle. Strengthening her shields, she slipped the sedative into her pocket. *You must be feeling much better,* she said lightly, and pushed open the door of his bedchamber.

Dervlin perched on the edge of his great bed, thin white legs dangling, scowling at her. "No thanks to you," he said sourly.

Feeling the heat in her cheeks, Alyssa said nothing and passed him one of the account books; allowing him to see her distress only made him worse. She turned to leave.

"Oh, no, you sit down until I have a chance to look everything over." He waved one hand at the day couch.

She settled on a silk cushion by the hearth, arranging her silk skirts into graceful folds, though why anyone had bothered to teach her the fine points of ladylike behavior when her family meant to give her into the hands of this monster remained totally beyond her understanding. Restlessly she twirled the huge green kori-crystal on the Alimn birth ring around her middle finger, watching as he scanned the line of entries. "Would you care for something to drink, my Lord?"

His finger stopped halfway down the page, and then the old man narrowed his eyes. "Thought you could hide this, did you, you conniving little nit?"

She steadily returned his gaze, refusing to let his intense golden eyes make her flinch. "I'll ring for some tea."

Ignoring her, he returned to his examination, stopping only to mutter to himself occasionally.

After a moment a servant cautiously thrust her gray-haired head through the door. "Ketha tea," Alyssa said stiffly. The old servant nodded and withdrew abruptly, like a tree barret bolting back into its hole.

Alyssa sat there, lacing her icy fingers together and listening to the low crackle of the small fire laid in the hearth until she thought she would go insane. All the while, her husband flicked through page after page.

When at last old Jayna, using her broad back to push open the door, came in with the heavy silver tray, Alyssa crammed a knuckle between her teeth to keep from crying out. Then she rose and reached for the tray. "I'll take it, Jayna."

The old chierra stared back at her with those unreadable dark eyes. "My Lady?"

"I said, *I'll* take it!" Alyssa fixed the old woman with a frosty glare.

Jayna hastily bobbed her head and settled the tray in Alyssa's hands. "Be there anything else I can do for you, my Lady?"

"You can *leave*," Alyssa said, turning her back on the servant. Bracing herself against the weight of the heavy tray, she walked over to set it on a bedside table. Behind her, she heard the door click shut. "Shall you have sweetener, my Lord?" she asked over her shoulder as she slipped her hand into her pocket and fingered the cool square shape.

Dervlin only grunted. She palmed the bottle and removed the wooden stopper. How much? she asked herself, then heard Dervlin snort behind her back.

"By heavens, I'll have your heads for this, both you and that overeager nephew of mine! Who gave you permission to buy Old apple seedlings to replant the orchards?"

Feeling her stomach knot with fear, Alyssa knew she

didn't care if she *did* give him too much. Better that and then it would really be over, just as Jarid had promised!

"Don't you remember?" She fought to keep her voice from trembling as she poured the dark contents of the tiny bottle into his cup of tea. "You planned the orchard with us, just before you—got sick."

"Got sick? That's a good one." His heavy face creased into a scowl. "You were probably in on it with the little skivit, at that!"

She braced the steaming, aromatic cup between her two hands and turned to pass it to her husband. "Don't be ridiculous, Dervlin. You're perfectly aware that the Lady Haemas and I have never had much in common."

"Bah!" The old man stared at the cup for a moment. "Are you saying my daughter isn't good enough for you?"

Alyssa sighed and allowed just a trickle of exasperation to leak through her shields. "Really, you mustn't say such things." She reached for his hand. "Now drink your tea while it's hot. I don't intend for you to exhaust yourself and have a relapse."

He returned to his study of the account books, but didn't resist as she settled the cup of hot tea into his hand. Then he stiffened. "Twenty measures of Pa Naud silk in various colors?"

Alyssa's face went cold.

"This House hasn't bought twenty measures of silk in the last three generations!"

"I won't allow you to excite yourself this way," she said coolly. "I'll come back when you're feeling more reasonable." She turned on her heel.

She heard him slide off the bed behind her. "Just who do you think you are to walk out on me?"

Her hands clenched until her nails pierced the skin of her palms. Her breast heaved as she stopped, trying to control the white-hot anger that flashed through her. "I am your *wife*," she said through stiff lips. "Though, by the Blessed Light itself, I would give anything that I were not!"

The stoneware cup flew over her shoulder and smashed into the door in front of her. The dark tea trickled down in small rivulets to pool on the floor.

Alyssa fingered the empty gray bottle in her pocket, then wrenched at the latch and escaped into the hall.

Haemas rested on her knees in the wet grass, taking deep lungfuls of the clean night air. When her heart had slowed somewhat, she wiped her face with the back of one hand and found her cheeks wet with tears. Shivering, she locked her arms around her knees and wished for the warmth of a fire to take away the night's damp chill.

Answering flamelets leaped up eagerly in the back of her mind. No! she told them angrily. I will not have it!

The flames remained, crackling stubbornly just out of reach.

Closing her eyes, she fought back panic and tried to remember what Kevisson Monmart had told her to do. The flames licked joyfully at the edges of her mind and the smell of smoke permeated the air.

Small sister-ter-ter . . .

She leaped to her feet and looked wildly around the dark glade. Inside her head, the flames laughed in little sizzling pops and blazed higher.

It is only your fear-fear-fear . . .

The echoing voice made Haemas dizzy. She pressed her fingers to her temples.

. . . that makes them strong-strong-strong.

Heat charged through her body, at first merely warming, but then quickly progressing into a burning that ran from the soles of her feet to the top of her head. Yellow flames sprang up in the brambles and the foliage overhead. "Kevisson?" she cried, backing against a tree trunk.

Fear is not your enemy.

The flames' hot breath came from all directions now. She cringed at the center of a fiery circle.

Fear is the little mother at your side, keeping you from harm.

Think of fear like a mother? She wiped the smoke-tears from her blistering face, then sank down against the tree and closed her eyes. She'd never had a mother. Anyah Killian Sennay had died nearly sixteen years ago giving her birth.

Know fear as an old and trusted friend. . . .

Trust? Trust was a word she never thought of in connection with anyone except the oldest chierra servants. Jarid had always called her a "little skivit" because she was afraid of everyone.

Although you must let fear guide you, it should not control you.

She'd never been in control of anything, except perhaps that last night. Her mind cringed again at the memory of her father's dead body sprawled at her feet; the flames inside her mind reached hungrily.

She wrapped her arms around her head. It was too much, and she lacked the strength to care anymore. Let the flames burn her into ashes. No matter how far she ran, no matter what she did, nothing would ever alter the horror of what she had done.

He may yet live.

"What?" The soothing certainty of the voice gave her strength. Forcing open her eyes, she felt the flames retreat, little by little. In a few moments, nothing was left but wisps of smoke curling pale against the blackness of the night sky.

Chapter
Eighteen

Bitter, fiery liquid burned down Kevisson's throat. He choked, then flailed weakly at the slab of bark pressing his lips.

"Drink the rest of it, damn you, or I'll hold your high-and-mighty nose!"

The bark cup tipped again, spilling the remainder of its bitter contents into his mouth. He pushed it away and gasped for air. "Stop—that!"

A shaggy-haired chierra man sat back on a rotting log and regarded him with a pair of startling blue eyes. "Now! What did you do with that light-haired girl?" The fire shifted and spit sparks. Nightmare shadows flickered over the surrounding trees and brush.

Kevisson tried to sit up, but slipped back. His vision doubled for a second. "What in the name of Darkness is that bloody stuff?" The acrid aftertaste was nearly gagging him. "Ummit sweat?"

"I made it a bit strong on purpose." The man was cradling a richly worked sword across his knees, and he looked affronted. "Though I suppose, properly speaking, I should have let you die rather than waste perfectly good assafra on the likes of you."

"I think I would just as soon be dead." Kevisson glanced over the man's shoulder; he recognized the keiria thicket and a lightning-split trunk a little beyond, so he hadn't been moved, and as nearly as he could tell, his captor was alone.

He reached out a tendril of thought for the other's mind, then felt the world go muffled and gray around the edges. His energy reserves were still too depleted. He sighed. "I don't suppose your kindness could extend to some food? I seem to have—overextended myself."

The chierra flicked the sword point into the bare hollow of Kevisson's neck, drawing a bead of bright-red blood. "The *girl*, old sod, and none of your flashy Kashi tricks." He lifted the sword higher, caressing Kevisson's jugular.

Kevisson hesitated, remembering Jarid Ketral's response to his query about Haemas: *dead*. Could that really be true? He tried his mental link to the girl, then broke off as his vision dissolved into gray fog again. "I—" His eyelids weighed as much as an entire mountain and it was a struggle just to breathe. From far away, he heard vague rustles and the chierra swearing under his breath.

A few minutes later, something hot was thrust into his hand. "Now, sit up and eat, damn you."

He forced open his eyes and juggled a piece of steaming whiteroot wrapped in husk.

"Suppose that's not good enough for the likes of you!" The man pushed impatiently at the black hair dangling in his face, then balanced the heavy sword across his knees again.

Kevisson made himself sit up, then took a tentative bite. The cold knot in his stomach eased as he swallowed. "Thank you."

"Don't go thanking me, *your Lordship*." The man ran a grimy finger along the sword's gleaming length. "I want the girl." He scowled. "She's worth a rare bit of gold, that one, and I'm not letting the likes of you cheat me out of it."

Feeling his energy level beginning to rise at last, Kevisson settled back and chewed slowly. "I can find her, but I have to build my strength back up. Mindsenses take a lot of energy."

The man glowered at him. "Is that so?"

Kevisson swallowed the last of the whiteroot and began to sense the shape of the other's mind. Sifting at his surface thoughts, he picked out the chierra's name. "Cale Evvri." Kevisson wiped his hands on his breeches. "That's a chierra name, but you look more like an Outlander with those eyes."

"There's Outlander blood in my line." The blue eyes narrowed. "But Outlander blood runs as red as any other."

"Is that Ketral's sword?" Kevisson tried to sift deeper into the other's mind.

"The very same sword that were dropped on my foot."

Kevisson glanced at the crudely splinted foot and winced. "Sorry."

"You said that already." Cale eased his foot to another position. "Are you going to find the girl for me, or do I have to punch in that smug Kashi face of yours?" He frowned. "Although you do look darker than any Motherless Kashi bastard I've ever seen."

Kevisson's mouth tightened. "There are rumors of an old indiscretion in my family, too."

"The girl, old sod." The sword tip swung up to nick Kevisson's neck just below his ear.

"All right, I'll—I'll take you tomorrow." Kevisson felt his way through the other's mind, trying for motor control. A wave of giddiness washed over him, but he fought it off. There! He found the proper synapses and flashed a message to the chierra's arm to release the sword.

"Hold out your hands." Cale fished in his pocket and came up with a leather thong.

His head spinning from the effort, Kevisson stimulated the synapse again.

"Damnation!" Radiating impatience, the chierra man seized his wrist and looped the leather thong around it.

Kevisson sank back, his head pounding.

Windsign watched the small one curled up on the ground. She was lovely, after the fashion of her kind—smooth of skin, long-limbed, so solid and helpless, so young. Increasing her mass, the ilseri descended to the slender branch arching over the sleeping girl. *Perhaps we should wait for another.*

And how long will it be before one comes? Summerstone's impatient mind imaged the grove empty and silent as time wove its relentless way onward. *The mountain males never allow small ones of power to come alone down here in the living land.*

Windsign could not argue with that. Although the dark, quiet-minded ones sometimes ventured into the forest, she had never even seen a sister of this golden-hued breed before, and her memory went back a good three Interims before Summerstone's. She listened to the small one's dreams for a moment, troubled by repeated images of fire and death, fear and guilt. *This one has borne much in her short time.*

The girl tossed restlessly in her bed of soft grasses, throwing first one arm over her eyes, then the other. Her face contorted as she cried out, then bolted up, staring wildly about the moon-shadowed glade. Windsign heard the roar of flames in her mind, saw the blackness of grief and pain.

Fear is natural. Summerstone sent soothing images of sun and shade and the sweet voice of the morning breeze into the small one's mind. *Fear is but a sister whispering in your ear to keep you from danger.*

Confusion and loneliness filled the small one's mind. She put her hands to her head, fighting the suggestion.

Small sister, you must rest. Dream of— Summerstone hesitated, rifling through the girl's mind for a comforting memory, then settled on a narrow black muzzle and tufted ears. *Yes, dream of our brave, clever shadowfoot.* She sent the feel of its smooth, thick coat and the rumbling warmth of its company into the small one's thoughts.

The mountain child's eyes fluttered. Gradually she relaxed back into the nest of soft grasses that Summerstone had woven for her.

Windsign waited until the young mind was drawn back down into dream images again, more peaceful ones this time. *You see? This one is flawed. She will never survive what we ask of her.*

It is for her kind's survival, as well as ours. Summerstone called to a passing lightwing and held out her finger for it to perch.

You see how her people have failed her. Even by their simple standards, she has not been properly trained.

Summerstone abandoned the treetop, increasing her body's mass until gravity bore her down to the grass-carpeted forest floor. She knelt by the mountain child's head and smoothed back the fine moon-gold hair from the still face. The skin was warm beneath her touch, and soft as a sunbeam, but as her fingers trailed down the delicate neck to the girl's shoulder, she felt the wrongness of torn muscles, inflamed nerves. She sent a pulse of healing energy through her fingertips into the painful area and probed the fragile body further. There was damage in the brain tissue, too: neural pathways seared, nerves overloaded and unable to function properly. This child had fought beyond her strength, and yet Summerstone sensed her potential was great. She concentrated, pouring as much healing energy through the damaged area as the small one's cells could take.

That is not enough. Windsign watched from above. *There is still some dysfunction.*

That is all she can stand for now. Their bodies are very fragile.

Yes. Windsign paused. *Perhaps too fragile. You saw how she lost her way in the nexus.*

That does not matter. I will teach her. Summerstone's voice rang with the stubbornness of living gray stone. *Then she will return to her kind in the mountains and end the danger.*

She is too afraid. Windsign decreased her body's mass and drifted on the night breeze, losing sight of her sister and the small one beneath the trees below. *It might be kinder to let this one fade away, before her own fear kills her.*

Jarid squinted up at the twin towers of Tal'ayn spanning the split crags of gray rock ahead. Blast that simpering shebavval Alyssa! He watched the gold-and-green banner flap in the morning breeze with a hot anger burning behind his pale eyes. Obviously his uncle still lived.

Shouldering his saddlebags, he took a deep breath of the crisp late-spring air and followed the familiar path that wound around the Old apple orchard onto the grounds of the ancient House. So far, he'd passed no workers, which meant Alyssa had at least managed to arrange for his unobserved arrival.

Reaching the tiny side entrance in the north wing, he tried the door and was relieved when it swung smoothly inward without a creak. Just on the other side of the threshold, Alyssa waited, her green-gold eyes wide.

"Oh, it is you!" She flung herself onto his surprised neck.

He stared down at the bright gold plait that circled her small head like a crown. "We do not have time for this, *Aunt*."

She released his neck, sliding down his chest. "You're not still angry with me about Dervlin." Shiny tears welled up in her eyes. "I really did try to—to do it."

Turning away from her silently, he closed the heavy door and threw the latch. "It doesn't matter now."

She glanced down the darkened hallway. "What are you going to do?"

"I'm going to see my uncle, of course, like a dutiful nephew."

"Oh." A knuckle strayed to her mouth. "You'll find him very—restless."

"Hide these." Jarid handed her the saddlebags. "And stay away from Uncle's chambers for the time being. I'll have enough trouble covering for myself without worrying about you." He brushed past her in the narrow passageway. "And have some roast savok with berrysauce sent to my room. I haven't had a decent meal since I left."

Although he didn't look back, he felt her bewilderment follow him down the passage. She might as well get used to it, he thought. Her usefulness had just about come to an end.

He encountered few servants on his way to the family wing, and those he did meet simply bowed and backed out of his path. Their minds revealed no real awareness of his absence these past days.

Good. That meant less work for him to do. Slipping off to his own rooms, he washed his face and hands, combed his hair, and donned fresh clothing. Ten minutes later, he was outside the master suite, easing his shields to overhear his uncle's thoughts within.

Damnation, boy! If you want to come in, just say so! Quit sniffing around.

A wave of nausea rolled through Jarid's stomach and cold sweat broke out on his upper lip. He blotted it with his sleeve. Blast that spineless Alyssa for not finishing the job when she had the chance! Locking his shields as tightly as he dared, he pushed the door open.

"I wouldn't be too quick to come in here, either, if I

were you." Tal was wrestling with the arm of his overtunic. "Not after the way you and that sneaking wench have been wasting my gold!"

Jarid crossed the outer chamber and lounged in the inner doorway. "And what has Aunt been doing this time?" He let just the slightest hint of boredom seep through his shields.

"Don't try to make out that you weren't involved in this, too, right up to your washed-out eyes." His uncle's florid face disappeared as he forced the black garment over his head. "You've been after me to put in an Old apple orchard for too long for me not to recognize your thieving hand in this."

A knowing smile drifted across Jarid's lips. "Rest assured, Uncle, if I ever should be tempted to get in your way, it will be over something more important than a few worm-eaten fruits."

His uncle paused, staring at him with powerful golden eyes. He felt the sudden weight of the old man's probe against his shields. He glanced down at his hand, examining the nails with as much nonchalance as he could summon.

"Damnation and everlasting bloody Darkness!" The pressure eased off as abruptly as it had begun. The old man sagged gray-faced against the four-poster bed. "Thought I'd never see the day . . . when I couldn't crack open a young whelp . . . like an overripe melon."

Jarid sighed. "Nor I, Uncle." He walked across to the bed, supporting the old man by the arm. "But if you overdo, your recovery will of course take much longer."

Tal resisted him for a moment, then fell backward, wheezing. "Where . . . have you been, anyway?"

He pulled up a chair. "Been, Uncle?"

Tal opened his eyes. "The last few . . . days. Blast it, boy, I've . . . been sick, not dead."

Jarid scratched his chin, then shook his head. "I've been right here, looking out for Tal'ayn until you're recovered." He brushed at an invisible speck on his sleeve. "I couldn't leave you unprotected."

His uncle's eyelids closed for a second. "You're in on it with . . . her, aren't you?" He swallowed hard and took a deep, gasping breath. "She knew the Council would never approve her for my . . . heir on her Naming Day, so—" He broke off as a spasm of coughing racked him.

Jarid poured a glass of water from the carafe by the bedside and handed it to him.

No, Uncle, he thought, *I* knew the old fools would be ecstatic once they measured her Talent and found the skivit measuring Plus-Six or better—much too ecstatic to think of accepting me in her place. "We've been through this a hundred times." He schooled his tone to patience. "When I realized what the little wretch was up to, I stepped in and saved your life. Surely you must remember some of that, now that you're better?"

"Nothing." His uncle's voice was faint. "I . . . remember nothing of that . . . night."

Standing beside the old man's bed, Jarid watched until his uncle's chest rose and fell in the evenness of sleep. As long as the old nit remembered nothing, he thought, it wouldn't hurt to keep him around for a few more days . . . just for appearance's sake.

He fingered the well-tempered steel sheathed at his waist and smiled.

The song rang with the chattering of water running over rocks, backed with the sweet edge of a crystal wind chime. Haemas lay aware of the music long before she woke enough to wonder where she was.

You have been sleeping in the Great Forest, small sister.

Opening her eyes, she gazed up into the deep green of winterberry leaves. She lay in a snug nest of soft spring grasses under the arching boughs of the grove of huge trees. "Kevisson?" she asked, although the voice in her head hadn't sounded like the Searcher. Only the breeze shuffling the leaves answered her. Then she stopped in wonder. Whoever it was, she had *heard* the mindvoice without any physical contact. She was better somehow— and her shields were back in place. She felt rested and strangely invigorated, almost whole again.

She sat up and picked the bits of grass out of her hair; some of the pieces were charred and black. The flames—so she hadn't dreamed that.

No, small sister, that was of this spacetime.

Her heart thumping, she backed against a tree, glancing warily around the grove.

Think not of fearing. Think of living.

"Who are you?" Haemas demanded. "Jarid?"

No males are permitted in this songful sacred place, the voice insisted primly, and although there was no sound to that voice in her head, there was something of the strange music she'd heard earlier.

Not Jarid, she told herself, and not Kevisson, but then—who?

Summerstone, the voice said, and Haemas's mind filled with the image of gray stone cliffs washed by a river at its bending.

Windsign, another voice said, sending her the caress of the wind against her face on a balmy summer day.

"Where are you?"

Later, small sister. There is much that you must learn.

Rise, Summerstone said. *Eat of the Mother's fruits. Your struggle last night was long and difficult.*

Haemas slowly rose to her feet and saw a pool in the center of the grove, ringed with carefully worked white stone inset at intervals with large ilsera crystals. Steps descended into the clear water on one side, and next to the steps she found a pile of sweet yellow callyts and succulent purple nasai, as well as several fruits she did not recognize.

After tasting an unfamiliar green fruit, she wiped at the dribble of juice down her chin. "Was it you, then, in the sanctuary?"

That was an Otherwhen, Summerstone's voice replied. *A dangerous place in which to be lost.*

The memory of her own waxen, dead face made Haemas stop with the fruit halfway to her mouth. "How can I be dead there and yet alive here?" She swallowed hard.

That was a When that either might have been or might yet become.

"And my father?"

Nothing answered save the murmuring of small living things and the whisper of the leaves.

Chapter
Nineteen

"Darkness and damnation, Kniel!" Birtal Senn choked on a mouthful of tea that tasted like dishwater. He regarded the mug with disgust. "Why don't you get some decent help around this mausoleum?"

Master Ellirt sipped cautiously at his own mug, then wrinkled his nose. "Bless me, I think it *is* dishwater, at least partly!" A low chuckle rumbled up from his chest. "I suppose they're training a new shift down in the kitchens and they forgot to rinse. Well, they'll get the hang of it—after being forced to eat their own cooking for a few days. I'll have some proper tea sent up."

Senn set the mug aside. "I fail to see anything so bloody funny about it."

"You wouldn't—" Ellirt turned his sightless face away from the fire and smiled. "—unless you'd spent a few absolutely terrifying boyhood days having to eat your own abysmal cooking as well as put up with the complaints of everyone else in Shael'donn."

"Eat my own cooking?" Senn drummed his fingers on the arm of the high-backed chair. "Don't be ridiculous!"

Ellirt sighed, then bowed his white-haired head and rested his chin on his folded hands.

"Let's get back to the subject." Senn leaned forward. "I want you to attend the next Council conclave on temporal transfer."

The cheerfulness fled Ellirt's round face. "We've already discussed that."

"We haven't had enough full Talents for a quorum since Tal was injured." Senn took the poker and prodded the burning logs into a new configuration. "We've felt for some time now that we're close to a breakthrough. I want you to assist in the power relay."

Ellirt rose stiffly and edged around his chair, one hand resting on the back to guide him. "I'm not up to that anymore."

"Don't tell me you're afraid!" Senn watched impatiently as the Shael'donn master crossed to his cluttered desk in the corner and fumbled through a drawer.

Ellirt turned back to him, his cheeks flushed, his jaw set. "You're bloody right I'm afraid! How many more men do you have to lose in this insanity before the Council gives it up?"

"We haven't lost a man in—" Senn stiffened as an unbidden memory flashed through his mind: an agonized face being drawn inch by inch into throbbing blueness. "—in over two years."

Holding a long, slender object, Ellirt angled back to his seat. "You forget I trained Yjan Tal Alimn myself." He held out the flute in his hand. "He made this for me several months before he died."

Senn wove his shields more tightly as he stared at the rich warm brown of the polished wood. "Looks like Old oak."

"It is." Ellirt ran his fingers over the glossy finish. "Grown in unmixed Old soil at Alimn'ayn." His sightless eyes roved the room as though he were staring at something Senn couldn't see. "He was only sixteen and it was a brutal death. I heard every one of his last cries, even here at Shael'donn. We all did, down to the youngest student. I have nightmares about it still."

"If we give up now," Senn said tightly, "then Yjan's death will have been in vain."

Ellirt's gnarled hands gripped the back of the chair. "It *was* in vain!"

Even through his rigid shields, Senn felt the blast-furnace heat of his old friend's anger.

"It's all stupid and pointless! What will the Council do with this new toy of temporal travel if they do make it work—use it to subjugate the rest of the Lowlands all the way to the Cholee Sea?" Ellirt rubbed a hand across his forehead, seeming to sink in upon himself, suddenly old and tired.

Senn closed his eyes, holding a tight rein on the part of him that wanted to seize the sightless man by the shirt and shake some sense into him. Closeted here with nothing but boys and landless teaching masters for company, Ellirt could afford to be impractical and unworldly. Those who had the responsibility of a House couldn't. "We'll use it for research."

"Research!" Ellirt snorted. "Research into the tactics and disposition of outlying chierra holdings, no doubt!"

"I have no doubt that we might find some—military applications."

"The Council has already cut off a bigger piece of this world than it can hold." Ellirt thrust the wooden flute unerringly at Senn's chest. "Here, take it. Let it remind you of Yjan Tal Alimn."

Senn took the flute between two fingers as if it were made of fire.

"Yjan was a fine boy." Ellirt turned away. "And I've always felt he would have been a great man. Now, please leave while I can still remember why we are friends."

Thrusting the flute deep into his pocket, Senn snatched up his cloak and stalked out the door.

Fear is a natural part of continuing for your kind, Summerstone's soothing mindvoice continued, *just as much as joy and suffering, disease and health.*

Haemas trailed a hand in the crisply cool water of the pool, catching an occasional winking glimpse of orange sun overhead through the shifting leaves. "But the flames—"

You punish yourself.

A breeze whispered through the interlocking tree branches, bringing the scent of moist earth and growing things. Haemas leaned forward and rested her head against her bent knees. The memory of what she had done burned like a red-hot coal, and yet, try as she might, she could recall nothing of what had been in her mind that night—no reason, no motive. "You told me he might not be dead."

She felt the cool green brush of the ilseri's touch against her thoughts, oddly soothing, somehow not intrusive. A long silence passed, filled with only the creak of limbs swaying in the wind.

In your mind, he both is and is not, Summerstone said finally. *I cannot explain.*

So no matter what Summerstone had said before, she didn't really know. The breath caught in Haemas's chest. He probably was dead, had gone to his funeral pyre days ago while she wandered the Lowlands in a guilty daze. Flames leaped up behind her eyes, bringing the acrid smell of smoke. She clenched her hands until her nails pierced her palms, until her vision was only a white buzz and pain was all she had left to hold on to.

No, you cannot throw yourself away. Windsign flooded her mind with a cool green strength that left no room for anything else. *You are needed here.* Haemas felt a barrier being set up, energy diverted. The fire faded into gray ashes. A sudden, strange quiet pervaded. Dimly she still sensed her fear and guilt, but they were outside somewhere, held at bay like a hungry bavval circling a campfire. She drew a long, shaky breath.

So, said the other mindvoice, *now we begin.*

She heard the faint tinkle of crystal.

We shall teach you to walk the pathways of When as only a sister may.

The crystalline vibration increased, shrill almost to the point of pain.

You must attune your thoughts.

Haemas felt the ilseri nudge her brain, and the sound diminished until it was bearable again, more like the crystalline music on the wind that had lured her from Kevisson's campsite. She closed her eyes, sensing currents of force flowing around her; their source was the same crystals used by the Kashi for travel since the beginning, but this was a different frequency. Her heart pounded. Had this power always been there, waiting to be unlocked, and she just hadn't known how to look?

Focus on the pathways, Summerstone said softly. *Match the energy of your thoughts to them.*

In her mind, it seemed she stood in the center of a vast circle of dancing blue lines radiating outward into infinity.

If you look carefully around the nexus, you will find the lines of Truewhen.

Her heart beating faster, she opened her eyes. The writhing lines all seemed the same, although they led to a thousand scenes, each one varying in some degree from the ones on either side.

Think of where you wish to go, whom you wish to see.

Home, Haemas thought, and the scenes shifted. Now some lines led to a wall of silver-gray rock softened by greenery. She recognized a familiar ummit-shaped geyser spraying hot water and steam up into the frost-edged air— the thermal garden at Tal'ayn.

At the end of one pathway, she saw a tall, willowy woman strolling with a chubby-legged girl-child of about two. The air was frosty and their breath puffed white. Their cheeks were pink with the cold and exercise, and they both had hair of an unusual pale gold. She started down that line, drawn to the woman's serene face.

No, small sister, that—

She took a second step, and then her boot trod on the fine crushed gravel of the Tal'ayn garden walkways.

The woman, dressed in an ankle-length dark-blue tunic over soft flowing breeches, had her hair braided loosely down her back. She glanced over her shoulder. "I didn't know we had company." She bent down and slipped an arm around the wide-eyed child at her side. "Look, Haemas, we have a visitor."

The little girl clasped her mother's hand with small delicate fingers, gazing up at Haemas with eyes the color of spun honey.

The woman's oval-shaped face smiled. "Are you a Killian? You certainly have the look of one."

Haemas stepped forward, taking a deep breath of the faintly sulfuric air emitted by the geyser and thermal pools. "Yes . . ." It seemed that she had to force the words to come from far away. "On my mother's side."

"I'm Anyah Killian Sennay, although I suppose you already know that." The woman scooped her daughter up into her arms. "You must sit down and tell me the news. My husband receives so little company at Tal'ayn these days."

"The—news, my Lady?" Haemas looked at the wriggling child nestled inside Anyah's arms—perhaps the child she might have been.

Anyah motioned to a seat on the bench and settled next to it with her small daughter balanced in her lap. "Well, those do look like traveling clothes."

Haemas glanced down at the torn and stained tunic she wore, realizing how many days it had been since Kevisson had tossed it at her in Dorbin.

"I've embarrassed you, haven't I?" Anyah's face fell. "Dervlin is always telling me I talk too much."

Male voices erupted from behind the garden wall, then grew louder. A younger, more golden-haired Dervlin Tal than the one she knew burst into the garden, followed by another man.

"Damnation, Anyah, I've told you not to bring the girl down here so much! I don't think it's healthy—" His voice broke off as he caught sight of Haemas. "And who in the hell is this? Another one of your endless Killian cousins? I told you I don't want them here."

"Dervlin, please." Anyah rose, her face a frozen mask, and set the child on the gravel path behind her. "There's no reason to be rude."

The pathways, Haemas thought numbly, she had to find the pathway back to the grove and Summerstone and Windsign. She opened her mind to listen for the vibrations again, but met only the probing thoughts of Dervlin Tal.

Why are you sniffing around here? his mind thundered at her. *Has she been complaining again?*

Without thinking, Haemas threw her shields up against his relentless pressure and backed away. He followed, his face creased in concentration; then the probing abruptly ceased.

Dervlin mopped his brow. "It's that damned Killian blood. Looks as frail as a house of sticks, but you can't beat it for sheer power."

"That's most complimentary, Dervlin." Scarlet heightened Anyah's graceful cheekbones as she regarded her husband with a frosty stare. "I'm sure I don't need any reminders why you accepted me."

Now! Haemas thought. She had to find the way back.

She opened her mind again cautiously and sensed the glimmering of a path.

Dervlin's golden eyes narrowed. "What's going on here?"

Haemas listened, catching the crystalline music of the way back. She took one step on the shining path that opened up before her.

"Where do you think you're going!"

Glancing over her shoulder, Haemas saw Dervlin Tal reaching for her arm. Breathing deeply, she focused her thoughts, setting each foot directly on the shimmering blue line of power.

Yes, small sister.

She took a third step, then looked down. At her feet lay the pool and the five glowing ilsera crystals fading back into quiescence.

"Go ahead and kill me. I'm not going another step." Kevisson collapsed on a fallen tree trunk and stretched out his weary legs. The late-afternoon sunlight slanted down through the canopy of leaves, dappling the ground with orange-gold light.

The ummit saddle creaked as Cale leaned forward. "How much farther?"

"Too far to get there before sundown." For the tenth time that day, Kevisson reached out to get a foothold in the other's mind and failed. What in the bloody Darkness was wrong with him? It was like trying to seize a fistful of water. He shut his eyes and rubbed the aching spot in the middle of his forehead.

Cale hiked his leg over the ummit's hump and slid down its shaggy side. "Well, I guess we might as well make camp. At least we be close to water here."

Kevisson gathered an awkward armful of dead, parchmentlike leaves with his bound hands, then dumped them on the grass under a large-leafed spine-wood tree. Settling down into the crackling leaves, he sighed; one lingering aftereffect of his overdoing was the need for extra sleep. A few minutes, he told himself, and then he would jump the chierra when he was off-guard.

He closed his eyes and listened to the afternoon breeze

ruffling the leaves overhead, the chittering of a tree barret . . . even the slight shifts on the log made by the other man. Just a few minutes . . .

A faint crystalline tinkling invaded his mind as he drifted, just the slightest hint of wind chimes. He found himself listening for something more in that sound, something meant especially for him. It seemed that he sat up and looked around.

The girl's face appeared before him on the breeze, smiling as the breeze swirled long light-gold hair around her moonlight eyes. The image startled him even as it faded. She had smiled, he thought numbly. He realized that he had never once seen her smile. It made her seem older, and hinted at the dazzling woman she would become.

He stared after her and saw a towering winterberry tree standing over a crystal-clear pond ringed with white stone, and then the currents of sleep swept him away.

"Isn't it time you found a wife, young man?" Lord Senn settled back from his desk and looked Jarid over like a prize saddle beast. "Some biddable young thing with a large dowry, and perhaps true-gold eyes to counter that damnable Killian pallor."

Jarid let a self-assured smile flow over his lips, but inside his shields, he burned. He would see a day, and soon, when no man would dare mention that name to his face.

Lord Senn's own eyes, burnished gold flecked with gray, blinked. "Well, enough of that. I asked you here to see if you would help with our temporal experimentation." He turned back to his desk and rustled through a stack of papers. "I thought I saw your name listed on the attendance at several conclaves last year."

A tingle jolted through Jarid's spine. At last! he thought. "Yes, my Lord." He forced his face to remain impassive. "My uncle took me along several times last winter."

The old Lord found the list he was looking for. "And I see you assisted in the power relay the second time. Very good." He pushed his thronelike chair away from the low desk. "We have need of some new blood in the circle, now that Dervlin is—" He broke off, looking embarrassed.

Jarid allowed a note of sadness to escape his shields.

"The healers insist this is just a temporary setback," he said with intentional insincerity.

"Well, of course!" Senn looked shocked. "I never meant to suggest otherwise, but in the meantime, would you like to join us in his place?"

"I would be honored."

"It would be better if you just observe again today." Senn put his hands behind his back and gazed at the fire in the hearth. "I'm sure you realize there is a certain amount of risk."

Risk for you, old man, Jarid thought exultantly, and for the rest of the Council. Once he'd unlocked the secret of temporal transfer for himself, he would travel the timeways on his own and arrange things to suit himself—starting with the long overdue demise of Uncle Dervlin and the transfer of Tal'ayn into his own deserving hands.

"Rest assured, Lord," Jarid said gravely, "you can count on me."

Windsign floated above the unaware child, anchoring herself in the grove by the tip of one finger against a twig. *She did not discriminate Truewhen from Otherwhen.*

But she found her own way back this time. Summerstone still felt hopeful. *It is a beginning.*

Windsign sent the image of thick gray fog muffling the forest. *If this small one cannot do better, we will have to find another.*

There is no time left to try again.

A shudder suddenly rippled through the grove, writhing through soil, trees, pool, and air. The light-haired girl below looked wildly around and clutched the grass. "Summerstone?"

A feeling of violation passed through Summerstone. The crystalline vibration coarsened into painful discord, and a second shudder gripped the grove.

Is it already too late for this When? Summerstone looked to her sister.

Below them, the human child had thrown herself against the ground, holding fast to the grass with knotted fists. She stared at the pool with horrified eyes. "What is it?"

Summerstone gazed down the shimmering pathways generated by the ilsera nexus. Visible at the end of most pathways now lay the maelstrom of time disruption, a yawning blue whirlpool crackling with the breached energies of When.

She increased her mass, sliding between the frightened child and the vision of Whens to come, pulling the child's face to her own pale-green breast.

Feeling the shaking body, so curiously solid, Summerstone remembered her own long-distant time of childbearing and sons. At this density, she could even feel the girl's warm breath on her skin. *Do not look*, she told her. *Those Whens may never come to be.*

A last temporal shudder ran through the grove and the clanging discord slowly faded. The child drew a long, ragged breath. "What was it?"

Summerstone ran her fingers over the girl's silky hair. *The males of your tribe attempt the pathways again.*

The child raised a face tracked with wetness to look for the first time at the ilseri. Her strange, pale-gold eyes widened and she backed away.

Summerstone felt her shock, but there was no time to make this meeting between their two kinds easier. *Unless you help us, everything in this When will die.*

"Me?" The girl's pale face lost what little color it had. "But—I don't even understand what that—thing—was."

We will try to teach you, and then you must make your kind understand before time itself shatters and passes away.

Chapter Twenty

"What if I went back into the past," Haemas asked, "and changed something?"

Summerstone's calm green presence flowed through her mind. *Like your mother's death.*

Haemas remembered Anyah's arm curled protectively around her small, shy daughter, and her soft, abashed expression when she'd thought she had inadvertently embarrassed a guest. Haemas would have given everything to grow up under her gentle guidance, but Anyah had died giving her birth, a difficult fate to remedy. Perhaps if an additional healer had been called, or a better one . . .

She sighed, then glanced at the tall, green-skinned ilseri reclining beside her in the grass. The Old Ones were curiously like humankind, having two arms and two legs and a round head covered with vaguely hairlike green tendrils, but much taller, and no human could ever have risen into the breeze and floated away as Summerstone frequently did.

Amusement emanated from the ilseri, although her facial expression never changed.

"So," Haemas said, "what if I could prevent Anyah's death? What would happen to now—this When?"

The one you altered would become an Otherwhen while this reality and its past would remain the same.

Haemas watched a winterberry leaf nearly as green as Summerstone's skin fall into the still waters of the pool and skim the surface. "You mean she can never be saved?"

She is well and happy in a number of Otherwhens.

Turning away from the pool, Haemas sighed. "Then what good are the pathways?"

The pathways exist for themselves, like the sun and the stars. They were not made for ilseri or humans.

Dark, knobby tree trunks appeared through the wispy white drapings over Summerstone's body as the ilseri dispersed her mass and allowed the breeze to lift her.

Haemas stood, head tilted back, squinting up into the sunlight after her. "Then why should I learn to walk the pathways if nothing can be changed?"

Summerstone's body grew more diffuse until Haemas could see the outline of every limb and blue-green leaf through it. *They must be guarded from disruption.*

Haemas thought of the maelstrom whirling at the end of the timelines. A cold, sick feeling washed over her.

Even now the males of your tribe work to unravel the secrets of When.

She turned around, but Summerstone had drifted out of sight. "If they can't change anything, what does it matter if they succeed?"

When your species first came to this world, we offered the crystal for travel from Where to Where. We ilseri are born male and remain so only to a very young age. Consequently, our males lack the power to enter the timelines. Your curious species, however, exists in either one form or the other, and some of your males develop mindpower of an impressive degree. Male-energy cannot align with the pathways.

"And if they enter. . .?" Haemas whispered.

If they succeed in entering the pathways with enough strength to resist disruption, then they will disrupt the timeways instead and bring the maelstrom into this When.

"But I don't see how I can stop them. They aren't going to listen to me."

You must control the nexus. Summerstone paused, and Haemas heard her call to the ilseri crystals submerged around the pool. They responded, singing like a chorus of tightly tuned lute strings. The water's surface shimmered with blue fire and the circle of lines sprang into being. *Try again. Seek out the mountain males who would tamper with the energies of When.*

Haemas closed her eyes and reached out with her mindsenses, trying to sense the correct line out of what had to be thousands. They writhed like lightning, flickering, coiling, never still for a second, terrifying in their instability and fragility.

Like this, Summerstone said, and Haemas sensed the ilseri sorting through the possibilities for some undefinable quality.

Haemas dropped her shields and followed, mentally reaching for it, too, not even able to say what it was. At the end of the line to which the ilseri led her, she felt a presence: many men gathered together, a few of them vaguely familiar, and a searing buildup of psionic energy.

There, Summerstone said.

Haemas opened her eyes and saw an assortment of bowed gold and gray heads, a circle of crystals spread before them. The details were obscured by the crackling blue fire of the nexus, but she could almost make out their strained faces. The song of the crystals sharpened into painful screeching. One white-haired man stood, his lined face contorted, then stumbled toward her. *No!* Haemas cried. *You can't do this! Stay out!*

He glanced up and she sensed a surge in the psionic energy the others were feeding through him. The crystals shrilled until she thought her head would split. She swayed, clenching her fists, barely able to see or think. *You can't enter the timeways, not ever!* she told him. *It would be the end of everything!*

He squinted, mouth open; then his legs wilted. He turned and groped his way back to a chair.

Haemas raised her shields, shutting off her awareness of the nexus. Her heart raced. How many more times would they try before they finally succeeded and destroyed the very fabric of time? She braced her back against a towering winterberry tree and tried to think. There had to be a way to make them listen.

Pausing to snatch up a shawl, Alyssa glanced up the long narrow stairway to the family courtyard. Yes—she could still feel Jarid's mind up there.

Her cheeks burned as she remembered how he had brushed her aside when he'd arrived back home because her old fool of a husband hadn't died. Well, that was more his fault than hers. If he'd done the job right to begin with, neither of them would face this problem now!

Winding the filmy green shawl around her head and shoulders, she lifted her long skirts and set off away from the courtyard stair.

A sneeze sounded explosively behind her. She froze in midstride, then collected herself and turned to see Dervlin round a corner, struggling to put one arm through the sleeve of his barret-down jacket.

"There you are." His face was ashen but for two spots of feverish color in his cheeks. "Have you scheduled the musicians yet?" His fist finally emerged from the end of his sleeve, but he made a poor figure in clothing that had become too large for him since his illness.

She released her full skirts and clasped her hands before her. "Dervlin, I'm sorry, but I haven't the faintest idea of what you're talking about."

He threw her a withering glance. "Don't even try to pretend that you don't remember."

She tried to read his surface thoughts, but could pick up nothing. "Remember what?"

His eyes were flat and cold, as if he were no longer even human. "The Lady Haemas's Naming Day."

She stared numbly at her husband's rigid face. "Haemas? But she's—"

Yes. Dervlin caught her wrist in a viselike gripe. *What about her?*

Alyssa fought back the tears that sprang into her eyes. "I was only going to say she's not here." She pulled at her wrist but his fingers bit into her tender flesh.

No, he said, his intense golden eyes boring into hers. *There was something else in your mind, just for a second.*

She gasped as he wrenched her arm back, then took a deep breath, trying to regain her composure. "Dervlin, stop it! You know what Healer Sithnal said—you'll make yourself ill again."

"You'd like that, wouldn't you?" He shoved her against the stone wall, then released her wrist. "Then you could run after every man who came within twenty miles of this House!"

She cradled her throbbing wrist and straightened her

spine. "I will take care of the Lady Haemas's Naming Day arrangements, my Lord, if that is your wish."

He stood, his legs braced apart, and glared at her, strain and weariness thinning his face to the bone. For a split second, she caught an undercurrent of doubt and loss leaking through his still-patchy shields.

"See that you do," he said finally, then, wheezing, started up the staircase. "And do it right! If I look weak, they'll take the Council leadership away from me. I can't have anyone saying Tal'ayn didn't do it right!"

Watching his slow progress up the worn stone steps, she smoothed a bright-gold curl out of her face. He *had* lost his mind, after all. She pulled the shawl from her shoulders; the delicate green fabric had torn on the rough-cut stone. Fingering the hole, she nodded angrily to herself. If the old nit wanted a Naming Day ceremony for his missing brat, then by the Light she would provide one he would never forget, and might he have much joy of it!

A tree barret climbed halfway down the trunk, bobbing its short tail as Haemas emerged dripping from the pool. She held out a bit of leftover fruit to the compact brown creature. It hesitated, sniffing, then whisked back up the tree, its feet scratching furiously on the bark.

She sighed. Windsign and Summerstone had drifted away to do whatever ilseri did on their own—perhaps eat or sleep—and the grove felt empty. Leaning over to pick up her wet clothes from the edge of the pool, she caught a glimpse of something white and fluttering caught on a low tree limb.

Abandoning the dripping tunic and breeches, she padded through the lush spring grass in her bare feet. It looked to be the same material in which the ilseri clothed themselves. She drew the white fabric along her cheek; it was soft as the finest velvet and oddly warm. She wrapped it around her shoulders and it clung to itself, adhering to make a garment of sorts.

She looked down at the front where she had drawn the two edges together; not even a seam was left. As she watched, the material divided and flowed up her outstretched arms to make long, trailing sleeves. She moved her right arm, realizing that, for the first time since she'd fallen on Kith Shiene, her injured shoulder didn't hurt.

She ran her hands down to her waist and the material followed, shaping the garment to her contours. Even Alyssa had never worn anything so fine. The thought of her stepmother spoiled her mood, though. Sinking to the ground, Haemas wrapped her arms around her knees and stared up at the roof of whispering leaves. No matter where she went or what she did, her thoughts always came back around to Tal'ayn and the wreckage of her life.

Over in the pool, the five pale-blue ilsera crystals inset into the pristine white stone flickered. Summerstone had told her to remain alert for another attempt on the timeways, so she eased her shields to catch the faint crystalline song. The pathways sprang up around her, shimmering blue lines that led to misty outlines of people and buildings and landscapes.

Rising, she saw the thermal garden again and Anyah walking with her daughter in the frosty air, but she couldn't even let herself think about visiting that time when there was so much danger in the here and now. Then her attention was caught by a scene near Anyah's garden: a sturdy, serious-faced youth and a white-haired man sitting on a bench under a tree in golden late-afternoon sunlight, talking. A huge sprawling keep of rough brown stone rose behind the walled garden, and rust-colored leaves lay scattered ankle deep on the ground. The boy's profile turned toward her, somehow familiar. She edged closer to get a better look.

He glanced up and stared in her direction with golden-brown eyes that matched his thick curly hair.

It's Kevisson Monmart, she thought, and *that*—she stepped forward again, drawn by something for which she had hungered without knowing—*that* must be Shael'donn where so much learning and knowledge were available, where life revolved around something more than the High Houses' endless jockeying for inheritance and succession.

Shaking his head, the boy turned back to his companion, who had a craggy, lined face but a surprisingly gentle manner. The old man smiled, saying something she could not hear. Then he rose and walked through a wrought-iron gate in the garden's stone wall.

She would go there just for a second, Haemas told herself, then come straight back. She took the final necessary step on the shining blue line of power. Her foot descended onto bleached, frost-nipped grass.

The boy's dark-gold head snapped up. "I thought I heard something!"

Haemas shivered and drew a fold of the silky white material into a hood against the crisp fall air. Woodsmoke from a dozen chimneys drifted lazily across the clear green sky and playing boys shouted somewhere on the other side of the grounds. "That's Shael'donn, isn't it?"

"How did you get in here?" Kevisson laid the book aside and studied her with penetrating eyes. "Did you climb the wall? The only entrance is behind me, and I know you didn't come in that way."

She felt his mind pressuring her shields. Her heart pounded and her bare toes curled in the dead grass. "Are— you one of the students?"

"Yes." A touch of grimness crossed his face. "And you needn't look surprised. No matter what you've heard, I'm *not* a chierra." His shields slipped and she caught a brief glimpse in his mind of tight-lipped anger over the constant allusions to his dark coloring, the continuing taunts, the open rejection—all answered by his bitter pride. He picked up the leather-bound volume and leafed through it. "I don't have time for this nonsense. You've had a good look at me. Now go away."

She was astounded; in all the days they had spent together, it had never occurred to her that he might have problems of his own. She looked away, unsure what to say to him—none of this matters? Someday you'll be a highly trained Searcher and work for the Council of Twelve? Someday I'll be in desperate trouble and you'll save my life? She shook her head; it all sounded foolish.

Kevisson slammed the book shut. "All right, then, I'll leave and you can have the bloody place to yourself!" His dark-gold eyes smoldered.

"Please." She stepped forward. "Don't go yet."

"I know. Everybody loves a trained animal—

'Shael'donn's pet chierra,' I've heard that often enough."
Setting his jaw, he angled around her.

"No, please." She held out a hand. "Someday we will
meet and . . ." She struggled for the words, knowing how
ridiculous she must sound.

Kevisson advanced on her and she found herself backing
away. "Just who in bloody Darkness are you, anyway? I've
never heard of any House letting its daughters go about
dressed like—that."

"I'm sorry. I shouldn't have come here." She looked up
at the brown stone towers of Shael'donn rising behind the
wall. "I shouldn't have come." Turning around, she reached
with her mind again for the crystals' song.

"There's that sound again." He cocked his head, looking
around the garden. "Like before."

"Don't listen," she said without looking at him. "It's not
for you." She took the first step on the shimmering blue
line, and her foot seemed to be somehow both booted and
bare as it crunched on the fine crushed gravel of the
Tal'ayn garden pathways. The sulfuric smell of the steam
vents and thermal pools filled the air.

"What do you mean, it's not for me?" Kevisson demanded from behind her.

Before her a woman dressed in an ankle-length dark-blue
tunic over soft flowing breeches glanced over her shoulder
and smiled. "I didn't know we had company."

Haemas put a hand to her head, staring around her; the
ghostly image of the thermal garden at Tal'ayn obscured
Kevisson and Shael'donn.

Kevisson's hand gripped her shoulder and she spun
around. "Where did you come from?"

At the same moment, Anyah knelt and slipped an arm
around the child at her side. "Look, Haemas, we have a
visitor."

"What *is* that chiming noise?" Kevisson insisted.

Haemas drew away from his touch. "I—I have to go."
The duality of voices and places dizzied her. How had she
crossed into Anyah's When, too? She tried to concentrate
on aligning with the pathway back to Summerstone's grove.
She took a second step on the line but seemed only to draw
nearer to the garden at Tal'ayn.

Anyah smiled. "Are you a Killian? You certainly have the look of one."

The wrought-iron gate squeaked open and the old man hurried up to place one hand on Kevisson's shoulder. "It's all right," he said to the boy quietly, then turned to Haemas. "Well, my dear, how have we come to have the pleasure of your company?"

Haemas wavered, caught between two realities.

"I'm Anyah Killian Sennay, although I suppose you already know that." The woman scooped the child up into her arms. "You must sit down and tell me the news. My husband receives so little company at Tal'ayn these days."

"The—news, my Lady?" Haemas faltered.

The old man's eyes wrinkled in a smile. "I don't think that I've ever been mistaken for a lady before. You seem unwell, my dear. Perhaps you'd like to come inside and lie down."

"No!" She closed her eyes, trying to sort out the vibrations that would lead her back to the grove.

"Can't you hear it, Master Ellirt?" Kevisson asked. "That strange sound—almost like music?"

"Please forgive me," Anyah said softly. "I didn't meant to be so forward."

"You mustn't listen to that!" Haemas opened her eyes and found Anyah/Ellirt reaching out for her. Sick and shaking, she lifted her foot again and set it down on what seemed to be the right line, although with everything so *double*, it was impossible to be sure.

Her foot touched the soft spring grass and she looked around at the comforting dark shapes of the trees, then saw her own pale face reflected in the pool at her feet.

Cale scooped up the last of the tart keiria berries he'd picked earlier and popped them into his mouth. Across the campfire, the Kashi sat brooding out into the darkness, his bound wrists propped on his knees.

A sudden rustle in the dimness overhead made Cale jump to his feet. "What was that?"

The Kashi's strange eyes, so dark for one of the high-and-mighty mountain Lords, swung back to him as the leaves moved again, and then sharp claws scrabbled against bark. Cale swallowed and ran his fingers over the gleaming sword blade. He sank to the ground, closer to the crackling fire.

The Kashi smiled slightly, then closed his dark-gold eyes. Cale balanced the sword on his knees while he reached for another stick for the fire. More than once in the past few days, he'd had the distinct feeling the Kashi was just playing with him, that he could take control of the situation any time. He knew full well what Eevlina would say if she were in his place—wait until the devil was asleep, then bash his Kashi brains in.

High overhead, a branch suddenly dipped, and Cale heard a twig snap. "Mother above!" Easing the sword into his right hand, he craned his head, trying to get a glimpse. "What in the seven hells is up there?"

The Kashi shrugged.

Cold sweat dripped down Cale's temple. Something made a sudden scraping leap, but he could only see the swaying branches and a couple of dislodged leaves drifting down. Then an earsplitting snarl rattled his eardrums. Holding the sword's wicked point ready, he whirled to face the source, above and to his left. The beast screamed again.

Cale glanced at the Kashi, who was gazing thoughtfully up into the leaves. "It's you, isn't it?" He leveled the sword at the other's chest. "You're calling the blasted thing just like *she* did!" He licked his dry lips. "Well, I'm not going to the next world alone! I'll take you with me, you yellow-eyed bastard, if you don't call that Motherless creature off right now!"

With a great leap, the lithe black beast sprang from the overhanging branch to land between the two men and the fire. Tufted ears flattened, tail lashing, it glared from face to face, rumbling a low snarl all the while.

Kevisson stared at the sleek, whiskered muzzle for a long moment. "She's not here."

"Who's not here?" Cale demanded.

The Kashi's face was pale and drawn. "Who in the name of Darkness do you think?" he muttered, never taking his gaze off the silsha. It blinked its hot yellow eyes, then lowered its head to snap up the rest of their dinner, downing the whole barret in one flash of gleaming white fangs.

"Dammit!" Cale felt the muscles in his sword arm tremble with fatigue. He eyed his quiver and bow lying on the ground on the other side of the fire.

"Don't bother." Kevisson used his bound hands to scratch his face. "I don't think it intends to hurt us, as long as we don't interfere with it."

Gathering its muscular black haunches, the silsha leaped back into the tree, then draped itself over the lowest branch, bathing them in its steady yellow gaze.

Kevisson stood slowly. "It's here for a reason."

"You did call the damned thing!" Cale let the sword tip fall into the dirt, then leaned on it to limp around the fire.

"Actually—no." Kevisson grimaced wearily in the waning firelight. "Because if I did have any control over it, believe me, you'd have been silsha-fodder long before now."

Chapter
Twenty-one

Dervlin heard old Jayna's chierra mind fussing as she hurried up the hall to announce the unwelcome visitor. It was pointless, of course. Even in his present condition, he'd known the instant Aaren Killian came through the Tal'ayn portal. Dervlin's hand trembled as he leaned against the polished Old oak mantelpiece and gazed down into the shifting flames in the hearth. It was too damn late in the spring for such a big daytime fire, but his so-called accident had left him weak and easily chilled.

Some of that fateful night had begun to come back to him: how he had sat at dinner while Alyssa and Jarid prattled on. His daughter had arrived late, then barely touched her plate. She had merely sat there, her white-gold hair caught in a neat braid, somewhat withdrawn, but not unusually so. He had brought her up to keep silent unless she had something sensible to say, which she rarely did. He pressed a hand over his eyes, trying to remember. Had he missed something, some hint of what was to come?

Haemas had gazed across the crockery at him, her odd, light eyes so like her mother's that he found himself uncomfortable and looked away. And then—what? He'd reached for a knife to slice an excellent ebari roast—

At that point, his memory jumped to five days later when, disoriented and mindburned, he had regained consciousness under the ministering hands of a healer. It infuriated him to have to depend upon secondhand accounts of the whole affair. He wanted to know exactly what had happened and why!

Jayna rapped, then eased the massive door open. He caught the aroma of spice cake baking down in the kitchens. "Company, my Lord."

"Tell that Killian bastard to—"

"He *said*, your Lordship, he weren't going away until you spoke with him." She gripped the door's edge with work-reddened fingers, staring pointedly at her feet. "He says he's come to—"

"I know what he wants!" Dervlin glared at her. "And it's none of his concern!"

"We have a contract, Tal!" The heavy door banged inward and struck the wood paneling. Aaren Killian appeared in the doorway, and Jayna's head prudently withdrew.

Dervlin scowled at the golden-haired man. Fifteen years his junior, Aaren Killian had in full measure that disquieting, long-legged vitality possessed by the entire Killian clan, the springy step of a finely blooded horse that could run all day. Dervlin had detested him for more years than he could count. Still, Killian'ayn wielded a lot of influence these days, and he had finally agreed to a marital alliance to increase Tal'ayn's backing in the Council. "I see Killian manners have not improved."

Aaren Bramm Killian glanced around the room with his light eyes. "No more than Tal hospitality."

Dervlin eased down into his wing-backed chair before the hearth. "No one asked you to come, Killian."

"I couldn't get anyone in this drafty barn to keep me apprised, including your young snip of a wife." Killian yanked a chair away from the desk by the window and sat opposite him. His expression was confident, overbearing. "I want to know what's become of the girl."

"That's none of your damned business!" Dervlin roused himself enough to meet the other's eyes of pale-amber ice. "She's not of age yet!" He fumbled in his pocket for a pipe, disgusted at the weakness dragging at him. "That matrimonial contract is probably worthless anyway. Even if the Council does locate her, I have no idea what action they'll take."

Killian laughed, his big voice booming in the enclosed space. "You aren't still holding on to the ridiculous fiction that an unNamed fifteen-year-old girl attacked and nearly killed you?"

A numbing iciness crept into Dervlin's fingers and toes and made its way up his arms and legs. "Get out," he said wearily. "She's not yours until, and unless, she's first Tested, and then Named."

Killian rose to his feet and loomed over him, radiating strength and health. "Just remember, Tal," he said softly, "if this is your way of trying to back out, it's value for value in this life. You've had partial payment already, probably more than she's worth. We expect the girl to be delivered at the proper time."

"If it's at all possible, you'll have her." Dervlin rubbed his jaw. "Don't forget Killian'ayn owes me yet."

"Their firstborn son will bear the surname of Tal." Killian's lips twitched. "Although I can't imagine how you persuaded your daughter to go along with that. And how do you think that baggage you call 'wife' will like raising your grandchild?"

"I don't care what she likes." Dervlin turned his eyes back to the fire. "It's about time the insolent wench was good for something."

The flames bent as Killian opened the door, then resumed their measured feeding on the wood.

It is not possible to walk two places in the same When. Windsign projected images of Haemas lost in a universe of glimmering blue. *Alignment is only possible with the vibrations of one When/place at a time.*

Haemas watched the ilseri's hazy green body float casually above the tallest tree in the winterberry grove, wishing she, too, could just thin herself and fly.

You must take more care, small sister.

An ummit grunted somewhere close by. Haemas heard twigs snapping, and the plodding four-beat footsteps of something large and heavy. She froze against the trunk of the nearest tree, then caught a fragment of thought—human thought.

The shadowfoot has brought your companions. Summerstone drifted out of sight. *We find them interesting.*

Haemas wrapped both hands around a low overhanging branch and scrambled up into the thick blue-green foliage. Below, an ummit's triangular muzzle nosed through the brush. She crouched on a smooth limb, trying to make out the two men astride the beast, one black-haired, the other lighter.

"Water!" The black-haired man slid down the ummit's shaggy gray side and hobbled toward the pool, using an unsheathed sword as a cane. He was broad-shouldered, wearing a faded blue-green shirt and leather breeches. Haemas's fingers tightened around the branch: It was Cale.

"I wouldn't bother that pool, if I were you," the other cautioned. "It's an ilseri artifact."

Haemas peered down through the leaves in astonishment. The second man was Kevisson Monmart, his face scratched and smudged, his clothes tattered. She rested her chin on her knees. What were they doing together? And why were Kevisson's wrists bound? Why hadn't they both simply gone home?

They search for you, small sister. Summerstone drifted down through the leaves and bark, her diffuse mass making no sound. *Neither will go back without you.*

Leaning heavily on the sword, Cale stared down into the pool. "Looks like water to me, old sod."

Kevisson slid off the ummit, steadying himself with his bound hands. "Go ahead, then." He craned his head around the grove, warily studying the trees. "Of course, the last time I encountered one, I ended up forty miles and twenty hours away from where I started."

Cale sank wearily into the grass, holding one leg out stiffly before him. His shaggy dark hair fell into his eyes and he raked his fingers back through it. "Do you think that black demon is still following us?"

Haemas glanced back at Summerstone's indistinct face. *He looks so tired.*

They have traveled far.

Kevisson walked around the ummit, his steps slow and heavy. "I don't know."

Haemas shivered as his mind reached out and brushed her shields. He rotated, his golden-brown eyes searching the foliage.

"Haemas?" He tipped his head back and gazed up through the tightly clustered leaves directly at her.

Her heart thumped wildly. She clung to the limb with indecisive fingers, then swung down, landing softly on her bare feet in the thick grass. The ilseri fabric settled in soft folds around her legs.

"Mother above!" Cale leaped to his feet, then grimaced painfully and swore under his breath.

Haemas winced as the pain in his foot beat at her.

"What in the name of Light are you doing here?" Kevisson blurted, stepping toward her. His face was gray with exhaustion. "That last night . . . the flames . . ." He strained at the rawhide cords binding his wrists. "Jarid Ketral thinks you're dead."

"Never mind about his high-and-mightiness here." Cale limped in front of the Kashi and balanced on his good foot. "All he can offer you is more of what sent you down here in the first place. Come back with me." His dark face grinned crookedly at her. "Don't you want to live free without anyone telling you what to do and how to do it?" His blue eyes sparkled.

Kevisson faced off with the chierra. "She doesn't want to stay in this Light-forsaken place, living like a blasted tree barret."

You have come to a branching, Windsign said. A few faint crystalline notes tinkled, like wind chimes striking randomly in the breeze. *You must decide.*

Kevisson raised his hands to his head, grimacing.

"Decide what?" Haemas demanded of the ilseri. "Decide if I'll go back to the Highlands and let the Council punish me for something I can't even remember doing, or if I can leave behind what's happened and live with Eevlina, stealing horses?" The crystalline chimes strengthened.

"It's the ilseri, isn't it?" Kevisson reached for her with his bound hands, his face pinched. "We have to get out of here!"

Examine the timelines, Windsign said. *Each of these males would select a certain destiny for you, just as the ilseri would mark a different path. But you, small sister, must choose the line you will walk.*

The vibration ascended into a higher pitch. Kevisson fell to his knees, his eyes clamped shut against the pain. "So— loud," he murmured. "How can you—stand it?"

Cale collapsed into a forlorn heap on the forest floor, arms curled over his ears. Haemas glanced worriedly from one to the other, her mind attuning itself to the vibrations as Summerstone had shown her. She felt the lines radiating from the nexus centered in the pool, forming an infinite circle around her into When.

Decide.

She raised her eyes and gazed down the dancing lines. At the ends of many lay the boiling maelstrom. And at the ends of most of the rest, her father's dead body rested on a bier surrounded by fluted bowls of blue chispa-fire—often next to the body of his daughter.

Naming Day! Jarid's lip curled back in disdain as he sidestepped another chierra carpenter carrying lumber for tomorrow. Tradition dictated that the ornate Naming stand must be built on the day it was used, then destroyed before sundown. His lips tightened. What a waste. He remembered his own ceremony: no stand and certainly no guests beyond the single witness required by law. No one had cared to celebrate the Naming of a bastard Killian son.

Late for the temporal enclave, he took the stairs two at a time and burst out into the warmth of the late-afternoon sun. A light wind ruffled his hair as he glanced around the courtyard. Alyssa was nowhere to be seen, but he detected her floral scent. Not today, he told himself, and especially not this close to his uncle. The peppery old coot was making a miraculous recovery, and would no doubt miss very little from now on.

After shutting the heavy door, Jarid strode purposefully to the portal housing. If the Light was on his side, he could be off to Senn'ayn before she intercepted him. But, just as he reached the foot of the portal, she stepped out from behind the framework of carved wooden beams, swathed in a long black shawl. He crowded past her onto the covered platform.

Jarid, we have to talk! She surged up the steps after him.

Setting his jaw, he turned around and gazed down at her strained face. "Why, *Aunt* Alyssa!" He made a mocking half bow. "Forgive me. I thought you were one of the maids."

She slipped the coarse black fabric down to her shoulders

and her burnished-gold hair gleamed in the sunlight. "What are we going to do? He says he will have the brat Named!"

"What brat?" He took her soft shoulders and pushed her firmly out of the portal. "He would have to find her first, and even then he would only be Naming a ghost."

She clung to his sleeve with desperate fingers. "How do you know? You never saw her body."

"I *know*!" He stared down at her small hand. "And just now I'm late for something more important than you can possibly imagine. You must forgive me for rushing off, *Aunt*."

"Don't call me that!" Her green-flecked eyes glittered with unshed tears.

He seized her delicate wrist and exerted pressure relentlessly until she released his sleeve. "Why not? You are united with dear *old* Uncle Dervlin, are you not?"

She rubbed her wrist and her golden eyes narrowed like a cornered silsha's. "I'll tell!" she hissed, backing away. "I'll tell Grandfather everything you did!"

"*We* did, my dear." He smiled thinly down at her white face, then opened his mind to catch the crystals' vibrations. "Don't let me keep you from your preparations for tomorrow. I'm sure you're very busy." He concentrated, matching the resonance in his own mind, then altered it for the portal at Senn'ayn.

Alyssa's bitter face faded from view, replaced by the iron grillwork of the Senn'ayn portal. He ran a finger over the corroding black metal. When *he* was master of Tal'ayn, he would have nothing but Old oak from Alimn'ayn, damn the cost.

A nervous chierra manservant in red-and-black Senn livery bowed as Jarid stepped down, then guided him to the meeting room where everyone was waiting.

Lord Birtal Senn's silver head rose as Jarid entered the large study. "About time." He grunted. "I thought we might have to give it up for today."

"Please forgive my tardiness, gentlemen." Jarid removed his cloak, handing it smoothly to the waiting servant. "I was detained at Tal'ayn—details about tomorrow's Naming."

"Naming, indeed!" Lord Himret Rald locked his hands

over his paunch and leaned back in his chair before the gleaming expanse of the wooden table. "And I suppose we're expected to show up for this farce."

Jarid took the remaining seat on the opposite side, across from Senn. "I hope you'll all be patient." He let the slightest hint of embarrassment leak through his shields. "Uncle just hasn't been the same since—"

Senn stared across the polished wood at Jarid. "Is there actually going to be a Naming? I was under the impression the Andiine Searcher never located the girl."

Jarid shifted uneasily in his chair, looking down at his reflection in the shining dark wood. Finally he raised his head and met Senn's gray-flecked golden eyes. "The only tactful thing I can say, gentlemen—and please don't repeat this—is it would be a kindness if you did not attend tomorrow."

Rald snorted. "I thought so!"

Several other golden and silver-streaked heads around the long table nodded. Jarid pushed his satisfaction deep within his mind where no one would read it.

Senn rapped on the wood. "Gentlemen, please." He glanced down the table, meeting each pair of golden eyes in turn. "We must return to the business at hand." He straightened in his chair. "If you will remember, at our last meeting we were very near a breakthrough. It was the general consensus that our lack of a full quorum in the power relay was the only factor blocking us from total success."

Again the heads nodded.

"With the acquisition of young Jarid Tal Ketral to fill his uncle's seat, I believe we have remedied that situation." Senn placed his hands palm-down on the smooth wood. "Shall we begin?"

The chierra servant standing ready at the floor-to-ceiling windows drew heavy drapes against the light. Then he handed the old Lord a large box of Old pine, bowed, and left the room without a word. Jarid heard the snick of the key turning in the lock.

Senn opened the box and removed, one at a time, seven fist-size ilsera crystals. He passed them around the circle so that every second man had one before him, then gestured at Lord Rald. "Himret, are you willing to attempt the transfer?"

Looking solemn, Rald nodded his balding head and pushed his chair away from the table to stand. Jarid followed the others' lead, throwing open his mind, striving to match the crystals' vibration. Traveling between portals was so automatic now that he did not really have to think about it. What the conclave needed, however, was very different. They were attempting to coax a much higher vibration from the crystals—a painful one, vastly more difficult to follow.

Fighting to keep his shields open, he matched the nerve-racking sound in his own mind, feeling the others strive to do the same. In the center of the table, a circular pattern of indistinct blue lines began to form, radiating outward.

Without warning, disruption snaked through the grove. The crystalline vibrations phased almost instantly from music to dissonance, much worse than before, racking Haemas's mind with the incompatibilities. Looking down the timelines in every direction, she saw only the yawning blue maw of the maelstrom, bristling with unleashed energies. She realized they must be very close to entering the nexus.

Follow the disruption to its source, Summerstone said urgently. *Make the males of your tribe understand they can only destroy everything if they persist in broaching the pathways.*

Haemas could not even feel the grass beneath her feet. She stretched her hands out before her, lost in a blue universe of pain. "I tried before. They're not going to listen to me. Why haven't you made them understand?"

They cannot hear our voices, Windsign said. *We have never been able to make the males of your tribe hear us.*

Fire seared every nerve in her body. She pressed her hands to her temples, fighting to raise her shields before her brains boiled. Then the suggestion of living gray rock surfaced inside her mind, and the pain dropped away.

She stood ankle-deep in cool blades of grass; the leaves rustling in the breeze made the only sound. Breathing in shuddering gasps, Kevisson and Cale lay curled into knots on the forest floor, immured in their own private agonies. The shimmering blue lines writhed through the ilseri nexus, making the grass and the trees seem to undulate beneath her feet.

You must stop them.

Haemas turned around and took one hesitant step. The pool at the center of the grove was obscured in dark, angry blueness. Her heart thundering in her chest, she took a second fearful step—and glimpsed a form standing before her, clearer than the last time. White-haired and trembling, an old man anchored the center of the crackling disruptive energy, his golden eyes staring at her. His lips moved, but she heard no sound.

She recognized him this time. It was Lord Rald, an acquaintance of her father.

You must stop this! she told him. *You are destroying the timeways!*

His eyes widened for a moment as if he heard her, but then she heard his mind still calling for more power. He took another step on the writhing blue line, then clasped his head and collapsed like an empty cloak. The line beneath him disappeared into nothingness. The grove reverted to sanity.

You made them understand, small sister?

Haemas wrapped her arms around her ribs and stared at the nexus where Lord Rald had stood just seconds before. The breath rasped in and out of her lungs as she fought to control her fear. "No," she said. "Something else happened."

Then they will try again.

"Yes." Haemas knelt beside the motionless forms of Kevisson and Cale in the grass. "They probably will."

Lord Rald lay on the floor, head to knees, breathing in shallow, ragged gasps. The shrill, discordant voice of the wrenched crystals wound down and down. Jarid stood beside the old man, staring numbly at the wall where, for a second, he had seen his cousin's face.

Senn unlocked the door and shouted to the servants waiting in the hall. Then he gripped Jarid's shoulder. "That was quick thinking, young man, when you broke the relay." He mopped at his red forehead with an embroidered sleeve. "A few more seconds and we might have lost him."

Servants rushed into the room with a litter, followed by the Senn healer, dressed in the traditional black of his calling. Senn urged Jarid out of the way as Healer Falt knelt to run practiced fingers over the old man's head.

At length he looked up at Senn, his tawny eyes angry. "This is too hard a game for the older members. You need a younger man for the focus." He motioned to the servants to load the unconscious man on the litter.

Senn released Jarid's shoulder and backed wearily into a chair. "But we've tried that," he muttered almost to himself. "Young men lack the necessary control, but now you say older men cannot handle the level of power required." He shook his head. "It will be at least a day, perhaps longer, before we can try again, but there has to be an answer. We are so close!"

Jarid thought of the skivit's hated face floating just out of reach, then distractedly toyed with his disordered bright-gilt hair. "Would you allow me to try, my Lord?"

Chapter
Twenty-two

Coolness trickled over Cale's hot face and down his neck. He felt himself rising involuntarily toward the thundering pain centered behind his eyes and tried to go away again into the soothing darkness. A winterberry-scented breeze danced over his skin.

"Are you sure he's all right?" a distant voice asked.

He drifted, afraid of the agony he had fled before, the shriek of shattering nerves, the imminent splitting of his head. Coolness bathed his face again and his eyes slitted open. A glimmer of sunlight filtering through the leaves above stabbed deep into his brain. He groaned and clamped his eyes shut.

"Try to sit up." The voice was urgent. "Windsign says you have to get away from here."

"Return to the Mother, you mean," he croaked. The throbbing in his head had a definite beat, like the big drums at Harvest Festival. He pressed trembling hands over his eyes. These Lords were insane, daring to call things into being that were outside nature itself. If he lived to be a hundred, he would never forget the cold terror of the awful roaring blueness that had threatened to swallow the world.

Warm fingers touched his temples and he felt a *presence* within his skull where no one else had any right to be. He shrank from it, but there was nowhere to run.

"No," she whispered. "It's all right."

Blackness beckoned as a startling pressure built within his head, a half-painful pushing against—something. He gasped and the pain faded away. The relief jarred him with its abruptness; he lay there, limp with surprise, his right cheek pressed into the cool grass and his head spinning.

An arm braced his shoulder and urged him up. Weak as

a newborn calf, he pried his eyes open again. A blurred white face hung over him, then resolved itself into the Kashi girl. "Mother above!" Cale whispered. "What happened?"

She sat back on her heels and met his blinking gaze with those baffling pale eyes that never gave him a clue to what she was thinking. "You have to leave before they try it again. This close to a nexus, you might not survive next time."

He gazed past her at the little pool rippling in the breeze. It was only water now, but he remembered it before—a crackling, writhing, fiery blue gateway into hell. Just looking at it made him afraid. He lurched to his feet, biting back a curse at the stab of pain in his broken foot. An arm's length away, the Kashi man lay crumpled and motionless, his face drained of color. "Is he dead?"

"He's sleeping." She brushed a lock of white-gold hair out of her face, and he saw lines of strain between her eyes. "Summerstone says it's the best thing for him now."

Cale glanced over his shoulder. "Who's Summerstone?"

She knelt in the grass and picked up the gleaming length of the sword he'd taken from the Kashi. "This is Tal'ayn's crest." She ran her fingers over the device etched on the silver hilt.

Hobbling over, he snatched it from her hand. "That's mine now!"

She stared at him until he could have sworn he felt her inside his head again. He had a flash of that terrible ride from Dorbin at the Kashi Lord's side, the sun beating down on his face, trapped in an unresponsive body while his mind gibbered in terror. His face heated.

"You're fortunate to be alive." Her expression was grave. "Jarid rarely makes mistakes."

"I suppose I could say the same, then, about you." He ducked his head and wiped the sword clean in a fold of his shirt. "He were almighty anxious to get his hands on you, too." He shuddered. "I won't never forget the nasty feeling of him using me."

Her face was solemn. "The ilseri sealed your mind against that sort of meddling after you followed me into the forest. No Kashi will ever command you again."

Cale put a hand to his head. "You mean something else has been tromping through my mind besides you and that Lord fellow?" He turned away. "Makes me feel like a damn public road."

Her warm fingers closed around his wrist. "I have to shield you for a few seconds to take you back. Windsign and Summerstone have shown me how."

He tried to pull away, but, at her touch, blackness danced at the edges of his mind, weakening his knees. His heart pounded as the shimmering blueness sprang up again, but the noise was quieter this time, almost tame. "Close your eyes," she said in his ear, and though he tried to resist, his eyelids sagged. She drew him forward and he stumbled after her, feeling a disorienting wrench. She pulled him one more step, then another, and released his wrist.

He straightened, blinked, and smelled the smoky tang of meat roasting over an open fire pit.

"And where in the seven hells have you been?" a familiar voice bawled from behind.

Cale turned around and stared across the fire into Eevlina's bristling gray eyebrows. His mouth dropped open but nothing came out.

"Fine way to treat your poor old Gran," she continued, one hand perched on her ample hip, "sneaking up on a body like that! You got no consideration for nobody."

He limped to the huge hollow tree trunk in which Eevlina made her home and felt the rough bark with a wondering hand.

"And I suppose all them horses you was supposed to steal are tied up just out of sight behind them trees over there?" She advanced on him, her walking stick firmly clenched in an upraised hand.

"Horses?" Cale swallowed around a large knot in his throat.

Eevlina stopped in front of him and looked him up and down like a haunch of suspect meat. "I always knowed blue eyes was unlucky, and on a manchild to boot!" Her brow furrowed. "I told your mum the day you was born that what she wanted with a manchild was beyond me, but she wouldn't listen to her poor old mother, no indeed!"

Cale suddenly remembered Haemas, but the Kashi girl had vanished as if she'd never been there at all.

It seemed to Kevisson that he heard Haemas Tal calling him from the other side of the world. His head was filled with shards of blue ice; he couldn't remember what had happened or how he came to be lost in this cold, dark place. She called again and he struggled to answer; she was his responsibility and he had let her down, along with Master Ellirt and the Council.

"You have to try harder." Anxious fingers bit into his shoulders. "Kevisson, please! You can't stay here."

He put his bound hands to his head and groggily opened his eyes. "Haemas?"

The girl breathed a deep sigh and sat back. Her lips were tight with strain, her eyes dark-hollowed. She raked her fingers back through the tumbled mass of her unbraided hair. "We have to go."

He gazed around the rapidly dimming grove; the last rays of sunset were just fading above the trees. "At—night?"

"We have to leave before they try again, and I can't carry you." She bent over his swollen wrists and picked at the knotted rawhide tie. Her pale hair brushed his face, silken, scented with winterberry.

He shook his head. "They?" She peeled the tie away; he rubbed the angry red indentations in his wrists, wincing as the circulation returned. "Who—what are you talking about?"

"Come on." Haemas stood, straightening her back wearily. "I'll tell you when we get to Shael'donn."

"It's days from here to Shael'donn," he protested as she levered him onto his unsteady feet.

"Not through the nexus." She steadied him, then looked toward the pool. "Let me shield you, then I'll explain as much as I can."

"Shield *me*?" he echoed stupidly. "You? But—"

"Be quiet." Her light brows knit together. "I've only done this once and I have to concentrate."

Kevisson watched her profile as she drew him toward the stone-edged pool. Her pale skin was luminescent in the deepening dusk, and yet, despite her obvious fatigue, she was more confident than he'd ever seen her—as well as in full possession of her mindsenses. What had happened after she left him in the forest? Was this really the same terrorized, damaged girl he'd trailed all the way from the Highlands? She seemed transformed, older, someone else entirely.

The faintest jangling of crystal began. He flinched back from the pool.

Lower your shields, she said clearly into his mind, startling him. *And then it won't hurt.*

He hesitated as the crystalline vibrations climbed higher, setting his teeth on edge and exacerbating the dull ache in his temples. He rolled his shields back with a convulsive shiver. The sound cut off immediately as her mind softly enfolded his.

Icy, prickling blueness formed around them, the same terrible blueness that had nearly swept him away before. She stepped into it, but he hung back.

She turned, her body bathed in crackling, scintillating blue fire. *It will be easier if you don't look.*

This wasn't real, he told himself; nothing about this nightmare Search could be real. He must be lying under a tree somewhere in the deep forest, thrown by that wily black Lenhe mare, his head split open and his life ebbing into the dirt.

"Please." It was only the voice of an ordinary young girl. "Trust me for just a minute, and then we'll be at Shael'donn."

"Shael'donn," he murmured and closed his aching eyes. Her fingers closed around his arm again, urging him forward into who-knew-what.

Well, he wouldn't mind walking into Darkness itself, he thought, if it meant he could sleep at Shael'donn tonight.

The same two Third Form boys were flipping spoonfuls of berrysauce at each other again. What were their names, Ellirt wondered irritably—Tiqery and . . . ?

He sighed, then told Brother Alidale to have that particular pair of youngsters scrub the dining hall floor after the evening meal was concluded.

Although it wasn't really that long ago, he told himself, laying his fork down, that Alidale had been cheerfully throwing mush around this very same dining hall. As the years wore on, mounting into the tens, life seemed to mire Ellirt down in foolishnesses instead of letting him attend to the problems that really mattered. Food fights, indeed! He picked up a piece of baked whiteroot and turned it over in his fingers. He was too old to spend his last days worrying about how much food wound up on the floor instead of in—

Master Ellirt?

His hand froze halfway to his mouth.

Master Ellirt, could you . . . come outside?

He sensed several boys staring up at him from their tables down on the main floor. Ellirt smiled benignly at them and popped the whiteroot in his mouth. *Kevisson?*

Yes, Master. I'm . . . in the walled garden.

I see. Ellirt reached for his napkin and wiped his hands. *Is there some reason you don't want to come inside?*

It would be better, Master, if you came to me.

Stay there, Kevisson. I will be down as soon as possible. Pushing his chair back from the table, Ellirt turned to Brother Alidale on his right. "You will see to that little matter," he said quietly, "concerning young Tiqery and—" He frowned; then his memory finally produced the name he had been seeking. "And Sanner!"

Amusement radiated from Alidale's mind, although his tone remained disapproving. "Of course, Master Ellirt."

"I have something to take care of." Ellirt put one hand on Alidale's shoulder and edged behind him along the wall.

"Do you want one of the boys to come with you?"

"No, thank you." His inner-sight was superior to normal sight in the darkness. "I should be able to manage." The noise from the dining hall followed him as he made his way down the corridor.

Young Brirn Lockne had door watch this night. Ellirt smiled pleasantly at the boy as he approached. "Unlatch the door for me, Brirn. I need to check on something."

"Outside, Master Ellirt?" Brirn's voice was surprised. "By yourself?"

"Not to worry, rock barrets rarely go after dried-up old

carcasses like mine." Ellirt clasped his hands behind his back and turned his face to the door.

"Are you going to be out long, Master?" the boy asked breathlessly as he tugged the heavy bar out of the braces across the door.

"No, I should be only a moment." As the door closed behind him, Ellirt cast his special Sight out through the night. The crisp evening air bathed his face with the soft spring smell of callyt blossoms. He sensed that Lyrdriat, the smallest moon, had drifted out from behind the clouds to cast its pale-golden light over the landscape. Ellirt sighed. Moments like these made him wish again that Fate had permitted him true vision. Inner-sight was useful, but he was well aware from occasional peeks through other people's eyes that merely finding one's way and seeing true beauty were not the same.

He shivered and thought momentarily of returning for a cloak against the rapidly cooling evening air. Then he chuckled. Getting old, he told himself. He set out toward the garden, easily navigating the crushed gravel path where a sighted man would have needed a lantern to find his way. Just as he reached the garden gate, he felt Kevisson's familiar, sensible presence ahead of him, but the younger man's mind was muted, almost distant. And someone else waited behind the wall, too—someone Ellirt didn't recognize.

The gate creaked open on its rusty hinges. Must have that seen to, he chided himself.

Just on the other side, a figure moved to meet him. "Master Ellirt!"

"Kevisson, lad!" Ellirt moved forward to clamp his hands over the younger man's broad shoulders. "I was beginning to think we had lost you to the Lowlands."

"At some points, Master, that very nearly was true," Kevisson whispered hoarsely. An aura of numbing weariness surrounded him.

Ellirt tightened his grip, reading the Searcher's low energy level much more clearly now. Kevisson had little reserve left. "But what of your Search for the young Tal? Lord Senn has been deviling me for answers."

Kevisson glanced over his shoulder and again Ellirt sensed someone behind several smaller callyt trees. He extended his mind toward the unseen figure: It was a young woman, or a girl. . . .

He turned back to Kevisson. *Haemas Sennay Tal?*

Yes, Master. He rubbed his forehead.

Why didn't you tell me you had found her? Ellirt's mind whirled like a top. *And how did you use the portal without anyone noticing?*

We didn't come through the portal. Kevisson swayed under the old man's hands, then caught himself.

The grass rustled as the girl stepped out from behind the trees. Ellirt could tell she was taller than he had realized from the image in her father's mind, long-legged, slim and graceful, and dressed in something flowing. She touched Kevisson's shoulder. "I—I have to go now."

"Where?" Kevisson seized her arm. "Not back to Tal'ayn?"

She flinched, and Ellirt caught a startling glimpse of flames in her mind. "No, back to the grove."

She was almost as exhausted as Kevisson, he realized, yet as tightly strung as a lute. He read Kevisson's desperate wish to keep her here at Shael'donn, and agreed. After having expended so much time and energy to find her, they couldn't let her disappear again. This whole matter had to be cleared up. "Why not stay with us for a few days, my dear, just until everything is straightened out?"

She turned back to him, and for a second he studied her through Kevisson's sight. Her eyes were so light they might have been frosted gold; she had the Killian coloring, inherited through her mother, which in combination with that unusual white-gold hair was a possible sign of a rare and particularly powerful strain of Talent.

"He's *dead*." She pulled away from Kevisson. "That can't be 'straightened out'!"

"Your father?" Suddenly the latest gossip among the great Houses of the Highlands came to Ellirt's mind. "Not only is he alive and very worried about you, he's holding your Testing and Naming ceremony tomorrow at Tal'ayn. The rumor is he's gone quite mad over this whole affair."

"Then it's—" The breath caught in her throat. She backed away, seeming smaller. "It's *not* true, but why—"

"Why what, my dear?" Ellirt moved closer.

"Why do I remember him cold and dead at my feet?"

He heard tears in her voice and laid a hand on her arm. Her skin felt icy through the sheer material. "Perhaps it was only a bad dream."

"Was it a dream, then, that I attacked him?" Her tone was bitter.

"There was an attack, but he recovered."

She radiated desolate lostness. Ellirt wished he did have that cloak so that he could fold this child into it. "Come inside, just for a little while, until you warm up. Perhaps I can help you sort this all out."

She stared at his hand. "I'm to be Tested and Named tomorrow?"

"Yes."

"But I can't stay." Her voice was only a strained whisper. "They may try again, you know, any time. I have to be ready."

Ellirt put an arm around her shoulder, pulling her toward the gate, sensing the weary Kevisson following behind on leaden feet.

"You don't remember me, do you?" she asked as they walked.

"Remember you?" Ellirt shook his head. "I'm sure we have never met, although I have known your father over the years."

"I don't know why I asked. I knew it was true." She sighed and reached for the latch on the gate. "The minute I entered your past, it shifted into an Otherwhen. There isn't anywhere to go ... no place I can hide."

What a strange child, Ellirt thought behind his shields as their feet crunched along the gravel path back to the main building. What in the name of the Light had been going on up there at Tal'ayn all these years?

Chapter
Twenty-three

Alyssa gazed up at the golden crescent of Lyrdriat, suspended over the bridged towers of Tal'ayn, and shivered. She had only brought a light shawl and the late-spring Highlands wind cut through her like a knife. What was Jarid thinking, to call her outside like some chierra servant girl?

Her cheeks heated as she thought of his imperious summons this afternoon, as well as the other slights and brushoffs he'd heaped upon her since his return from the Lowlands. She would suspect he'd found someone else if she hadn't been certain he'd never find another Kashi bride combining her bloodlines, beauty, and Talent.

Yellow lights still shone in the windows of the kitchen down on the ground level as the final preparations for tomorrow's ceremonies continued. She thought of the waste of food and decorations prepared for the Naming of a ghost and jerked her shawl closer around her shoulders. Lord of Light! Was she doomed now to spend the years tied to a madman?

Something reached up behind her and tapped her shoulder. She whirled around and a hand clamped roughly over her mouth.

Don't bother screaming. It's only me. Jarid's pale eyes glittered down at her in the moonlight.

She shoved his hand away. "How did you do that?" she whispered fiercely. "I didn't even feel your mind."

"Oh, I have a few tricks left to show you yet." He laced his fingers through hers and drew her through the waist-high Old apple seedlings. "We need to go farther, though. I don't want to be in Uncle's range."

She stumbled after him in her light slippers. The thought

of Dervlin catching them together was enough to choke back the rest of her complaints. They passed the far edge of the orchard and began to climb through the surrounding jagged gray rocks. "I'm not dressed for this." Alyssa felt she was panting like a field hand. "Why didn't you warn me to wear something suitable?"

Jarid looked down at her. "Because someone might have seen you dressed that way and told Uncle." He turned back to the rocks and continued working his way upward. "Besides, we're almost there."

Watching his tall, lean body disappear over the stone ledge, Alyssa's eyes narrowed. How dare he expect her to scramble about in the dirt and rocks like some Houseless urchin!

Jarid's head, black against the indigo night sky, reappeared above the rocks. "Hurry up!" He held up a bottle. "I brought wine, as well as food and—" He paused. "—a silsha-fur throw."

Alyssa glanced down at her precisely shaped nails, gleaming faintly in the moonlight, and sighed. Well, perhaps she could wear gloves at tomorrow's ceremonies. Then she shook her head. There weren't going to be any ceremonies anyway. The brat was dead.

"Alyssa!" The cork popped.

"All right!" she snapped, hitching her long skirts up with one hand. "I'm coming."

Ten minutes later, scratched and dirty, she pulled herself up to the last boulder and looked over. Jarid lounged back on one elbow on a blanket spread in a small hollow, holding a glass of wine in one hand.

"You seem to be out of shape, Aunt," he said, eyeing her over the top of the goblet.

Alyssa collapsed on the boulder, rubbing her scraped and bruised palms together. "I'm not some chierra wench you can just order around, Jarid Tal Ketral. I am a well brought up Lady."

"Indeed you are." He handed her the goblet and poured another for himself. "And you never let me forget it."

She sniffed the wine before taking a sip: sweet amber callyt from several years ago, a tolerable vintage. She took a small sip and let it burn a fiery trail down her throat.

Jarid laughed. "I know I'm being a terrible tease, but I just couldn't resist." He patted the blanket beside his long legs. "Say you'll forgive me."

His bright-gold hair shone in the moonlight, one lock dangling in his eyes in the most boyish way. "You've been very cruel." Alyssa combed her fingers through his thick hair and tilted her head back for another warming sip of the amber wine.

His arm reached up and enfolded her waist. She bent her knees and settled on the blanket beside him, enjoying his warmth against the briskness of the spring night.

"I have to be. Otherwise Uncle Dervlin would suspect us and everything would be ruined." He traced the line of her jaw with his forefinger all the way down to the pulse point in her throat. "You're good at shielding, but not that good."

She jerked away from his touch. "Then when are you going to get rid of the bloody old fool? I don't know how much more of this I can stand!"

"Tomorrow, as a matter of fact." He drained the glass and reached for the wine bottle. "Drink up."

She tipped her own goblet and savored the wine's bite on her tongue. The twisted knot of anger and frustration in her stomach eased. The wine was a more unusual vintage than she had first thought, unexpectedly potent. Above her, the frosty stars wheeled as if a giant's carriage were rolling across the heavens. "How—are you going to d—do it?" Her lips had grown numb.

He laughed and pulled the glass from her stiffening fingers, then smoothed a wisp of hair back over her right ear. "Me, Aunt?" He smiled, and his strong white teeth glinted through the dimness. "No, it's you, Birtal Senn's grand-daughter, who will send Dervlin Tal down into Darkness. And what a scandal that will be! I can hardly wait to watch the Houses scramble to take advantage of your little, shall we say, indiscretion."

Waiting in Master Ellirt's rooms, Haemas drew the scratchy wool of the borrowed cloak more closely around her shoulders. The small study off the bedchamber was sparely furnished, but made comfortable with shuttered windows and a blazing fire in the hearth. Still, she felt nervous and edgy with Kashi minds murmuring all around her. She'd never been this close to so many of her own kind before. If they were aware that she was here, if they had any idea what she had done—

Her hands clenched. She couldn't think about that, or she would lose the control for which she had fought so hard and the flames would come back. She tucked her feet up in the overstuffed chair, rubbing the aching muscles in her neck. Down in the garden, she had let herself be lulled for a moment by Master Ellirt's assurances, but it was just a ruse. Her father was dead by her own hand and she was in danger as long as she stayed in the Highlands. As soon as she knew Kevisson was all right, she would go back to the ilseri.

A light rap sounded, and then Master Ellirt opened the door. His craggy, weather-seamed face was creased with worry. She rose. "Kevisson?"

"He's sleeping now. I had one of our healers attend him, but it seems there's really nothing much wrong except malnutrition and exhaustion."

"I'm glad." Haemas sank back down on the wing-backed chair and turned her eyes again to the flickering yellow flames. "In spite of what I've done, he tried to help me."

"Kevisson understands better than most what it is to be friendless." Ellirt pulled up another chair and eased his bulk into it. "You've had a very rough time, haven't you?"

She listened to the crackling fire for a moment, feeling waves of weariness sweep over her. How long had it been since she'd slept? She rested her head against the padded back of the chair. "You want to know what I did to my father."

His face was grave as he folded his hands across his well-worn leather belt. "Actually, I think it's more important for *you* to find out what happened."

Her fingers tightened on the chair's arms. "I already know." The wrenching memory swept back over her again: the pallid hand brushing the toe of her boot, Jarid's laughter.

Ellirt shook his white-haired head. "You only know what you *think* happened."

"You're trying to trick me!" A knot of shame and guilt

closed her throat. "He's not holding a Naming tomorrow because I killed him!"

"He isn't dead." Ellirt leaned forward in his chair, projecting calm concern. "Come look in my mind and see for yourself if I'm lying."

She felt the old man's shields dissolve before her and stared at him with disbelieving eyes.

"Are you afraid to find out?" he asked gently.

She stood hesitantly, letting the cloak slip off her shoulders to the floor. "I'm—not very good at this."

Come and see, little one. I have nothing to hide.

Haemas stretched a trembling hand toward the wrinkled head, closing her eyes as her fingers brushed his temple. The brightness of his mind lay before her: a great golden House with many rooms, all the doors standing wide open.

Suddenly Lord Senn's gravelly voice froze her heart. "Send me a Searcher, you old rock barret—the best you've got."

"Is someone lost?" Master Ellirt's voice inquired.

"It's the Tal brat. She's half killed her father and run off to the Light-knows-where."

"Very sad," Ellirt said quietly. "Of course Shael'donn will be glad to help."

The conversation faded; then she caught Alyssa's familiar floral scent.

"Master Ellirt!" Alyssa's voice was light and airy. "You should have told us you were coming."

"I've come to see your Lord husband, my dear. Perhaps there's something Shael'donn could do for him yet."

"Oh, he's much too weak for visitors, Master Ellirt." Haemas felt Alyssa's hand under Ellirt's elbow. "But it was kind of you to come all this way."

And then, even as Alyssa's voice faded away, Haemas heard her father's angry voice.

"Damnation, Kniel, I want her brought back!" Dervlin Tal coughed and moved restlessly under the covers.

"We're doing our best, Dervlin. You know that," Ellirt replied.

"Well, your best isn't good enough, then!" She sensed how her father attempted to rise, then fell back against the pillows. "Put a real man on the case," his hoarse voice rasped. "The little skivit has to be brought back by her Naming Day or—"

Haemas snatched her hand away as if she had grasped a burning brand. She heard a great roaring in her ears. "He was dead," she said as her heart thundered against her ribs. "I *saw* him. He was!"

Ellirt stood and felt her icy fingers and face. "I'm an old fool," he murmured, turning away from her and rummaging through his shelves. A moment later, he pressed a small glass into her freezing hands. "Sit by the fire and drink this." He eased her into the chair, then wrapped the cloak around her shoulders once more.

The room seemed dim, his words distant and unreal. Haemas couldn't move, couldn't think. Ellirt pushed the glass to her lips. She took a sip, then choked as the bitter liquid burned down her throat.

Ellirt patted her on the back encouragingly and nodded. "That's better. I should have foreseen what a shock that would be."

"He's not dead." She stared numbly at her shaking hands. The ghostly flames of her fear and guilt laughed in the back of her mind. She shivered.

"No."

Every corner of her mind felt frozen. "How can that be?"

"Drink another sip of that brandy." He guided the tumbler back to her lips.

She swallowed, struggling not to cough as it brought tears to her eyes.

Master Ellirt settled across from her, the firelight casting shifting shadows over his concerned features. "Now, then," he said. "What we must do next is find out what really happened that night. Do you have the courage to go that far?"

"I only know what I remember," she said slowly. The brandy was melting the cold knot of ice in her middle, creating instead a creeping warmth in her fingers and toes. "If that's not what happened, I have to know!"

"I can help you look within and find the truth." He made a triangle of his thumbs and forefingers. "If you are willing."

"But the ilseri." Suddenly she blinked and looked at the door. "I have to go back."

"We'll talk about that later." He reached out and trapped her hand between his two gnarled ones. "Think, little one. Maybe you are responsible for what happened, but my instincts say not—and, if you didn't strike down your father, someone else did. The High Houses are always at each other's throats. He could still be in great danger."

"But I've relived that night a thousand times since—" She bit her lip, trying to shut away the chilling vividness of the dead body sprawled at her feet. The flames crept smoldering through her mind. She drew a long shuddering breath.

Master Ellirt's tiny golden eyes, almost hidden in the folds of his face, reflected the firelight. They seemed to see straight into her, although she knew he could not.

"It will take a skilled and clever Talent to find the truth of this puzzle." He lifted a white eyebrow. "Fortunately for you, my dear, that is exactly what I am."

Haemas knotted her fingers together to keep them from trembling. Guilt and shame yammered at her—if she let him into her mind, he would see what she had done for dark, unspeakable reasons she couldn't even remember. Deep inside, in spite of everything, she still *knew* she had killed him.

"We might as well begin." Blunt fingertips brushed her forehead. "There's nothing to be afraid of."

As her eyes fluttered, Summerstone's voice came back to her.

Fear is but a sister whispering in your ear.

Yes, Haemas thought, but this time her fear was whispering that something horrible lay buried deep beneath the flames' smoldering anger.

She felt Ellirt's no-nonsense presence hovering near. *Center down,* he ordered. One by one she blocked her other senses, seeking that quiet place in her mind where nothing of the outside could intrude. Gradually her tight muscles relaxed, and the sounds of the fire, her own breathing, and her heartbeat faded.

Now let me find the way, he told her. *Go deeper, until*

*you can see that night. Don't be afraid. Whatever happens,
I'll be with you.*

She felt her thoughts blurring, drifting. . . .

Family dinner . . . she stood at the dining room door, her
palm pressed to the satiny wood.

Ellirt watched Haemas clasp her cold, white fingers together as the old chierra seneschal, Pascar, opened the massive door. Jarid turned his light eyes to her—eyes so much
like, yet totally unlike her own. "Come in, cousin."

She glanced at the long table. "Where's Father?" Only
Alyssa, her stepmother, and Jarid, her orphaned cousin,
were waiting to eat.

Something was wrong. Pascar moved quietly around the
huge table, lighting the tall, twisted candles for the evening
meal. Jarid's eyes followed him impatiently. "Out!" he demanded as the last flame took hold. Pascar dropped his
brown chierra eyes and bowed, then closed the door behind
him.

Haemas slid into her accustomed place. Jarid lounged
back against the intricately carved wood of his chair and
stretched his arms over his head like a carnivore limbering
for the hunt. "You want to know where your father is,
skivit?" He winked. "Why should you care? He's never had
any use for you."

Alyssa's amused eyes gleamed over the hand she used to
mask her smile.

Haemas realized her own hands were clenched around
the table's edge. With an effort, she dropped them. "I don't
believe I'm hungry," she said faintly, holding her shields
very tight so no sense of her unease would escape. "Please
excuse me." Nodding to her stepmother, she began to rise.

"Not so fast, cousin." Steel rang in Jarid's arrogant
voice.

Without meaning to, Haemas found she had dropped
back into her seat.

"I have a little something for you." Jarid's sense of interest in her became stronger, sharpening into something
closer to ownership. "Something that I trust you will not
find unappealing."

Haemas tore her gaze away from Jarid's compelling, ice-pale eyes. "I want to go."

"Very well, then, skivit, by all means go." His tone mocked her. "But first, you must drink a toast with us."

Frozen, she watched as his steady hand poured deep-red tchallit wine into the green crystal goblets set before each place. His sense of triumph was so strong that she knew he was not even bothering to shield. Jarid handed one goblet to Alyssa and the next to Haemas, reserving the last for himself.

All three portions came from the same bottle, yet the moment her hand closed around the slender green stem, Haemas knew with certainty that something was wrong with it. Her hand jerked away from the goblet as if it had burned her.

Candlelight reflected on the green crystal as Jarid raised his goblet high. "A toast to the Heir of Tal'ayn."

Alyssa rose beside him, her hand draped casually over his shoulder. "To the Heir!" she agreed merrily. Watching each other, they sipped the bloodred liquid.

"What's this, cousin?" Jarid turned the full force of his magnetic gaze to Haemas. "You won't drink with us? We can't have that."

The compulsion to drink flowed over her, more powerful with every passing second. She closed her eyes, fighting his will, gripping the arms of her chair until her fingers were numb. Abruptly her cousin showed her a gruesome vision in his mind: her father lying dead on the floor.

"Father!" Haemas gasped. "I won't let you!"

Casually Jarid doubled the force of his compulsion. Her hand crept toward the cup. "But," he said softly, "you've misunderstood. You know a touch of Foreseeing runs through the Tal line. No, I'm afraid my unstable cousin is the one who will do that."

The struggle generated a white-hot haze inside her head, through which she could just barely see her hand as it closed around the goblet's green stem again.

Jarid nodded his approval. "Just one sip."

She picked up the cup and moved it to her lips—

Haemas blinked, slid out of her seat, confused, and then stopped as her toe bumped something. Her father sprawled at the foot of the table on the plush burnt-orange rug, one gnarled finger grazing her boot. Her throat ached. She wanted to run, to scream, to do anything but just stand there, gazing down at his curiously white and empty face.

"What's the matter, skivit?" Jarid asked from behind her. "Having second thoughts?"

She tried to turn around, but her body wouldn't answer.

Jarid walked into her field of view and nudged her father's still body with his boot. The gray-haired head rolled loosely. "Going after your own father like that." He crossed his arms and smiled his familiar crooked smile, as always, in perfect control. "And at such a tender age, too, only fifteen. Not even properly Named. Whatever will the Council say?"

Every muscle in Haemas's body ached with her effort to move. "I don't understand," she whispered. "What's wrong with him? What—what happened?"

Jarid raised an eyebrow at her. "You killed him, of course. I always knew it would come to this."

Enough! Ellirt told the girl. He reached a trembling hand up to wipe the sweat from his brow, even as the other remained on her temple. Lord of Light, that was like sticking his naked hand into a bavval den!

He leaned over Haemas Tal's bent head. *Sleep*, he said into her mind, then monitored to be sure she didn't resist; he sensed great depths of untrained Talent in this one. He would have liked to work with her. If only she'd been a boy . . .

Forcing his thoughts back to the problem at hand, he poured himself a tumbler of brandy, downing half the fiery liquid in one gulp. How much of that had been real? He paced the floor, replaying the chilling incident in his own head. What exactly had Jarid Ketral done to her mind? Then he knew: There had been an instant when time had jumped ahead. That had to be the edge of a false memory.

Retracing his steps back to her side, he pulled the other chair close. This was liable to turn into a very long night, he reflected grimly. He laid one hand on the girl's forehead. *You will sleep until I tell you to wake,* he told her firmly. *No matter what happens.*

And with that, he stiffened his resolve. First he had to play that disgusting scene again all the way up to the crucial time-skip. He placed her at the door once more, feeling her panic as the sequence began a second time. Nonetheless, it had to be done. He monitored closely as the events replayed exactly as before, down to the last glint of candlelight on the crystal.

She picked up the cup and moved it to her lips—

Stop, Ellirt commanded. It had to be here—some sign of a seam that covered the gap in memory.

The edge, though, was buried unexpectedly deep, and when he did at last uncover it, he blanched at the still-tender scars of a recent injury.

For all his assurances to the girl, this lay beyond his skill. If he tried to force her to remember, he might damage her mind further. When Kevisson had first found her in the Lowlands, he'd reported that she couldn't shield or hear his mindvoice. Seeing the burned pathways now for himself, Ellirt realized it was a wonder she had even survived, much less recovered to this point.

To resolve this, she needed someone who had been there that night, who could pick out a single thread of falseness so the rest would unravel like a piece of poorly woven cloth.

And there were only three candidates.

Chapter
Twenty-four

The tables laid out in the courtyard steamed with spiced nutcake and freshly baked Old apple pastries. Dervlin caught the exotic aroma of hot cinnamon as he stalked past, but he had no appetite for the cook's fancy dishes.

He felt like a fool. What had made him so bloody certain the whelp would show up? The Light knew she'd never failed to disappoint him down through the years, starting with her birth—an event that had cost him the woman who should have borne him a dozen strapping sons by now. Why should this day be any different?

Blueness flared within the portal as more guests arrived. Dervlin squinted across the courtyard at the richly garbed pair, then turned away scowling. More damn Killians. It seemed the entire clan intended to be here to eat him out of House and larder.

Shouldering his way through the bright silks and satins of the murmuring crowd, he realized that, except for Aaren Killian, none of the High Househeads had come. His face heated at the implied insult. They obviously thought he was finished.

Up on the ceremonial stand decorated with white anith flowers, the chierra musicians struck up another traditional tune. Dervlin couldn't put the ceremony off much longer; the milling crowd had already eaten its fill from the delicacy-laden tables and was growing increasingly restless. He scanned the faces again, but there was still no sign of his missing daughter.

A glint of burnished-bright hair and a gleaming white silk gown embroidered with silver roses drew his eye over by the foot of the stand. Alyssa, he thought sourly. What was the sullen wench up to now? Had she tired of batting her eyes at the Bramm'ayn younger son he'd seen her pursuing a few minutes ago and gone after larger game?

"Nice weather for a Naming."

Dervlin looked over his shoulder into Aaren Killian's amused light-gold eyes.

"I invited a few extra guests." Killian fell in beside him, wearing a tailored vest and shirt of embossed dark burgundy, resplendent, as always. "It seemed a shame to let all these fine preparations go to waste."

Dervlin drew his cloak around him and glanced in the direction of the stand. The worried priest was motioning to him.

"Looks like it's time to start." Killian clamped his big hand on Dervlin's shoulder and squeezed. "Good luck."

Jerking away from his touch, Dervlin gave the taller man a smoldering glare. Then he ducked his head and pushed through the jostling onlookers to the steps.

The priest met him with troubled gold eyes. "Has the young Heir arrived yet, my Lord?"

Dervlin looked out over the crowd of Kashi faces below and tasted the mental atmosphere, which vacillated between condescending amusement and pity. Not one of them believed Haemas was going to come. Why, he asked himself again for the thousandth time, why had he thought she would attend?

"Dervlin?" Alyssa slipped up to lay her soft hand on his arm. "Won't you come inside now?"

It must be his so-called illness, he thought. Perhaps he hadn't really recovered. He had never behaved so irrationally before. Bowing his head, he let her draw him away from the edge of the stand.

Then surprise rippled suddenly through the crowd. Faces turned like flowers tracking the sun to the portal where the blueness of transfer still shimmered faintly. A stocky, white-haired old man stepped out of the carved wooden housing. Dervlin squinted. Damn if that face didn't look familiar. Then he recognized the head of Shael'donn, Lord High Master Kniel Falt Ellirt. And, at his side, a young girl stood framed in the open portal housing, tall and slender, with undressed white-gold hair tumbling down her back.

The stand seemed to fall out from under Dervlin's feet; he swayed, unable to force air back into his lungs.

"But she can't be here!" Alyssa's fingers convulsed into the flesh of his arm. "Where in Darkness did she come from?"

Dervlin stared icily down at her clutching hand. "Well, she is here, so you will have to bear your disappointment."

His daughter, wearing glimmering white that accentuated her paleness, stepped down from the portal. The brightly dressed crowd, now whispering and staring, parted as she padded on bare feet across the gray flagstones.

How could the brat have come barefoot for her own Naming? Dervlin thought irritably. And the gown was odd, too, almost indecent, fitting her slender body in no style he'd ever seen before. Where in the name of Light had she been all this time?

The waiting guests fell silent, but their curiosity beat at his shields in mounting waves.

Haemas crossed the interminable space to the ceremonial stand, looking neither left nor right, her gaze fixed on his face as if she'd never seen him before. Even Alyssa fell back as the girl ascended the steps, her hand skimming the anith flowers' opalescent whiteness. Then she stood before Dervlin, nearly as tall as he, even in her bare feet. "Father." Her light-colored eyes were unreadable.

Dervlin swallowed, then made himself hold out his hand. He would deal with her part in his so-called accident later. For now, he had to carry through with this farce and satisfy the terms of the betrothal contract. "Welcome to your Testing and Naming, Daughter."

Making no move to take his hand, she stared back at him as the breeze stirred the long unfettered hair around her face. She looked older than he remembered, and weary, and strained.

"Are—are you really well?" she asked.

Alyssa burst forward, her fine features rigid with indignation. "No thanks to you!"

"This isn't the time for that." His voice was gruff. "Let's get on with the ceremony." He straightened his gold-encrusted tunic, then motioned to Aaren Killian, who was to stand witness to her Testing.

Killian stepped forward and bowed slightly from the waist. Haemas's startled eyes flickered at him.

The priest sidled closer with a pained expression on his face. "My Lady, if we might get started now?" He motioned for Haemas to take her place before him.

She blanched, then breathed deeply and shook her head. "I—can't."

Dervlin Tal's jaw dropped. "Why in the name of Darkness not?"

"You're sure that you want to do this, boy?" Lord Senn's golden eyes bored into Jarid's. "After yesterday, you must understand the risks."

Jarid tightened his shields to hide his overwhelming certainty that he could not only handle but control the temporal power locked into the gleaming ilsera crystals. Then, shrouding himself in a mask of humility, he nodded at the older man. "I understand, of course, Lord, but I am at your service."

"Good lad." Senn patted him on the shoulder. "Gentlemen." Senn met every pair of golden eyes seated around the long table. Then his mouth tightened into a hard straight line. "Where is Aaren Killian?"

"My Lord." A younger man with red-gold hair and the same pale eyes as Jarid stood and bowed slightly to the older Lord. "Lord Killian begs your forgiveness, but he wished to witness the Testing at Tal'ayn today. He sent me in his place."

"Damnation!" Senn scowled back at him. "And which one are you?"

"Kimbrel Alimn Killian, Lord." The young man sank back into his seat.

Jarid felt his blood heat. Kimbrel was Aaren's youngest son, and Jarid's half brother, and fully half the Highlands knew it. And of course his own mother, Danih, had done nothing to disprove the Highlands' wagging tongues when she had borne him at Tal'ayn and then, less than a year later, taken her own life.

He schooled an expression of cool indifference over his face, seething inside. Wait just a little longer, he counseled himself. He would show them what he was made of, and then they would pay—everyone would pay for shaming him.

Senn placed his hands palm down on the dark shining wood. "Shall we begin?"

Heads nodded around the long table, and the seven pale-blue crystals were removed from the velvet-lined box of Old oak, passed down, and positioned in the correct pattern.

Senn glanced at the chierra servant waiting unobtrusively near the door. The brown-haired man crossed to the window to draw the drapes, then bowed low and left the room, locking the door behind him.

"Yesterday, brothers, we nearly reached our goal. Today . . ." Senn glanced around the oblong circle of every conceivable shade of golden hair. "Light willing, today we will crack the secret of temporal transfer."

Excitement crawled up Jarid's spine. Soon, he told himself, very soon.

Haemas gazed at her father's craggy face, noting the dark shadows under his red-rimmed eyes, the thinness of his shoulders under the ornate gold-worked tunic. But he *was* alive! she told herself, hardly able to believe it, even standing here before him. She glanced down at Master Ellirt. Somehow, the blind man felt her gaze and nodded back at her.

"I—can't remember what happened that night." She clasped her hands before her, uncomfortably aware of the crowd of Kashi minds swirling against her shields. The crowd below shifted, murmuring. "Can we go inside and talk?"

A muscle twitched in her father's cheek. "Not now." His voice sounded hollow. "We have to begin the ceremony."

Perhaps she should just go along with him, she told herself. Then later they could be alone and she could learn what had really happened.

"We have a contract, Tal." The pale-eyed Lord who was to witness her Test seized her father's arm and spun him around. "You said she would be Tested and Named today!"

"And she will!" Dervlin Tal's icy rage enveloped her. "If I have to tie and gag her myself!"

His eyes narrowed and she felt his will battering against

hers, trying to breach her shields and compel obedience, even in front of a whole courtyard of witnesses. She went cold inside. Nothing had changed between them. He was the same, in spite of everything that had happened.

The circle of Kashi threw their minds open to the crystals' emanations and coaxed them into the unfamiliar frequencies. Jarid winced as the sound quickly shifted into the painful higher range and continued to ascend. He sensed the other men laying their energies open to him, waiting for him to draw the tremendous amount of power he would need.

In the center of the table, the same circular pattern formed, surrounded by thin blue lines radiating outward. Around him, the power relay strengthened, securing him in a net of raw psionic energy. The coruscating blue lines beckoned and Jarid stood, letting the conclave's power feed through him, feeling the vibrations thrumming inside his aching head until he could hardly think.

Looking around the full circle of possible paths, he glimpsed faint outlines of people and places at the ends of some; at the ends of many others was the same puzzling dark-blue mass seething with angry energies.

At the end of one line, though, he saw a female figure—Haemas again? Jarid took one step toward her, then gasped as the power he drew sizzled along his nerves.

Lord Senn's face was rigid with strain. "Can you transfer, boy?"

The crystals shrieked inside Jarid's head. He grimly laid himself open for more power and managed another step. The scene at the end of the line solidified, and the figure turned. Blinking in surprise, Jarid froze. He knew that sad-eyed face framed in bright-gilt hair from an old portrait that hung in his rooms. It was Danih Kentnal Tal, his mother.

Gritting his teeth against the searing influx of energy, he forced his foot forward.

"No!" Alyssa's voice hissed at Dervlin's elbow. "She's not worthy of a Name!"

Haemas blanched. A contract—for her? No one had ever asked if she was willing, or even brought up the possibility.

The grating mix of envy and fear and anger and greed around her intensified, smothering her until with great effort she managed to shield everything out, retreating to soothing silence deep within her own head. Had she really desired this man's approval, the respect of these people? All of that seemed part of another lifetime.

She was shielding so tightly that at first she missed the crystalline ringing, but the now-familiar shimmering blueness around the portal caught her eye. Softening her shields, she tried to listen beyond the angry mishmash of emotions around her.

It was happening again. Although the portal crystals were not set in the configuration of an ilseri nexus, they still were sensitive enough to pick up the disturbance. Blue timelines twisted and writhed across the courtyard through the unperceiving Kashi and chierras alike. Haemas's nerves were wrenched with distorted vibrations that had the intensity of overtuned lute strings about to snap.

Couldn't they feel it? She swayed, then caught herself on the tall corner beam, crushing anith flowers beneath her hand. Her father, Alyssa, and the pale-eyed man all stared at her, frozen in place.

The crystalline shrieking phased into an agonizing higher register. The blueness surrounding the portal thickened into a darker muddy blue; somewhere in the Highlands the timelines were being torn apart.

Leaping down from the ceremonial stand, Haemas tried to align her mind with the vibrations, to trace them as Summerstone had told her. But they were so dissonant that it was like trying to catch lightning in her bare hands.

The blueness abruptly faded, although the pain still seared along his nerves. Trembling, Jarid stood knee deep in grass in a mature Lowlands orchard somewhere in late summer. Around him, the heavy-leafed nasai trees bowed low under their burden of ripe purple fruit, and the scent of newly mown hay filled the air. He reached out a hand to the smooth, gray-barked trunk in front of him.

A voice came soft and low. "I thought I heard someone."

"Don't be ridiculous, pet," a male voice answered. "There's no one else here."

Jarid stared numbly through the branches at the pair: Danih with her golden hair fashioned into a single braid coiled on her head and a tall richly dressed man with eyes of amber ice.

She pressed his larger fingers between her two hands as though they were a great treasure, her bronze eyes seeking his pale ones. "Take me with you."

"You know I can't." He stroked her braided hair and pressed her head to his chest. "Ketral'ayn would protest and the Council would have the right to revoke my charter. I could lose everything."

"I want to go back to the Highlands." Her large eyes glistened with unshed tears. "I can't bear it on this wretched farm another day!"

He didn't answer.

Danih put her hands on his shoulders and stood on her tiptoes, staring into his face. "Please, Aaren!"

Aaren Killian! Jarid felt the long-controlled anger flash through him like wildfire, aggravating the already staggering pain of Transfer until he thought his head would split. "Don't beg!" He darted out from behind a tree. "Don't you dare beg that bastard for anything!"

Aaren thrust Danih behind him and drew his dagger. "And who in the name of Darkness do you think you are?"

Jarid hesitated, then caught a faint crystalline ringing. The pain in his head redoubled as blueness laced the air around him.

Aaren and Danih stared at him through a whirling dark-blue wall crackling with energy. Jarid put both hands to his skull, fighting to control the renewed surge of power, as well as the frightening dissonance that threatened to tear his brain apart.

The seething blueness thickened before him until he could see nothing. Struggling for breath, he turned back and glimpsed the misty outlines of the conclave room behind him. Gathering his will, he made his feet take one step along the shimmering blue line, then another, and at last, one more.

The room solidified around him, and he fell to his knees, summoning his shields against the frightening flow of power still directed at him.

The relay faded. Senn left his chair and knelt beside him. "Are you all right, boy?"

Jarid glanced up into the older man's drawn face. "Yes."

"Where did you go? What year was it?" Senn put a hand under his arm and levered him back into his seat.

Taking a deep, steadying breath, Jarid looked down the table at Kimbrel Killian's exhausted face. "It was the past, my Lord. I'm not sure of the exact date."

"Wonderful, my boy!" Senn clapped him on the back. Approval washed over him from all sides of the table.

"As soon as we've all rested," Jarid said, "I want to try again."

Chapter
Twenty-five

Haemas sank limply to the portal floor, the breath sobbing in and out of her chest. The cessation of pain had been so sudden that she couldn't comprehend it for a moment. But nothing of the disruption remained except a hollow ringing in her ears.

"Are you ill?" An unfamiliar bejeweled woman dressed in dark-green silk leaned over her. A dozen more white-faced onlookers peered over the woman's shoulder and through the open latticework of the portal housing.

The memory of the dissonance still rang in Haemas's bones; her every nerve throbbed as if flayed. "No-no-no." She flinched as her words seemed to echo.

"Then you must return to the stand." The woman reached for her arm. "Your father's calling you. The ceremony is already running quite late."

Shrinking back, she thought she would scream if anyone touched her, and she lacked the strength to use the crystals to transfer.

Master Ellirt hurried up and crowded the woman in green aside. "What in the name of the Blessed Light was that?" He bent low, but made no move to touch her.

Haemas locked her icy fingers together, shivering as reaction to the near catastrophe set in. "You heard it, too?"

"Only through you." He crouched beside her in the portal's shade, ignoring the whispering onlookers. His expression was haggard. "Evidently you've become sensitized to a whole new frequency that the rest of us don't normally perceive. I was maintaining a light link, in case you needed me, and it almost took my head off."

"It was very close to—" She broke off, not sure how to

explain. "—to the end of everything. I have to go back to the grove!"

"To the ilseri?"

Haemas put a hand on her throat, trying to steady her ragged breathing. "They—say Kashi are causing the disruption."

"Which Kashi?" Ellirt's face darkened.

"Some of the men, I'm not sure just who—but yesterday, when this happened and Kevisson almost died, I saw Lord Rald in the nexus."

"It has to be the Temporal Conclave." Ellirt lowered his head and ran spread fingers over his white hair. "They only try once each meeting, and even that is too much for some of them. It should be safe for you to stay for a few minutes and talk with your father. Then I'll take you to the Conclave. Perhaps together we can talk some sense into them."

Haemas could feel Dervlin Kentnal Tal's angry presence all the way across the courtyard. What if he hammered at her again? She wasn't sure she could stand against him after what had just happened. "Shouldn't we go to the Conclave now?"

"Your father may still be in danger," Ellirt said gently. "Only you can say."

The false memory leaped back into her mind—the terrorizing moment when her father had sprawled dead at her feet. She shuddered, fighting the fear and guilt and smoldering anger still buried under images that had never happened. Perhaps just a few more minutes wouldn't matter. The portal's ilsera crystals lay quiescent now, humming their inaudible crystalline song. Pulling herself up, she stood and looked out over the sea of golden Kashi heads.

Ellirt moved aside to let her pass. "What of your cousin Jarid? Is he here?"

"I don't know." With so many mental presences crowding around, it had been all she could do just to keep everything screened out. "Alyssa is here, but I haven't seen him."

"Strange." Ellirt offered her his arm. "With all the trouble that rascal has gone to, I wouldn't think he would miss this farce."

Rascal, Haemas thought—what a pale word to describe her handsome cousin. She stepped down from the portal, hesitantly laying her hand upon the old man's arm. The contact felt warm and comforting, and she found she could bear it after all.

Once more the people fell back before her, even as their minds clamored for an explanation of her outrageous behavior. Unbidden images flashed into her head before she could shield them out: a barefoot, dirty-faced urchin draped in a bizarre length of white material . . . a disrespectful young whelp who had defied her father . . . a coward who had struck him down, then run away.

She straightened her back and rubbed at her face with the back of her free hand.

Never mind, Ellirt said. *It's only a smudge, hardly worth bothering about.*

He dropped his arm as they approached the stand, and she went on alone, forcing herself to meet her father's gaze as she ascended the steps again.

"Shall we begin the Testing now, Lady Haemas?" The priest's concerned gold eyes blinked at her as he shifted his weight beneath the braid-encrusted ceremonial cassock.

She turned to her father. "Can we go inside?" Fear hammered at her stomach; perhaps something even worse lay buried beneath the false memory. What *had* she done? "I want you to read my memory of what happened that night. It's—not right."

"No!" Alyssa's delicate features contorted. "She nearly killed you before, Dervlin! Don't listen to her!"

Dervlin Tal glanced down at his wife and his mouth tightened. "You don't want me to listen to her? I find that very interesting." He glared again at Haemas, his heavy gray brows meeting over his nose. "If I do, will you go through with the ceremony?"

Haemas glanced at the priest, then the pale-haired man at his side who was studying her as if she were a prize mare. "If you still want me to."

He rubbed one hand across his chin. "And you'll allow me control?"

She nodded.

"Then open your shields, dammit, and let's get on with this!" His irritation washed over her.

"Here?" Haemas looked over her shoulder at the restless crowd.

"Yes, here, or not at all!" His gaze was flinty.

Trembling, she closed her eyes and dissolved her shields, summoning up yet again the hateful memory that had haunted her. Fingers pressed against her temple.

She stood at the dining room door, her palm pressed to the satiny wood.

Haemas clasped her cold, white fingers together as old Pascar opened the massive door into the dining hall. Jarid turned his light eyes to her—eyes so much like, yet totally unlike her own. "Come in, cousin."

She glanced at the long table. "Where's Father?" Only Alyssa, her stepmother, and Jarid, her orphaned cousin, were waiting to eat.

What is this garbage! Dervlin's mind bellowed at her. *You know damn well I was there when you came in, late as usual!*

Something was wrong. Pascar moved quietly around the huge table, lighting the tall, twisted candles for the evening meal. Jarid's eyes followed him impatiently. "Out!" he demanded as the last flame took hold. Pascar dropped his brown chierra eyes and bowed, then closed the door behind him.

Haemas slid into her accustomed place. Jarid lounged back against the intricately carved wood of his chair and stretched his arms over his head like a carnivore limbering for the hunt. "You want to know where your father is, skivit?" He winked. "Why should you care? He's never had any use for you."

Alyssa's amused eyes gleamed over the hand she used to mask her smile.

But I was there, blast it, sitting next to that simpering excuse for a wife! Dervlin's irritation flooded through Haemas's helpless mind.

Haemas realized her own hands were clenched around the table's edge. With an effort, she dropped them back onto her legs. "I don't believe I'm hungry," she said faintly, holding her shields very tight so no sense of her unease would escape. "Please excuse me." Nodding to her step-mother, she began to rise.

"Not so fast, cousin." Steel rang in Jarid's arrogant voice.

Stop this nonsense! Dervlin ordered, but Haemas, caught in the unfolding memory, could only ride the current on through.

Without meaning to, she found she had dropped back into her seat.

"I have a little something for you." Jarid's sense of interest in her became stronger, sharpening into something closer to ownership. "Something that I trust you will not find unappealing."

Haemas tore her gaze away from Jarid's compelling, ice-pale eyes. "I want to go."

"Very well, then, skivit, by all means, go." His tone mocked her. "But first you must drink a toast with us."

Frozen, she watched as his steady hand poured deep-red tchallit wine into the green crystal goblets set before each place.

My best Nivan tchallit! The little bastard would never dare!

His sense of triumph was so strong that Haemas knew he was not even bothering to shield. Jarid handed one goblet to Alyssa and the next to Haemas, reserving the last for himself.

I was there, dammit! Dervlin's anger burned like a hot poker inside her head. *It did not happen that way! What are you trying to pull?*

The moment her hand closed around the slender green stem, Haemas knew with certainty that something was wrong with it. Her hand jerked away from the goblet as if it had burned her.

That—

Her hand jerked away from the goblet—

—never—

Her hand jer—

—happened!

Haemas felt herself flung into blackness as she shattered and pieces of herself spun away into emptiness . . . lost . . . nothing to hold on to . . .

* * *

Deep in the velvety darkness, a dream waited for her. Haemas looked up and realized that Pascar stood by the dining hall door.

His familiar old face wrinkled into a sympathetic smile. "Late again, my Lady?"

"Third time this week," she said, trying to catch her breath. "Have they started yet?"

Pascar reached out and twitched her collar down, then nodded. "I be feared so, my Lady."

Haemas smoothed down the fine flyaway hair around her face. Just let Alyssa guess she'd been running again and she would never hear the end of it. "All right, Pascar." She folded her hands.

The massive oak door swung back on its well-oiled hinges. "Decided to join us, have you, whelp?" Her father stuffed a chunk of roast savok into his mouth.

Alyssa shot her a sideways look out of large green-gold eyes, allowing a sly smile to steal across her red lips. *So kind of the child to drop in*, she confided to Dervlin without bothering to shield.

Haemas's face warmed. Not again, she chided herself. It only makes Alyssa worse when she knows she's upset you.

Pascar crossed the room and pulled out her chair. Not daring to look the old chierra servant in the face, Haemas slid into her place and unfolded her napkin.

Across from her, Alyssa cut her roast into precise, tiny bites, then speared one with her fork and chewed it thoughtfully. Pascar swept Haemas's plate up from the table and filled it from the steaming dishes at the sideboard. Then he lit the tall, twisted green candle before her place.

Haemas watched Alyssa's perfectly chiseled features through the wavering candle flame for a moment. Every movement her stepmother made, down to the last flick of her wrist, was so graceful that Haemas felt like an ummit every time she saw her.

"Not hungry, skivit?" Jarid stretched his arms behind his head and stared at her through slitted pale-gold eyes. "You know you have to keep your strength up for the big Testing."

Pascar picked up the stem of her green goblet, filling it

with sweet callyt wine. Dropping her gaze, Haemas buttered a piece of spicy, dark nutbread and took a bite. Why did Jarid always bring up her upcoming Testing? No Tal had ever failed.

Now, nephew. Alyssa smiled fondly at Jarid's high-cheekboned face. *Don't tease the child. You know how it upsets her.*

"Both of you, shut up!" Her father's fist crashed on the table, making the silverware clatter. "A man can't hear himself think with the two of you always babbling in his head!"

Alyssa wiped the corner of her mouth with the most delicate of gestures. "Please forgive me, Dervlin." She motioned at the servant. "Have some more of this excellent wine."

Dervlin stared moodily at the goblet in front of him as Pascar poured the amber wine, then snatched it up and downed half the contents with one swallow.

Jarid smiled thinly. "Yes, it is good, isn't it, Uncle?"

A heavy air of expectation ran through the room, making Haemas feel itchy and uncomfortable. She pushed the slice of roast savok first to one side of the etched Tal crest on her silver plate, then to the other. "I'm not very hungry tonight," she said finally. "Please excuse me."

Jarid rose and placed his hands flat on the table's gleaming surface. "You're not going anywhere!"

"It's no good!" Alyssa crumpled the napkin between her hands and threw it to the floor. "She didn't drink enough!"

"It doesn't matter." Leaving his place, her cousin paced around Alyssa's seat to peer into his uncle's face. "*He's* had plenty, and he was the only one that mattered."

Haemas could not take her eyes off her father sitting there, staring slack-jawed into his empty goblet. Alarmed, she scraped her chair back and stood up. "Father, are you all right?"

Sit down!

Without her meaning them to, her knees buckled. She sank back into the chair.

Now stay there. Jarid's sense of triumph rolled over her. *I'll deal with you later.*

Haemas's mouth was dry, and the room seemed to swirl

around her. The wine must have been laced with something—a drug? Haemas tried to watch her father. A dark form rustled near the sideboard. She glanced out of the corner of her eye; it was old Pascar, standing in the shadows.

"Well?" Alyssa abandoned her chair and slid her hand up Jarid's shoulder. Her voice was sharp. "Can you do it?"

"Stop whining and let me concentrate." Jarid shrugged her hand off, then reached for his uncle's brow, just under the fringe of gray hair. At his touch, the old man's eyelids fluttered; then he slumped heavily to the table.

Haemas tried to shout "Stop it!" but her voice came out in only a hoarse whisper. Gripping the chair so hard that her knuckles stood out, she levered herself up. "Leave him alone!" The walls whirled sickly around her.

Sweat beaded out on Jarid's forehead as he glanced at Alyssa through slitted eyes. "Will you—shut her up?"

What was Jarid trying to force him to do? Supporting herself with numb hands on the table edge, Haemas stumbled toward her father.

"And just what do you think you're going to do?" Alyssa reached across and shoved Haemas to the floor.

"No!" Dervlin's eyes forced themselves back open and he gasped for air. "Never! . . . Tal'ayn will . . . never go . . . to a Killian . . . bastard!"

"Think again, old man!" A vein bulged in Jarid's forehead as he leaned over the old man. "Acknowledge me as your heir or die, it's all the same to me. I'll just eliminate my poor backward cousin, whom no one will miss anyway, and then I'll be the only possible Tal left. Either way, I will have what I want."

Haemas pushed herself up to her knees and saw Pascar glide out of the shadows toward Jarid's back, holding something low to his side that reflected the candlelight.

Shoving Dervlin back against the chair, Jarid seized his hair and forced the lolling head up. "Cede Tal'ayn over to me! I am more of a Tal than that sniveling brat will ever be!"

The old man's eyes rolled sideways, looking up into Jarid's enraged face, and he laughed with a terrible chest-rasping wheeze. "You're nothing . . . but a . . . bloody Killian bas . . . tard. . . . The whole world knows . . . that!"

Then die, you old fool!

Feeling the strength of Jarid's gathering blow, Haemas threw her mind at his, knowing full well that she was no match for him. *No!* she cried, seeking to thrust herself between him and her father. *I won't let you!*

The room dissolved into a reddish-gray haze of pain as Jarid struck her down. She heard him laughing from someplace far away. "So the skivit has teeth? Who would have thought?" A booted toe prodded her ribs. "Don't be in such a bloody hurry. Your turn will come."

Through her pain, Haemas could still feel her father's drugged mind shielding weakly against her cousin, his life-force ebbing with each passing second.

"Will you hurry up?" Alyssa's voice demanded. "You said it would be easy!"

Haemas summoned the strength to open her eyes and blinked foggily up from the floor at the still forms of the two men, the young gilt-haired one and the old gray-haired one, as they wrestled, mind against mind. The air around them crawled with psionic energies.

Huddled next to the massive dining room door, Alyssa watched the struggle with overbright eyes, her hands knotted into the green silk of her skirt.

Haemas forced herself to her knees, then gasped as the room spun again, twisting her stomach into knots. Her father was straining now to resist, his reserve strength nearly burned away. An irregular black shadow appeared over Jarid's shoulder, and she squinted up at it, trying to make it out.

It was Pascar.

"Danih . . . should have let me feed you to the stream." Her father stiffened with pain. "I told . . ." His voice was only a whisper. "She . . . begged me . . . My fault . . . I gave . . . in."

Shut up, old man! Jarid's rage thundered through Haemas's mind.

She saw the gleam in Pascar's hand as it rose over Jarid's golden head, then flashed downward in the same instant that Alyssa's scream rang through the room. Her cousin looked up and redirected his mental attack to the old chierra servant.

The carving knife dropped from Pascar's hand and he crumpled to the floor, already dead as he fell.

"You fool!" Jarid turned to Alyssa. "Now the whole House will come!"

Haemas stretched out a hand and touched her father's cold cheek, feeling the small spark that still burned deep within his mind.

"Kill *her*, then!" Alyssa's normally well-bred voice came out in a screech. "Kill her before they come! What could they do but let you inherit?"

Jarid glanced down at Haemas and let a thin smile play across his lips. "No," he said, "I have something better in mind."

He leaned closer and twisted her wrist in a cruel grip. *Imagine that.* His triumph saturated her drug-weakened shields. *Killing your own father—whatever will the Council say?*

His jeering face faded into a white-hot haze of pain.

Chapter
Twenty-six

A voice drew her out of the beguiling blackness, comforting . . . familiar.

Haemas . . .

She let it guide her back to the sensations of her own body: a strong arm supporting her shoulders, the air cool against her face, the warm tracks of tears down her cheeks.

"That's better," the voice said beside her ear—still familiar, though spoken rather than thought.

Her eyes fluttered and she blinked up into Master Ellirt's worried face. He removed his palm from her forehead.

"It was Jarid who attacked my father," Haemas whispered, the ugly scene fresh in her memory now. "And Pascar who saved him." Guilt washed over her. It had been old Pascar who had lain pale and dead at her feet all this time, Pascar who had given his life to save her father—as she should have done.

Dervlin Tal grimaced and turned away, his eyes bleak.

Ellirt braced her so she could sit up. "What of Jarid Tal Ketral?" he asked the onlookers in a businesslike tone. "Is he here?"

Her father glanced over to Alyssa's drained face. "Well? Where is he?"

Her stepmother's small fingers knotted together. "You can't possibly believe her!" She backed away, her chin quivering, her green-gold eyes wide with shock.

Seizing her wrist, Dervlin stared down at her colorless face. "Where is this damn Killian *bavval* I've been fostering all these years?"

"I don't know where he went!" Tears spilled down her face as she tried to pull away from him. "He wouldn't tell me!"

The pale-eyed man who had earlier claimed a contract for Haemas stepped forward. "He's attending the Temporal Transference Conclave at Senn'ayn this morning in your place."

"That's impossible!" Dervlin thrust Alyssa roughly into a pair of gaping chierra musicians and glared at the other man. "They wouldn't dare replace me with that Houseless bastard!"

"They already have." A faint amusement glimmered in the man's cool amber eyes. "It's a well-known fact that the Lord of Tal'ayn has not been the same since his— accident."

Temporal Transference? Haemas blanched. Jarid was involved with the timelines, too? She leaned her forehead against her knees, still dizzy, and worried. The priest, her father, Master Ellirt, Alyssa, the strange pale-eyed man— none of them would exist much longer if the conclave at Senn'ayn penetrated the timeways again, but . . .

She tried to swallow around the icy lump in her throat. Jarid had nearly killed both her and her father, then played with her memory as if she were nothing more than a servant girl. He'd bested her at every turn. What would he do to her now if she followed him to Senn'ayn and tried to stop the conclave?

You don't have to do that. Master Ellirt's thought reached out to her, warm and comforting. *We'll alert the Council members at Senn'ayn. That should end the Conclave for today, and they can take the young wretch into custody there.*

But across the courtyard, the faint musical hum from the crystals sharpened and Haemas's head snapped up. It was too late—they were starting again! Struggling to her feet, she stumbled down the steps and fought through the baffled onlookers. The air rasped through her lungs and black dots danced behind her eyes as she tried to reach the portal before the vibrations distorted beyond use.

As she stepped into the open housing, she glanced back at the Naming stand. Everyone was watching her, astonishment written on their faces. Only one figure moved—a small, shapely woman wearing a white gown embroidered with silver, advancing toward Dervlin Tal's unprotected back with a glittering koral-hafted dagger clasped in both hands.

Father! Haemas reached for her father's mind, but the dissonance climbed another note and it was impossible to focus her mental cry. Any second now it would be too late to transfer and then everything would be lost. She closed her eyes, throwing what strength she had left into one more frantic attempt. *Father! Look behind you—Alyssa!*

Dervlin Tal stiffened, then turned around as the knife descended, flashing in the sunlight.

Heart pounding, Haemas concentrated, altering the vibrations to shift her to the portal at Senn'ayn. The familiar tingle washed through her, then faded, while the terrible crystalline dissonance remained.

She swayed and caught herself against the black grillwork of the Senn'ayn portal.

This time, Jarid promised himself, he would master the secrets of temporal travel. Despite the indifference and disdain of his uncle and everyone else, he would become the most powerful man among the great Houses, the Highlands—perhaps even all of Desalaya.

Lord Senn rapped his knuckle on the satiny dark-red wood of the table. "Brothers." His silver eyebrows arched. "It's time to try again."

The small groups of men sitting and standing around the library drifted back to the oblong table. Jarid slid back into his place at Senn's left, his eyes on the box of Old oak and its seven perfect crystals.

Senn laid his hands reverently on the carved container and looked at Jarid. "This time we will manage enough power to send you to a place of your own choosing. I'm sure of it." Removing the lid, he cradled each pale-blue crystal in his lined palm, then passed it down the table to be laid in the precise pattern. When the last one was positioned, he drew himself up, his gray-gold eyes confident. "Now, brothers, we will remake our own history."

Each member in the power relay threw his mind open to the crystals, matching the strangely pitched frequencies they emitted in this pattern. Jarid lowered his shields, drawing the power into his mind like a whirlpool. Already the faint, telltale blue shimmer radiated outward from the crystals. If the Council's theory was correct, the times and places available for transference depended on the person at the focus. He should be able to choose.

It was the future he wanted to see—what would become of him and Tal'ayn and even that mindless bauble, Alyssa. Pushing back his chair, he stood, the vibrations shrilling through his mind. Sweat beaded on his forehead as he struggled to shunt the rising pain aside and concentrate, seeking the line that would take him into tomorrow. Then he caught a mist-shrouded glimpse of the twin crags of Tal'ayn and the arching bridge between them. In all the Highlands and Lowlands put together, no other structure matched them.

Behind the gray stone, the setting sun was painting the sky a brilliant red-orange. And at the foot of the holdings he could see a mature orchard—no doubt his Old apple grove, planted just these few weeks past!

Straining to channel the psionic energies, he set one foot on the blue line that led to that scene, then another.

The Senn'ayn servants in their gaudy red-and-black livery gaped at Haemas as she ran through the House, but the color of her hair and eyes guaranteed her passage. The crystals' agony drew her upward through the branching halls. Her breath was coming in shallow, chest-straining gasps when she pounded past a massive door attended by a single liveried servant. The middle-aged man gave her a startled glance with his dark chierra eyes as she passed.

Then she realized the dissonant thread had eased slightly; the conclave must be in progress inside that room. She turned and went back, gasping for air, her weary feet sinking into the plush rug.

The servant blocked the door. "I am sorry, Lady, but the old Lord himself bid me let none pass until he called."

The overstressed crystals shrieked through Haemas's mind, making it hard to hear anything else. She pressed her fingertips against her throbbing temples and tried to shut them out. "You must let me in! They're all going to die!"

The servant's square chin lifted. "I has my orders. No one gets into this room without Lord Senn's say so."

Haemas reached for the door latch, but he seized her arms in his large-knuckled hands and pushed her firmly back. Inside the locked room, she could feel the crystals' painful crescendo climbing higher and higher. Her head spun, and she stared at the man in frustration. He was too big; she'd never get past him, unless—

She closed her slim fingers around his wrist and at the same time reached for his unshielded mind. *You must let me pass. Lord Senn is calling for me. Can't you hear him?*

His brown eyes widened. "Begging your pardon, your Ladyship!" His heavy face went red as he fumbled at his belt for the key. "I swear I didn't hear him before!"

The door swung open, and the man flinched back from the hellish, coruscating blue energies as Haemas shoved past him. None of the straining, pain-lined faces at the table gave any sign they were aware of her; they had all turned inward, concentrating their psionic energies into a single source, from which someone was powering an attempt to broach the time pathways. Jarid was nowhere to be seen.

This close to the power relay, unrelenting pain burned along her nerves, a demanding, hungry thing, and she could feel the violence of the maelstrom. It was very near this timeline now, overclose. She caught sight of a tall back disappearing into the shimmering blue mist at the end of one writhing line. She saw the crystals on the table and started to remove one, but realized that if she broke the pattern, she would just trap the dissonant energies within the timelines. The only answer was to force him out before the maelstrom took them all—even though that man must be Jarid.

She struggled to follow him as the line swerved before her, then whipped back across the room. She heard her own breathing, harsh and irregular, as she managed one step, then a second. She squinted desperately against the eye-searing glow, then finally found the line and took the third and last step.

The blueness under her bare feet faded into the stringy yellow of winter-blasted grass, and the frost-laden air took her breath away. She blinked up at the red-orange glow of the setting sun. Ahead of her rose the twin crags of Tal'ayn,

black against the brilliant sunset. Inside her head, the
stressed crystals still shrieked their agonized song.

"No!" An anguished cry rose from the low path leading
to Tal'ayn just below the rocky bluff where Haemas stood.
Dropping to her knees, she looked down and saw two figures leave the house. A man with bright-golden hair ate up
the path with long, purposeful strides. A slighter figure, the
same shade of gold in her hair, rushed after him. "Please,
no!" She caught up and clawed at his arm.

The man, carrying something wrapped in a blanket, elbowed her away. "Go back to the house!"

The voice froze Haemas's nerves; it was her father as a
much younger man. But what was he doing, and where was
Jarid? Turning around, she hurriedly picked her way down
the rocky path to the rolling plain below. If these two were
here, then surely Jarid was close by.

"Dervlin, you can say he's *yours*!" the woman cried.
"Anyah is ready to swear it!"

Haemas flattened herself against the gray rock as the pair
passed just below her and entered a callyt orchard, now
leafless in early winter. Then she hurried after them.

"I won't pass a Houseless bastard off as my own son!"
The bitter wind whipped her father's angry voice back to
her.

"Then I'll take him." Defeat colored the woman's voice.
"We'll go away. No one will ever know."

They sounded much nearer. Haemas thought they must
have stopped, but there was still no sign of Jarid. Pain skit-
tered along her nerves with the effort of walking this When;
it hurt to breathe, to hear, even to see. How long could
Jarid remain here before everything disrupted?

"*I'll* know!" Her father's voice was grim. "Go back to
the house, Danih, and stay in your room. I'll deal with you
and that Killian son of a bitch later."

The thin wail of a baby split the air. Haemas peered
through the spiny brown branches, trying to see.

"I won't let you!" The woman's voice had a shrill, desperate edge to it.

"Damn you, get out of the way! You should have
thought about this before you dishonored your husband and
your family!"

The baby's crying rose another octave.

"And what were *you* thinking of when you gave me to Ersal Ketral?" the woman flung back. "You had to know what a filthy beast he was!"

"You just weren't enough of a woman for him!"

Haemas crept closer through the stiff, dry grass, using the trees for cover. At the edge of the orchard, her father and the unfamiliar woman struggled over the wailing, blanket-swathed bundle in his arms. Just beyond them ran the mountain-fed stream that supplied Tal'ayn, glimmering red-orange under the last rays of the setting sun.

Hair spilled over the woman's shoulders like molten gold as she fought for the child. Haemas remembered the old stories Jayna had told her down in the kitchens without her father's knowledge—Danih had been her father's sister, now long dead.

Her aunt—and Jarid's mother.

"Dervlin, you can't!" Danih threw her body over the child and clasped it convulsively to her breast. "You know the law! He's Kashi! With both Tal and Killian blood, he's bound to be strongly Talented! Give him to the Brothers at Shael'donn, if you must!"

"I'll give the little bastard to the *lraels*!"

At that Haemas glanced up through the winter-bare limbs and saw the scavenging flyers already circling overhead, their leathery black wings slicing through the crisp air.

A twig snapped to her left. She reached out with her mind and met Jarid's white-hot anger. Recoiling, she clung to a tree trunk for support.

"As our mother should have given *you*, then!" Danih spat, turning smoldering golden eyes up to Dervlin.

Haemas could feel her father's stunned surprise.

"Have you ever wondered why she had no place for you in her heart—you, the only living son she ever bore?" Danih fixed Dervlin with a flinty stare. "The truth is she bore *no* living son, and you were always indelible proof of that sorrow."

Dervlin's hands slipped from the child and he half fell to the dead grass, his face gone white. "You lie!" His voice was a hoarse whisper.

"Does the name of Enya Falt mean anything to you?"

Danih lay her cheek against the sobbing child's face.
"When Mother couldn't provide an heir, Father generated
one down in the Lowlands, then brought you home for her
to raise. 'Not even from a Highlands House,' as she used
to say."

Dervlin Tal sat in numb silence as his sister regained her
feet, cradling the babe. She arranged the blanket around the
wailing child's red face and looked back at her brother, radiating contempt. Then she turned toward Tal'ayn.

"Don't think this is finished, Danih!" Dervlin flung after
her rigid back. "I'll see you pay for the dishonor you've
brought upon this House!"

Haemas heard crashing in the knee-high grass, then saw
Jarid rushing toward the lone figure at the stream.

Jarid! she called to him before realizing.

He stopped and glanced over his shoulder. Shock crossed
his face; then his lip curled back in a sneer. "Well, if it isn't
the skivit. I didn't know the Darkness gave up its dead that
easily." He looked around and clenched his sweaty fists.
"Although that scene could have passed for Darkness itself."

The shrilling vibrations redoubled, and Haemas realized
it was his nearness. Fighting the pain, she forced herself to
move closer. "We have to leave before—"

The same agony was mirrored in his high-cheekboned
face. "If I can't kill him in my own time, at least I can do
away with the son of a bitch here!"

"It won't make any difference!" Haemas clenched her
hands, fighting to make her lungs breathe, to keep from
crumpling to her knees. Pain sang through every cell in her
body. "Nothing will change!"

Jarid wavered on his long legs, then laughed hoarsely.
"Just think. If I kill him in this time frame, you'll never
even be born!"

The dissonance hammered through Haemas's head. "It
may not have even happened this way! This may only be
an Otherwhen." She swallowed hard, blinking at the dark-
blue mist thickening in front of her eyes. "And if you in-
tervene, this will only shift into an Otherwhen. You can't
change what has already happened!"

Jarid put one hand to his head, his face ashen, his forehead furrowed. She could feel him trying to fight off the frightful buildup of dissonant energies. "Watch me!" he snarled, then staggered through the leafless trees toward the stream.

The younger version of Dervlin Tal stood on the bank, trim and fit as the father she knew had not been for many years. He watched them with narrowed suspicious eyes. "Who are you? Why are you sniffing around my land?"

The air was growing dense and increasingly difficult to breathe. Haemas forced her rubbery legs after her tall cousin. Electric blueness whipped through the space around her, and the ground seemed to writhe beneath her bare feet. *Jarid!* she called. *You must come away now!*

Ahead of her, Jarid's tall form stumbled against a tree, then recovered. How could he bear the dissonance? Another few seconds of the head-splitting pain and she herself would be beyond caring how this affair ended.

Jarid closed with her father on the bank of the stream. For a second, the two men hung there together, outlined black against the orange-red of the setting sun. Haemas saw Jarid's hands clench around her father's neck; then a burst of mental energy dazzled her even where she stood, yards away, and Jarid sagged heavily into the yellow grass.

Dervlin Tal watched with bemused eyes as she wrenched at Jarid's limp arm. As she touched him, the dissonance increased, a thousand out-of-tune lute strings screeching inside her head.

"Get up!" she shouted at him through numb lips. "We have to go back!"

Jarid blinked at her, confusion written in his face. Then he managed to stumble onto his feet and swayed against her, fighting the pain. She took a step forward, trying to align herself with the line enough to go back. Jarid started to follow, then slumped against her shoulder, his pale eyes rolling back in his head. The whirling blueness around them darkened, obscuring the stream, Tal'ayn, and her father.

"Try!" she screamed at Jarid, her fingers digging into the arm she'd looped across her shoulders. "You have to try! I can't take you by myself!"

Even as she said it, she knew he could not. His mind had

been weakened from the effort of coming here and the dissonance, and then dazed by the stunning blow he'd received from Dervlin. Even his shields were down.

The increasing blue darkness roared in her ears as they hung there together. Then the reality finally penetrated her conscious mind: His shields were down. *She* could shield *him*.

Closing her eyes, she concentrated on wrapping around his mind as Summerstone had shown her. Nothing of his disrupting energies must escape. She stepped forward again and he stumbled after her. Danih's angry face floated through her mind. *If it were not for me*, Haemas found herself thinking, *she would still live*.

But that wasn't right; she'd been born years later. That was Jarid's thought. Haemas shook her head, then dragged the dead weight of her cousin another step forward. Had the roaring lessened? She was afraid to drop her shields and find out.

Anger . . . sorrow . . . rage . . . Emotions burned through her like white-hot pokers. *What right had those smug old men to keep him, a Tal, from his rightful place as heir of Tal'ayn?*

She recoiled from the violence of his mind. Her shields slipped and the dissonance around them was so great she feared that they would both be ripped apart. Drawing his hurtful, seething mind close again, she thickened her shields and tried to summon strength for a final step.

Hatred raced snarling through her mind, hatred of her Killian blood and her pale eyes, so like his . . . loathing for himself because of what he was and what he could never be . . . and above all, greed for Tal'ayn, her birthright, the one thing they would never let him have.

She embraced his hateful, scalding mind, then managed one more step and fell to her knees. His body slipped from her exhausted arms and flopped to the floor.

For a terrifying moment, she huddled there, shields locked, fearful that when she looked up, there would be nothing but the awful yawning blue maelstrom.

A hand touched her shoulder. Taking a shallow breath, she opened her eyes and looked up into the dark-brown eyes of the chierra servant.

Chapter
Twenty-seven

Dervlin Tal's impatient strides burst through the anxious, whispering knots of servants and endless Senn mothers, cousins, wives, and daughters gathered in the halls of Senn'ayn. They scattered out of his way, then stared after him with wide, worried eyes. Lord High Master Ellirt puffed in an effort to keep up. "The healer said you should rest," he repeated to Tal's back.

"Damn healers don't know nearly as much as they think they do!" Tal snapped without slowing. "It's just a scratch!"

Ellirt sighed and followed him around a corner. The so-called scratch from Alyssa's blade seemed rather more like a gash to him. And even though Healer Ekran, who had been representing the Healer's Guild at the ceremony, had tended the wound after Alyssa had been subdued, Tal had refused to wait long enough for him to do any real healing. Now Ellirt sensed the seeping warmth of blood beneath the thick shoulder bandage.

The word from Healer Alimn was that she was all right, he said to Dervlin. *I don't think we really need run.*

Silence descended between them like a closed door. Very well, Ellirt thought, shut everyone out. Why should things be any different from the way they had always been?

Tal's carpet-muffled steps swerved into an open doorway. A dozen strides behind, Ellirt cast his mind ahead: Haemas was in that room, and Jarid Tal Ketral, as well as others, and many of them had fared badly.

Ellirt followed him into the large library and picked his way through the shocked onlookers. The air was thick with the smell of heated metal and the stench of burned flesh. He halted at a long table where Birtal Senn's head rested on outstretched arms. The palms of his upturned hands were

scorched. Ellirt touched the man's temple with his fingertips; nothing remained of the old friend of his long-ago
childhood but an empty husk.

Several more men seated around the long table radiated
pain and fear and confusion. Ellirt placed his hand on the
sleeve of Kimbrel Killian, one of his former students, and
reached out with his mindsenses to assess the damage. The
young man flinched, and, through his tattered shields, Ellirt
glimpsed the raw agony that had seared his mind. Overload
burn. He withdrew, shuddering.

The man next to Kimbrel slumped in his chair, his head
lolling to the right, his sightless eyes staring at the ceiling.
It was one of the older Sennays, Ellirt wasn't sure which.
He shook his head, appalled at the waste of lives.

"Get up!" Dervlin Tal's voice, shrill with anger, rose
above the muffled confusion in the room. "Get off the
damned floor and face me like a man!"

Ellirt made his way to the corner where Jarid Ketral
sprawled on his back across the thick-piled rug with the
Senn healer kneeling at his side. His eyes were closed and
his raspy breathing was shallow.

"You made him what he is!" Haemas Tal pushed between her father and her unconscious cousin. "Now leave
him alone. He'll pay for what he's done, but if you had
ever given him one moment of understanding—or even
respect—we might not be here like this."

Ellirt could feel the frightening fury boiling through Tal's
mind. *Not now.* He gripped the other man's shoulder. *And
not here. This should be resolved between the two of you in
private.*

Petar Alimn, the Senn healer, straightened and rubbed his
forehead wearily. "I've done what I can for the moment,
but he's very weak. He will need rest and constant looking
after for a few days. I can arrange for care here at
Senn'ayn."

Ellirt drew the healer aside. "The Council will want to
question him when he has recovered," he said in a low
voice. "See that a guard is kept on his door round the
clock—a *Kashi* guard."

The healer nodded and motioned to a pair of chierra servants waiting with a litter. "Take this one up to a guest bed-

room. I'll be there in a few minutes." He crossed the room to Kimbrel Killian's side.

Haemas retreated as the servants moved in with the litter, then clutched a chair as her knees buckled.

Tal reached for her arm. "You're coming back to Tal'ayn with me." His voice was brusque. "We'll discuss this later."

The girl jerked away from his touch, her head held high. "I think not."

"You will come home and behave like a proper daughter for a change!" His anger lashed out like a whip.

Ellirt sensed that the girl's energy reserves were almost gone. He moved quickly to her side. "The Council will also have a number of questions for the Lady Haemas. If she wishes, she can go back with me to Shael'donn until Senn'ayn selects a new representative and a quorum can be seated for the inquiry."

Go home and see to your wife, Dervlin, he added. *I'm afraid Alyssa will have much to answer for, as well.*

A tremor passed through Tal's body. Then he turned and stalked out of the room, his shoulders rigid.

Haemas waited until he was gone, then sank bonelessly into the nearest chair and buried her face in her hands. Her breath came in long, shuddering gasps. From behind, Ellirt laid a monitoring hand across her forehead; her skin was cold and clammy, and in her mind he felt a dark, spinning exhaustion, threatening to pull her down into unconsciousness.

"It's all right," he murmured. "Let go now. You're safe, and everything will sort itself out." With a sigh, she sagged back against him, close to collapse.

Supporting her shoulders, Ellirt motioned to the nearest servant. "Bring the Lady Haemas some keiria tea," he said, "and make it strong." The servant bowed and dashed out the door.

He took her icy fingers in his, trying to lend her his strength. How had she even survived? Somehow she had managed to channel psionic energies at levels that had killed half the grown men in this room and incapacitated the rest—all of them men who had received the best training the Highlands had to offer.

At his side, a pair of servants loaded Senn's lifeless body

on another litter and crossed his limp arms over the motionless chest. Such a waste, Ellirt thought—and for what? What good could any of this possibly have done the Kashi Houses?

Jarid Tal Ketral's pale eyes stared straight ahead as two sturdy Rald younger sons, armed with brightly polished swords and daggers, led him before the Council of Twelve. An air of nervous anticipation rippled through the assembled spectators, both male and female, drawn from every High House in the Highlands. Arranged around the clerestory ledge of the circular chamber, twelve fluted urns of mind-conjured chispa-fire cast a sickly blue pallor across the prisoner's face. His eyes were fever-bright, his skin almost translucent. The Ralds positioned him before the Council's dais, then stationed themselves at the door.

Seated between Kevisson Monmart and Master Ellirt in the back, Haemas shifted restlessly. Jarid had haunted her whole life, poisoned her relationship with her father, and tried to kill her, yet she remembered his raging despair when she'd enclosed his mind with hers and found their thoughts mingling; in that searing moment she had seen, beneath all the hatred and anger, the most miserable soul she had ever known.

Dervlin Kentnal Tal led the High Lords into the chamber and assumed his place at the center of the half-circle, his mouth thin and determined. "Brothers, today we must pass judgment on this Kashi who comes before us."

The remaining eleven heads, ranging in hue from white to the purest shade of gold, nodded. Haemas noted how Aaren Killian lounged back, his elbows braced on the arms of his ornate leather-upholstered chair, and gazed at Jarid over locked fingers. This was as much his fault as anyone's, she thought. Jarid might have had a chance if Killian had acknowledged him as his son and raised him at Killian'ayn. She closed her eyes, seeing Danih's agonized face as she fought for the despised, wailing child cradled in her arms.

"You know from my own testimony, and that of the Lady Haemas, that Jarid Tal Ketral has violated every vow given at his Naming." Tal's intense golden gaze swept the room. "And he professes no repentance concerning his crimes."

A savage smile flashed across Jarid's haggard face.

"Will any here speak for him before sentence is pronounced?" Tal looked to the man seated at the far right end of the half circle. The Lord of Chee'ayn shook his head. Tal turned to the next in line.

One by one, each High Lord shook his head.

Lastly, Tal looked to the Lord of Killian'ayn, who spread his hands on the shining oak. Then Killian's fingers knotted into fists and his head gave a tight, nearly imperceptible shake.

"Through the consensus of the Council, then, I must pronounce the maximum sentence allowable, short of execution." Dervlin Tal squared his shoulders. "It is our decision that Jarid Tal Ketral have his mindsenses burned out, then be remanded to the Lowlands to work the remainder of his natural life at hard labor."

A hint of amusement leaked from Jarid's mind. *I'll see you in Darkness first, old man!*

The onlookers gasped as Jarid flung a bolt of psi energy with murderous intensity at the two Ralds by the door. The pair staggered, then wilted to the floor without a sound.

On her feet and shoving through the startled crowd without even thinking, Haemas headed toward the dais. She felt the energy disperse about the chamber, the backwash prickling through her mind.

Dervlin Tal stumbled to his feet as Jarid turned back to him. Her mind screamed at Jarid. *No!*

She could feel Jarid's concentration as he summoned what strength he had left after that first stunning blow. Haemas pushed through the final row of white-faced spectators gaping at the prisoner.

Coward! she flung at Jarid. *It's me that you want to kill! It's always been me! Take me!*

Dream-slow, he turned in a half crouch to face her, his high-cheekboned Tal face ablaze with hatred. *You would have been next, cousin.* The blue chispa-lights danced in his eyes. *But if you can't wait your turn—*

The buildup of energy in his mind was blinding. Fear knotted Haemas's stomach. He would never be able to channel so much, and she would never be able to shield against it. Sweat ran freely down her face as she stood before him, paralyzed by fear. It wasn't fair, she thought, staring into Jarid's feral eyes. He was going to win after all.

He always won.

She recalled Summerstone's words: *Fear is but a sister whispering in your ear to keep you from harm.*

She closed her eyes and took a deep breath, remembering the hard-won knowledge she'd acquired fighting her fears. Fear was meant to guide, not control.

Jarid laughed. *Now, skivit,* his mental voice hissed at her, *shall we settle the inheritance of Tal'ayn once and for all?*

Think not of fearing, Summerstone's voice spoke in her memory. *Think of living.*

Haemas suddenly became aware of the sweet edge of crystalline vibration that always sang below the level of ordinary perception. She dropped her shields and wrenched her mind into alignment with the courtyard portal crystals, darting down the first blue line that appeared to her.

In the middle of the room, Jarid flung his bolt, then stared fixedly at the spot where she had stood. He hesitated, puzzlement written on his face, then doubled over and collapsed to the floor.

Haemas retraced her steps and closed off her awareness of the ilsera vibrations. The people closest to her started and stared.

"There she is!" someone cried.

Haemas glanced around the room. Several Lords were kneeling beside the Ralds, but everyone else was looking at her. Jarid's still body sprawled in the middle of the Council's half circle.

"It's all right," a male voice whispered in her ear. She whirled and looked into the concerned face of Master Ellirt. "He collapsed after you disappeared." He shook his head. "Nice trick, that. Probably saved your father."

She swallowed hard. "Will he . . . ?"

"I don't know, child." He took her arm. "There's the healer. You must ask him."

Haemas let the old master guide her back to Jarid, where a man dressed in healer's black knelt at his side. Her cousin's eyes were closed and a sheen of perspiration covered his waxen face.

The healer's brow was furrowed as he concentrated, one hand resting on the fallen man's forehead. After several minutes, he shook his head and stood.

Haemas forced the words out. "Will he live?"

Before the healer could speak, Jarid's pale eyes, so like hers, slitted open. "Stupid—skivit." His voice was only a hoarse whisper. "Can't—you get any—thing right?" Then his eyes closed and his head rolled limply to the side.

The healer touched her shoulder. "He was still weak from the accident at the Temporal Conclave. The energy he drew for even the first blow was too great. The second only speeded his inevitable death."

Haemas gazed down at Jarid's colorless, empty face. He looked more like a little boy now than a full-grown Kashi warrior.

The healer gazed down at the body. "He must have known this would happen."

The memory of her time in the Lowlands flashed through her mind: those terrifying days when she had been both head-blind and head-deaf from her struggle to save her father. She remembered the terrible claustrophobia of being locked inside her own head without control of what power remained, a danger to herself and others. No doubt the healer was right; Jarid had known what would happen. She would rather be dead herself than return to that half-alive state.

Master Ellirt laid a warm hand on her arm. She let him lead her away from the sorrows buried in that room.

Speaking in low whispers, the crowd of Kashi men and women drew aside as she and the blind Master of Shael'donn passed.

Dervlin opened the door of Master Ellirt's study when his daughter knocked. Her pale-gold eyes studied him with cool indifference. He met her gaze, then turned away and gestured at the table where Aaren Killian waited to work out the details of the coming matrimonial.

She brushed past him. "I have no intention of fulfilling the contract."

Dervlin saw Killian smile from the opposite side of the table, then felt anger burn through his veins. "You have no say in the matter! It is a father's duty to contract his children's marriages."

Haemas crossed to the window and gazed down onto the Shael'donn grounds. She wore shimmering green today in the casual style she had always preferred, over his objections: a long, loose tunic over soft flowing pants, in sharp contrast to the more formal gowns Alyssa affected. The sunlight transformed her waist-length hair to a mass of spun white gold. A pang knifed through him. He had known that hair in another, happier life, and that high-cheekboned profile. She was Anyah, her long-dead mother, all over again. When had she found the time to grow so tall or graceful? He couldn't think how it had happened.

His throat was suddenly dry. "A child owes obedience to her parent!"

Aaren Killian's mouth tightened. "And how will you make her obey?" He pushed away from the small table and stood, pulling black leather gloves out of his belt. "Killian'ayn renounces the contract, Tal. I'll have a list of the amounts and goods you owe me by tomorrow."

Dervlin stared at the younger man for a moment, stunned by the loss of face implied if he could not force this through. Would he even be able to hold on to his leadership in the Council? "Give me a few days," he said. "I suppose she's had a bad time, but she'll get over it."

"A bad time?" Killian threw back his head and laughed. "You could call it that." He studied Haemas's slender form. "Even so, I could almost be tempted. Killian strength seems to have bred true in this one, and she carries herself well. She and Kimbrel would have made a good cross."

Dervlin pushed his chair away from the table, wincing at the twinge from his shoulder wound. "Then wait. She'll come around!"

Killian shook his head. "She's been touched by the ilseri. How would Kimbrel keep her at home?"

Dervlin watched him go. The bastard was right. Who would want an unNamed, disobedient girl who consorted with ilseri—no better than animals, in his opinion—and who could apparently just disappear into Darkness-knew-where any time she damn well pleased?

"I hope you're satisfied!" He whirled on his daughter as the door closed behind Killian's back. "No House will have you now!"

"I don't intend to marry." She spread her fingers in the golden light streaming in through the window. "Master Ellirt said I may remain here at Shael'donn and study."

"Shael'donn takes no females!"

"Go home, Father." Her voice was low. "You have Tal'ayn to see after, as well as Alyssa."

"Alyssa Alimn Senn is no longer Lady of my House!"

Haemas turned her pale-gold eyes to him, and a shiver of fear ran up his spine. Those were Anyah's eyes, he thought numbly. How had this child come to look at him with Anyah's calm, indifferent moonlight eyes?

"Alyssa should be your penance." The reflected sunlight danced orange-gold in his daughter's eyes. "If you could give her the forgiveness you have never given anyone, not even yourself, then perhaps you would finally be able to find some peace."

"Stuff and nonsense!" His hands closed over the carved wooden arms of his chair. "I don't know what you're talking about."

"No," she said, turning her gaze back to the window, "and I don't suppose you ever will."

He sat there for a dozen breaths, wanting to know what she meant almost badly enough to ask. In the hearth, the fire hissed; then the logs shifted, settling into the ashes.

He rose and walked to the door of Ellirt's study, overwhelmed by frustration and anger. "Don't think that this is over yet!" He put his hand on the knob. "We'll see what the rest of the Council has to say!"

Epilogue

Kevisson Monmart's hand steadied Haemas's shoulder as they moved through alternating strips of sunlight and shadow under the lattice-covered walkway. She glanced up at his expectant face, then hesitated when they reached the edge of the Shael'donn courtyard. Rain had fallen during the night, but now the sun shone down bright and strong, making the scattered puddles glitter with a rainbow intensity. Lyrdriat's pale gold wafer rode high in the eastern sky, almost translucent in the strong sunlight.

The entire complement of Shael'donn's Andiine Brothers and Masters waited in the middle of the courtyard in neat rows—Master Ellirt's doing. Classes had been dismissed for the morning so the staff could assemble for her Testing. She knew it was intended as an honor, but she hung back, skittish and uncomfortable.

Kevisson bent close to her ear. "Forget about them." He squeezed her shoulder. "Master Ellirt is just trying to make a point. He wants witnesses who will testify that you belong here with us."

Haemas drew a deep breath, remembering her struggle down in the Lowland forest, where it had taken all the strength she could summon simply not to burn both herself and Kevisson into cinders with her out-of-control abilities. "It's—too soon. I'm not ready for this."

If you're not, then I don't know who is. Besides, we're measuring potential today, not training, he said into her mind, and his confident warmth cheered her. He looped his arm through hers and escorted her across the wet cobblestones to face Master Ellirt.

The Lord High Master was robed in traditional white with a gold-embroidered stole of a deep maroon around his

263

neck. "It's all right," he said softly. "I haven't lost a candidate yet."

She lowered her head. "What—do I have to do?"

"Close your eyes." He reached out and unerringly passed his hand over her face as her eyelids descended.

How did he manage that without sight? She took a deep, centering breath and tried to relax.

I'll show you someday. His mental tone was touched with amusement.

She felt his hands on her shoulders, warm and familiar. *Open your shields and let me find the way. I'm an old hand at this.*

Haemas let her shields dissolve, knowing she was safe with him. She felt the whisper of his mind against hers, and then a dark-green coolness carried her away from the warm sun beating down on her face, the dankness of wet stone, the pressure of his hands. The coolness became a green-black river that picked up speed until it was roaring, bearing her faster and faster toward something she couldn't even imagine.

A faint light glimmered ahead in the darkness, intensifying rapidly until it was a searing, silver-green brightness that burned everything dross and unnecessary away—all her fears and anxieties, doubts, needs. There was only the overpowering Light and its comforting warmth. She felt indescribable joy in that timeless second as she and it merged into an exquisite blending of cool green fire and self.

As the searing glare faded from her mind, she wavered on the balls of her feet, dizzy, unable to think of where she was or what she was supposed to be doing. She pried her eyes open and blinked in the golden morning sunlight.

Kevisson steadied her with a hand on her arm. "By the Blessed Light, I've never seen anyone go that far before!"

Lord High Master Ellirt dragged a sleeve back across his sweaty forehead. "Well, the next time the Council wants someone of this magnitude Tested, they can bloody well do it themselves!"

The Test. Suddenly remembering, she looked anxiously at the waiting faces of the Andiine Masters and Brothers. Had she passed?

Ellirt winked a sightless eye at her. "I think that we can

safely say your level of Talent will be acceptable." He turned to Kevisson. "Do you agree, Searcher?"

"Plus-Eleven ..." Kevisson seemed to consider, his face solemn. "I suppose it will have to do." Then he extended his hand, revealing a black obsidian ring in his palm.

She reached out and took the familiar circlet of carved stone between her fingers.

"Lord Senn gave it to me when he authorized the Search," Kevisson said.

Haemas pressed the birth ring between her palms. The memory of Anyah's smile flashed through her mind and brought a sudden tingling warmth against her skin.

Master Ellirt nodded. "And as you have now *finally* been Tested and certified to possess Talent of a high degree, you qualify for membership among the Kashi'an, the People of the Light. In coming forward to be Named, you are required to leave the days of childhood behind you. Now, before these witnesses, will you Name yourself and enter adulthood?"

Lifting her face into the streaming sunlight, Haemas began to speak, but then a faint crystalline hum edged its way into her consciousness. Startled, she glanced at the simple Shael'donn portal of native spine-wood and saw the telltale glimmer of blue.

A sharp black nose emerged from the blue mist, followed by the lithe, velvet-black body of a full-grown silsha.

Small sister.

"Summerstone!" Haemas glanced around the courtyard for the source of the words, but neither of the ilseri were visible.

It is the custom of your people to take a name on this day so that all may know you.

Haemas dropped to one knee as the silsha bounded across the courtyard to butt its huge head against her chest.

You are sister to the ilseri now. We wish to give you a name in token of that sisterhood.

The pale gold of Lyrdriat seeped through Haemas's mind. *We name you—Moonspeaker, our sister who shall speak for the ilseri among your kind.*

Resting her hand on the silsha's silken head, Haemas

looked up into Master Ellirt's wary face. "The ilseri also wish to give me a name."

"Oh—yes, the Old People." The corners of his mouth quirked upward. *I just hope you realize how livid the Council is already over the thought that their wives and daughters might learn to transfer across time while you insist none of the men ever will. Well, get on with it. We'll taste that bread after it's been baked.*

She smoothed the white bodice of her Naming gown. "I Name myself among the Kashi, Haemas of Shael'donn, and among my ilseri sisters I take the name of Moonspeaker."

The silsha growled contentedly, low in its throat.

Master Ellirt shook his head. *And now I suppose this—beast—is to be a permanent fixture.* He sighed. *As with the rest, it's going to take some getting used to.*

DEL REY DISCOVERY

Experience the wonder of
Discovery with Del Rey's newest
authors!

. . . Because something new is
always worth the risk!

TURN THE PAGE FOR AN EXCERPT
FROM THE NEXT *DEL REY DISCOVERY*:

THE END OF FAME

by Bill Adams and Cecil Brooks

Chapter One

The dead emperor wears a mask, but I know better than to lift it and see his face. I can't quite recall the details of the legend, but I know I mustn't do that.

"The ring is closing."

An impersonal voice reverberating from the outer sphere, as if an attendant were telling me it was time to leave.

But there is no exit. The room's solid gold wall curves around me in a perfect and unbroken circle. I look up. Above two meters the wall ends, not in a normal ceiling, but in a transparent glass bubble, beyond which burn the billion naked stars of deep space, so many that they light the room.

It is a small chamber—but wasn't it larger a moment ago?—and empty except for myself and the dead emperor. He lies in his bier, a strangely dramatic figure in his moldy and decaying military uniform, though he is no larger a man than myself and I see no sign of the great red beard of legend. Of course, there might be something under the silver mask.

"The ring is closing.
The bubble must burst."

The room *is* growing smaller, that's what it means—even now, the circular band of golden wall contracts with the deep moan and shriek of metal under stress. And, above, the glass of the bubble dome begins to shiver. A little more pressure and it will shatter; hard vacuum will reach in, blow me apart before I can even suffocate, and freeze-dry the fragments as they fly. Only the dead emperor can save me.

That's the legend, sort of like Arthur's: the once and future savior king. The anointed hero who fell on the way to the Crusade, but who waits in a cavern of glass while crows circle in the sky to watch the world for him, his red beard weaving round and round the bier until it reaches the seventh coil, when the world will need him again and he will awake . . . and I know his name:

BARBAROSSA

Why does it hurt to say it? Has the air already begun to leak from the shrinking room? There is a crash like thunder, and a crack flashes across the dome, the shape of lightning and just as white against black space, and above the violated-airlock hiss comes that disinterested goddess voice—Domina's voice:

"The ring is closing.
The bubble must burst.
And the crown must pass."

The crown, yes! If I were wearing his magic crown, I'd be the immortal, unkillable one. There's still time, though the curved wall of gold is almost touching me, while crack after crack snakes across the bubble ceiling. Standing to one side of the bier, I bend over the corpse and grip the emperor's crown with both hands, ignoring the wisps of dead hair that brush at my wrists like spider's legs—and lift.

But the crown is heavier than I expected. Gold, not spired like most medieval crowns, but rising in crenelated tiers like the layers of a labyrinth, and it's really a helmet, all of a piece with the mask that covers the face. If *mask* is the word—a flat sheet of silver that now mirrors my own desperate eyes, my bared teeth as I strain to remove it. And meanwhile the hiss of escaping air has become a roar, above which I can faintly hear:

"The ring is closing,
The bubble must burst.

270

And the crown must pass
From the last—
              to the first."

As the walls snap tight around the bier to make a big gold coffin, forcing me up and on top of the corpse, to crouch over his clay and bones in an obscene posture as I yank and yank at the crown and the mask, and the bubble bursts above me, a trillion shards of glass suspended like snowflakes for an instant before the explosion of escaping air hurls them at the stars, and now the vacuum of space is coring my lungs like razors of ice as I bend and strain—

—and the mirrored front of the helmet is a centimeter from my face when it suddenly comes free, leaving me eye-socket to eye-socket with *his* face, the face I feared, the last face I'll ever see—

And I wake the hell up, of course, my heart ringing in the darkness like fists against the hatches of a sinking ship.

Chapter Two

I lay there a moment, stewed in sweat, trying to catch enough breath to curse with, and telling myself I wasn't really going to die. I may have been born a hundred and twenty-two years ago, but physiologically I'm just thirty-five. And in excellent shape—below the neck.

They're called trauma nightmares. Want one as good as mine? They're expensive: First you have to sign up for a deep-space trip, say, one of those exploratory missions they ran a century ago, the ones that analyzed the stars at near lightspeed so that ships can flit between them faster than light today. Since such a mission will last for years, they'll want you to spend much of the time in suspend-sleep, your body functions slowed, your brain protected from sensory-deprivation insanity by extremely vivid and pleasant dreams. And here's the catch. Someone must sabotage the glass coffin that feeds you your suspend-sleep dreams, must leave it running for weeks on end without the reality checks of regular wake-ups, leave you spinning and spinning those realer-than-real sensuous dreams until it's too late. Until, when they finally drag you out of the tank, you have lost the ability to tell the difference between reality and dreams.

And then for the rest of your life—if it *is* your real life—you'll have rich, recurring nightmares so striking I've often thought of numbering them and putting them into verse, like Stephen Vincent Benét. And when you wake up, you'll never be sure you've really woken up. You'll never feel that solid floor beneath your feet, not ever, ever again.

No floor tonight. But I had to stand up anyway, on plush carpeting—a reminder that I was in the capital city of the planet Troudeserre, a guest of its garish but luxurious Romana Clef Hotel. I turned on the light and went to the bathroom.

My wristcomp showed the time in local minutes. 2310. I'd be a little late, but maybe that would save my life—maybe I'd be captured if I followed the plan. And then again maybe I had already been to the meeting, and would soon wake up for real in a secret cell somewhere, with interrogators warming up the brain probe just outside the door. Fuck it; I erased two days' growth of beard with ultrasonics then cleaned my teeth.

I dressed and stepped out into the hotel corridor.

"Watch where you're going!"

An African lion with yellow eyes and a flowing mane elbowed past me in a red velvet smoking jacket, Cleopatra clinging to his other arm. Not a dream, not a dream. Avoiding the elevator—the hollow-bellied dropping sensation would have been redundant—I walked quickly down the red-carpeted stairs past a musketeer, a pig-woman, a Column marine colonel, and a blonde fairy with transparent wings.

It was the Feast of Pope Joan, a local mardi gras. Conventioneers who visited Troudeserre during the week-long celebration were encouraged to join in all the masquerades at night. I, too, wore a mask; but I'd come to Troudeserre to take it off.

The hotel lobby gaped before me, vast as a city plaza, and thronged with wild animals, supernatural beings, and historical figures. Most of them were Column civil servants staying at the hotel for the Ministry of Mercantilism convention. In the afternoons they attended seminars on ways to maintain interstellar tariffs despite the Consultant's latest trade reforms, but at night they partied at the hotel's main ballroom or at other revels elsewhere in the city. A few commercial groups—tobacco traders, software guildsmen—had reserved smaller banquet rooms of their own; the hall I approached bore the banner WELCOME ACCREDITED DEALERS OF UR-TERRAN ANTIQUES.

None of the party-goers looked at me or at the porter who stood holding the red velvet rope at the entrance. But he couldn't control a glare of accusation—almost outrage—as he surveyed my costume and my mask.

I was wearing the monkish habit of the Master of a Kanalist lodge chapter, with a gold labrys pin at my throat. My cowled robe was black fractal silk—admittedly eye-catching in that bright lobby, like a hole in the light. As for the mask, it was latex, not too lifelike but recognizably modeled after Schaelus's bust of Evan Larkspur, the most famous Kanalist of them all.

Altogether, it was just the outfit to wear—in a hotel full of vacationing government officials—to a secret meeting of the forbidden Kanalist underground. But the porter didn't appreciate the joke.

"At least take off the mask," he hissed, as a giant panda, a Medusa, and an Iron Brotherhood mercenary swept past us on the way to the ballroom.

I shook my head. I'd had the mask made to order. While it suggested Schaelus's romanticized Larkspur, it more closely resembled the real thing. Now that I'd placed it over my naked face with no other disguise, I would only remove it after the right build-up, and under the lights of the stage and the eyes of the crowd.

The porter frowned and took a last glance at the invitation I'd handed him. But there was no way he could tell I'd stolen it from a dead man months before. He unhooked the velvet rope and sent me past him with a jerk of the head.

The corridor past the curtains was short; another hotel porter—and secret Kanalist—stood at the far end. He put his hands over his ears as I approached, but I didn't get the hint. I could hear party sounds from the banquet room beyond him: loud drunken talk, cries for a waiter, the choppy chant of a piano, and a few songsters trying to keep up.

But halfway down the corridor, between two banks of audio speakers artfully camouflaged against the wallpaper, those convivial sounds broke down. Unnatural shrieks, jagged arpeggios, and barks of static drilled into me. I raised my hands to my ears, but as I passed the last of the speakers, the weird electronic cacophony spun itself back into something human: the sound of a lecturer, of listeners coughing and moving in their seats and murmuring to one another. This was the actual sound from the banquet room, I realized—before the wall baffles had computed which vibrations to add and which to cancel out in order to create party noises for the benefit of listeners in the lobby.

Neat. Perhaps this chapter actually knew what it was doing. And why pick the hotel that catered to the Column's own government employees? Because every room there had been swept for surveillance bugs beforehand by the Shadow Tribunal—the Column's courtesy to itself. There was plenty of security around, of course, but it was facing in the wrong direction.

After all the false leads I'd followed, after all the little groups that had smelled inconsequential, crankish, or government-infiltrated, these signs of intelligence had convinced me to risk everything on this so-called Pan-Kanalist underground. It was that, or crack up under the constant pressure of the trauma nightmares. Two years before, on an optimistic high, I'd thought myself cured, and had made certain grandiose plans; but when those plans had fallen through, the nightmares had returned, worse than ever.

It was time to risk everything on one cast of the dice. Tonight I would show my face—Grandmaster, or nothing.

The inner guard acted sharper than the first one. He shook his head at my get-up, but smiled and said, "Funny."

Then his eye caught the gleam of the gold ring on my finger. "Are you really a Master?"

I nodded, although my chapter of the order had been burned to the ground a hundred years before.

"Please take one of the reserved seats in the front row," he said. "You're probably the last to arrive, anyway—the meeting has already started."

I went past him into the banquet room.

The hall was hung in dark green curtains and tapestries so stylized they might have represented a funeral, an orgy, or a dog-washing. The crowd of two or three hundred impressed me immediately; although they were all in costume, they radiated thoughtfulness and purpose. They looked young enough to be audacious, old enough to be responsible, with a nice mix of bookish heads and athletic bodies. Here and there the broad, farmer's face of this woman or the sardonic smile of that man drew my eye with the mysterious gravity of natural leadership; and more often I saw what was even more valuable, the eager attentiveness of natural followers. It looked like the briefing for some elite military group, but without the uniforms and muscle-flexing.

Someone had done it for me, someone with fantastic resources at his or her disposal. I was looking at the cream of the underground movement.

And they were looking at me, some taking in the seeming joke of my outfit and mask at a glance and turning away with a laugh, but others whispering to their neighbors with an earnest excitement that puzzled me. I found one of the empty front-row seats; I didn't want to make a scene—yet.

The speaker didn't notice me, as he was too busy gauging the effect of his words on the fringes of the audience. He was good—tall, velvet-voiced, with commanding eyes and a bald head so shiny you'd swear he waxed it. But I felt he wasn't the real leader—rather, a professional recruiter, one more feature of the brilliantly assembled package.

He had been speaking of Kanalism in general terms when I entered. Introductory remarks.

"And now that recent archaelogical discoveries have unearthed the original Kanalist initiation maze, we can *prove* that Kanalism has been around since the earliest colonies of lost Mother Earth, over a thousand years. Its founders took advantage of a secret trove of alien technology to attain financial and political power behind the scenes of our civilization. To the individual, Kanalism offered wholeness, self-mastery, a leasehold on the universe. To the community, it offered individual liberty as the highest value of government.

"By structuring itself as a secret society, a semireligious fraternity, Kanalism risked the charge of elitism. But for centuries, the Old Rite strategy served us well. Sons and daughters of the great families were imbued with our ideals, encouraged to find the natural leaders and hidden talents among the lower classes—to raise them up, treat them as brothers and sisters, and lead them to Kanalism in their turn.

The crowd, I noted, was beginning to show signs of restlessness. They must have expected some preaching to the choir, but Freeman Slickdome was beginning to push the limit.

"And what were the ideals that motivated them? No one had put them more succinctly than a poet and playwright who lived a hundred years ago. The one great voice who spoke up for the Old Rite when the Reformers destroyed the Federal Alignment and almost succeeded in burying true Kanalism for once and all. Evan Larkspur."

I would have thought this just more standard rah-rah boilerplate, but for some reason the crowd stirred with new interest. What could they know that I didn't—about Evan Larkspur?

The lecturer smiled and leaned forward on the lectern. Sometime during this next speech, so slowly as to be unnoticeable, the houselights went down, his spotlight came up, and the narrow stage behind him vanished into blackness.

"A hundred years ago," he said, "the most prestigious of colleges was the university of the planet Nexus. The great families of the commercial empires competed to send their smarter children there; while the university's Kanalist lodge, the oldest public temple and by then the most influential in Kanalism, provided scholarships for boys and girls from the farthest fringes of the human sphere.

"Oddly enough, Larkspur qualified on both counts: his grades were of the highest, and, while he was penniless, his family name had been the most prominent on Wayback, the tough frontier world of his birth. Historians have speculated that he originally joined the Order to further his own social advancement. A young man who wants to write verse plays had better have rich patrons. But it was Kanalism's rich lore that seduced him; and the legendary Summerisle, who had been Master of the Nexus U. chapter for decades, was grooming him to take over that lodge when, a hundred and two years ago, Larkspur wrote his masterpiece.

"The Nexus U. chapter had already gone rotten from within. Under the Federal Alignment, the great families of colonial days had been in slow but inevitable decline, unable to maintain control of the new fortunes that keep sprouting from nowhere in a free market. What they wanted was a powerful new central government. Their model was what we now call the First Column—a small subfederation of planets within the Alignment. On the Column worlds, government-franchised cartels run by the 'right' people suppressed business competition, and kept the masses quiet with a deft mix of welfare programs and secret police. Sound familiar?

"Summerisle had recruited a number of young Columnards in hope of converting them, but they converted the rest of the Nexus chapter instead. They spoke of a Reform Kanalism that would get behind the Column movement, of an elite that would give the 'little people' the order and security of strong government.

"Larkspur, of course, believed in making people greater, not littler. And so, as his contribution to the struggle within his chapter, he restated and reaffirmed all the true Kanalist ideals in his verse play *The Enchanted Isle*. Many of you know that play by heart—but perhaps not the marginal notes on his original manuscript. This is what he wanted to make his Nexus classmates realize as they saw it performed:

" 'Once you know that you were born a king, that this world is your forest and its creatures your deer, all else falls into proportion. You will not want to be warlord or warden or hoarder now, nor ward heeler, nor whore. The only politics not utterly beneath you is noblesse oblige, the helping hand to those who have not yet remembered that they are your peers.

" 'I've done my part there. I have crept through a maze of errors to find that the golden Kanalist thread is still in place. We took the right steps all along, and said the right words, and nothing remains except to remember that they mean just what they say and are true: the secret of Everyman's noble birth is that it lies outside history, and can be reexperienced at will, like memory itself, like a work of art.' "

This still seemed too boring a digression for a political rally—but it suited my own purposes perfectly. Simply a question of when to interrupt—when to take over.

The lecturer took a dramatic pause.

"But Larkspur, and those of his party, failed. Some perished bravely in the revolution—Summerisle, for instance. But before the outbreak of fighting, the Reformers had already made things hot for Larkspur on Nexus. Looking for a positive way out, he'd joined the Alignment's navy, and signed on board a survey mission to obtain praeterspace access data for new stars. During the four to six years the survey would spend at near lightspeed, thirty or forty years would pass for those he left behind. And Larkspur was optimistic enough to believe that while he was gone, the Reform movement would fizzle out; his enemies in the great families would grow older and wiser, or perhaps get themselves killed; and he himself would be forgotten. It seems funny to us now, but he thought of the plays and poetry he left behind as juvenile apprentice work—he intended to start his literary career afresh when he returned.

"Of course, he never did return."

The lecturer paused to pull at a glass of water. I couldn't help looking around in the darkness, trying to weigh the mood of the crowd. What was Baldy up to? You don't summon revolutionaries from a hundred planets to give them a lecture on Dead Poets of the Pre-Column Era. Where was the "Down with Column tyranny, Up with Liberty!" stuff the situation called for? And why was this dangerous-looking crew waiting for it so meekly?

"A hundred years have passed," the lecturer said—finally getting down to cases? "I don't know much more about the history of that century than you do—they don't teach it in school. During the first few decades, the great families extended the constitution of the First Column over the whole human sphere, and they didn't care how much blood they shed. The Shadow Tribunal rose to its current eminence among secret police forces. And it must have been about thirty years ago that the Consultant to Intelligence Affairs, an obscure naval officer, managed to obtain executive authority—or dictatorship, whatever you want to call it—over the Column. And what happened to Evan Larkspur?"

I groaned at the renewed digression, and someone shushed me. They'd get their Larkspur update soon enough, from me; I wanted them *militant* first—

"His survey ship, the F.A.A. *Barbarossa*, never returned to the human sphere, apparently lost to an accident. Meanwhile, Larkspur's plays—mere college entertainments—soon found universal recognition. Are they actually so brilliant in themselves, or is it just that he picked the best classics of old Earth literature to retell? Or is the real appeal the legend of Larkspur himself—the tales of sex and violence and politics surrounding his Nexus University career, his Byronic life and mysterious death—the artist as rebel and prophet?

"Personally, I believe that it was the early Column attempts to suppress his works that made them so famous; nothing sells like a banned book. Eventually, of course, the Column changed its policy. They took the line that Larkspur was a Columnard at heart—that it was the Old Rite he fled from, not Reform. Now every political and religious faction claims Larkspur for its own. And everyone cherishes a forlorn little hope.

"Larkspur could still come back."

The mask seemed to tighten against my face as the hairs on the back of my neck stood up. Was this a trap after all? Or was it somehow . . . something *worse*?

"There's no reason why the *Barbarossa* couldn't have spent an extra year near lightspeed, which would translate into decades of our time. Evan Larkspur could still come back, a century after he left—only a half-dozen years older than when he departed at twenty-two. *And why would this matter?*

"First of all, he'd be rich beyond the dreams of avarice. Any survey—especially one of that duration—would return with p-space access data for stars we cannot yet travel to: thousands of stars, meaning hundreds of new planets to colonize or mine, a vast fortune.

"Second, he'd be the idol of every liberty-loving man and woman, outside government and in—the perfect figurehead for a new revolution. Even our long-divided Kanalist underground would unite under the oldest and most knowledgeable of living Masters.

"And third, he'd have powers that I am revealing to you for the first time tonight. Because, just before Larkspur left for deep space, Master Summerisle entrusted him with the great secret of the Nexus University chapter—"

"No," I heard myself say. *He could not know this!* This time I was not only shushed, but the hawkfaced man sitting next to me in the dimness half reached for something in the folds of his Satan costume; I shut up, but I could barely hear the lecturer's next words over the roar in my head. *No one could know!*

". . . now called the White Book. Handed down from the first Kanalists, and known to no other chapter, the White Book contains the one true history of our order. It also teaches an advanced alien technology, considered too dangerous for men to know. Summerisle had sworn an oath upon everything he held sacred never to use the Book as a weapon—but Larkspur had not."

Excitement was rustling into the dark room like a night tide. Baldy grinned fiercely.

"You've heard the rumors, or you wouldn't be here tonight. They are true. He is back, he is safe on the planet Venezia. He has the resources, the power, the secrets to bring down the Column and its Consultant. *Evan Larkspur has returned.*"

And he stepped back. He extended one arm to his side, hand outstretched. And slowly, someone walked into the light—a figure almost made of light.

"No," I said again, standing.

Young, not yet thirty. Not exactly like Schaelus's famous bust—or the mask I wore—but recognizable all the same. "Greetings," he said—

—continuing to talk obliviously as I stiff-armed the hawk-faced man when he tried to interfere and vaulted onto the stage. "No!" I cried, and chopped my hand at the lying face—

—and the hand disappeared into it for an instant before the Larkspur image broke up and flickered away—a hologram!

I slapped a little pistol from Baldy's hand before he could level it at me and dropped him to the stage with the old Alignment Navy knuckle to the solar plexus; six like him couldn't have stopped me from going through with the plan that had barely kept me sane all those weeks. I faced the audience—someone turned up the houselights, and the crowd was on its feet now, scared and baffled—and tore away the Larkspur mask to reveal my Larkspur face.

"I'm *here*, now!" I roared. "The real Evan Larkspur! What you wanted to say to him, say to *me*!"

And they said it, the hawk-faced man and a half-dozen other agents strategically placed throughout the crowd and the two men in Shadow Tribunal uniforms standing over unconscious Kanalists at the houselight controls; almost in unison, they said, "You're under arrest!"